HIDDEN
DRAGONS

EMMA HOLLY

Hidden Dragons

Emma Holly

Hidden Dragons is an approximately 92,000-word novel.

ISBN-10: 0988894335

ISBN-13: 978-0-9888943-3-4

cover photos: istockphoto.com/Geber86,
shutterstock.com/Shukaylova Zinaida

OTHER TITLES
BY EMMA HOLLY

The Prince With No Heart

The Assassins' Lover

Steaming Up Your Love Scenes (how-to)

The Billionaire Bad Boys Club

Hidden Series

Hidden Talents

Hidden Depths

Date Night

Move Me

The Faerie's Honeymoon

Hidden Crimes

Winter's Tale

Hidden Dragons

CONTENTS

PROLOGUE

The Last Dragon

THE great bronze dragon circled the red desert, leathery wings spread to block the stars. Her name was T'Fain, and her sinuous, whipping tail was longer than her body—though that was long enough. Twenty grown men could stand on her dorsal ridge, assuming they had the stones. Black spines as sharp as razors thrust from her supple back, each worth more than a king's ransom to poachers. No armor known could withstand the piercing power of these spikes. When crushed to powder for a tincture, they counteracted illness and poisons. The dragon's tail was another marvel. If severed, it—and all her limbs—would regenerate.

Then there was the fiery breath *draconem magister* could produce. If used in conjunction with certain spells, water could not quench these flames, only magic of equal strength. What they touched would burn up in instants or smolder on for days—a gruesome passing, by all reports. Though dragons didn't possess the level of sentience of man or fae, their minds were wonders too, capable of executing complex strategies without oversight. Understandably, the beasts had played a role in all the realm of Faerie's important wars.

What few understood was that *draconem's* greatest value lay in its loyalty. The phrase "faithful as a dragon" was not empty. Where dragons loved, they loved with all their hearts. They would not betray their masters or let them come to harm. Many dragon keepers claimed to love their beasts better than their wives.

Despite being a woman, this was a sentiment Queen Joscela understood perfectly.

At a signal from its trainer, the dragon she watched tonight dropped silently to the arid plain. The fact that T'Fain was the last of her kind lent her grace poignancy. Puffs of dry dust burst up—first from the deadly back claws and then the front. The huge scaled body dwarfed the man who'd called her, but the fae was in no danger. The beast hunkered before him as obediently as a dog, glowing ruby eyes fixed lovingly on the being who'd imprinted her as a hatchling. She lowered her scaly head to bring her gaze level with the man's.

The dragon could not anticipate the sacrifice that would be asked of her.

The dragon master was aware. As a member of the secretive Dragon Guild, his family's bloodline was as pure—if not as royal—as Joscela's. At the moment, his face was masklike, his movements stiff and self-conscious. Dressed in fireproof leather from hood to breastplate to hip-high boots, he stretched a gloved hand to rub the dragon between her eyes. T'Fain let out a *chirr* of pleasure, wisps of steam trailing from her nostrils. The trainer stepped back, his attention shifting toward the king to whom his family owed allegiance.

King Manfred was the fae of the hour—of the century, to hear him. Hundreds stood behind him in quiet ranks, soldiers for the most part. As if these troops weren't enough for his dignity, a traveling throne splendorously supported his royal butt. Elevated on a platform set on the sand, the seat glistered with electrum and precious jewels. For five decades, ever since this last dragon had been hatched, Manfred had badgered the High Fae Council over how he thought the precious resource should be employed. Finally he'd won his way. As regally as if *he'd* trained the dragon, Manfred nodded toward his sworn man.

Queen Joscela watched all this from above, from the deck of her floating ship. Magic and not hot air buoyed the vehicle's black and tan striped balloon. Keeping her company at the rail were her personal guards, her hand servants, and her most trusted advisers. Though this was an important night, no wine casks had been opened. She most definitely hadn't triumphed in the long debate with the High Council. This, however, didn't mean she was willing to miss the show.

Those royals who felt a similar reluctance bobbed in the airspace above the plain, each elaborate vessel declaring the uniqueness of its sponsor. Here was a ship that resembled a daffodil, there one entirely formed of gears. All were lit by torches or faerie lights, but not all were festive. Some of Joscela's peers had sided with Manfred and some with her. She consoled herself that few would actually delight in the pompous bastard's ascendency.

Of course they'd abandon her quick enough, now that his star had eclipsed hers.

"If Manfred's head swells any bigger, it will explode."

This comment came from her Minister of Plots. Ceallach stood closest to her shoulder, a smooth and handsome male who'd been her lover for many years. He served in both capacities very well.

"We should be so lucky," she murmured back.

"It's not too late to arrange for a hell dimension door to open and swallow him."

The plain below was dotted with portals, this being the best place in Faerie for forming them. Most were invisible, created too long ago and used to seldom to be active. Others were so popular they had duplicates throughout the realms. These glimmered on the edge of vision, ghost doors to alien existences. Despite their proximity, it was too late to shove Manfred through one—as they both were aware. Joscela's opposition to her rival's plan had been too public and impassioned. Should any ill befall the ruler, suspicion would fall on her.

She touched Ceallach's hand in thanks for his support. "With the way my luck's run lately, we'd send him to a bunny realm."

She sounded bitter. Ceallach squeezed her fingers.

She appreciated that, though her hatred for the puffed-up sovereign knotted darkly inside of her. *I won't let resentment consume me*, she swore. Manfred didn't deserve any more victories.

A stir rippled through the crowd at her vessel's rail.

"Oh joy," Ceallach said. "The idiot is rising to make his speech."

Manfred was a handsome faerie: black-haired, black-garbed, with flashing silver eyes and a sensual mouth. His greater than normal height—further raised by the throne's platform—commanded attention. Then again, if he hadn't known how to present himself, he couldn't have bested her.

"Countrymen," he began in a resonant spell-enhanced voice. "Neighbors and fellow fae. Tonight is a momentous occasion, one many of us fought long and hard to bring about. Tonight we undo the narrow-mindedness of our forefathers, who saw only the backwardness of the human realm and not its value. They closed the door between our worlds, but tonight we re-open it. Those who were stranded among the humans can now come home. Those who wish to visit the human world will have that option. The reason for this is simple. Tonight we do more than our ancestors ever could. Tonight we create a Pocket behind the portal, half fae and half mortal—a place of stability, immune to the magical anarchy that threatens our less fortunate regions. Plodding though they are, humans anchor reality, a service the wise among us know we can no longer live without. I do not exaggerate when I say the Pocket is our future."

"Well, it's certainly his future," Ceallach observed dryly. "And that of anyone who likes conditions exactly as they are."

Joscela pressed her lips together but did not speak. They'd talked of this before. Ceallach knew she agreed with him. The dragon master must have believed Manfred's argument. No matter if he were Manfred's vassal, she couldn't see him going along with this otherwise.

A gust of wind buffeted her ship, forcing her to grip the rail or be knocked off balance. Ceallach's arm came protectively around her back. Because flashing one's wings in public was bad form, hers were flawlessly spell-folded beneath her gown. Ceallach knew they were there. His bicep tightened, reminding her of the pleasure of having him stroke them. His fingers were capable of great delicacy, his tall body fair and hard. Joscela shuddered at the memory of many intimacies.

"Cease," she whispered as his hand squeezed her waist. She didn't need the distraction. Events were progressing down on the plain. Manfred's cupbearer jogged across the sand toward the dragon master, a ceremonial chest tucked beneath his arm like a suckling pig. Going down on one knee, the youth extended it toward the man.

Not wanting to miss a detail, Joscela whispered an invocation to extend the focus of her vision. The magic snapped into place with spyglass clarity, bringing the scene closer. A muscle ticked in the keeper's jaw as he stared at the cupbearer's offering. The chest was electrum and heavily enchanted, the alloy of gold and silver good for retaining spells. When the keeper opened the flowery lid, slender beams of light spoked out.

Involuntary gasps broke out as people identified the object the beams came from. Nestled within the padded red velvet was a quartz crystal sphere. Joscela would have given her right arm—at least temporarily—for ten minutes alone with it. That clear orb contained the blueprint for the proposed Pocket: the magical rules by which it would be governed, its capacity for expansion. As Manfred's staunchest opposition, Joscela hadn't been invited to participate in planning. He and his cronies wanted to stack the new territory's deck in their own favor, to suit their own agendas. Though this was to be expected, the exclusion offended her more than any of Manfred's slights.

To ignore the genius of a mind like hers was criminal.

Manfred was too enamored with his grand experiment to consider how dangerous humans were. The race seemed weak and easily dazzled compared to fae, but their very susceptibility to fae glamour seduced their superiors. Mixed blood children brought shame to proud families—nor were Joscela's concerns theoretical. Just as fae had been trapped beyond the Veil when it dropped, humans had been trapped here. Her sensibilities rebelled at the results. Pure humans could be useful, but halves? And quarters? They were a mockery of what fae were supposed to be, always causing trouble or getting into it.

As a wise fae once said, a little power is a dangerous thing.

The dragon master removed the crystal from its nest of velvet.

The dragon nosed it, smart enough to be curious. Joscela wondered how the keeper felt to stand so close to the ancient beast. She'd never had a dragon. Once every queen possessed one, but their number had dwindled by the era in which she'd assumed the throne. Some compared the creatures to dolphins in intelligence, others to small children. Though they couldn't speak, they understood commands. Crucial to tonight's proceedings was the magic that packed each cell of their huge bodies. Pure magic. Old magic. The very magic the one-time gods used to form fae reality. Never mind combating poison or piercing good armor, the spell power within one dragon could create or destroy worlds.

Compared to that, burning enemy villages couldn't measure up. Every hatchling was a weapon someone, someday wouldn't be able to resist deploying.

Though the dragon's playful nudge nearly pushed him over, the dragon master didn't scold or shove her off. Perhaps he couldn't bear to with so little time remaining. He braced his back leg instead, closed his eyes, and composed himself.

As if sensing the seriousness of the situation, T'Fain settled back onto her forelimbs. Her keeper held the sphere between them. As he connected his mind to it, the crystal began to glow. The detail Manfred and his cohorts had encoded into the quartz soon poured into him. The keeper's eyes moved behind their lids. Unlike inferior races, pureblood fae could grasp immense amounts of knowledge, each bit as clear and accurate as the rest. This dragon master's lineage endowed him with yet another skill: the ability to communicate with his charge telepathically.

The dragon's wings twitched as the river of information hit her awareness. Fortunately, like her keeper, she could hold it. Comprehension wasn't needed, only accepting what was sent. The beast seemed to be doing exactly that. Her upper and lower lids closed over her ruby eyes.

At last the transfer was complete. The keeper set the empty crystal on the cracked sand, then gently clasped the dragon's cart-size muzzle. The creature blinked as if emerging from a dream.

"Be," the keeper said softly in High Fae. "Be what I have shown you."

He let go and stepped back. T'Fain shook her body and raised her wings, not for flight but in display. The keeper retreated faster. Despite her misgivings, Joscela couldn't deny a thrill. It wasn't every day one witnessed new realities being born. The dragon tilted her great bronze head as if listening to faint music. Joscela's heart thumped behind her ribs. If she'd been in the beast's position, she'd have been screaming or belching flame. The dragon didn't seem upset, merely attentive. The keeper turned and ran.

Joscela wasn't prepared. Possibly no one was.

Like a star exploding, a blinding brilliance replaced the bronze dragon. The power blasted Joscela's hair back, and her ship jerked to the end of its anchor line. She couldn't tell if the tether snapped, because her senses were overwhelmed. Lightning swallowed the world around her, rainbow sparks dancing in the white. Her ears rang with alien chords. The air was so thick with power it felt like feathers against her skin.

He's killed us, she thought. *The dragon keeper wanted us all to die.*

Even as this possibility arose, the sight-stealing radiance ebbed. Her vessel was still aloft, still anchored, though she'd been knocked onto her ass on the wooden deck. Everyone around her had, from what she could see through her watering eyes.

Ignoring the disarray of her long silk gown, she stumbled to the railing to see what had transpired below. The scene she discovered made her smile unexpectedly. Manfred's fancy throne had toppled over with him in it. He didn't appear hurt, but half a dozen shaky soldiers vied comically with each other to help him up. Everywhere she looked, fae pushed dazedly to their feet. The dragon was gone. Her death had produced that great white light.

Joscela focused on the spot where T'Fain had been standing. Beside her, Ceallach pulled himself up as well.

"Look," he said, a note of grudging awe in his voice. "The new portal is forming."

She'd already seen what caught his attention. The opening was round or would be when it finished coalescing. Years might pass before the doorway was mature enough to use. For now, streaks of green and brown and blue swirled like clouds within the aperture. Though she'd had no part in its design, she understood what was happening. The essence of the realm of Faerie was outfolding into the human world, blending with it to form a combined reality bubble. Silver glimmered and then disappeared at the top of the portal's ring—a pair of dragon wings taking shape, she thought.

"The sacrifice succeeded," she observed, though this was obvious.

"The dragon master should find that some comfort."

"That presumes comfort matters. The last living reason for his bloodline's existence was just wiped out. The protectors among the Guild can hire out as mercenaries. Gods know what purpose he and his kin will find."

Ceallach put his hand on her arm, and they gazed at the man together. The dragon's trainer had run as far as he could from the explosion. Now he stood on the sand, a solitary figure looking grimly back toward the forming door. Char marks streaked his face and leathers, as if he alone had passed through real fire. The soot obscured his expression, but still . . .

"Shouldn't he be more devastated?" she asked Ceallach quietly.

When she glanced at her companion, one corner of his mouth tugged up. His intensely blue eyes met hers, and the grin deepened. "I believe he should, my queen."

Joscela's heart skipped a beat. "Perhaps the rumors are true."

"Perhaps they are."

Though willing to believe almost anything of her kind, Joscela had discounted the whispers as wishful conspiracy theories. If they were true, however . . . If more dragon eggs existed, hidden away by the fae whose calling it had always been to train them . . .

If that were true, all might not be lost. Joscela could transform her present disgrace into victory. She could undo everything Manfred had accomplished. As to that, she could undo him.

The increasing warmth at her side told her Ceallach had shifted closer.

Unwilling to risk any associate but him hearing, she spoke in a spell-hushed voice. "We must discover everything we can about this dragon master."

"Yes, my queen," Ceallach agreed in the same fashion.

He laid his hand over hers on the silver rail. They were royals—cool thinking and strategic. It wasn't their way to let their emotions run rampant. Nonetheless, both their palms were damp with excitement.

"We'll have our work cut out for us," she said, meaning the caution for herself as much as her confidante. "The Dragon Guild is as good at keeping secrets as the nobility."

"Better." Ceallach flashed a wolfish grin. "Nobles come and go. Dragon masters have survived whoever sat on the high throne. If someone held back a clutch, it won't be discovered easily."

Joscela longed to grin in return. She could always count on Ceallach relishing a challenge. Instead, she returned her gaze to the chaotic scene below, her expression carefully composed to queenly placidity.

"Good thing we have forever to rewrite destiny," she observed.

CHAPTER ONE

CASSIA Maycee was home again.

She came to this realization on the roof of her deceased grandmother's downtown penthouse. Her three best friends sprawled in their swimsuits on the fancy lounge chairs to either side of her, as if a time machine had transported them from high school. Because Cass's gran had been more lenient than their parents, they'd often hung out here. She'd splurged on a climate spell, so though it was late October, the terrace was summery. Above the ephemeral shield, stars twinkled like diamonds on black velvet. Ripples glowed invitingly from the lap pool, though no one was swimming. To the east, a flock of young gargoyles played airborne tag around the Pocket State Building's spire. Their joyous swoops were medicine to Cass, allowing her grief to lie on her as softly as the blood-warm air. Her grandmother was at peace, her life having been full and rewarding.

Cass was tempted to stay up here forever.

For twenty-two strange years she'd lived as a human among humans, cut off from the magic of the Pocket. She'd done it because she loved her fully human mother and because her father, who wasn't human at all, impressed upon her the fact that human lives were short. Cass was half faerie and could expect to live centuries. She'd probably still be out there if her mother hadn't remarried and her maternal grandmother hadn't left Cass her estate. Even in death, Patricia Maycee could move mountains. One of the few arguments she'd ever lost was when her daughter divorced Cass's father and moved Outside.

I don't belong here, Cass's mother had pleaded. *I'm not like the rest of you.*

Patricia Maycee had been aghast. The Pocket had grown up around her ancestors. Their original family farm was smack dab in its center. Since that time, Maycee descendants had flourished in this city.

Not Cass's mother, however. She'd hated magic the way some women hate spiders.

"Oh my God, this is delicious," Cass's friend Jin Levine broke into her thoughts to declare. "I'm an excellent bartender."

Cass turned her head on the lounge chair cushion to smile at her. Rarely lacking in confidence, Jin was half gold elf and half human. Her skin was a creamy tan, her short-cropped hair twenty-four karat. Dressed in a tiny blue and green bikini—which she looked awesome in—Jin was sipping the rainbow-colored cosmo she herself had whipped up.

"We need a toast," her cousin Bridie suggested. Her golden hair was long. Aside from that, she was enough like Jin to be her sister and probably closer than the real thing.

Jin sat up and raised her glass. "Here's to the half-and-halfers. Now that we're back together, may we never lose touch again."

"May we never take each other for granted," Bridie added.

"May we never run out of hot men to ogle—"

"or chocolate—"

"or comfort-spelled Jimmy Choos."

"Crap," Rhona interjected into the elf cousins' riff. Her newly adopted werefox son was trying to squirm off her lap. "No, Pip, cosmos aren't for one-year-olds!"

Cass had to grin. Leave it to Rhona to bring them back to reality. Straddling the fence between cute and pretty, she was half human and half werefox. Jin might have made up the name for their clique—which they'd thought extremely clever as tweenagers—but Rhona was its glue. She made peace and planned birthday parties, not to mention telling *the* best lies to parents. She was the good girl none of their folks thought would deceive them.

Jin and Bridie were the wild girls, of course. Cass hadn't really had a role. "Snow White" was what classmates called her, for her raven hair and her soft blue eyes. She hadn't been especially bad or good. Boys liked the way she looked, but Jin and Bridie were the ones they chased, the ones they knew would be fun. Cass's faerie blood intimidated people, though as far as power went, she couldn't call on much. Boys hadn't been in danger of ending up as toads.

Maybe "the quiet one" was the closest she'd come to a label.

To go by his excited babbling, Pip wasn't likely to have that problem. Cute as a button and very wiggly, he stretched even farther across his mother's front. Activated by his attention, the rainbows in Rhona's cosmo danced.

Cass hopped up before he could knock the glass over, plucking it from the table beside his mom. "That's just too pretty, isn't it?" she said. "Next time we'll buy Cointreau without enchantments."

Pip let out a wail as his object of desire escaped.

"I should have gotten a babysitter," Rhona said, bouncing him worriedly.

"No," the others denied in unison.

"Cass *had* to meet him," Bridie assured her. "We shouldn't have brought alcohol."

"Well, *I* need alcohol," Jin said with her wonderful throaty laugh. She flicked her short golden hair with matching manicured fingernails. "You wouldn't believe what I put up with at work today! Boy bands behaving badly are no picnic."

Bridie smacked her cousin's thigh with her hand. "Like I wasn't right there with you."

The cousins hosted a popular TV show called *As Luck Would Have It*. Each episode related an amazing escape from danger or stroke of good fortune.

"Between the two of us, you got the patience," Jin informed her cousin. "Therefore, you don't need to complain."

Rhona laughed, which thankfully distracted her son from his distress.

"Ma, ma, ma," he burbled, patting her cheeks with chubby palms.

"Oh my God," Rhona choked. "Every time he calls me that, I tear up."

"Aww," Jin and Bridie chorused in unison.

"To Rhona's wonderful new addition," Cass said. Still standing, she toasted her with the rescued drink. "No little boy could have a better mom."

Rhona blushed. "I hope so. Since I adopted him, I swear I feel like an idiot at least twenty times a day."

"There's a lot to learn," Bridie said, patting her knee reassuringly.

"Anyone can see you're good for him," Jin put in. "He's totally normal and healthy."

Pip had been one of the city's infamous "little miracles." Prevented from shifting to his fox form by a genetic flaw, his parents had abandoned him to a bogus adoption agency. The criminals who ran it sold him and other children like him for use in dark rituals. Pip had been lucky to be rescued—and to end up with Rhona. Interestingly, a couple boys they'd known in high school, now detectives with the RPD, had been instrumental in saving them.

"We should toast Cass," Rhona said with her trademark thoughtfulness. "Maycee's brave new leader."

"Oh I'm not that," she denied, startled to hear it put that way. "The department stores run themselves. I'll just sign a check or cut a ribbon occasionally."

"Don't be modest," Jin scolded. "Everybody knows your gran kept the board in line. If it weren't for Patricia Maycee, who knows what shape the chain would be in?"

Cass's human grandmother had protected the hereditary family business like a bear guarding cubs. She'd been tireless in the quality she demanded *and* in enforcing her concept of fairness. The idea that Cass would follow in her footsteps was alarming. She didn't have her gran's passion for commerce. As far as she knew, she didn't have that kind of passion for anything. Cass curled her toes in her bright flip-flops, wondering if she'd put a damper on the evening by saying so.

She was spared deciding by the distant chime of the doorbell.

"Food," Cass said when they all looked at her.

Aware the delivery guy was waiting, she grabbed a cover-up and hurried across the terrace to the French doors. Apart from mini-lights, the portrait hall behind them was dark. As she moved down it, Cass felt the absence of her friends. Ever since she'd returned, her gran's apartments had seemed spooky. She didn't know why. When she was a girl, she'd thought this the safest place in the world. Her maternal grandmother doted on her, turning every visit into a special treat. Though she could be stern with others, when it came to her granddaughter, no sin was too big for Trish Maycee to forgive, no opinion too ridiculous for her not to take Cass's side.

"That's what grandmothers are for," she'd liked to say.

She'd died at 112, peacefully, in her sleep. No way would her spirit linger maliciously.

I'm just missing her, Cass thought, trying to explain her creeps.

A shadow slunk across the cross hall like smoke, jolting her pulse into overdrive.

"Mew?" it inquired politely, changing direction to wind around Cass's ankles.

"Sheesh," she gasped, laughing at herself. She bent to scratch her grandmother's cat Polydora behind her ears. The feline was gray and bony and very affectionate. "You scared me, skulking around like that."

Cass continued to the front entrance with the cat treading on her heels. Poly must have smelled the delivery. The cat was a fiend for pepperoni with extra cheese.

Fortunately, the pizza guy hadn't given up. He did look bemused as she opened the door to him. "How ya doin'?" he said, handing the boxes over. "I never knew there was a house up here."

His confusion was understandable. *Up here* wasn't a normal apartment building. Up here was the top floor of the downtown Maycee's.

"Our family has a tradition of living above the store."

"Hah!" he said, seeming to appreciate her joke. "That's thirty plus tip for two large pies."

Rather than try to juggle the boxes, Cass levitated her ResEx card from her cover-up's pocket. The delivery guy didn't bat an eye, used to customers from all magical levels. He plucked the card from the air, swiped it through his reader, released it, and wished her a good evening.

When she closed the door, she was alone again.

"Mew!" Poly demanded.

"Okay," she said, a little too glad the cat was there. "Follow me to the roof, and you can have a slice."

To her surprise, Rhona was waiting outside the terrace doors. Jin and Bridie had taken charge of Pip and were playing a game of crawl dodge on a soft stretch of grass. Evidently, Jin thought a one-year-old didn't need to see cleavage. She'd pulled a silky wrap over her bikini. Maybe more things than Cass knew had changed while she was away.

Pip squealed with delight as his playmates evaded him.

Sensing something was up, Cass gave Rhona her attention. Her friend bit her lip before she burst out with it. "Did you have a chance to talk to your dad?"

Rhona wanted Cass's dad to serve as Pip's faerie godfather. In their belated wisdom, Resurrection's fae overseers had decided the city's "miracle babies" were entitled to extra protection.

"I spoke to him on the phone this morning, but like I warned, I'm not sure what he'll decide."

Rhona's cute-pretty face fell slightly.

"If he doesn't come through, the Founders Board will assign someone."

"I know," Rhona said. "I just hoped it could be your father. Sometimes purebloods are *brr*." She hunched her shoulders and made a shivering sound. "Your dad isn't like the rest of them."

For a fae, her dad was a sweetie, but that was sort of the problem. "He's concerned he's not powerful enough to protect Pip like he deserves."

"How can he not be powerful enough?"

Cass wondered how to navigate this question. Resurrectioners tended to assume all purebloods were super powerful. In some cases, this was true. In others, not so much. The misconception wasn't one the fae wanted to clear up. Though they'd created the Pocket, most remained aloof from its citizens. They merely visited or lived in their own enclaves. To marry a human the way her father had was practically unheard of. The impression her dad had given Cass was that the match hadn't mattered because his power level was modest. Whether this was true, she couldn't say. Even as a child, she knew direct questions were unwelcome. Purebloods had issues about lying—and about sharing personal information. Because truenames could be used to weave harmful spells, she couldn't even swear she knew his real surname. Her mother hadn't taken it after they married.

"Uh," Cass said. "I'm sure Dad is just being careful. He's always been fond of you."

A wash of pink colored Rhona's cheeks. "I'm sorry," she said. "I didn't mean to push."

The blush caused Cass's eyes to widen. Not wanting to think too hard about what it meant, she chafed her best friend's arm. She didn't touch people often—another habit from her father. Faerie dust rubbing off on others could be awkward. "I'll talk to him again when I see him in person. If he can't do it himself, maybe he'll recommend someone."

"Sure," Rhona said. "That'd be just as good."

Cass couldn't help but notice her old friend's gaze remained stubbornly lowered.

Luckily, the awkward moment was cut short. "*Pizza!*" Jin growled like a weretiger. "Pizza!" Bridie agreed, and they ran over with Pip laughing.

Setting up on the outdoor table was like old times.

Who remembered the soda?

What does your Gran do with all these forks?

Really, Cass? You want us to eat on the good china?

"Please," Cass insisted. "Gran would like knowing we're using it."

Bridie snorted out a laugh with her mouth full of hot pizza. "She wouldn't have liked knowing how many plates you un-broke for us."

"I'm sure the practice using my magic helped. I'm quite good at unbreaking now."

"Ooh." Jin pointed Cass's way with a celery stick. "Remember the concealment spells you used to do for me? My mom never understood why my skirts were twice as short when I got home from school."

"I remember trying to 'conceal' Tony Lupone, so he could sneak into your bedroom."

"That so didn't work," Bridie hooted, jostling her cousin's arm. "And you were so busted."

"Those Lupone boys were hot," Jin declared airily. "If Tony hadn't secretly been gay, it would have been worth it."

Cass gasped. "Tony the werewolf is gay?"

"Tony the werecop, and—yes—he is. He came out a few months ago."

"Noo. He was a total flirt. His brother Rick must have had a cow. Unless . . ." Cass hesitated. "Unless he's gay too?"

"That truly would be cruel." A small smile played around Bridie's mouth. "As far as I know, Rick Lupone is a hundred percent hetero."

"Not that it's my business," Cass said hastily.

"No." Jin grinned like her cousin was. "There's no reason he'd be your business."

"I don't still have a crush on him."

"Of course you don't, and of course you're completely uninterested in the fact that he's single. Not even dating, from what I hear."

Cass's human half blushed too hot for comfort. Hoping the girlish reaction would go away, she placed one slice of pizza on a gilt-edged plate and set it on the ground. Poly leaped on the treat as if Cass hadn't fed her less than an hour ago.

To be fair to the cat, if Rick Lupone had been laid out for Cass, she'd have leaped on him too.

She'd had it bad for the hot werewolf. He'd been a jock in high school but not stupid. Sweet, sexy and just plain big. Mile wide shoulders. Long solid legs. A butt that did dangerous things to a pair of jeans. Never the most outgoing, Cass had gone mute if he so much as looked at her. Reams of diary pages immortalized her yearning. How decent he was amazed her, how kind, how unlike any other male! His younger brother, Tony, though charming, always struck her as a player. Rick the paragon was a gentleman.

She'd dragged her friends to every sporting event he'd played, ducking behind their shoulders if it seemed like he'd catch her watching.

What made all this more pathetic was that he barely knew she existed.

Once, at a vending machine, when she'd run out of change, he'd bought her a candy bar—a random act of kindness for a girl she doubted he knew by name. She was pretty sure she still had the caramel SnickErrs. Mummified probably, at the back of her treasure drawer.

Jin and Bridie hadn't understood why she didn't just spell Rick to fall for her. She'd had the juice but couldn't bring herself to use it. Half fae or not, she'd had a human girl's romanticism. Love shouldn't be magicked. Love should be genuine.

Memories of how he'd thrown her teenage hormones into a tizzy distracted her from the dinner talk. She nodded and laughed when her friends spoke to her, but Rick's awesome biceps and killer butt took up the lion's share of her thoughts. All these years later, he still made her thighs sweaty.

She wondered if he was as fit as he used to be. As a cop, that seemed probable. Was he harder now? Had he seen things that put an edge on his old sweetness? Suddenly Cass was glad for the cover-up she'd pulled over her bathing suit. Her nipples had tightened at the thought of him being grown.

Maybe *he* was the one who'd put a charm on her.

Almost before she knew it, Jin and Bridie were clearing plates and making noises about how early they needed to be at the studio tomorrow.

"This was the best!" they exclaimed with an enthusiasm she couldn't doubt. "Let's do it again real soon."

They flattered her more than they realized. Cass hadn't assumed they'd automatically fall back into friendship. "I'd like that," she said sincerely.

Her eyes were teary. Knowing she didn't hug, Bridie squeezed her sleeve quickly. "We missed you too, sweetie."

While the glamorous Levine cousins called the elevator, Rhona paused in the entryway. Pip was a momentarily quiet bundle on her hip. Like most fox shifters, Rhona was strong but petite. Holding Pip evened out the weight of the humongous baby bag on her opposite shoulder.

"I'll catch up," Rhona promised when the door hissed open and Jin looked back at her. "I want to talk to Cass a second."

"All right. We won't let the limo pull off without you unless we see Channing Tatum and need to shadow him."

Jin was kidding. Hollywood actors didn't know about the Pocket.

"They have a limo?" Cass asked as the doors slid shut.

"The network supplied it. It's a hot pink stretch with *As Luck Would Have It* spelled out in white glitter."

Cass snickered. "That sounds about their speed."

Pip flapped his arms and babbled, apparently having decided she needed to pay him more attention. He was covered from head to toe in pizza grease and grass stains. His little "Kiss Me!" T-shirt had ridden up his round tummy.

"Do you want sparkles?" Cass teased, poking his belly button. To entertain him, she shot two from her fingertip. He liked that so much he squealed.

"Oh my God," Rhona moaned. "Look what a mess he is! I put a bib on him, I swear."

"He's just what he ought to be," Cass assured her, carefully kissing his sticky palm. Pip settled back against his mother, his big brown eyes wide and curious. Cass didn't think she'd glamoured him. Babies were susceptible, but she was cautious. "I'll spell a box of baby-safe detergent for you tonight. It'll lift the stains right out. I got plenty of practice at that sort of thing when I was Outside."

"You could do magic there?" Rhona asked, the first of her friends to inquire about her time away directly. "You didn't have to go cold turkey?"

"It takes longer to recharge beyond the border, but I could do it if I focused."

Rhona hiked Pip higher. "Being out there must have been difficult."

"Sometimes." The answer was enough of an understatement that her left temple throbbed. Too often, living Outside had been miserable, like missing a limb no one else believed existed. "I'm glad I got to see my mother happy. I didn't know the person she truly was until I was there with her. Her whole personality opened up."

Rhona nodded sympathetically. Her relationship with her mother was strained sometimes. Mrs. Burke had definite opinions on her firstborn's life choices. "I'm not sure I could leave Resurrection. I'd be afraid the mundanes would hunt me every time I changed form."

Due to the dominance of were genes, Rhona would have been able to shift. Shivering in reaction, she hugged her boy closer.

"You'd learn to cope," Cass said. "All you'd need is a strong enough reason." She stroked Pip's mussed hair, then touched her best friend's cheek. Rhona's mouth fell open. She was unused to Cass being demonstrative. Cass dropped her hand and smiled. "What did you hang back to talk to me about?"

Rhona shook herself from her daze. "I just wanted to make sure you'll be okay alone tonight. Your grandma's place is big for one person. Pip and I could stay if you feel lonely."

"I'll be fine," Cass said. To her surprise, pain stabbed her sharply behind one eye. Clearly, she didn't believe her own words. She was experiencing the standard faerie reaction to telling lies. She did her best to keep her expression impassive.

"You sure?" Rhona asked.

"You should go," Cass assured her, neatly avoiding the question. "You don't want to upset Pip's new home routine. Poly will keep me company."

She pushed the elevator call button for her friend, waving farewell and smiling as they stepped in. Pip's floppy wave back was adorable. "Bye-bye," he piped quite intelligibly.

"I'll call you tomorrow," his mom promised.

Cass blew a kiss as the doors shut her off from them.

Alone once more, she felt the silence of the store beneath her. It was half past nine, and shopping hours were over. Her fae senses picked out a security guard patrolling menswear two floors below—a reformed demon, if she read his energy correctly. Cass hadn't adjusted to the sharpness of her perceptions since she'd returned. Her skin prickled with aliveness, too sensitive for comfort. Compared to this, she'd been wrapped in cotton batting for two decades.

Poly yowled for her to come back to the apartment.

Cass did so and locked up.

"You and me, cat," she said.

She fought an urge to check her old treasure drawer. She'd kept it here to avoid her mom's snooping. Was Rick's candy bar still there? Surely wondering was silly.

"Twenty-two years," she said to Poly. More than time to get over a teenage crush.

She turned instead to Gran's study, where Patricia Maycee had stored her geological specimens in lighted cabinets. Collecting them had been a lifelong hobby. Larger rocks were displayed on antique tables, getting dusty in her absence. The stones weren't magical, just pretty or interesting. When she was little, Cass had loved playing with them. As she opened one of the creaky glass fronts to revisit that pleasure, Poly hopped onto the couch and curled up.

A shiny tumbled sodalite drew Cass's fingers to stroke it. Hadn't Gran owned a selection of polished eggs? Different colored agates, she thought, culled from each of the Pocket cities around the world. Cass pictured the drawer in her mind. It had been wide and shallow and lined with felt.

She turned to see which of the cabinets matched her recall . . .

As she did, another memory surfaced. She was six or seven, her hands dimpled with plumpness. Dressed in pink corduroy overalls, she knelt between a tree's big roots. It was dark, and she was alone. She dug through the cold damp dirt with a garden spade, chucking shovel after shovel from the hole like her life was at stake. A chill rippled down her spine at the image, worse than when Poly had startled her in the portrait hall.

Something bad lurked down the path from her.

Hide, she thought—or remembered thinking. Hiding was very important.

She and the cat jumped a foot when a knock sounded on the door. Cursing her over-stimulated nerves, Cass went to answer it.

Her dad was behind it, the welcomest visitor she could have imagined.

His hug was formal but wonderful. Cass never worried about overwhelming him with her power.

"Daughter," he said, pushing back from her.

"Father," she answered in the same fond tone.

They smiled at each other.

"You look well," he said. "Unharmed by your time Outside."

He looked amazing, but that went without saying. Whatever their age, purebloods were the definition of beautiful. Her father was tall and solemn. His close-shorn hair was raven black like hers, his eyes the same dreamy blue. The faintest lines scored his well-cut mouth as parentheses. Unless he damped the effect with glamour, he sparkled constantly.

"Come in," she said, gesturing with a shadow of his grace. "I've got pizza left if you're hungry."

"I won't stay long," he demurred politely. As if she'd left a trail he could follow—which perhaps she had—he strode into the crystal study she'd come out of. He stopped in its center and looked around. Whatever he sought he didn't appear to find. His rosy statue lips thinned slightly. The response made her curious.

"Did you want something, Dad?" she asked.

He turned to her, the movement naturally elegant. "I brought a gift for the werefox boy."

He hadn't brought the gift in a bag. No pureblood worth his salt would tote things around that way. They created carrying pockets by folding reality. Her dad lifted his hand with his thumb and finger pinched together. In a literal blink of her eye, a baby's mobile dangled from his hold. Fluffy lambs and ducklings circled each other, so dear and sweet no new parent could have resisted it.

"That's darling!" she exclaimed, knowing he'd fashioned it. By profession, her dad was a toymaker. "Dad, you know you could have brought this over when Rhona and Pip were here."

"I could not," he said a trifle sternly. "It would have been rude to intrude upon your reunion when I'm not able to fulfill the favor she wished of me."

Her dad had funny ideas about manners, but Cass didn't press him to reconsider. He could be as stubborn as her grandma.

"Orange juice?" she offered, knowing this was a rare weakness. "I dug out Gran's old juicer."

"That would be lovely," he said gravely.

She returned with glasses for both of them. Faeries got a little drunk on fresh squeezed fruit, especially purebloods. Her father sipped his consideringly. She noticed he'd worn a business shirt and blue jeans for his visit. On him, they looked as nice as a tuxedo.

"Your grandmother was a fine woman," he announced. "She lived a life any human could be proud of."

"Yes, she did."

"You will miss her."

"I expect I will," she agreed.

He set his drink on a dusty table. As soon as he took a seat in an old armchair, the cat jumped into his lap. With soft absentminded movements, he petted Poly into feline ecstasy. Cass sat on the sofa across from him. Though her father wasn't an open book, she recognized his behavior as working up to something.

She didn't mention he hadn't asked about his ex yet.

After a minute of no sound but Poly's purrs, the man she knew as Roald le Beau gave her his full attention. She was fae too, but his blue gaze hit her like a laser.

"I suppose you'll sell this place soon," he said.

Shock slapped her. What did he mean, he supposed she'd sell? She'd only gotten home yesterday. Didn't he know she was staying?

"Dad." She pressed her palm to her heart. "I'm not selling. I'm moving in."

He was too startled to hide his horror—which wasn't at all like him. Fae didn't show emotions that openly. "You're moving in? What about your mother?"

"Mom is happy in Ohio. This new fellow she married is nice. She certainly doesn't expect her thirty-nine year old daughter to stay with her forever."

"You're still a child."

"Maybe to you, Dad, but not to her. She thinks like a mundane now, like she's forgotten this place exists. Even when we're alone, she never talks about anything magical."

This didn't seem to hurt his feelings, no more than her mother's had seemed hurt during their divorce. All at once, forty years of her parents' weirdness became too much for her.

"Dad," she said, determined to be direct. "Why in the world did you two get hitched?"

"Why do you ask?"

"Because you don't make sense as a couple. You got on better with Gran than Mom. Did you even love her?"

"I love you."

Cass appreciated that, but it didn't answer her question. She lifted one eyebrow.

"Very well," her father said. "Your mother was extremely pretty. I suppose I was lonely."

"But you *married* her."

"For you, darling," he said. "So you'd have two parents."

A muscle twitched at his temple. "I didn't exist when you married."

Her father smiled, slow and sweet and so beautifully Cass understood what non-fae must feel when purebloods glamoured them. "You existed for me."

The tic was gone. He was telling the truth as he believed it.

"Now," he said, aware that he'd disarmed her. "Why don't you tell me about your evening? I'm interested to hear what your old friends have been up to."

~

Cass's father was a great listener. A glow would spread out from his attention, as warm and safe as a down blanket. Cass still floated on it as she prepared for bed. Her room was exactly as she'd left it. Her gran had preserved it, from her gargoyle night light to her tulle-draped princess four-poster. Each year in February, she'd come back and spent a week in it: her and Gran's After-Christmas, as they called it. Cass's mother hadn't joined them. She hadn't liked the reminder that this place existed. At the end of every visit, Cass and her grandmother would hug a long time.

I don't care about your damn glamour, her gran would say. *I couldn't love you one sparkle more than I already do.*

She'd felt fragile in Cass's embrace that last time, a rickety little human using up her store of years. Cass had suspected there wouldn't be many more visits. She hadn't guessed there wouldn't be even one.

No tears, she told herself, slipping under the covers and dashing one away. She was going to be happy in Gran's penthouse. That's what Trish would want for her.

She explained to Poly which pillow she could have, then pulled the sheets to her neck.

I'm loved, she told herself. *It only feels like I'm alone here.*

Not ready to sleep, she thought about her friends. Jin and Bridie were as fun as ever, happy with their work and lives. Seeing Rhona with Pip was lovely. If anyone could pull off single motherhood, it was her. Rhona had talked about wanting kids when she was one herself. With Gran for an example, Cass intended to spoil Pip every way she could think of.

Maybe one day she'd have a kid herself.

That idea tugged Rick Lupone's image rather embarrassingly into her head. She grumbled and squirmed on the mattress, sorry she'd thought of him. So what if his gorgeous arms were designed for propping his massive chest over a bed partner? The chance she'd find herself under it was slim.

"Slim to *none*," she said, hoping the warning would sink in.

Fearing it wouldn't, she closed her eyes.

She didn't think she had time to fall asleep, much less to have a dream.

Even so, suddenly she was fleeing down a long dark tunnel. She'd been running for a while. Her lungs were burning, and a stitch stabbed her rib muscles. Ahead of her, on the tunnel's raw concrete walls, evenly spaced lights formed rings that disappeared into a black distance. Behind her, footsteps pounded—gaining on her, from the sound of them. She couldn't afford to be caught like this. She had to protect the keeper. She searched desperately for a hatch she could escape through, or maybe the next station. Nothing was close enough. There was no way out and no way to call for help.

Unless . . .

She had magic. She could summon her replacement. The universe would provide. That was Law, no matter how far from home she was, no matter how distant the nearest member of her bloodline.

A crash yanked Cass awake again. Across the bedroom, a photograph of her father had fallen from the wall. Poly sprang up on the pillow and made the eerie low-in-the-throat growl scaredy cats were prone to. She'd puffed up her fur as well, though she still looked a bit scrawny.

"C'mere, you," Cass soothed, pulling the cat to her. Poly stopped growling and butted her.

The picture's hook must have broken. It was probably old enough.

She'd snapped the Polaroid when she was a kid, surprising her dad at the workbench in his shop while he spelled a small stuffed rabbit. The picture was the only likeness of him she had. He didn't like being photographed. As she recalled, he'd asked her to destroy it. She said she would but had changed her mind at the last minute. Some days her dad was more approachable than others, but she'd always adored him. If this was the only picture of him she'd get, she couldn't relinquish it.

Hoping it wasn't damaged, but reluctant to get up and check, Cass lay down on the bed again. Her heart rate decelerated more slowly than the cat's. Fortunately, Poly didn't mind the extra petting. Soon enough, they both settled.

You're safe, Cass promised her rattled self. *You're home and you're safe and everything's all right.*

Her head throbbed a little, but that didn't mean her doubts should be listened to. A doubt was just a doubt, not a harbinger of danger.

"Sleep," she murmured, putting some juice in the self-order.

This time, she did so without visions.

CHAPTER TWO

IT was four in the frick a.m. on a Saturday, early shift for the Lupones. Rick was driving to work with his brother Tony in his reliable gray Buick. The sky was clear and the streetlights hazy, the glow they shed on the shuttered shops undisturbed by man or beast. The city might never sleep, but the Lupone's 'hood definitely did. River Heights was solidly blue collar, a bastion of cops and shifters, in various flavors.

"God, I need more coffee," Tony grumbled as Rick turned on Saltpeter.

His younger brother hunched in the passenger seat, knees drawn up between him and the dash. Normally, they rode with the rest of their team in the squad's response van. This morning, Rick decided he wanted to talk in private to his sibling. He wasn't sure why the car seemed the best place for it. They lived a mere floor apart in the same 1910 brownstone.

But maybe the car seemed good because Tony had nowhere to stalk off to if Rick annoyed him.

Rick glanced over at him, trying to gauge his mood. His brother looked scruffy. And sleepy. Rick couldn't tell if the weariness in his face was grumpy or carnal.

"Do I have Faerie O's in my hair?" Tony asked without turning.

"What?"

"You're staring at me."

Rick returned his attention to the nearly empty road ahead. "I just wondered. You were out late last night."

"I went to a bar."

He hadn't gone to O'Doul's, their neighborhood cop hangout. "And?"

"And what?" Tony snapped. "I'm not hung over. It's four in the frick a.m. You want sprightly, you need a sprite for a brother."

Rick laughed in spite of this convo not starting out so well. "I'm trying to ask if you met someone nice."

He'd thought this was an okay way to put it, but evidently not. Tony stared at him like he'd gone crazy.

"You haven't had a date since you came out," Rick explained.

Tony gave him the stare a few seconds longer. "That you know of," he said darkly.

"Have you been dating?"

Tony frowned at the edging of rain spots on the windshield. The car wasn't bright, but Rick thought he might be blushing.

"Tony—"

"You know, Rick, if you were getting laid yourself, you wouldn't worry so much about my sex life."

Rick not getting laid was true, but that was nothing new. Ironically, he wasn't as smooth with the ladies as his brother. The real source of his concern was that Tony had come out in a city of notoriously macho supes. This wasn't San Francisco. Not stepping on the wrong boots was going to be a challenge—and never mind finding happiness. Rick had taken some time to adjust to the news himself. Now he wanted Tony to understand his big brother supported him.

"You could tell me if you met someone special," he tried again.

"Oh God," Tony moaned.

"You could," Rick insisted. "I wouldn't be rude to them."

"Just give me a chance to get my sea legs, would you?"

Did this mean Tony hadn't popped his gay cherry yet? Or what if it meant he was sleeping with every Tom, Dick and Hairy he tripped over?

Rick had reached the end of the D Street Bridge. Gripping the wheel with way too much tension, he turned at the four-way light onto Elm. Unsure if he should drop the subject, he shifted in his seat. Try as he might to be open minded, there were some doors he didn't want to look behind.

The radio crackled, causing Tony to snap upright.

"RTA requests assistance," came the dispatcher's voice. "10-34 M at the Elm and Fifth north station. Witness describes two perps going at it with long swords."

RTA was the Resurrection Transit Authority. A 10-34 M was an assault in progress that involved magic. The subway stop the dispatcher named was only two blocks away. Rick and Tony weren't uniforms. They weren't obliged to take the call. Like most cops who liked excitement, they damn well were tempted.

"Swords," Tony mused, giving Rick a look he had no trouble interpreting.

"Not unheard of," Rick said. "But intriguing."

Tony grabbed the radio. "Car 65 responding. We're two minutes out, no more."

"10-4," Dispatch acknowledged. "Be advised the suspects are fae."

Rick's adrenaline pumped higher. Faeries with swords. This *would* be interesting.

Tony reached into the back seat to grab their vests, which were both bullet- and magic-resistant. Once his own was secure, he readied Rick's for him to slip into. "You packing electrum loads?"

"Yup. You got your depowering charms?"

Tony said he did, and Rick swung the wheel hard right. The Buick hopped the curb like a bunny at the grassy Elm and Fifth Plaza.

Rick's vest fastened with Velcro straps. He had it halfway on before he was out. They slammed the Buick's doors behind them, and then he and Tony were loping across the plaza in nearly the same strides. The lights that marked the north subway entrance weren't broken out. Rick's inner wolf caught a whiff of blood, but the scent wasn't from nearby.

"Maybe the fight started underground," Tony panted.

He wasn't winded; he was amped up.

"Be careful," Rick said, and then—like some huge sparkling dove startled from its roost—the faerie burst up the subway stairs.

People talked about stunning beauties, but for pureblood fae, the meaning was literal. This guy was a slender angel: silver hair, electric blue eyes, grace like a song spun from bone and muscle. No glamour dimmed his glory. His skin was white and shot sparks where it was exposed. His centurion-style armor leathers were plain brown but, boy, did they show off how perfectly shaped he was. For a couple seconds, as Rick took this in, his mind was blank of anything but awe.

The giant long sword the faerie held ran with gore.

The pureblood seemed surprised to encounter him.

"Fuck," Tony cursed, seeing Rick was frozen.

The escaping fae could have come at them. Killed them too, possibly. Werewolves weren't harmless puppies, but even exhausted from a fight, the fae radiated more power than either of them had been this close to. Luckily, rather than attack, the pureblood cut left—too tired to fly across Elm Street but moving fast.

"I got this," Tony cried, peeling off after him.

Rick didn't think he'd catch him, but his heart still stuttered. Tony was the baby. "Call for backup!"

"Will," Tony threw over his shoulder, across all four lanes by then. "Find out who he gutted!"

A gutting seemed likely. Rick followed the strengthening scent of blood down the subway stairs. Resurrection's public transit ran twenty-four/seven, but the staff station booth was empty. As he jogged toward the turnstiles, a human woman in a waitress outfit ran up to him.

She appeared desperate for someone to help her.

"She's dying!" she cried frantically. "I called the ambulance, but I don't think they'll arrive in time."

She? Rick thought, vaulting the locked turnstile. He'd assumed the battling fae were men. Had a bystander been injured? He flashed his badge at the scared woman. "Is anyone still fighting? You see any weapons beside the swords?"

She shook her head. "The other faerie ran away. He stuck his sword straight through her. The RTA guy is giving her first aid."

"Okay," Rick said. "Stay here. I'll have questions for you later."

He left her wringing her hands and urging him to hurry. He hoped this meant she'd hang around long enough to give a statement. A second broad flight of cement steps took him to the platform. There, a burly guy in a blue RTA uniform pressed a big wad of bandages against a slender female's midsection. Rick suspected her delicacy was misleading. Power mattered more than size for faeries. This one lay on her back near the tracks, her black-garbed feet edged into the yellow hazard line. Nearby, the plastic case for a first aid kit was clamshelled open. Rick didn't see the sword she'd been fighting with.

The RTA guy's expression as he looked up conveyed what he thought of his patient's chances of survival.

"Thank God," he said huskily. "Are the EMTs behind you?"

Rick had no joy for him on that score. He heard the sirens approaching, but they were miles away. He turned his wolf senses around the platform and down the tunnel. They confirmed what his eyes told him. The threat was over. The woman lying on the cold station floor was fallout.

He stepped to the subway employee's side. The woman was a pureblood faerie but in no danger of stunning him right now. Clearly in pain, she moaned with her eyes screwed shut. Her fist was clenched beside the subway guy's wad of bandages, as if she wanted to shove him off but knew he was trying to help. Her wound looked too grave to staunch. She'd been stabbed at an angle all the way through her torso—and maybe sawed at for good measure. Though it was cool in the underground, the RTA guy hadn't dragged out the first aid kit's heat-reflecting blanket. Maybe he hadn't dared let up on the pressure he was using. The blood that pooled under the injured woman was turning to faerie dust.

That wasn't a good sign. Rick had seen faeries die before. Those heaps of sparkles were all they left behind.

Not sure what else to do, he knelt. Though it seemed pointless, he added his left hand to the RTA staffer's white-knuckled two. The injured fae let out a noise that made him feel bad for trying. She wasn't wearing armor, leather or otherwise. Looking a lot like a ninja, a black silk tunic and matching pants clung to her pain-tensed form. The cloth's gold dragon pattern was familiar.

Knowing he might only have minutes, he wrapped his right hand gently over the woman's fist. Her skin was icy under his.

"Ma'am," he said. "Can you tell me who attacked you?"

His voice penetrated her pain stupor. The female faerie opened her eyes.

Her irises were as black as obsidian, her lashes a sable fringe over which two diamond teardrops welled.

"*You,*" she said, blinking the jewels away. "Thank the gods you've arrived."

"I'm a cop," he said, wondering if she mistook him for someone else. People did that before they passed sometimes, probably because they wished their loved ones were there. "Hold on for us, okay? Medical help is on the way."

She winced, then fixed her gaze on him. "You're the one. You have to protect her. You need to warn her she's in danger."

"Who's in danger?" he asked softly.

Her eyes cut to the subway guy, as if she didn't trust the very person who'd been trying to save her life. Her fist turned beneath Rick's hand. Her delicate fingers opened, the subtle movement pressing their palms together. Her hand wasn't empty. Something rounded and metal pushed against him.

"You'll know," the faerie said, silently urging him to take it. "You know already. The universe chose you for a reason." The faerie coughed, the sound a crackling inside of her. "Don't trust anyone. They're watching."

Rick couldn't control the gooseflesh that swept his shoulders.

"Shit," said the RTA guy. The faerie's wound had begun to glow. A scent like a field of flowers times a thousand rose pungently around them.

"Hang on," Rick pleaded, wanting her to live more than he could explain. "I'm a shifter. I have energy you can draw on to heal yourself."

He didn't know if this would work, but offering seemed worthwhile.

The faerie smiled like a resigned angel. "I thank you for your kindness, but the sword our enemy stabbed me with was spelled. The moment the enchanted steel pierced my heart, he doomed me."

"The EMTs are *here,*" Rick insisted, hearing the ambulance screech up to the square above them. The faerie's eyes were glowing at their center like her wound was. "At least give me your name. Who we should notify."

He should have known no faerie would tell him that.

"Be brave," she said. "You must not fail as I have. The destiny of your city depends on it."

A number of things happened simultaneously.

The faerie's body dissolved in a bright burst of radiance. Robbed of his support, the RTA guy fell forward, catching himself on hands now buried to the wrist in fine sparkles.

"Shit," he breathed in a mix of dismay and awe. The faerie's shimmering remains were beautiful.

They were also too volatile to last. Rainbow trails drifted from the heap as it began to evaporate. The subway employee gaped, barely noticing the four gear-toting EMTs who clattered down the stairs onto the platform.

"Shit," said one of them—the word of the hour, Rick guessed. "Get that canister working, stat!"

One of his colleagues pulled a sleek handheld vacuum from a big shoulder bag.

"No," Rick said, jumping instinctively to his feet.

"We're licensed to do this," the first medic insisted. "Faerie dust doesn't retain forensic evidence."

This hadn't been Rick's objection. Still in protector mode, he hadn't wanted the faerie harmed further. He stepped aside reluctantly, frankly uneasy watching the EMTs suck the dissipating remnants of his victim into a hose nozzle. He knew faerie dust was an irreplaceable component in many medical treatments—and quite hard to come by. The medics weren't being ghoulish, just practical. They knew better than he did how many non-fae this dust would help.

"Shoot," Tony said, just then arriving at the foot of the platform stairs. A cluster of uniforms followed him. He had called for backup apparently.

"You okay?" Rick asked. His brother looked fine, just out of breath.

"I lost Sword Guy." Tony shook his head dolefully. "I mean, no surprise, but I hoped I could stop him from catching his magical wind longer. He disappeared himself about a mile from here, outside that motorcycle repair on Elm. I requested a department psychic to see if he left any trace of where he went."

This was good thinking. Fae were hell to nail for crimes. They glamoured witnesses, they disappeared, and they poofed away evidence. Hopefully, this one had been in too much of a hurry to erase his tracks completely. If he had, it could save the night from being a total loss.

"We'll escort whoever they assign," said one of the uniforms.

Rick nodded. His throat felt tight, so he cleared it. "Anybody see a waitress up on the next level? She called the bus, she said."

"Compton's taking her statement," the same uniform answered.

"Good."

Sensing he was off, Tony stepped closer to his brother—not to touch but just to be near. It was something pack did without thinking. Rick was glad for it right then.

"I'll talk to you," he said to the dazed transit guy. The big man was shivering slightly from his ordeal. "We'll get you a coffee, and go over what you saw. I assume you can get me access to the station's surveillance."

The man said he could, steadying a bit at having a task to do.

"Where's the female's sword?" Tony asked, thanks to his cop's aversion for leaving dangerous weapons unaccounted for.

Rick kicked himself for forgetting. "I don't know. I didn't see it when I came in."

"We'll search the tracks," assured the uniform. "We had Transit halt the trains."

Out of reflex, all the cops glanced around—as if the missing sword were going to conveniently reappear. As they did, Rick realized his hand was fisted around the metal object the faerie had passed him. It was evidence: his only evidence right then. He started to show it to Tony, then remembered the faerie's words.

Don't trust anyone. They're watching.

Tony wasn't anyone of course, but who knew what else might be lurking invisibly? With its policy of letting any race that could play nice qualify for visas, the city had no shortage of sneaky residents.

Rather than show his hand, Rick shoved his fist into his pants pocket.

~

The detective squad Rick and his brother worked for operated out of a magically warded basement bunker in their precinct building. Their cousin, Adam Santini, was their alpha and lieutenant. Werewolves comprised the bulk of the RPD. Organizing squads along pack lines made such instinctive sense few cops ever questioned the arrangement. Rick was Adam's second—his beta, as it was termed. He liked the position. Adam was a good leader as well as someone he cared about. Having his best friend's back plus authority over the others suited Rick's personality. To him, being number one was too much pressure. Being number two was perfect.

Watching Adam fall in love and get married the previous year had required some adjusting. Luckily, Rick was over that. Adam's wife Ari had become his friend as well, and her bringing a new baby into the pack made both him and his wolf feel good. When it came down to it, Rick was a simple soul. He wasn't prone to brooding or bad moods. He loved his family, his pack, and his job—pretty much in that order. As long as they were safe, he could deal with a change or two.

Weird though this case was on its surface, it seemed unlikely to threaten that.

On the other hand, if they had stumbled over a fae conspiracy, best to keep the information within the family. The first thing Rick did after entering the squad room was walk straight to Adam's office, yank out his bottom drawer, and activate the anti-eavesdropping charm Adam kept stored there. Per usual, Adam had been hanging in the squad room with his men. He followed Rick into the windowed office. Seeing his second making himself at home, he snorted humorously.

"Should I shut the blinds for you?" he offered.

"Sure," Rick said, knowing his alpha was too secure to take offense. "At the least, we'll want it dark to watch this footage."

He stuck a thumb drive into the port on Adam's computer. By this time, the squad had squeezed around Adam's desk to watch. Silence reigned while the faeries fought like Errol Flynn on steroids. Considering the combatants were more or less superhuman, it didn't surprise that the clash ranged from the tracks to the platform and the steel-beamed ceiling. Both faeries had meant business, the action moving so fast that more than once Rick had to slow the playback. The video ended with the EMTs arrival.

Tony whistled in regret for all of them. "Now I'm really sorry I didn't get Sword Guy. That lady faerie was badass."

"Does her outfit look familiar?" Rick asked. "I swear I've seen it before."

"Maybe," Adam said unsurely.

Nate Rivera, their snazziest dresser and maybe their sharpest tack, snapped long fingers. "*Mini-Dragons to the Rescue!* Evina's kids are obsessed with that cartoon. That black costume is what the dragon keepers' protectors wear."

Just last weekend, Nate had married a weretiger. She had two kids already, whom Nate was adopting.

"The dragon keepers' protectors?" Adam repeated.

"There's a Dragon Guild on the show. The keepers train the dragons, and the protectors safeguard them." Nate sounded sheepish for knowing.

"That's right," Tony said. "Ethan watches that all the time."

Ethan was Tony and Rick's nephew. Like most kids, he loved dragons. Rick had seen snippets of the show himself every Sunday he babysat.

"So . . . what then?" Adam said. "Our vic is a mini-dragon fanatic?"

A tingle took hold of Rick's shoulders. "Maybe she's a member of the actual Dragon Guild."

"Dragons are extinct," Adam said. "The big ones, anyway."

"They're extinct *here*. We don't know everything that goes on in Faerie."

"What I miss?" Carmine asked from the door. The final member of their squad was an uncle figure, a good-natured stocky older wolf who'd once been their only married detective. He'd been questioning a suspect in another case. Rick assumed he'd finished.

"Scooch in," Adam said. "And shut the door behind you."

Carmine's bushy brows shot up at the extra security measures. He listened attentively while Rick went through his account again. The longer Rick talked, the more unsettled he was by his own story. The sword fight in the subway couldn't be all there was to this. Resurrection's mysterious fae founders must be up to something.

"That's what she said?" Carmine asked when he finished. "You have to protect some woman, and the destiny of the city depends on it?"

"She might have been nuts," Tony suggested, seemingly for the hell of it. He'd braced his back against Adam's shelves of procedural manuals. He was relaxed now, easy among his pack. "Faeries live so long sometimes they go bonkers."

Barring death by violence or misadventure, faeries were immortal.

"I've heard rumors that in their own realm, they occasionally get so tired of their lives they erase their memories. Actually self-induce complete amnesia."

This contribution came from Nate. Third in the pack hierarchy, he sat on the corner of Adam's desk, one alligator-booted foot wagging where he'd pulled it across his knee. Some might consider his posture—and his position—presumptuous, but that was Nate for you. Rick had learned not to get his back up every time Nate got big for his britches.

Adam reinforced who Rick was in the pecking order by addressing him directly. "Did the fae seem crazy to you?"

"No." Rick was careful not to deliver his opinion as if it were established fact. "A little dramatic, but not unhinged." His hand was still in his pocket. He hesitated, then decided to pull out the object his fingers were curled around. "She gave me this before she died."

He opened his palm, looking at what he held for the first time himself. That was weird, he realized. Logically, he should have peeked by now.

"Are those brass knuckles?" Carmine asked, leaning forward with the rest.

They certainly looked like it. They had four finger holes, plus a bracing loop on the bottom to fit the palm. Short sharp spikes topped the circles, guaranteeing being punched by them would do damage. Incised runes marked the metal's curves, suggesting more mystical defenses. Oddly, though the faerie's hand had been slender, these rings were suitably sized for him.

"I think they're electrum," Tony said, one finger stretched toward the silvery gold metal.

Rick didn't jerk his hand away, but he should have. The instant Tony's fingertip connected, a spark the size of a walnut zapped out at him.

"Ouch," Tony said, electrocuted fingertip in his mouth. "You didn't warn me that thing bites."

Rick looked at it. "I didn't know it would."

Because he was Nate, Adam's third tried to touch it with the same results.

"The pureblood keyed it to you," Adam concluded.

"But why?" Rick was utterly flummoxed now. He was an ordinary wolf, not the sort a faerie would involve in anything important.

"Because you're 'The One,'" Carmine teased, quote marks obvious from his tone. "You're supposed to warn some chickie she's in danger."

"I swear I have no idea what she meant."

"Don't you?" Adam peered at him. "She claimed you already knew who the woman was."

"That doesn't mean I do!"

"Put them on," Carmine suggested. "Maybe the pureblood keyed the answer into them."

"What if it isn't safe?" Rick said, feeling uncomfortably hemmed in. "If the knuckles are enchanted, maybe one of the department psychics should vet them first."

Even as he made the suggestion, his fingers closed over the faerie's gift.

His brain was at war with his instincts. They didn't want anyone touching this thing but him.

Adam didn't miss the unconscious gesture. He put all his alpha soothing into his voice. "Hang onto to them for now. You know there are no coincidences in Resurrection. We'll follow what leads we've got, and maybe an answer will come to you."

Rick opened his mouth to repeat his denial. Before he could, a tiny tickle of something nudged the back of his awareness. It was like trying to remember the words to a song he'd caught himself humming. Rick *almost* saw a face. A scent came with it, a sensation of old longing. Muscles tightened in his chest. He realized his groin was heavy and hot, like he was about to throw wood.

Sheesh, he thought, startled by the reaction. Rick was a normal guy. He got boners, sometimes for no reason. This, however, reminded him of the instant hard-ons he'd been plagued by in high school. God, they'd driven him crazy. As he recalled, they'd been inspired most frequently by one particular pretty girl.

No, he thought to himself. No way could she be involved in this.

"I'll hang onto them," he agreed, wanting out of Adam's crowded office that second.

"Good." Adam's gaze sharpened. He must have sensed more going on than Rick was saying. "Let us know if you come up with something."

Rick's penis twitched. He feared *coming up* with something would be the problem.

~

The squad had other crimes to investigate besides Rick's fae-on-fae violence. Carmine had caught lead on a vampire homicide—or re-homicide, Rick supposed. The undead were famous for big egos and short tempers. Carmine asked Nate and Rick to back him up while he questioned the case's primarily nocturnal witnesses. Carmine was good with people, getting them to talk, putting them at their ease. Rick and Nate were mostly along as muscle. They returned to the precinct around daybreak. When Rick checked his email, the report from the uniform who'd interviewed his witness was waiting.

Sadly, the waitress hadn't heard the sword fighting faeries speak. She knew no reason for the altercation and couldn't describe the surviving pureblood even as well as Rick. Officer Compton, who Rick guessed had a sense of humor, noted she'd expressed the wistful opinion that the male had been "too gorgeous to breathe around."

Rick doubted he'd get an ID from that. If their killer didn't keep a home in the Pocket—and even if he did—purebloods weren't in the system like other folks. No birth certificates, no taxes, no credit cards required. What they were was the *abracadabra* to open any door. Thinking back to his brief glimpse, Rick was inclined to believe this pureblood wasn't a regular visitor. He'd seemed wild to Rick in ways he couldn't put his finger on. Fae familiar with the city weren't that alien. Occasionally, they even went native. Rick was willing to bet this male spent most his time in the Old Country.

Which left Rick pretty much nowhere.

The psychic who swept the motorcycle repair shop came up empty as well. The killer had disappeared his trace and himself. She was able to assure Rick he was highborn. According to her, juice like his wasn't common to lower ranks.

So now Rick had a—maybe—royal fae conspiracy, possibly involving dragons, and perhaps a risk to their fair city.

Stymied, he stacked his feet on top of his cluttered desk. The nearest cop in the squad room was Nate. He sat at the desk in front of Rick's, tapping his phone after hanging up a call. His dark ponytail—just one of his vanities— was so neat and glossy it looked polished.

He must have been aware of Rick staring. Without turning to look, he balled up a piece of paper, threw it over his shoulder, and hit Rick in the head with it.

"Don't think too hard," he teased. "You wouldn't want your brains to run out."

Sometimes Nate was lucky he was Rick's cousin.

"Sorry," he said, swiveling around to catch Rick frowning. "If it makes you feel better, I asked Evina to gather up Abby and Rafi's *Mini-Dragon* DVDs. The cubs will be ecstatic when I tell them I have to watch them for work."

He did make Rick feel better, though not out of revenge. Rick was willing to admit Nate's brain was worth consulting.

"It's a cartoon," he said, not wanting to get his hopes up.

"Sure it is." Nate leaned forward across his knees. "On the other hand, according to my Oogle search, the original showrunner was a pureblood. Maybe there's a thread of truth behind the stories."

"Mini-dragons are actual creatures. They're just aquatic."

"More truth than that."

Nate was being less jokey than usual. Maybe marrying his tigress had made him more of a team player. Rick fought off a pang of jealousy. Before Evina, Nate had defined *ladies' man*. Of all the pack, Rick was probably the least committed to bachelorhood. And now only he and Tony were unhitched. No matter what challenges his little brother faced, considering Tony's natural charisma, Rick probably shouldn't count on having company long.

The stupid brass knuckles dug into his hip. Ignoring them, he rocked his chair squeakily. "What did big dragons do that was so special? Besides chowing down on virgins and setting villages on fire."

"Dunno," Nate said. "All I've read are fairy tales."

In Rick's experience, they weren't much better than cartoons. He glanced at his watch. Two thirty. Normally, he wasn't eager to knock off work, but today he was restless. Making his decision, he swung his legs down and stood.

"I'm going home. Maybe I'll do some research there. Call me if anything new breaks."

"You okay?" Nate asked, tilting his head at him.

"Fine," Rick said. He didn't know what to think of the sudden ache that jabbed behind his left eye.

~

Rick's place took up the second floor of the narrow brownstone he owned with Adam and Tony. He had a door—and a lock—though you wouldn't know it from the way the others made themselves welcome. The space inside was comfortable but messy. Because he hadn't done it that morning, he took his usual trashbag around the kitchen and living room, clearing up the stuff he should have tossed right away but somehow never did. Takeout cartons disappeared into the green plastic maw; Adam's newspaper minus the sports section; Rick's subscription to *Police Monthly*. Those empty bottles had to be Tony's. Rick eyed the fanciful label suspiciously. He certainly didn't drink "Cracked Pumpkin." The name sounded like something trend-conscious Nate would dub the next big thing in craft beer.

On a roll, he nearly threw away baby Kelsey's squeaky bath duck. What was *that* doing here? Ari and Adam hadn't brought the baby down in days. Unless Ari had borrowed his washer-dryer while he was out. She kept telling Adam *he* should try doing laundry for three people one load at a time.

Rick smiled as he perched the rescued duck on his mantelpiece. Ari was a pip. Being married to an alpha didn't cow the human at all. Done now, he looked around the room with a sense of accomplishment. Not spotless but much better. Nobody could say he was too slobby to be a good boyfriend.

He went cold as a terrible idea hit. His weapons closet. Had it been locked when Ari came down with the baby? He ran to check, relief flooding his whole body when he found it secure. He'd remembered. And he'd never, ever forget. He knocked his brow against the wood to make sure the intention would sink in.

What was that he'd been thinking about being a potentially good boyfriend?

He let out a sighing laugh. To be a good boyfriend, first you had to find someone you wanted to be good to.

He straightened, positioned across from his dining nook, where he kept his at-home workspace and computer. His brain felt too fried for research. A shower and an hour of shuteye should cure that. Chances were, his killer faerie was unreachable already.

When he returned to his bedroom, clean and clearer of head, he saw he'd tossed the contents of his pockets onto his unmade bed. Sun from the two broad windows winked off the brass knuckles.

It was like they were mocking him.

Fine. He'd put them on and see what happened. He could "research" while he napped. If some magical message had been encoded into the metal, his decidedly non-magical werecop brain would be more receptive.

He didn't bother dressing, simply got into bed and lay on his back. His fingers slid easily through the electrum rings. Nothing happened, though the knuckle-dusters felt like they'd been made for him. He flexed his fist to test them. Still nothing. They were just cold metal.

Resigned to feeling foolish, he pulled up the sheets and closed his eyes. His body hummed from the day's events. Surprising that glittery fae . . . running into the subway . . . watching the female die . . .

You know already, she'd said. *The universe chose you for a reason.*

Clearly, she'd mistaken him for someone more in touch with the mystical.

He shifted onto his left side, his muscles itchy, the hand that wore her gift curling around the palm bar. His cock was hardening, but he ignored it. He was tired of jacking off, tired of a life where everyone but him had someone awesome to come home to. So what if he wasn't as exciting as his friends? He was a decent guy. Not ugly and not a loser. It shouldn't be that hard for him to find a partner.

Sleep snuck up on him gradually. He thought back to high school, where more than one girl had chased him. He'd fooled around with a couple, but they hadn't been keepers. He'd had his eye on someone so out of reach she might as well have been made up. Had he established his romantic pattern then? Was he doomed to only want women he had no chance of snagging?

And the dream was on him. He recognized the hallway at North Heights High, dull tan lockers stretching forever in either direction. In front of him was his locker from senior year: 1212 with the sticky lock. Not that he wanted to open it. Snow White was in the way. She had her back to the dinged up metal, like she meant to keep him from the schoolbooks he'd stowed inside.

"Want a bite?" she asked. She showed him a ruby-skinned apple. She'd already taken a chomp, her red lips glistening as she licked them.

Jesus, she was hot. Her glossy black hair fell in waves over her smooth shoulders, her soft blue eyes too mesmerizing not to get lost in. Like all her kind, she was tall, as elegantly curved as an X-rated fae princess. Her legs were so long and graceful they made him hurt.

"Where are your clothes?" he gasped, stunned by her bareness.

"Gone," she answered, doe-eyed and innocent.

She didn't even look slutty naked. Her pussy hair was a perfect triangle, her breasts snowy velvet knolls tipped by strawberries. He swallowed. She was wriggling her bottom against the locker, like maybe she was horny. That idea was too much for his libido. His erection shuddered inside his jeans, the frickin' Pocket State Building of hard-ons. Only she revved him up this bad, like he'd die if he didn't get his cock inside her.

Maybe she wanted to kill him. She caught her full lower lip in her pearly teeth.

"Come on, Rick," she coaxed, surprising him by knowing his name. "Don't you want a taste of this?"

She meant the apple, but he wasn't interested in that.

"I want you," he groaned, the truest true confession he'd never made. "If I don't have you, I'll go crazy."

Her eyes were bold, her irises glowing like an excited wolf's. She slid her silky arms up around his neck. "Take me," she purred. "I've been waiting for you to wise up."

He kissed her like he was starving. He was naked too then, maybe from her magic. She hiked herself up his body, long legs tightening around his waist. He meant to wait. Girls needed to be ready to take guy his size. Then her nails dug into his back, and he just couldn't. He shoved his cock all the way into her wet pussy.

She felt so good his vertebrae tried to melt.

"Oh my God," he said, breaking free of the kiss to pant. Overwhelmed with desire, he pressed her harder into the locker. Her breasts were soft on his chest, her sex hot enough to burn. She squirmed those tight walls around him, making him even more insane. His tip was squashed deep inside her. Fourth of July sparks shot up it.

"You're big," she said breathily. For a second, he feared he was too much for her. "I like that. I want you to protect me."

Rick's cock threatened to have a seizure. Growling low in his chest like the wolf he was, his hands clamped around her bottom. He drew his hips halfway back to thrust.

"I'll protect you," he vowed. "I'll fucking protect you good."

His eyes snapped open before he could slam in. Shit. Talk about wet dream *interruptus*. A monster erection pounded in front of him, as huge and desperate as if he'd been having sex for real. His right hand was trying to grasp it, but the damn electrum knuckles were in the way.

He could hardly get them off fast enough.

"Shit," he hissed as he gripped himself.

He pulled two-handed all the way up his pole. God, he was close, like he'd been teased for hours and needed to come or die. Unable to hold back, he spit on three fingers and rubbed the head. His neck arched with pleasure. That was it. That was . . . He rolled onto his back so he could fuck his right hand while his left fingers rubbed. He grunted, grinding his butt cheeks together and thrusting compulsively. His cock was steely, the hot spot at the base as itchy and tender as if someone else were there. All werewolves had a gland there, one that turned their sensation dial to ten if it switched on for a partner. His bulbus shouldn't feel like this when he was alone, but it was driving him crazy. He pumped faster, tightening his fingers, making sure they squeezed as tight as they could on the achy spot.

His hand was big, but his stiffened cock was longer.

"Unh," he said, his scalp nearly lifting off.

He twisted his grips like he was opening a jar, one on his swollen base, one on the slippery crown. A bundle of sheet was caught between his thighs. It strafed his balls like a woman's nails.

"Cass," he gasped. "*Fuck.*"

His orgasm blasted off. His hips snapped up for it, jism shooting like a fountain onto his chest. The pleasure was sharp and hard and left him as mellow as melted caramel when it trailed off.

His panting breaths were loud in the empty room.

I said her name, he thought. Cass's name. Snow White. The breathtaking unattainable bane of his high school existence.

This wasn't the first time he'd jacked off to fantasies of her. It was, however, the first time a mysterious dying faerie told him he already knew the person he was meant to protect.

It might not really be her, of course. Rick might *want* to play her knight in shining armor because he wanted her. His own wish fulfillment could be obscuring the true message. Then again, what if it *was* her, and he convinced himself not to help? Could he live with the consequences of letting her be hurt?

He groaned aloud at the conundrum. One thing he knew for sure: going to see Cass Maycee would be embarrassing.

CHAPTER
THREE

CASS couldn't swear things looked better in the morning, only that she was determined to tackle them. A cautious walk across her bedroom brought the first knockback. The picture of her father, which had fallen down last night, lay in a compact puzzle of its own broken glass. Careful not to endanger her bare feet, Cass fished it out by the frame. Though this was unharmed, part of the photograph was blackened, as if the paper had smoldered and then gone out. Her father no longer sat at his worktable, caught in that long-ago moment of creation. A rough edged smudge replaced every bit of him.

Dismayed, she touched the carbonized shape with her fingertips. She didn't know who would have done this except for him. Indeed, perhaps this was what he'd been looking around for in Gran's study. He should have reminded Cass she'd promised to destroy it, rather than summoning up the juice to do it long distance.

But maybe he thought she'd fail to follow through again. He must have realized how precious the photo was, how it symbolized their connection. This saddened her even more. Did he truly mind that she loved him like a human? Not cool and remote and proper but complicated and messy.

"I still love you, Dad," she said stubbornly. "Burning this picture doesn't give you your way."

Poly reminded her with a head butt and a yowl that it was time for breakfast.

The little bell on her collar jingled. That was funny. Cass didn't remember hearing it yesterday.

"Aaow," Poly insisted.

"Oh fine," Cass said. "At your service, your highness."

Once the cat was happy, Cass squared her shoulders to face her second source of anxiety: the dolorous Maycee portrait hall.

Her gran had been obsessed with her ancestors. Behind her back, Jin and

Bridie used to call her the Mayflower Madam, a nickname they'd probably understood too well for twelve-year-olds. The tall barrel-ceilinged corridor ran the length of the penthouse, more than sufficient wall space for hanging every Maycee Gran could dig up. The earliest were near the foyer. The original farming family each had their own oil portraits, painted by Resurrection's version of Rembrandt Peale.

As a girl, Cass had wondered how they felt—those presumably practical-minded tillers of the soil, swallowed without warning by an unfamiliar reality. They'd been the first residents of the Pocket, before faeries or demons or any of the descendants of the Stranded who'd gradually found their way to this supe haven. As the city rose, magically and otherwise, Maycees stood ready to greet newcomers, happy to show them around and sell them whatever staples they might require. Gran's relatives had excelled at commerce from the get-go.

Cass smiled at Isaiah Maycee, the patriarch of the first Maycees, prosperous and proud in his Victorian business suit. The vibe the portrait gave off was barely there, probably coming more from the painter than Isaiah. This, she concluded, wasn't what she'd come to find.

She drew a slow breath and focused, trailing three-quarters down the hall before her willies jumped out at her. She'd paused at a photograph of Agnes Maycee, taken during the era of beehive hairdos. It must have been new. Cass didn't remember seeing it on previous visits. Agnes's frosted bubble-gum pink lipstick did nothing to improve her smug half smile. Aside from not liking her expression, Cass couldn't say what was wrong with her. The photo didn't feel haunted; in fact, its subject might not be dead.

"Don't care," Cass muttered and focused herself again. She spun a camouflage around the picture, something she'd always been good at. When she was done, the picture looked like a bundle of greasy cardboard, safe to toss down the trash chute to the furnace without some janitor being tempted to rescue it.

That business taken care of, Cass fulfilled her promise to Rhona to spell a couple boxes of baby-safe detergent with extra stain-lifting power. She fixed her own breakfast next, a slightly pathetic bowl of Wheaty Charms. She ate them standing at the acre-long kitchen island, switching on Gran's TV to keep her company.

Clearly, she needed to get a job. She'd had them when she lived Outside. Being nothing but a department store heiress was already boring her.

For two whole seconds she thought about adopting like Rhona had. That idea didn't feel right for her. She had a maternal streak, but it wasn't as strong as her best friend's. Cass wanted something more like a *purpose*, something she'd be proud of when her long half fae life eventually wound down. Her gran had felt that way about the family stores. Cass had no clue what would inspire her.

Lost in thought, she put her empty bowl in the dishwasher. The news had come on the small TV. A human in a waitress outfit was being interviewed by a reporter. Cass was watching WQSN, so the extra energy the interviewer radiated was probably shifter.

"It was the scariest thing I ever saw," the woman declared breathily. "Two pureblood faeries trying to kill each other with big long swords. If I hadn't been riding the train so late, I would have missed the whole thing!"

"Did you fear for your life?" the handsome newscaster asked.

"Absolutely!" the woman said, clearly more excited than fearful now. "It was like an action movie, the way they flew and flipped across the platform. The male was amazing. I could hardly breathe watching him. Of course it was sad when the female passed. She was so beautiful. I'd never seen one of them up close before."

"Sheesh," Cass muttered, switching off the program. *One of them.* Why did non-fae have to be so weird about purebloods? She could tell the woman wasn't thinking of what she'd seen as having happened to real people.

~

WQSN's interview with the waitress was all over the radio in Rick's car. This didn't make him happy. True, he hadn't told the cop who questioned the witness to warn her off blabbing to the press, nor would a warning necessarily have stopped her. Knowing this meant he couldn't chew out Compton or even himself too much.

He simply hated when homicides became public entertainment. The end of a person's life was due more respect.

When the radio announcer promised more details coming up, Rick clicked the program off. The tease was a lie at least. No one had anything of substance to divulge—including him, sadly. Anyway, it wasn't worth losing his cool over.

He had other reasons for doing that.

A search for Cassia Maycee on his home computer had yielded a long article on the death of her grandmother. For a human, Patricia Maycee was quite the luminary. Businesswoman. Sponsor of charities and the arts. Interestingly, only Cass was mentioned as a "survived by." Rick was under the impression Patricia's daughter was alive.

He could have been wrong. After Cass left Resurrection, he'd sworn off glomming onto every story about the Maycees he came across. What would have been the point? She'd been beyond his reach when she lived in the same city.

She's still beyond it, he told himself. No matter what that faerie had or hadn't been telling him.

Nervous, he tapped the wheel with restless fingers as he turned into the public parking beneath Resurrection's main Maycee's. The faerie's knuckle-dusters were once more in his pocket. He'd knocked them on the floor during his crazed masturbation session. Naturally, they hadn't broken or poofed away. He couldn't be that lucky.

The memory of how intensely he'd blasted off inspired an unwelcome stirring between his legs.

"Fuck," he cursed, parking the Buick with a small screech.

He was partially hard by the time he unbuckled and climbed out. Pressing the button for the store's elevator brought him up all the way. He wasn't even certain Cass was staying at her grandmother's. Coming here was a what-the-hell long shot.

By nature, werewolves ran hot. Despite the plummeting October temperatures, Rick had dressed in old jeans and a long sleeve T-shirt, plus a light sport jacket to cover his shoulder rig. He buttoned it with a grimace, not cold but needing its length to conceal the effect his old crush had on him. The elevator took him as far as Twelve, at which point his cock was shoved so tight against his zipper he had to work to walk normally.

Rick's pack had answered calls here a time or two. He'd been aware the Maycee matriarch lived here. The security station was where he remembered, in a corporate looking atrium with a sunburst-patterned terrazzo floor. A horseshoe desk on a platform sat in its center. The rent-a-cop behind it looked up from his surveillance screens.

"RPD," Rick said, badging him. "I need to speak to Miss Maycee."

The rent-a-cop studied his badge and him. "She expecting you?"

"No," Rick said. His pulse picked up at the indicator that she was here. "I'd appreciate it if you'd ring her for me."

The guy didn't argue, though he also didn't promise him entry. Picking up his phone's receiver, he pressed a speed dial button.

"Miss Maycee?" he said after a short delay. "This is Security on Twelve. There's someone from the RPD to see you, a Detective Lupone. Would you like me to send him up?"

Somewhat embarrassingly, a bead of sweat rolled down the channel of Rick's spine. His wolf-enhanced hearing told him the guard's announcement was met with silence. After two heartbeats, it ended.

"Lupone?" said a muffled but familiar voice.

The effect this had was ridiculous. Waves of chills chased each other along Rick's vertebrae. His cock throbbed, his jeans front stretched enough for a couple socks to be stuffed inside. The sudden roaring in his ears prevented him from deciphering Snow White's next comment.

Fortunately, the guard heard it. "She'll see you," he said to Rick. "The residence's elevator is at the end of the hall behind me. Just press the 'P' button."

Exiting the private elevator was disorienting. Whatever he'd been expecting, it wasn't this. The Maycee penthouse wasn't some modern loft; it was a mansion in the sky. The floor his worn running shoes landed on was marble, the walls to this—antechamber, he had to call it—paneled in impossibly beautiful tigerwood. Two exquisite Chinese vases, both as tall as he was, both valuable antiques, flanked either side of the residence's double door.

Shit, he thought, hitching his jacket straight on his shoulders. He was so out of his depth here.

He jabbed the bell before he lost his nerve.

Then he braced himself to see Cass.

"Coming," she said from behind the door.

A second later, she opened it.

He wasn't prepared. All the time in the world and all the sensible intentions couldn't have accomplished that. Rick was no faerie groupie—never had been and never would be. Fae beauty was too cold for a hot-blooded wolf like him, too arm's length and elitist. Cass, though . . . Cass married vulnerable human sweetness with faerie perfection. Yes, she had the reserve all faeries did—the effortless air of being a notch or two better. Despite this, Cass's soft blue eyes invited a man to drown; they didn't demand it. Cass was *almost* real enough to believe in.

She was dressed in the fancy sweats rich people were fond of. Hers were navy with a white zipper. Helpless not to admire how they hugged her figure, his gaze traveled down her and up again. Her wavy black hair was wet. He wasn't sure, but it seemed shorter than in high school.

"Sorry," she said, her hand going to it. "I'd just gotten out of the pool when Security called."

She sounded nervous. Her velvety cheeks were pink.

"Actually, I'm sorry for intruding." He was proud of how steadily the words came out. He was *not* going to think about her swimming, possibly in nothing but her shimmery faerie skin. "I don't know if you remember me. I'm Rick Lupone, Detective Lupone now. We went to school together at North Heights. I'm working on a case, and your name came up."

He'd decided this was how he'd put it, rather than make himself seem crazy from the start.

"Oh." Her graceful hand, every bit as slender and tantalizing as he remembered, slid from her hair to her throat. "I . . . um . . . I do remember you, as it happens. Won't you come in?"

~

Rick Lupone was at her door. Given how recently she'd been thinking of him, that was too weird for words. And he wanted to talk to her about a case. What on earth could *she* know that would help him?

She was somewhat stunned by the fact that he knew who she was—unless he remembered because he'd looked her up in preparation for coming here.

"Would you like coffee?" she asked. "Or soda?"

He shook his head. She reminded herself this wasn't a social call. God, he looked good. He'd been tall in high school. Now he had to be six foot four—every inch of it honed muscle. His beautiful green eyes were as kind as she remembered, his dark brown hair as thick and shiny. Werewolves aged slower than humans, so of course it would be. He did seem a *little* older. More solid. More . . . rooted somehow. His chest was broader. His shoulders too. She started to feel heated between the legs.

"Could I take your jacket?" she blurted.

"I'm fine," he said politely. "Is there somewhere we could sit and talk?"

For a moment, she couldn't remember the location of a single room in her gran's penthouse.

"In here," she said, once her brain recovered from its stall. Rick preceded her through the archway into the big living room, striding through the various furniture groupings to the long line of arched windows. She knew why they'd drawn him. They overlooked Fifth Avenue and the Ramble in Resurrection's version of Central Park. Down below, leaves glowed with bright fall colors, the winding paths curving in and out of sight between the treetops.

"Wow," Rick said, leaning into the deep embrasure. The walls of this room were stone. That and the Gothic tracery on the windows made the space castle-like. Rick looked oddly right in the setting, despite his modern clothes. But cops were sort of like knights, she supposed.

"Gran liked her views," she said.

The sill was wide enough to perch on. Turning back to face her, Rick rested his hips on it. His eyes held hers, warming her deep inside. To her embarrassment, a spark of faerie glitter leaped off her hand. Hoping he hadn't seen, Cassie shoved it in the pocket of her Juiced Couture sweat jacket. For adults, faerie dust was a mild aphrodisiac. She didn't want Rick thinking she was trying to seduce him.

"About the case," he said, one wide shoulder braced on the window's glass. Sunshine lit his smooth olive skin. As if reluctant to continue, he cleared his throat. "What do you know about dragons?"

The question took her by surprise. "Dragons? Nothing especially."

"Nothing." He didn't sound like he believed her.

"I know what everyone else does of course. *Mini-Dragons to the Rescue* and all that. I assume that's not what you're here to ask."

"Your dad is a pureblood."

"Yes," she agreed slowly. If he wanted her to share privileged information about her father's people, this could get awkward.

"Didn't he tell you stories about the original race? The ancient dragons who sailed the sky like ships?"

She smiled. She couldn't help it. The way he put it was poetic. She seemed to have embarrassed him. Color washed onto his cheekbones.

"I've heard those stories," she said, pushing back her amusement, "but not from my father. He read me human books when I was a kid. He said he liked them better. He didn't talk much about the Old Country."

Rick was listening with more attention than she understood. "And you didn't think that was strange?"

She thought lots of things were strange, including the fact that in the last five minutes she'd exchanged more words with her long-ago secret crush than in all four years at high school.

"Faeries are private people. I assumed my father's memories of where he came from weren't sunny. If you think I'm some sort of expert, I'm afraid I'll disappoint. You might try the Dragonati. They claim their kind descends from the ancient ones."

Dragonati were eight-foot-tall bipedal talking lizards. They looked a bit like dragons, though opinions differed as to whether the species were related. For that matter, opinions differed on whether ancient dragons existed. Cass was inclined to believe, but a lot of residents of the Pocket dismissed them as legends.

Rick rubbed the back of one finger across very kissable full lips. "I'm not sure the Dragonati can be relied on to be objective."

The sun that struck the side of his face turned his dark lashes gold. He had great bone structure: not too pretty, not too rough, but a perfect blend of both. Cass struggled to keep her thoughts on track.

"I don't understand," she said. "What exactly are you hoping I can tell you?"

Rick let out a quiet sigh and dug in his pants pocket. When he'd sat, the bottom of his buttoned jacket had parted. His jeans weren't tight, but the denim displayed the same tantalizing fade marks that had fascinated her as a teenager. The thighs were lighter of course. His leg muscles were well developed. More distracting were the paler patches around his crotch, where the weight of his balls habitually rubbed the cloth. God, he had a substantial package. Cass shook her head to herself. Could he really be that hefty when he wasn't aroused? She could see the thickness of his penis pressing against his zipper and stretching down his pant's leg. The head was discernible—rounded and big and . . .

Arousal and awareness flashed through her like lightning bolts. He *was* hard. That was a full blown boner she was ogling. She must have dusted him without realizing, because he attracted her. Shit, this was embarrassing.

Face blazing, she yanked her gaze to his.

He knew what she'd been staring at. His darker skin hid his flush better, but it was there. Apparently, he wasn't going to mention her faux pas. He clenched his jaw—in annoyance or determination—and pulled his hand out of his pocket. Metal gleamed in the sun.

"Have you seen anything like this before?" he asked.

Her eyes saw the brass knuckle thingie he'd drawn out, but her brain couldn't quite catch up. It assumed he was referring to his prize-winning erection. *No, Detective,* she thought with slightly hysteric humor. *I've never seen anything quite like that.*

Cass was certain her friend Jin would have uttered the wisecrack aloud.

~

This interview was turning out even more awkward than Rick had feared. That Cass had seen Mt. Everest rising from his crotch was obvious. Ignoring his embarrassment and hers, he held out the electrum knuckles. Cass touched them before he could warn her not to. Nothing happened—or nothing to do with them giving her a shock. Her little finger bumped his palm accidentally. Tingles streaked through him so strongly he shuddered.

Rather than take the weapon from his hand, she brushed over it with her thumb and forefinger. "I'm not an expert on reading objects, but I can tell you this is millennia old. The runes are an obscure dialect of High Fae." She lifted her hand, her palm now hovering an inch above his. When she closed her eyes, the fans of her black-black lashes rested serenely on her cheeks. "The energy inside the electrum feels transformative."

"Transformative."

She nodded without lifting her eyelids. "That's the best description I can give. I can't tell if the enchantment is meant to change itself or something else. For what it's worth, these things have been keyed to match your energy. I assume you were given them as a gift?"

Deeply ingrained cop habit kept him from confirming this. "Are they dangerous?"

She shrugged and opened her eyes again. "Any magic can be. I don't sense an intent to harm you. The opposite, actually. If I were forced to guess, I'd say they were protective."

She'd spoken as casually as someone reading the newspaper, this sort of thing second nature to her.

"If I'm allowed to ask," she said, "where did you get them?"

This was his opening if he wanted it. He hesitated. Did he really want to share the cockamamie story of a dying fae *maybe* suggesting she was in danger and—also maybe—claiming *he* was her protector?

"Is this related to the faerie who died in the subway last night?" she asked.

Little hairs stood up on his arms. "Why would you say that?"

Again she shrugged, her eyes watching his closely. "I'm half faerie. We get hunches. Forgive me for saying so, but your reaction tells me I'm right."

"Yes," he admitted, oddly glad she'd pushed him to. "Here's the thing. When the faerie gave them to me, she implied her enemies were watching and that I needed to warn someone they were in danger. She failed, but I mustn't. She said the destiny of the city depended on me protecting this individual."

Cass was wide-eyed. "Who did she mean?"

"She said I'd know. Cass, I think she was talking about you."

"Me?"

Even if she weren't half fae and therefore bad at lying, Rick would have judged her astonishment as genuine.

"Yes," he said, studying her expression. "When I put the knuckles on, you were the person who came to mind."

"But I'm not in danger! Why would I be? I'm no one important."

"Are you sure? Nothing strange has happened to you lately?"

She crossed her arms. "I promise, you showing up here today is the strangest—" He saw the idea flicker through her face.

"What?" he said. "What just occurred to you?"

She grimaced. "A picture in my gran's portrait hall was giving me the willies. I camouflaged it and threw it out. And—"

"And?"

She tested his concentration by biting her lower lip. Thanks to her faerie nature, her mouth was naturally soft and red. "A photo of my dad fell off the wall last night. When I picked it up this morning, his image was burned out. I assume he did it. He doesn't like being photographed. So that doesn't really count as strange, just annoying."

Annoyance wasn't the sole emotion her father's action had inspired. Rick saw that from the way she dropped her eyes. "Where's your father now?"

"At his shop, I expect. He's a toymaker. Rick, he isn't important either. For a pureblood, his power is strictly low level."

He saw she believed this, but given everything that had happened, he wondered. Not being able to lie comfortably made most faeries experts at misleading.

"I think we should speak to him," he said.

She blinked, rapid and surprised. "He's very private."

"This could be important."

Cass gnawed her thumbnail. Was she afraid her father would refuse? He thought of his parents, who were always there for him—for anything or nothing. They loved him and Tony without limits, and he and Tony absolutely returned the sentiment. Adam and Nate, their honorary sons, received nearly the same treatment. Pack simply was that way.

Rick couldn't stop himself. He reached out to clasp her arm lightly. "Call him," he said. "Maybe he knows something you don't suspect."

She trembled when he touched her, a tiny vibration running through the surprisingly firm muscle beneath her sweat jacket's sleeve. Suddenly he realized she'd called him Rick, not Detective Lupone. She wet her lips, and his brain and body went haywire. Forgetting sense, he leaned to her. His hold on her arm was gentle, but she didn't pull away. God, he wanted to kiss her. Her breathing quickened, her soft red lips not completely closed. Her energy, the energy all living beings were surrounded by, began to sparkle the tiniest bit.

A pulse like a tapping finger drummed his cockhead.

"Oh," she said, jerking back from him. "I'm so sorry. I must have dusted you accidentally. I'm a little nervous this afternoon."

Her left eye twitched, so maybe this wasn't the exact truth.

Rick straightened up slowly. "I'm sorry," he said, his voice unavoidably husky. "You're very pretty. I always thought so."

Pretty was understating it. Whatever she thought of the term, it didn't calm her nerves. "Why don't I call my father?" she said, gesturing vaguely behind her.

Rick cooled his heels while she exited the room, presumably to make her call without him listening in. In an effort to avoid obsessing over their almost-kiss, which had left his blood simmering, he studied his surroundings.

The sunlit room was the size of a hotel lobby, overwhelming but beautiful. He observed lots of cream and gold, most of the color reserved to the large area rugs. Antique though the furniture was, it looked as if people actually sat in it. He knew Patricia Maycee had thrown a lot of parties: charity dos and musical evenings. Would Cass throw parties now that this place was hers? He tried to picture her sitting here alone. To him, that seemed lonely, but maybe these swank environs were what she thought of as normal.

A movement in the arched entryway caught his eye. A skinny gray cat was peeking in from the hall. She let out a startled *mew* as she spotted him, then dashed away with her collar bell jingling. Rick grinned. He had nothing against cats. They, however, didn't always like werewolves. And maybe they were right to be wary. Rick's inner wolf was experiencing a definite longing to give chase.

The thought of pursuing Cass's kitty around the giant penthouse amused him. He had to wipe a smile from his face when she returned to the living room.

"I'm sorry," she said, looking uncomfortable. "My dad wasn't answering his phone."

Rick wasn't sure why, but her news made him uneasy. "Why don't I drive you over to see him?"

"Oh no," she said hastily. "He's probably caught up in a job. I'll try him again tonight. If I can't reach him, perhaps we could meet at his shop tomorrow?"

He heard a plea in her voice. Could she really not rely on her father to welcome her phone calls?

Rick knew it would be rude to press, and that he had no official reason to. Her agreeing to provide an introduction to her father was beyond what he could demand.

He rose from the window and straightened his jacket. "Okay," he said. "I'd appreciate that. I'll call you first thing tomorrow."

She nodded, one hand holding her already zipped top together at her throat. "I'll just . . . show you out."

He accompanied her to the round foyer. The need to say something pressed at him. Maybe an apology for the almost-kiss? Or a confession that he was sorry she'd stopped him? No doubt Nate would advise him to ask her out for drinks. He opened his mouth, then remembered he shouldn't date someone from a current case. Not that Cass was a suspect. At least, he couldn't imagine what he'd suspect her of.

Before he could decide, they were at the threshold and she was opening the door. "You can call early if you like," she said. "The cat won't let me sleep past daybreak."

Her words gave him an excuse to look at her. Christ, she was beautiful. Her damp hair was drying in little curls, the exquisite oval of her face like an illustration for a tale of chivalry. Princes would line up by the hundreds to win her hand, no matter what dread deeds they were asked to perform.

Too bad Rick was a peasant.

"Okay," he said stupidly.

"Goodbye," she said and shut the door behind him.

His chest hurt, like he couldn't get enough air now that they were apart.

Don't be a sap, he snarled impatiently in his mind. *You aren't fricking twelve years old, and she isn't your princess.*

He stabbed the button for the elevator, then shoved his right hand into the pocket of his sport jacket. The electrum knuckles lay inside. Restless, he curled the tips of his fingers through the holds.

Heat like a match flame swallowed his entire hand. He cried out, too surprised not to. The heat dissipated as quickly as it had flared, but something had him around the wrist, something as snug as iron.

He yanked his hand out of his pocket.

What he saw dropped his jaw in shock. The knuckle-dusters were gone. An electrum cuff shaped like a Roman gladiator's circled his wrist halfway to his elbow. The same strange runes that engraved the rings on the knuckle-dusters marched in straight lines up it. Rick tugged at the thing, trying to get it off, but it might as well have been welded on.

"Shit," he hissed, taking a second to be grateful his hand hadn't actually seared to a crisp.

Whatever weird thing had happened, it seemed to be over. The metal was warm from his body, but not burning. The elevator's bell announced its arrival. Rick decided he'd go to the precinct psychic. Hopefully she could tell him how to undo the change he'd accidentally triggered.

Satisfied with his plan, he began to step into the waiting elevator. His feet had different ideas. Seemingly superglued to the marble floor, they wouldn't budge an inch, though he struggled hard enough for sweat to break out on his body.

"Damn it," he said, truly frustrated now. He looked over his shoulder to Cass's door. He'd have to call her out here to help him.

And then something else strange happened. As he turned, his left leg freed itself. A second later, his right did too.

Rick could add two and two, even if he didn't like what they summed up to. The faerie's gift wasn't letting him walk away. Apparently, it had decided he shouldn't leave Cass's side.

He experimented, trying to move toward the elevator. The moment he attempted it, his feet stuck in place again. If he turned toward Cass's place, they were free.

I don't believe this, he thought.

Not looking forward to explaining his return, Rick strode back to Cass's to ring the bell.

~

Cass had walked away from the door as soon as she locked it, mainly to prevent herself from leaning on it weak-kneed. Hearing the bell again took her by surprise.

Had Rick forgotten something? Or maybe it was like those movies where the hero turns back at the last moment to claim his kiss.

Get a grip, she scolded her runaway imagination. She opened the door.

Rick was behind it, looking sheepish. With his jacket sleeve pushed to his elbow, he held up his right arm. "Something happened to the knuckles when I touched them."

Cass choked on a startled laugh.

He glowered at her, as adorable as an angry five-year-old. "It isn't funny."

"I'm sorry," she said, starting to break up. "That looks like one of the bracelets Wonder Woman deflected bullets with."

"Haha. It won't let me walk away from you."

He demonstrated like a crazy mime. She covered her mouth to muffle laughter.

"Maybe you should come in," she said between snickers.

He came grumpily. "I have to call my boss. Let him know I probably won't be in next shift."

She let him do this in privacy.

"It appears you can walk around my house," she observed when he returned.

He grunted in acknowledgment, then shook himself. "Sorry. This isn't your fault."

"Some people would assume it was."

He looked at her, considering what she suggested. "No," he decided. "You wouldn't gain anything by it, and you're no prankster."

She hid her pleasure that he knew this. He was a cop. He had to be a good judge of character. "I don't think I can reverse what happened. The spell in those electrum knuckles was more sophisticated than anything I know how to do."

"What about your father? Could he get it off?"

"Maybe," she said unsurely.

"You realize this means you must be the person I'm supposed to protect, at least according to these things."

Cass's inappropriate giddiness faded. If she were honest with herself, she didn't totally mind that he thought he should protect her. The idea that she might really be in danger was less appealing. Plus, wanting to be protected wasn't exactly the hallmark of a modern woman. Shouldn't she prefer to protect herself?

Her expression must have been interesting. Rick broke into a laugh. "You are thinking hard." He touched her shoulder. The contact was light, but it grabbed her whole attention, pleasing her more than she wanted to let on. Luckily, he didn't seem aware. "Show me your kitchen. When I'm stressed, I take after my parents. I need to cook something."

~

Rick prepared a simple pasta dish with meatballs, an activity Cass watched as if it were the most amazing magic trick ever. The sparkling black and white kitchen was big enough for an army of caterers, apparently the only people who cooked in it. The cat—introduced by Cass as Poly—mustered the courage to accept one meatball from his fingers before streaking out again.

Rick felt like he had to coax Cass too. She was shyer than he expected, clearly unused to being around strangers. He remembered the group of girls she used to hang with—the half-and-halfers, they'd called themselves.

When asked, she told him what they were up to. The topic relaxed her, the affection she felt for them obvious.

"You really remember us?" she asked, digging into her plate with an appetite that gratified him.

"Why wouldn't I? You were the prettiest girls in school. And you always seemed like you were having fun."

They sat opposite each other at the black limestone island, perched on sturdy modern stools. Cass suddenly found chasing ziti with her fork highly interesting. "I didn't think you knew who I was."

His heart gave a funny skip. She sounded like a teenager when she said it: sweetly insecure. He wanted to bundle her up and hug her, not because of some stupid spell, but because *he* wanted to.

"Cass," he said, low and gentle. "Everyone knew you."

She nodded, her face still lowered, her fork jabbing at ziti. "I *was* the only half faerie at North Heights."

"That would never be the only reason to notice you."

She looked up. Oh those dreaming blue eyes of hers were killer, big and round and as innocent as a lamb. His ribs contracted around his lungs. He was getting hard again, with no hope of stopping it. He shifted on his stool, more than a bit enchanted by the color rushing into her cheeks. Had he gotten it wrong all those years ago? Was she attracted to him, despite him being a rough werewolf?

His idiotic circadian clock chose that moment to goad him into a huge yawn.

"Shit," he said when he managed to shut his jaw. "My schedule is upside down. I've been working graveyard shift with my squad."

Cass laughed, relieved by the change in tone. "I promise not to assume I'm boring you. Why don't I clean up here? Pick any guest room you like to sack out in."

The idea of Snow White cleaning anything seemed wrong.

"Shoo," she said before he could protest.

He didn't mind being given permission to explore. His wolf and cop halves were both snoopy. Though he was tired, he walked through the entire place, from the pool terrace to the snooty portrait hall to the wing with the eight bedrooms. The opposite corridor seemed more lived in. He found her grandmother's personal rooms shrouded in dust covers.

Because this felt like somewhere he shouldn't go, he retreated and kept walking. Some impulse told him to ignore the next few doors. The last in the hallway drew him. A delicious smell wafted from it, like field of wildflowers warming in the sun. His wolf would have been happy to roll in it. As he turned the knob, his electrum shackle hummed.

The tingle should have warned him to stop. Cass was inside the room— her room. She sat on a gauze-draped four-poster, slowly brushing her shiny hair. Dry now, it waved to her shoulders. In the millisecond before she noticed him, he saw she was gazing blankly at the wall across from her.

"Oh," she said, turning to look at him.

She should have been irritated by the intrusion. He'd have been in her place. He guessed her temper was slow to rise.

She put down her hairbrush. "The guest rooms are in the other wing."

"I was snooping," he admitted.

Her mouth slanted, a wry and very human expression. "You're as honest as a faerie. Do you know where everything is now?"

"More or less." Since she wasn't angry, he stepped inside and looked around. The decor was . . . romantic, lots of swoopy fabric and delicate furniture.

"Gran kept my rooms pretty much the same since high school."

Cass sounded embarrassed. Amusement tugged at Rick's lips. "You liked tulle."

"Way more than was good for me."

They smiled at each other. Something deep inside Rick went *ahh*. He ignored it determinedly. The window behind Cass was open. A breeze far warmer than normal for October belled her sheer curtains.

"I splurged on a climate spell," she explained. "For a gathering at the pool. The charge hasn't run out yet."

His imagination threatened to detour to her skinny-dipping again. "I'll just go back to the guest wing," he said.

He certainly meant to. His parents raised their eldest to be respectful of females. No acting like a wolf unless he was invited to. The problem was when he tried to leave, the electrum manacle stuck him to the carpet.

"Crap," he huffed.

Cass laughed softly behind his back.

"I don't understand this," he said. "The stupid thing let me wander all over your house."

"But you weren't just wandering. You were mapping the territory—checking its defenses for weak spots, I'll bet."

"Sure." Rick turned back to her, his leg muscles instantly relaxing. "That's what cops do. Are you saying this thing will let me move around if it believes what I'm doing is useful for protecting you?"

"If *you* believe it," she said. "Even magical bracelets aren't capable of thinking."

He frowned at the gleaming thing.

"You can sleep on my bed," she offered. "I'll sit and read a while."

"I'm not taking your bed."

"There's a trundle. My friends and I used to have sleepovers."

"If you try to braid my hair, I'm leaving."

Cass smiled like a cat in cream. "That's assuming your Wonder Woman gewgaw will let you escape me."

Her eyes twinkled with mischief, her enjoyment of his predicament obvious. He realized he liked that look on her.

~

Cass watched Rick toss and turn for ten minutes before she gave up pretending to read her book. He'd taken off his jacket and shoes. Seeing his big male body make a mess of her covers was incredibly distracting. "Is the bed uncomfortable?" she asked.

Rick flopped onto his back and sighed. "It's a nice bed."

"I didn't, um, accidentally dust you again?"

He turned his head toward her on the pillow. Even from across the room, his green eyes seemed hot. "It wouldn't matter." He lifted the chain that hung around his corded neck. "My Saint Michael medal is charmed to resist glamours. It's police department issue, and I'm pretty sure it's working."

"Oh," she said a second before his meaning sank in. She hadn't spelled him. He wanted her by himself.

That giant erection he'd been sporting was all him.

"Yes, *oh*," he said, rolling onto his side again. She didn't have the nerve to check him out between the legs. "I just plain want you, Cass. I wanted you the first time I laid eyes on you in high school."

The sudden heat that crashed through her left her speechless. She noticed how faithfully his long sleeved T-shirt hugged his chest and arms, how taut his muscles were and how big. He'd pushed his sleeves to his elbows. His face was flushed and glowy. He looked warm enough to want to peel the garment off . . .

"Um," she said, "me too?"

Her admission flipped a switch inside him. He smiled, slow and sinful and confident. On another man, that expression might have annoyed her. On him, it totally wet her panties.

He wasn't assuming anything about his chances that wasn't true.

He wet his lips and her nipples pebbled. "Since we're both in agreement, want to do something about it?"

"We shouldn't." The reaction was automatic, based on nerves and not logic.

"Shouldn't we?" he countered throatily.

"I'm . . . not very experienced."

The look in his eyes softened but didn't grow less steamy. "You don't have to be. Please come here and kiss me."

She wanted that. She was just so used to not touching, to not abusing the unfair advantage she'd been born with. As if he knew what would tempt her, Rick sat up and pulled off his shirt. His chest was even yummier than she'd thought. Golden brown, broad and tapering, layered with muscle and dark hair. His movements as he performed the partial strip tease were graceful, hinting at the animal power that slept inside him. And maybe his beast wasn't sleeping. As he undid the top button of his jeans, the first unmistakable embers of wolf fire lit up his eyes.

Then he lay down again. His six-pack drew attention even when he was lounging.

"See?" he said teasingly. "It's perfectly safe for you to come over."

Safe wasn't the word Cass would have chosen.

CHAPTER
FOUR

CASS hadn't lied about being inexperienced. She'd had a lover for six months when she lived Outside. Because the relationship ended badly, she hadn't tried to take another.

Rick's smile grew even gentler when he saw her hesitate.

The gleam in his hot green eyes was a different matter.

"I'm a captive audience," he pointed out, displaying his wrist cuff as evidence. "I couldn't get away from you if I tried."

His eyebrows went up and down so comically she smiled. Still she stayed where she was. "I'm not afraid, I'm just . . . rusty."

Rick stroked the covers with long tanned fingers, petting them like he would a cat. "It's like riding a bike, Cass. Only the first few minutes are wobbly."

"Oh hell." Surrendering, she crossed the rug to him. Her knees were already wobbly. What could it hurt if the rest of her followed suit?

He rolled onto his back as she reached the bed. His arms rested more or less harmlessly at his sides. Cass bit her lip and put one knee on the mattress, too aware of his glittering gaze as she swung her second knee over him. She looked down at him, and her heart nearly stopped. He had a hump like a faerie barrow at his groin. Her breathing got embarrassingly faster. His sped up too, his gorgeous bare chest rising and falling in plain view.

She couldn't recall wanting to lick a man's ribs before.

Once she was settled, he put his hands gently on her thighs. His thumbs rubbed her muscles through her sweat wear. The small caress provided more than comfort. Her nipples went so tight and hot the air felt icy.

"There," he said, his voice smoky. "That's not so bad, is it?"

It wasn't bad at all. In truth, it was wonderful. She shook her head to let him know she agreed. Then, to prove she wasn't a coward, she drew the fingers of both her hands down the hard center of his chest. His heart thumped beneath her touch despite his calm demeanor. His saint medal had fallen into the hollow of his strong throat, where it winked in time to his hastened pulse. Cass pushed her thumbs into the V created by the open metal button at the waist of his jeans. There, she stroked hair and skin, sweeping over a distended artery that pumped blood to his erection. His hips squirmed at her caress.

Knowing she'd excited him made cream run out of her body.

"Is this as far as you plan to open these?" she asked, flicking the gaping button to clarify.

Rick's nostrils flared, his keen sense of smell allowing him to scent her arousal. "My . . . friend needed . . . breathing room," he said, seeming to have trouble getting air himself.

"Your friend," she repeated, amused.

She'd rested her bottom on his thighs. Unable to remain motionless, his hips lifted high enough to lift her. "Sometimes he's a pain in the ass, but he feels like my friend now."

Maybe he was her friend too. She laid her hands on his bulging zipper. His eyes closed, pleasure crossing his face as she pushed her hold up the ridge. His response was unselfconscious. His skin flushed with enjoyment, one lip rolling between his teeth. She pushed up him lingeringly twice—plus once more just for herself. Mostly for herself, she slid her palms up his honed torso and around his shoulders. His skin was fevered, his strong shifter energy tingling under her fingers and up her arms. Faeries got touch-hunger, but this was more than that. For her, touching Rick was as big an aphrodisiac as her faerie sparkles would be to him. She thought about that tingling moving inside her pussy and couldn't contain a gasp.

Rick opened his eyes again. "Take this off." His hands shifted to the hem of her dark blue top.

She didn't have anything under it. She'd dressed too quickly after getting the call from Security. She dragged the zipper down anyway. Satisfied to let her take care of this, Rick returned his hands to her thighs. Perhaps without realizing, his fingers kneaded her. His gaze was glued to the parting garment, all guy when it came to some things, apparently.

The zipper opened all away. Cass wriggled her arms free one at a time.

"Whew," Rick said, focused on her swaying breasts. "That is a pretty sight."

His hands ran up her sides to them, whispering over the outer curves, first with his thumbs and then the backs of his fingers. She was half faerie. She knew her rack was nice. Not too big, not too small, with . . . well, saucy little nipples that appeared rouged against her snowy skin. What she hadn't known was that such a gentle touch could make her feel this way. Her nerves were sparking, her nipples aching for him to suck them.

"Cass," he said, just her name, low and hoarse. His gaze held hers, excited fires glowing in his green irises.

She moved his palms over her nipples and held them there.

She guessed he didn't expect that. He drew a quick breath and let it out shakily.

"Come here," he said, like it was life and death. "Come down here and kiss me."

She put her hands on the bed and let her weight sink to him. His fingers tightened where they cupped her breasts. Her heart was racing, her eyes open. His were too until their lips molded together.

His mouth was smooth, cushiony for a man. His head shifted angles, and suddenly her lips were opening.

His tongue slid inside as smooth as satin.

After all this time, he was kissing her. Her pulse started racing between her legs. Oh my, he tasted good. She had to kiss him back or go crazy.

He made a little noise, as if his pleasure was too much to contain. His arms came around her, her breasts now flat against his hard chest. The hump of his cock dug into her mound. Cass's thighs tightened by themselves, hugging her hips to him. Another noise broke from him, sending lovely shivers tripping down her spine.

He rolled her under him, then backed up and looked at her.

"You don't have to stop," she said rather breathlessly.

He smiled with the kindness she'd been remembering all these years. "Why don't we establish that I'm not going to unless you ask?"

That sounded both exciting and alarming.

"Okay," she agreed. "No stopping unless I ask."

He shifted his arm between them so he could slide his hand down the front of her entirely too warm sweatpants. She didn't have anything under them either. His smile grew broader as he discovered this. He was almost laughing, like he thought he'd won the jackpot. Cass couldn't mind his good humor, especially when three long fingers slid between her pussy lips.

"Mm," he hummed, probably because she was very wet.

His middle finger went into her.

She arched, unable to stop herself. The incursion felt so *good*, much better than she'd expected from her admittedly limited experience. A noise sounded in her throat, louder than the one he'd made.

"Good," he whispered and took her mouth again.

She really kissed him back this time, and this seemed to free him to show her what he could do. Wow, he was a good kisser—like twelve on a scale of ten. She couldn't get enough of him, not his mouth, not his body, not anything. She clutched his shoulder blades and rubbed herself against him, thrilling to the way he grunted and worked his hand deeper.

"Cass," he gasped.

His body writhed, especially at the hips. She drove her hands into his thick hair, pulling his mouth greedily closer. She loved how he grew hungrier, how his lips and teeth pushed at her harder. She didn't care that maybe this was racing ahead too fast. After all her years of playing it cautious, she wanted to let go with him.

She got her arm between them too. Going straight for what she wanted, she wrapped her hold around his erection and gave it a good firm squeeze.

He moaned in praise as she kneaded his pulsing length. His hand took a moment to regain its rhythm. When it did, it was even more purposeful than before. The pad of his thumb covered her clitoris, depressing the swollen button as he rubbed up and down. Cass's excitement jumped a couple rungs at once. The combined strokes got to her: his thumb going up and down, his finger delving in and out. Her passage tightened. She was going to come if he didn't stop, but that seemed okay. If he hadn't wanted her to climax, he wouldn't have been groaning so longingly.

"Shit," he hissed without warning, pulling his hand from her.

The withdrawal was careful, but it still shocked. He sat up, panting raggedly.

She touched his thigh, still clad in faded jeans. "What is it?" She swallowed. "Did I do something wrong?"

When he looked at her, his eyes were flames. "You did everything right, sweetheart. I got a little too excited."

He showed her his hands. Claws curved from them where he should have had fingernails. A shiver she didn't think was fear quivered over her tailbone.

"Oh." Her voice sounded strange, throaty and low-pitched. "I didn't . . . I didn't know you could change without a full moon."

"Usually I don't." He drew in a lengthy breath, trying to slow his respiration. "Under the circumstances, giving you a hand-job seemed like a bad idea."

"If you'd accidentally hurt me, I'd have healed. I have enough faerie blood for that."

"I don't want to hurt you."

Her hand was still on his thigh, and she found she didn't want to move it away. The intensity of his gaze as it locked with hers made her ache down low and melt. Maybe he knew. The breathing he'd tried to steady sped up again.

"So . . ." she said, teasing her fingertips along the inner muscles of his leg. "If you weren't giving me a hand-job, what would you like to put inside me instead?"

The question was blatantly suggestive—and so not *her* she could hardly say it with a straight face. Rick, evidently, didn't think it was too much at all.

"Jesus," he breathed, flushing darker.

Then he slapped one clawed hand atop his mouth.

Guessing what had happened, Cass broke into a chuckle. "Noo . . . Fangs?"

"You're a menace," he growled, hiding them with his palm.

"Let me see." She tugged at his wrist.

Reluctantly—even grumpily—he let it fall.

As considerately as she could, Cass peeled back his upper lip. "They're fine," she said, peering at them. Both his upper and lower canines had lengthened. She tested the points with a finger, deciding they weren't too sharp for safety.

"Are you done?" Rick huffed.

Cass was kneeling on the mattress now. She crossed her arms and smiled. "You're kind of prickly for a guy who's about to get lucky."

"Right," he said disbelievingly.

"I like you like this. Your fangs and claws are sexy."

"You're just being nice."

"Rick," she said, schoolmarmlike. "You do know what happens when faeries lie."

His brow had furrowed, but at this reminder his scowl eased up. "You want to have sex with me while I'm like this?"

"Some people would say I'm scary," she pointed out.

"You're beautiful."

He said it gruffly, like he intended to defend her against every faerie hater in the Pocket. God, he was cute. Her nerve recovering, she climbed out of the four-poster and shucked her remaining clothes. Rick's reaction to her nakedness was totally worth the courage stripping took.

"Boyohboy," he said, swinging his legs around to sit on the mattress edge. His erection bounced distractingly. "No, just stand there, please. My poor wolf brain needs a minute to take this in."

"Rick," she said, blushing with pleasure but embarrassed. It was hard to stand still while he ogled her.

His gaze traveled eventually to her face. "You're good enough to eat."

"So you're the big bad wolf?"

"You have no idea, sweetheart."

She liked the growl in his voice. "Take off your jeans. Being naked by myself is weird."

He started unzipping them sitting down, but quickly realized his sizeable hard-on presented logistical challenges. He stood, finished, and shoved the soft denim down his long and rather awesome legs. His boxer briefs followed in short order.

Cass's breath stalled a little. His whole body was breathtaking. He was what a man should be, she decided—from the hair on his legs, to the narrowness of his hips, to the sculpted breadth of his broad shoulders. His pecs were . . . and his arms . . . and, wow, he was really hung. Of course you couldn't really call it *hung* when it was standing up, but that was a fine manpole jerking at his groin like it wanted to leap at her.

A bead of pre-come welled from its tip.

"Cass," he said.

"Huh?" was her best answer.

His eyes crinkled with amusement, an interesting effect when paired with the fire in his irises. "I said I only brought one condom. It's a good brand— and charmed—but if you really want to have intercourse, it'll have to be just one time for now."

The words *for now* snagged her already addled brain. "What?"

"I'm aware faeries are . . . fertile with almost all races. You're only half, but I figured—"

He trailed off, and her thought processes caught up belatedly. "Oh," she said. "No. You and I couldn't— I'd have to do a special spell. You don't need a condom unless you want it for you. I'll probably dust you when I, um, you know. Some men find that uncomfortable."

Her cheeks were fiery. She'd never had this conversation with her Outsider human lover. He hadn't known what she was. She'd let him use condoms because it was easier than explaining.

"You're sure that's safe for you?" Rick asked.

"Yes."

"And you're not concerned about my size?"

She laughed, which seemed to take him aback. Maybe he was used to women worrying? "No. I mean, you are obviously big, but you won't hurt me. Faeries are very, um, adaptable."

His glowing eyes stared into hers a moment longer, his lovely mouth pursed consideringly.

"Should I come back over there?" she suggested, admitted hopeful.

He grinned and held out his arms. She walked into them and kissed him, naked body to naked body and sweat to sweat.

"Mm," he groaned into her mouth. His lengthened teeth made kissing interesting. They were hot spots, she gathered. She licked one fang, and his embrace tightened. A second later she was on her back under him on the bed. She couldn't believe how fast it had happened—and how gently.

"You used your werewolf speed on me," she gasped.

His kissed the crook of her neck. "Only for that. I promise I'll take my time over everything else."

His voice was half growl again. She wriggled at the undeniable thrill of his animal nature, her pussy so wet and achy she'd happily have taken all of him then and there.

"I'm half faerie," she said, trying to speak intelligibly as he nibbled across her collarbone. "I can go fast too."

He *mm-hm*'d against her skin, kissing the upper curve of one breast and then the other. Cass's back arched in anticipation.

Rick didn't disappoint.

"Oh," she sighed as his soft warm mouth settled onto her right nipple.

He pulled just hard enough with his lips and cheeks that she felt the spangle down to her toes. She felt it between her legs as well, which shot her impatience almost higher than she could stand.

"Rick," she said, fingers forking into his hair.

He switched to the other breast.

He was on one elbow. His other hand curled lightly around the side of her ribcage. The rooting noises he made had her squirming with arousal. As her legs shifted restlessly around his, his clawed hand tightened. When he realized what he'd done, he forced it to relax.

"No," she murmured, moving his hand to her unsucked breast.

He lifted his head. His irises were so bright they reflected off her skin.

"If you're self-conscious about what you are, I will be too," she said.

His eyes glittered. She couldn't read what lay behind them, but the emotion seemed important.

"Truly," she insisted a little shyly. "I like you as you are."

"I want you to enjoy this."

"There's not much chance I won't." Deciding he needed proof, she tilted her hips to him. The change in angle squeezed his cock against her warm wetness. Her folds parted for his thickness, the pulse in both increasing. A shiver of pleasure ran through his whole body.

Encouragingly, he dragged the tips of his claws lightly up her tight nipple. "I never thought this would happen. You and me. Together like this."

"But it has." Not quite liking his tone of awe, she squeezed her thighs around his hips. "Don't tell me the big bad wolf is afraid of my little fae pussy."

He laughed, a wonderful low male sound. "All right," he said. "Tell your pussy to get ready."

"She's ready," Cass promised. "She wants this big manly cock pushing your energy inside her."

One dark brow arched at her claim. Boldly, but watching her face for reactions, he drew his claws over her breast, down her side, and finally clamped them—not too hard—around her right buttock. His weight lifted from her, his big body shifting in preparation for entry.

"God," she breathed, then bit her lip in embarrassment.

"Hungry?" he whispered.

"Oh yes," she whispered back.

He reached between them to place his rounded glans at her opening. She made a little noise at the first contact.

"Jesus," he said. "You're going to kill me."

Then he pushed and went into her.

It was a long slow glide, the strength of his hips and thighs ensuring it was steady. The generosity of her arousal ensured he didn't have to stop. His cock was thick and smooth, throbbing more violently as it filled her up. Oh he stretched her good. Her spine arched with pleasure, her hands sliding up his muscled back to pull herself to him. If his cock weren't enough of a treat, his energy was *delicious*: stronger than a human's, wilder and hotter.

She absolutely adored that his cock was bare.

Considering how he trembled, maybe he adored it too.

When he was all the way in, he drew back and thrust again. He held at the end, squeezed to her limits.

"God," he moaned, his neck arching back and his eyes closing.

She knew what he meant. Having him inside her was heaven.

His hand tightened on her hip as he segued into another slow deep stroke. Cass moaned in reaction, her legs starting to climb his sides.

"One second," he said, not going at it yet.

He dropped his brow to the pillow, clutching the Michael medal around his neck. He whispered something too quick for her to make out.

"Was that a spell?" she asked, amused by the idea of him using magic on her.

"A prayer," he said, slightly embarrassed. "It's kind of my thing in the squad. I don't want to, you know, go too early for you."

He was so damn adorable it was hard not to laugh. She managed to restrict herself to a grin.

"I don't want to screw this up," he explained defensively.

She smoothed her hands up and down his back. "I want to give you pleasure too."

His face darkened in a different way. He let go of his medal, stretching that arm up to grip the mattress edge. He didn't warn her to get ready. She just knew she ought to. His hips pulled back, dragging his thickness to her brink.

Then he began pumping.

He didn't go fast or hard, but his thrusts worked on her as quickly as if he were racing. He was big enough to hit every part of her. She gasped as her pussy tightened, her excitement rising with every stroke. He made the most of his grip on the mattress and on her hip. She couldn't interfere with his movements, though she was soon thrashing. His steady strokes went exactly where he intended, at the speed he intended them to go.

He put a twist into each snap of his hips that drove her crazy. His body was so powerful, so agile and athletic. The simplest, most vanilla motion was incredibly effective.

She wanted to tell him to keep doing exactly what he was forever. Unfortunately, all her breath was taken up in panting.

She guessed he liked what he was doing too. His energy was intensifying, the tingles he shot off heightening, his cock hardening a fraction more inside her. The big muscle in his jaw tightened a second before he hitched his chest higher over her. His knees were bent more then, his thrusts lifting her slightly off the bed. Cass decided she liked this angle even better. Her hands slid to his waist and hung on.

"Good?" he panted, putting noticeably more *oomph* into each rhythmic plunge.

She couldn't speak. She writhed with pleasure, so close to peaking it hurt. He started giving her that lovely hip twist from his new position.

She came with a gasp, deliciously intense sensations contracting her pussy around him. Rick didn't mind that. Grunting at the feel of her on his cock, he spun the dial of his efforts up at least two notches.

"God," she groaned as her climax heightened as well.

He wasn't stopping there. He swung her up again, so that he knelt with her straddling his lap. That was the best of all. His hands were clamped on her bottom, lifting her up and down with that amazing control of his. She gripped his shoulders, her half fae aura beginning to sparkle uncontrollably.

He cursed as her magic hit him, then snarled and thrust harder.

She cried out, working herself crazily back on him. Her breasts bounced against his chest, the wetness of their bodies slapping together abandonedly. She enjoyed the noisiness of their coupling more than she thought she could, so excited she thought she'd burst. Another peak built swiftly inside her.

Rick's hard wolf claws bit into her soft bottom.

"Cass," he gasped. "Fuck."

Maybe she was dusting him too much, but she couldn't stop. His cock stiffened even more. He sucked a breath and changed angles one more time. Cass let out a helpless cry. His thrusts were getting her clit now, tugging and bumping it with each strong upstroke.

Flutters of orgasm quivered through her pussy.

"Unh," he grunted, losing it. He drove in all the way, face contorting, cock throbbing out long pulses of wetness. Cass came around them, hot sweet streaks blazing through her clit and pussy. The strength of her climax shocked her. She heard Rick choke out her name, felt him shoot harder and flood out of her.

Her body settled gradually. Rick was holding her, his cheek on her hair while hers nestled on his shoulder. Sweat covered both of them.

She felt peculiar, aware they'd shared something more earthshaking than she'd been prepared for—and with someone she didn't know too well.

Her Outside lover hadn't rocked her world this way.

"Wow," Rick sighed, slowly petting her hair.

She didn't know what to say in return. She pulled back and looked at him. His handsome face was flushed and relaxed.

His expression sharpened as she regarded him. "Second thoughts?"

"I don't know," she said, mindful of not lying. "That was . . ."

"Intense?"

"Yes."

He shifted his big hands to rub her back. "Maybe we shouldn't think about it too hard."

He sounded so hopeful Cass laughed. She climbed off him as gently as she could. Though he didn't protest, he watched her intently. "You *are* going to think about it," he predicted.

"I'm a girl," she said.

He sprawled back on his elbows, his fine male form unabashedly exposed. "You're also fae. Aren't they supposed to be more casual about sex?"

Was he hoping she'd be? She couldn't read his careful expression. "Maybe sometimes. I suppose it depends."

He yawned until his jaw cracked, then laughed at himself. "Sorry. It's been a while since I got lucky, much less had sex that good. I'm afraid you took the starch out of me."

She didn't feel like she'd done much at all—apart from going along with an amazing ride. Also, what did *a while* mean to a man as hot as him? Surely not as long as it meant to her. He was really good at lovemaking. That didn't happen without practice.

"I should let you sleep," she said.

He caught her arm before she could leave the bed. He softened the restraining gesture by caressing her with his thumb. "Stay. Please." He lifted his cuffed right arm and grinned. "This thing will certainly be happier if you're close."

Maybe she shouldn't have, but she allowed him to coax her down beside him. His chest was a hard pillow, but she liked it all the same. Bit by bit, his thudding heart slowed beneath her ear. He was asleep within two minutes, all guy when it came to that as well.

No teddy bear had ever been so warm to snuggle to.

You'd better not fall for him, she warned herself. When it came to love, her faerie luck tended to run crooked.

~

When Rick woke an hour later, not only was Cass still there, she was sprawled across his body like a blanket. She was tall but slender, and the difference in their sizes made him feel manly. He enjoyed that more than he should—just as he'd enjoyed her unexpected shyness about making love to him.

Realizing this, he frowned at the tulle-draped canopy above him. His fingers were curved into her silky hair, but he couldn't bring himself to pull them free. He'd been wishing he had someone special in his life. Casting Snow White in that role was ridiculous. Faeries were the rock gods of Resurrection, and half fae weren't far behind. Just last year, the *Pocket Observer* ran a survey of top male fantasies. One night with a part fae had edged out threesomes with lesbians. Given that Cass could have anyone she wanted, she could do considerably better than a blue-collar working stiff like him—and likely would once she adjusted to being home again.

Rick let out a gusty sigh. It was just his bad luck the sex had been fantastic.

A jingling noise jerked his head around on the pillow. Poly the cat was staring at him from the top of a flowered chair. He couldn't help but interpret her expression as baleful.

"You'll have to wait to get your spot back," he warned her quietly. "I'm not leaving this minute."

The cat made a sound that was amusingly grumble-like.

"Where's my shovel?" Cat muttered against his chest.

She hadn't woken. She was talking in her sleep. Rick laughed softly to himself. He found it reassuring that she was human enough for that.

CHAPTER FIVE

LE Beau Toys was on a city street so narrow only bikes and pedestrians could get through. Mostly residential, what shops there were boasted worn brick fronts and hand-painted signs. Rick drove Cass there first thing in the morning, a venture that involved her putting her high heeled designer shoe through a not-quite-empty Star's Brew cup. Someone—probably Tony—had left it in the passenger side foot well.

Cass was dressed like a businesswoman: tailored trousers, silk shirt, expensive fitted jacket with a single button to do up. When the coffee splashed her pants cuff, she let out a cry of dismay and immediately spelled it off.

She was good at little spells—not to mention nervous about seeing her father. Then again, the sartorial armor might have been meant to distance her from Rick. They hadn't woken up like lovers, their morning-after awkwardness impossible to miss. Rick didn't know how to overcome it, or even if he should try.

Because he had to park the Buick around the corner, they walked side by side up the slightly uneven sidewalk. Neither of them attempted to make chitchat. When they reached the address it was 7:02 a.m. Her father's toyshop still displayed its CLOSED sign. Rick peered up the narrow building to the apartment where Cass said her dad lived. Two windows, also dark, marked the front. Something was off. Rick could feel it. The little street was quiet, few residents stirring yet. He smelled them cooking breakfast, heard them running water and speaking softly to roommates or spouses. He called his wolf closer to the surface and realized what had alarmed him.

Roald le Beau's apartment was empty. No sounds. No food smells. No warmth or energy. Rick couldn't be certain until he did a search, but he was willing to bet no one alive or dead was in there.

"Do you have a key?" he asked Cass quietly.

"You aren't going in there without me." Her response was hushed. Like him, she'd noticed the offness in the atmosphere.

"Cass." He held her eyes sternly. "Give me the key to your father's place."

She gnawed her lip, then gave in and opened her smart under-elbow purse. "I'll hang back," she said as she passed him a pair of keys on a ring. "But I am coming up with you."

Rick would have preferred she remain outside but didn't see how to force her. Too, if her father was in there and just hiding magically, Rick might need Cass to announce him as a friend. Approaching purebloods without an invitation was rarely a good idea.

Resigned, he nodded curtly to her and drew his gun. He held it beside his leg for now. No point alarming the neighbors.

The first key she'd given him opened the shop's front door. The overhead light didn't work when she hit the switch, but other than that everything seemed normal. Le Beau's wasn't set up for browsing. Rick concluded custom commissioned toys were its mainstay. The shelves were a hodgepodge, the big worktable at the back the apparent center of activity. A half wall shielded the tool bench from the street window's view.

The variety of enchantments that had been spun there pricked thickly through Rick's arm hair.

"That's the door to the stairs," Cass whispered, pointing it out. "Dad's apartment is at the top."

"Stay here until I check it," he said, not wanting her caught on the steps with him.

She frowned, and he frowned harder. When she crossed her arms, he knew he'd won. Rick hadn't become Adam's second without a generous serving of natural authority.

The old wooden staircase was narrow, making him glad he'd insisted she stay behind. His nose twitched as he climbed. He smelled sawdust and drywall and maybe singed cotton. The butt of his Smith & Wesson was braced in both hands now. He wouldn't need Cass's key to open her father's door. As it came into view, he saw it was ajar. To judge by the splintering, the lock had been busted from the frame.

He blew out a silent breath to control his adrenaline. Peering briefly into the opening revealed no one.

"Mr. le Beau," he called quietly. "I'm from the RPD. Your daughter sent me to check on you."

No response came back. Rick shouldered the door open. He saw at once that the living room/kitchenette was a disaster zone. Refusing to let that distract him, he proceeded to each room gun-first and cleared it. The process was quick. These were humble digs for a faerie. One bedroom. One bath. One closet for storage. The only indulgence was a glassed-in sunroom for growing plants.

They and their soil had been dumped onto the floor.

Satisfied he was alone, Rick relaxed marginally and straightened. He fought an urge to whistle at the shambles that surrounded him. The small apartment had been ransacked to an extent he'd never seen before. Every piece of furniture appeared to be overturned. The walls were ripped apart to the actual studs. Holes gaped in the ceiling, and floorboards were torn up.

It was no wonder the stair had smelled like demo.

Rick spied numerous long scorch marks under the disarray—suggesting they'd been created first. This apartment had been the site of an epic battle, at least partially mystical. Certainly a spell had been required to prevent the neighbors from hearing it.

"Oh my God," Cass moaned, frozen in horror at the doorway.

She was pale by nature, but now she looked slightly green. Rick was about to reassure her he'd smelled no blood, then remembered a pureblood faerie wouldn't leave any. Their blood devolved to sparkles, and their sparkles were volatile. If her father had died here, he wouldn't necessarily leave evidence of it.

"Your father isn't here," he said instead.

She waded a few awkward high-heeled steps into the broken clutter. Her hands rose shakily to her mouth. "There was a fight . . ."

"Yes." He let her process this. "Afterward, it appears someone searched the place, probably whoever he fought with. Did your father keep valuables here?"

She shook her head, her stress making the gesture extra emphatic. "Dad didn't have valuables. His magic was his living. He didn't spell up extras like some fae do."

Rick was standing across the room from her in the upended kitchenette. Even the stove had been dragged from the wall. "This isn't where you grew up."

"No," she confirmed distractedly. "Dad moved above his shop after the divorce."

Her soft blue gaze came to his. "He's alive," she said firmly. "I'd know if he were gone."

He wanted her to hold onto that steel. "I agree."

Despite his intention, her eyes welled up and glittered. Maybe she knew he was being kind. Pressing her lips together, she turned her head away. His heart squeezed tight without warning. Her profile was the most exquisite—and possibly the saddest—he'd ever seen.

"I should look around," she said. "See if I can sense what happened here magically."

He allowed her to do so, sticking close by her side as she walked from room to room. More than once she appeared perplexed by what she found, though she didn't speak or touch anything. Rick observed no family pictures among her dad's belongings. There wasn't much of anything personal.

The furniture was so modest Rick could have afforded it.

The single bedroom was at the rear, overlooking an alley and the fire escapes of a similar stretch of brick buildings. As Rick looked out the window, a curtain in the structure directly opposite fell closed.

He smiled. Nosy neighbors were among his favorite witnesses. Giving in to the urge, he laid one hand on Cass's tense shoulder.

"Have you seen what you need?" he asked. "I think I've found someone we can question."

~

Mrs. Nemo was an elderly human woman with a touch of blue elf—as evidenced by the robin's egg luster in her otherwise silver hair. Within two minutes of being let into her home, they learned she was 120, had eight great grandchildren, and couldn't eat spicy food like she used to.

She served them coffee and store-bought cookies in her cozy parlor. Rick noticed Cass sat as gingerly on her little chair as him.

"Eat!" their hostess urged. "You're both too skinny."

Rick didn't know in what universe he qualified as *skinny*, but he thanked her for the refreshments. Then he steered the conversation back on topic. "About what you saw last night . . ."

"Oh *my* yes." She settled back into a cushioned chair that was exactly sized for her. "That was a to-do."

"Just start at the beginning," he suggested.

"Well, the faerie came skulking down the alley around midnight. I know because *Late Night with Kenan* had just gone off. That demon is handsome, don't you think?"

"He is," Cass agreed, the question seeming to be for her. Rick hadn't introduced her by name, simply saying she was his associate.

"How did you know the skulker was a faerie?" Rick inquired.

"He was too beautiful to be human," Mrs. Nemo explained. "And he was dressed funny. Like a Roman fighter with a leather breastplate and lace-up sandals. Also, when he climbed the fire escape, I saw him from the back. He had his wings hidden like they do, but I saw their energy glowing." She tapped her temple. "My bit of elf blood lets me see and hear more than plain humans."

"So he climbed the fire escape. Did someone let him in the building?"

"No. He magicked the lock on the window. There's a light on the landing, but he spelled it to go out."

If he'd disrupted the power in the building, that explained the shop's broken switch.

"Then what did he do?" Rick asked.

"We-ell," said their hostess, drawing out the word for effect—leaving Rick in no doubt that she relished having an audience. "He closed his eyes and chanted and put the whole street to sleep! It was an amazing spell. Pigeons fell over on their roosts. Probably a few people too, because I heard some thumps."

"But you didn't sleep," Cass said, speaking for the first time.

"I'm an old lady!" the woman crowed. "And a terrible insomniac. Apparently even purebloods can't knock me out."

Rick hid his amusement behind his delicate coffee cup. "Then what?"

Mrs. Nemo pointed toward the parlor window. "I figured something interesting was happening so I crouched at the sill. I didn't want the faerie to know I was awake. He called through the door to the nice toymaker who lives there. He said, 'Jig's up, keeper. Time to hand over what you've stolen.' And then he kicked in the door."

She nodded to herself as Cass stuck her thumbnail between her teeth. Their hostess didn't notice. She was focused on her memory. "That was quite a fight. I didn't see it until they got to the bedroom, but that was plenty. Karate kicks, and fireballs, and each of them throwing up magic shields to thwart the other. Both of them were so juiced their skin shot sparks like suns. Finally, the Roman faerie got Mr. le Beau up against the wall by the throat. 'Where are they?' he said. 'Where have you hidden them?'"

Rick shot a look at Cass to make sure she was all right. "What did the toymaker say?"

"He said, 'I'll die before I tell you.'"

Cass let out a little noise. She silenced herself by pressing one fist in front of her mouth.

"I thought he was done for," Mrs. Nemo confessed, her gnarled hands patting the chair arms.

"But he wasn't," Rick said, reading that in her expression.

"No, he wasn't. He was playing possum like the Outsiders say. He sagged in the other's grip, like he'd run out of steam, and the other faerie should just get it over with. Except he wasn't out of steam. He was spinning a spell. He had a quilt on his bed with a vine pattern. He made it come alive and used it to trap his attacker!"

"My . . . Mr. le Beau performed an animation spell?" Cass's tone was shocked.

"It was a beaut!" Mrs. Nemo confirmed. "The other faerie took half an hour to free himself. Naturally, Mr. le Beau was long gone. I suppose him escaping made the other angry. He tore that place to pieces like it was his personal enemy. A big faerie tantrum, it looked to me."

"Did the other fae take anything with him when he left?"

"Not that I noticed. He streaked off in the same direction as Mr. le Beau. A few minutes after that the pigeons recovered, and I went to bed."

"Mrs. Nemo," Cass said, drawing the old lady's gaze to her. "If you don't mind me asking, why didn't you call the police while this was going on?"

"But . . . it was faerie business," she said as if the answer were obvious. "Pretty girl that you are, I can see you have some of their blood in you. You must know how it is. Purebloods do what they please between them and them. If I'd called the police, they'd probably have got killed in the crossfire. No offense," she added for Rick's benefit.

Rick scratched his jaw with one finger, seeing her reasoning but unable to endorse it. "We're not without defenses," he said. "If something like this happens again, you really should call us."

"Oh," she said, slightly deflated. "I'm sorry. I didn't think."

Rick didn't have the heart to leave her feeling bad.

"Your report was very helpful," he said, rising from his too-small chair. "The RPD is grateful you were on watch."

~

Rick could tell Cass was in shock when they shut themselves in his car again. She didn't even check the floor for more trash landmines. Rick slid his key into the ignition but didn't turn it. He wanted to talk to her first.

After a few seconds of blank staring, Cass spoke. "My father *couldn't* have gotten the upper hand in that attack. He's a low level pureblood—a commoner by fae standards. Mrs. Nemo must have been confused about what she saw him do to that quilt. Vivifying inanimate matter is a high level ability. Maybe it was an illusion that he brought the vine to life."

"An illusion wouldn't have trapped the other fae while he got away."

"But it can't be true!" Cass knuckled her forehead as if it hurt.

"Look what you're doing," Rick pointed out gently. "That headache is saying you know it's possible. You knew you saw contradictions when you poked around his house."

"Damn it." She dropped her hand to her lap and scowled. Rick wanted to reach out and squeeze her fingers, but couldn't tell if the gesture would be welcome. She looked at Rick. Her emotions were so wrought up her blue eyes glowed slightly. "My father lied to me."

"Misled you," he corrected.

"But why? I wouldn't have said anything."

"My best guess is he's trying to protect you."

"From what?" she burst out. "What did he supposedly steal that the other faerie was so keen to recover?"

Rick was working on a theory he decided he'd rather not share right then. "Does your father have people he trusts in the Pocket, friends who might help him hide?"

"I'm not sure he has friends. Just customers. And me." Her frown turned thoughtful, her thumbnail between her teeth again. "He *knew* he might have to run. That's why he destroyed my picture of him. So I couldn't use it in a tracking spell. The photograph would have captured a bit of his essence."

She turned to Rick on the seat, one long leg tucked up under her. Rick had been with her all morning, but having her suddenly face him caused her half faerie gorgeousness to strike him with the force of a thunderbolt.

He fought not to let his breath go short. "When exactly was the picture damaged?"

She thought. "Early yesterday morning. The sound of it falling down woke me."

That would have been after the female faerie was killed in the underground. And possibly after news of the sword fight first hit the media.

"You're thinking the faerie who attacked my father is the same who killed the female in the subway."

"The descriptions are very similar."

"This one didn't have a sword."

"This one didn't *use* a sword."

"If my father knew he was in danger, why didn't he run before this Roman soldier fae found him?"

Rick touched the side of her face lightly. Her skin was velvet under his fingertips. "I expect your father didn't run before because he wanted to lead his attacker away from you."

Cass's lovely mouth fell open. Rick's groin tightened, but he ignored it.

"But my father trapped him," she objected.

"Your father must have known he'd get free, and that he'd be extra hot to chase him afterward—especially once he didn't find what he wanted at his apartment. If the soldier fae is as powerful as he seems, he probably could follow your father's energy."

Cass considered this.

"There's another thing," he went on. "The other faerie called your father 'keeper.' Whatever your dad is hiding, I think it's safe to conclude he's no commoner."

It was also safe to conclude his daughter wasn't as ordinary as she'd assumed. Keeping this to himself for now, Rick started the car engine.

This seemed to startle Cass. "Where are we going?"

"My place. I need a change of clothes and to touch base with my alpha."

"Rick—"

"You can trust him." He reached for her hand the way he'd been longing to. "Pack is always stronger together."

She let him squeeze her fingers for a few moments before drawing her hand away.

~

Her father was alive. That's what Cass needed to focus on. Not that he was in danger. Not that he'd lied to her. Not that Rick's comfort felt so good it frightened her.

She repeated this to herself all the way to his house.

He lived in River Heights, a nice family neighborhood in the city—a pack neighborhood, to a large extent—where everyone knew each other like on a TV show. Rick lifted his hand to three different people before they'd closed the distance between the curb and his row house's stoop.

If he noticed their heads swiveling back to her, he didn't let on.

"Chances are no one's home," he said as he unlocked the street door. "Well, Ari, Adam's wife, might be, but she'll be busy with Kelsey."

Cass didn't know who Kelsey was. Someone Rick was fond of, to go by his tone of voice. Maybe the child of Ari and Adam? She didn't want to ask. She felt out of place here, nearly as much as she had Outside. The interior hallway of Rick's building had an extra-male feel to it: a pack feel, she guessed, with the heightened testosterone that went along with wolves. Probably it was her imagination, but she almost thought she could pick out Rick's pheromones.

That seemed as good a culprit as any to blame her rather awkward arousal on.

"I'm on the second floor," Rick said, glancing back at her as he started up the stairs. Him being above her made him seem bigger. His shoulders filled up the stairway, his legs surely a mile long. She remembered how he'd held his gun by one thigh when they entered her father's shop.

His entire body had been in serve and protect mode.

Between her legs, nerves that shouldn't have reacted did.

You're just trying to distract yourself from the morning's shocks, thinking about sex instead of your worries.

She *wasn't* becoming obsessed with her old high school crush—even if it seemed like he'd crushed right back on her. Building too much on that would be silly. A crush was just a crush, the same as sex was just sex.

Really, really good sex, her libido reminded her.

"Coming," she said, when Rick lifted his brows at her.

Possibly she should have chosen a different word.

Rick stopped at the landing in front of his own door. "Huh," he said, flattening the fingertips of one hand against the panel. "I think my brother's in here."

"Your brother." She backed an unthinking step away. Her feelings were confused enough. She didn't need to meet his family. "Maybe I should wait in the hall."

Rick noted her anxiety. "It's just Tony. He won't bite. Not you, anyway. You're not his type."

His crooked half smile reminded her of Jin's scuttlebutt that Tony Lupone was gay. Rick didn't appear traumatized about it—just maybe a bit rueful.

"I, um, I'm not really good with strangers," she said. "Sometimes they react . . . oddly to meeting me."

"But Tony's not a stranger." Rick grinned like someone expecting to win an argument. "You know him from high school the same as you know me." He took her arm gently, but she dug in her heels.

"Scaredy cat," he teased.

"Wonder Woman," she retorted.

Rick gaped, then realized she was referring to his magical arm cuff. He laughed, not the least annoyed by her sharp response. "The gloves are off then," he said, seeming to look forward to this prospect.

Cass truly could not have said whether she was delighted or horrified.

Tony saved her from deciding—though not from her social anxieties—by opening the door himself. "I hear you out here," he said to his brother. A second later, he did a double take at her. "Whoa. Snow White."

Cass guessed this settled the question of whether he remembered her.

~

Rick wanted to smack his brother. He could tell Cass disliked her old nickname. "You want to step aside and let us in?"

"Uh, no?" Tony said, cutting a look at Cass. "We, um, made a bit of a mess."

"*We?*"

"Evina got called in to her station for a three-alarm building fire. Her mom's out of town, so I got drafted to emergency babysit."

"And you're not watching the cubs at your place because—? No, never mind. I know the answer. You didn't feel like cleaning your apartment enough for them."

"I didn't have time!" Tony pleaded.

Rick sighed. "Just move aside. Cass won't faint. She's already seen a worse mess today."

He thought she had, but his living room was running a close second. Toys and games were everywhere. His couch was upside down, what looked like his entire supply of clean sheets having turned it into a fort. Nate's adopted kids, six-year-old tiger twins Abby and Rafiq, lay on the floor by his front windows, studiously drawing with magic magic markers on a big shared sheet of white paper. The sun hit their dark curly heads, bringing out a hint of gold in the matching mops. An expected sense of satisfaction radiated through him from his wolf.

The kids were safe. All was right with the pack.

"Hi, Uncle Rick," Abby said without looking up.

Rafi was less blasé than his twin. He did look up, and his big blue eyes widened. "It *is* Snow White," he breathed.

This Abby had to see for herself. She sat up and goggled.

"Uh, I'm not Snow White," Cass said. "I'm just a half faerie."

Abby took this in. "Are you Uncle Rick's girlfriend?"

Rick felt his cheeks go ridiculously hot. "She's my friend-friend. We knew each other in high school. She's helping me with a case."

He was talking too much, so he stopped.

"You should ask her to be your girlfriend," Rafi said. "Clarence's dad says part faeries are hot stuff."

"O-*kay*," Tony interrupted belatedly. He took each twin gently by the arm. "Why don't I move you guys and your picture into Uncle Rick's kitchen?"

"We can hear in there too," Abby pointed out, weretiger ears being as sharp as wolves'.

"Pretend you can't," Tony advised briskly.

When Rick snuck a look at Cass, her lips were pressed together like she was holding in a laugh. He was glad that was her reaction, though it didn't totally cure his nerves over having the topic raised. He knew this kind of household couldn't be what she was used to.

"Sorry," he said.

"It's okay," she demurred. "Kids say things."

Her gaze met his, and his insides gave the most incredible swoop. Amusement lit her eyes, her fears for her father momentarily forgotten. The warmth he read in her beautiful face set his cock twitching.

Rather than risk another monster hard-on, he tore his gaze away. "I'm going to . . . change and catch Tony up on what's happened.

~

"Holy smokes," Tony whispered the moment they were alone in Rick's bedroom. "Is she The One?"

"The one what?" Rick asked, refusing to assume his little brother meant the term romantically.

"The person the dying faerie said you had to protect."

"Oh." Rick rummaged in his dresser for a clean shirt. "Yes, it's looking that way."

"Wow." Tony plunked his butt on the bed. "You and Snow White. Your high school fantasy."

"Her name is Cass," Rick corrected. "She's an actual person, not a storybook character."

Tony looked at him and smiled. "You still dig her."

Rick stripped off his slightly stinky shirt. "People don't say that anymore."

"That doesn't mean you don't feel it. You might want to shower, by the way. I can tell you and 'Cass' got sweaty."

Rick cursed, which stretched Tony's grin wider. He pretended not to see. "Call Nate while I'm cleaning up. I need to know everything he found out about dragon keepers."

~

72

"You owe me," Nate said as he strolled into Rick's place with his usual I'm-too-sexy-for-this-joint confidence.

"I owe you?" Rick replied.

"Okay, maybe you owe Carmine. He's pissed at me for ditching his vampire case to work on yours."

"Daddy!" squealed the cubs, streaking out from the kitchen to attack him.

Nate bent to pick both up at the same time. Rick was treated to the sight of the normally self-possessed werewolf beaming with pure delight. That he liked being called *Daddy* by his adopted kids was clear. A little chaos of explanations and news sharing ensued, after which Nate pushed them firmly in the direction of Rick's bedroom.

"Tiger nap," he ordered.

"*Daddy,*" the twins complained in unison.

"Go on," he said. "You know the rules for when grownups need to talk in private."

The cubs stumped off like glum French *chats* to the guillotine.

"You are the man," Tony said admiringly.

Nate shook his head. "Don't be too impressed. The little monsters will probably eavesdrop."

He looked serious, and that made Rick feel serious as well. "What did you find out?"

"Let's sit for this," Nate said.

Tony and Rick had turned his couch right side up. Cass was perched on one arm, seeming lost in thought as she stared out the front window. Nate stopped in his tracks when she turned around. There was no denying he was as dazzled as his kids had been. Snow White simply had that effect.

"Hello," she said, looking like she felt awkward. "I'm Rick's friend, Cass."

"Ah, right." Nate recovered his aplomb. "Nate Rivera. Nice to meet you. I, uh, take it you need to hear this too."

"Yes," Rick said—maybe too firmly. Nate gave him a weird look. He couldn't help that. This concerned Cass more than anyone.

Nate pulled a big armchair closer, leaving Rick free to sit beside Cass. She didn't move from the couch's arm, though her hands did tighten for a second atop her thighs. Being close to her felt good, like a drug he was getting addicted to.

"So," Nate said, leaning forward across his knees. "I went to see a professor of Faerie Culture at City U. I figured your question about what made ancient dragons special was worth getting an expert opinion on. According to Professor Pliny, true dragons could make and unmake worlds. They feature in a lot of fae origin tales, including the story of how the Pocket was formed."

"The Pocket isn't that old," Tony interjected from beside Rick. "Only a couple centuries."

"Right," Nate said. "Professor Pliny says according to recent legend, our reality was created from the death energy of T'Fain, the last true dragon to walk Faerie."

Nate glanced at Cass, but she shook her head. "I've never heard this story."

Nate studied her expression for a couple seconds before appearing to accept what she said. Cass didn't seem to mind being doubted as much as causing jaws to drop with her looks.

"Neither had I," Nate conceded. "But this professor seemed to know his stuff. He said the last dragon had a keeper, variously known as Justice, Saul and Zeke." He rolled his eyes at the list. "You know how faeries are with names.

"Anyway, the story goes that Justice or whoever was distraught over the loss of the beast he'd trained up from a hatchling. Supposedly, he disappeared into the Pocket shortly after its death, never to be heard from again."

Nate pinned Cass with another look, but she shrugged at him.

"What does this have to do with the guy who attacked Sn- Cass's father?" Tony asked.

"Professor Pliny said there were rumors—which he admitted could be wishful thinking—that T'Fain wasn't actually the last dragon."

"So this Justice guy smuggled a dragon into the Pocket? Those things are big. Wouldn't *we* have heard rumors it existed?"

"Maybe not if he'd smuggled eggs. Three eggs, specifically. They were known as the Sevryn clutch, after the cave in which they were supposedly discovered. The clutch was a myth even in T'Fain's time. Apparently, purebloods have conspiracy theorists too. They accused the Dragon Guild, who were supposed to answer to fae kings, of hiding the eggs to further their own agendas."

Tony pulled one sneakered foot above his knee. His running shoes were in worse shape than Rick's. "Don't dragon eggs have an expiration date?"

"According to the professor, they could last indefinitely. He says they won't hatch until conditions for it are right."

"Conditions being?" Rick asked.

"If we were talking about ordinary creatures, I'd say temperature and available food supply. Since we're talking dragons, who knows? The conditions could be entirely mystical."

Tony leaned back on the couch with his hand on his ankle and his foot wagging. "So some faerie or block of faeries wants to make their own version of the Pocket? Maybe one they can lord it over without interference from their rivals?"

"Professor Pliny suggested another possibility," Nate said. "That some people in Faerie want to *un*make us. Evidently, certain factions think Faerie should be Faerie, and Outside should stay Outside. They're very much opposed to our blended reality."

A shiver seized Rick's shoulders, rippling strongly across them. As if the response were catching, Cass shivered too.

"You're *sure* you've never heard of this?" Nate asked her.

"Positive. I'm half human. Faeries that narrow-minded wouldn't approve of me."

"And your father never suggested he might be this Justice-Saul-Zeke fellow?"

"*No.*" She jumped to her feet to make the denial, which even she seemed to realize was odd. "No," she repeated more moderately. "Admittedly, he wasn't completely forthcoming about his history."

She sat again and hugged herself. Rick edged his shoulder close enough to brush her side.

"Would you know how to train a dragon?" Nate asked, watching her closely. "Assuming a pureblood isn't required."

"I wouldn't have the first idea. My father didn't encourage me to practice magic. He said I'd have an easier time fitting in if I lived like humans. What tricks I know, I figured out myself through trial and error."

Rick looked at her. Her brow was furrowed but not pained.

"I'm not lying," she said, noting his attention.

He wouldn't have thought she was, except her pulse was elevated, the color in her cheeks high. *Something* was going on with her.

His wrist cuff tingled, reminding him of its existence.

"Maybe we should try to dig up more facts," he said. "All we've got now is speculation."

"We could put out an APB for Cass's father," Tony suggested.

"Let's hold off on that. If we did find him, we might inadvertently put him in more danger."

"And Cass as well," Nate said, eyeing him steadily.

"We shouldn't discuss this outside the squad," Tony added. Rick rarely saw him so serious. "If this is a faerie plot, they could have glamoured anyone to help them."

"Agreed," Nate said.

"Agreed," Rick concurred.

Somewhat to his surprise, Cass took a tight grip on his shoulder. He guessed she needed an anchor. Rick was glad it was him.

~

Cass wanted to rail that all of this was nonsense. Her father wasn't some famous dragon keeper from a tale. He couldn't have stolen a mythic clutch of eggs and hidden it God knows where.

The problem was, if the story were true, it would explain a lot.

She followed Rick to his little kitchen, where he took one look at the mess and cursed. "I just cleaned up in here!"

"Sorry!" Tony called from the living room. "I'll tidy before I go."

Nate had left already, to share the latest news with their pack alpha. Rick tossed a few empty juice boxes in the trash, then pulled a clean glass from the cabinet. He filled it with water from the tap and handed it to her.

"Drink," he said. "You look shaky."

She drank and she did feel better. "I forgot how good Resurrection water tastes."

He smiled. He was leaning against the counter close to her. Recently showered, he wore a fresh long sleeve shirt, which he'd pushed up to his elbows. Its deep green hue contrasted with the healthy ruddiness of his skin. Cass couldn't resist laying her hand over his breastbone.

His heart started beating faster the moment she covered it.

"Shouldn't we be doing something?" she asked. She meant since the world might be ending, but her voice was inappropriately husky.

Rick's gaze focused on her mouth. "Yes, we should. As soon as I figure out what that is."

He took the empty glass from her. Because that hand was now free, she flattened it on his chest as well. Heat sluiced through her, spreading outward from her sex. Rick's muscles were hard as iron under the soft T-shirt. He took a step, and turned, and suddenly *her* back was against the counter.

His body was a wall she didn't want to get around.

"Cass," he whispered. "I love the way you flush when you look at me."

She had no doubt she was flushed, especially when he wrapped his hands around her bottom and lifted her onto her tiptoes.

"Yes," she murmured, tipping her mouth to his.

The kiss he claimed seared every nerve in her lips and tongue. She kissed him back with the same heat. His hands began to knead her ass, pulling her against the big ridge rising at his groin. She remembered how his cock felt moving strong and thick inside her. Wanting that again, she slung one leg around his hip and hooked her arms up his back to grip his shoulders. He understood what she needed. He ground his hardness against her pubis and she ground back, both of them gasping out their lust as quietly as they could.

"Shit," he breathed, breaking free for air.

Because she could, Cass nipped the pulse that raced at the side of his neck.

He liked that. His green eyes flashed, the sudden bite of his fingers against her butt telling her his claws had slid free. The danger he theoretically posed to her made her hot. Too hungry to stop, she flicked her tongue over his upper lip.

He licked off the wetness she'd left behind. Cass couldn't help shivering at that.

"God," he swore, almost too soft to hear. "I want to fuck you till you can't walk."

She wanted to be fucked that way—probably more than once. Her panties were wet, her body itching to rub naked against his.

He must have read the readiness in her eyes. "We're not alone," he reminded.

She blinked. She'd actually forgotten Tony and the kids were there. Shocked at herself, she released Rick and dropped back onto the heels of her Manolos.

"Don't apologize," he said when she sucked in a breath to do so. He pressed one finger across her lips' center. The tingle that streaked through her at the contact was alarmingly pleasant.

She shut her mouth and nodded.

Rick let out a wistful sigh. "Let's get out of here. Maybe some fresh air will help me think."

She knew he was right. She also knew *thinking* wasn't what her body craved.

~

Rick seldom regretted his lack of alpha genes. Today he wondered if they'd have helped him know what to do. Adam didn't wait for things to happen. Adam made up his mind and took action.

For a millisecond Rick considered handing the lead to him. He couldn't do it, and truthfully he didn't want to. No matter how big the ramifications of this case, it had fallen into his lap for a reason. Cass had fallen there too, he guessed.

He certainly wasn't going to hand *her* over.

He stood on the sidewalk in front of his and Adam and Tony's house. Cass stood beside him, nervously rubbing the elbows of her nice jacket. She was the key to this, whether she wanted to face it or not: she and her father.

Rick's hand slid to the cuff that circled his right forearm, absentmindedly stroking it. The runes were subtle ridges under his fingertips. He and Cass were bound—by their pasts, by their attraction, and maybe by mystic forces he was too simple a wolf to understand. He thought about his own father. Marcus Lupone wasn't a huge personality. Not like Nate or Tony or Adam's wife. Rick's dad was steady and patient and affectionate. Rick remembered learning to cook from him as a kid. *Here's how you crack an egg, son,* he'd say, letting Rick ruin a whole carton until he got the hang of it. *Your mom likes them whisked nice and frothy. She'll show you how to roll out pasta. She's got a gift for that.*

Rick had learned more from his dad than his dad had known he taught.

He looked at Cass, who turned to look at him. He wasn't aware of what he was going to say until it came out his mouth. "I want to see the house you lived in as a kid."

Her cerulean eyes widened in their frame of black lashes. "Why?"

He didn't have a good answer, only a vague instinct. "Just humor me," he said. "Faeries aren't the only folks who get hunches."

~

To Rick, Enchanted Hills sounded like the name of a cemetery. In reality, it was a long-established, posh-to-the-nines residential enclave four miles outside downtown. Mainly humans inhabited the oversized Tudor homes, with a sprinkling of rich elf doctors and other white-collar professionals. The hills that gave the area its name weren't big . . . unless you were the lawn boy pushing the mower up them.

Cass had a good memory. Though she didn't seem to enjoy it, she directed him to her childhood street without faltering. Big elm trees lined it, their brown leaves mostly stripped by the last windstorm. Her family home was among the largest, set on a well-kept and spacious yard. A tall wrought iron fence guarded it, the thing substantial enough that Rick knew it meant business.

Keep out, riffraff, he thought as he parked out front. The message seemed to be getting through. The street was as quiet as a graveyard.

He couldn't imagine a slightly shy little girl playing on that perfect grass.

"We can't go inside," Cass said. "Mom sold the place before she left the Pocket. Other people live here now."

Her voice was tight. She was clutching her seatbelt's strap like she'd fight any attempt to unfasten it. Rick found her reaction interesting.

"We could ask the current owners if they'd let you look around. You could say you felt nostalgic."

"Why?" she asked stubbornly.

"Because we might find a clue."

"We won't!"

Rick cupped her cheek, and she frowned at him. "Why are you so sure it's pointless?"

"Because . . . I don't know why. I just am."

She'd clenched her jaw, so he stroked it with his thumb. He wished he didn't have to press her, but he was pretty sure he did. The signs of distress she was displaying didn't strike him as normal.

"Cass, your father fiddled with your perceptions. At the least, he misled you about his background. At the most, well, he's a pureblood. He's got a lot of mojo. I think it's possible he glamoured you."

"I'm his *daughter*. He wouldn't do that." A moment later Cass cried out, both palms flying to her forehead. "Crap," she said, breathless from the flash of pain. To Rick's dismay, she began to cry.

"Shh," he soothed, undoing her seatbelt and pulling her to him.

"Why would he do that?" she sobbed. "Doesn't he love me?"

It was a child's lonely cry, one he sympathized with even if he didn't know how it felt. Heart breaking for her, he rubbed her back. "Let's not jump to conclusions. We don't know the whole story."

"Shoot," she said, cutting short the storm.

Though he didn't want to let her push back from him, he released her. "There's Kleenex in the glove compartment."

She dug it out and blew. "You're being really nice to me."

This was said so forlornly he rolled his eyes. "Don't be stupid. You know I like you. More than like you, probably."

She turned to face him. Naturally, her pink nose looked good on her. She grimaced at herself. "I'm being pathetic."

"Well," he said. "Learning stuff like this about your father would shock most people. And you've been through a lot lately."

He rubbed her shoulder through her jacket and then her neck. That was a miscalculation on his part. Her skin was bare there, and her half faerie energy shot from it into his palm. Everything he'd wanted to do to her in the kitchen rushed back into his mind. He remembered how she'd nipped his neck like a she-wolf, how she'd clung to his shoulders and rubbed her crotch over his erection.

His cock jammed out in his jeans so swiftly it stole his breath.

"Oh God," she said, clearly suffering the same violent arousal. Her nipples pebbled behind her nice silk shirt.

"We shouldn't do this here. This is a public street."

"Right," she agreed. "I just—" Her gaze fell to his throbbing groin. "I just need to undo your zipper and touch you for one second."

He couldn't refuse her when she bit her soft red lip that way. He'd heard about faeries getting touch-hunger. "One second . . ."

"Or half a minute. You cut that kiss short. I didn't get to do what I wanted."

"What did you want?" His voice was raspy; pornographic, it seemed to him.

Cass's pupils dilated. Her hand dropped to his knee and progressed upward along his thigh, causing nerves to jump wildly in its wake. "This."

His heart pounded when she undid his jean's button. She took his zipper's tab between her thumb and two fingers. She pulled it down the hump of his erection, carefully but not slow, watching his eyes as his swollen flesh pushed his white boxer briefs through the opening. The stretchy cotton didn't dull the effect of the soft stroke she gave him.

Despite that undeniable thrill, he wasn't truly panting until she took hold of his briefs' waistband. She lifted it over him, allowing his trapped hard-on to spring out. Steadying the pulsing shaft in her hand, she bent to him.

Rick swallowed back a moan. This was definitely a high school fantasy. Her mouth surrounded his penis's head in warmth, her cheeks soft and clinging, one hand sliding smoothly into his jeans to cradle his still covered testicles. When she squeezed them, fireworks shot through his system.

He cursed, his fingers forking helplessly into the waves of her raven hair. He liked the length it was now, the way it whispered over him. The strands were silk, the clasp of her mouth doing crazy things to his arousal. She sank down his erection, her sleek tongue wetting and rubbing him.

No force on earth could have kept him from tightening his buttocks and thrusting an inch farther.

"Jesus," he gasped as her lips tightened and she pulled back up him.

His glans vibrated when her mouth popped off it.

"I'll finish you this way," she said throatily, her hand caressing the well-licked spots where her mouth had been. "Unless you'd rather take me instead."

A tiny uncontrollable explosion went off inside his brain, like phosphorus flaring. "Yes," he rasped. "I want to take you."

Possibly they both went crazy. Heedless of where they were, they started tearing their clothes open. Her jacket flew into the back. Her shirt. His shirt. Her trousers and panties. They muttered swear words as they bumped against the confines of the car. The old Buick was a boat, but they were tall people.

He thanked God the front had a bench-style seat.

"Hurry," she said, spreading her naked legs for him.

He felt like he dove between them; he was that desperate to get into position. Not there yet, he wedged one foot on the door behind him, the other leg bent up beneath her. He chafed her hips—reassuringly, he hoped.

"Is this okay?" he asked. "Are you ready?"

"Yes," she urged, her hands on his waist. "*Please.*"

The *please* just about killed him.

She placed the ball of one foot on the Buick's window and the other on the dash. If anyone walked out of their hoity-toity house, there'd be no doubt what they were up to.

In that moment, Rick simply couldn't care.

"God, I want you," he said.

She reached between them, her beautiful silky hand wrapping his raging cock.

His body quivered as she pulled him to her. He was as crazed for this as the first time, like every time he took her would be a miracle. The heat of her pussy was insane, the wetness, the way it twitched when his tip touched her.

Part of him longed to stay there and savor, but the wolf in him had to push.

"Oh," she said as he slid in.

His cock wanted him to pump like a madman. He gave her a hip swivel.

"*Ohh,*" she said lower than before.

"Yeah?" He did the swivel again, loving the results pretty much himself.

"Yes." This was a breathless gasp. "I like that." To prove it, she wriggled under him, one hand fumbling out to grip the dash.

The other pressed hot and flat on his sweating back.

He didn't have room to get fancy. The car allowed him one position, one method of stroking, one steady slope to climb toward increasingly powerful sensations. He'd never been bare inside a lover before her. His cock felt so good—his whole body, actually. He knew he wasn't going to stop, and that she didn't want him to.

He paid attention to *everything*.

The softness of her pussy around his thrusting cock.

Its strength when it contracted to pull his length deeper.

The little mewls she made when he did something pleasurable.

"Oh yeah," he praised, ducking to kiss her neck. "That's what I want to hear from you."

As sweet as she was to nuzzle, he couldn't stay bent there. She was too pretty a picture to ignore. He pushed up again to see her. He felt like he'd never watched a woman during sex before. Her breasts jiggled in their fancy bra cups with every stroke, their upper curves flushed with excitement. Tendons in her inner thighs tightened when he pulled his cock backward. When he pushed in to reclaim her, her entire being seemed to welcome it.

Her eyes . . .

Her eyes were his window to heaven, closing with bliss and then opening to search his. They seemed to ask the same questions he wanted to ask her. *What does this mean? Why are we so good together?* His chest ached from more than arousal, from more than his need for air.

Oh yeah, he didn't just like her. He wanted her to be his forever.

He couldn't worry about that then, not while his body demanded he drive it to completion. Seeming to feel the same urgency, Cass dropped her foot from the window onto his ass. He'd shoved down his jeans to take her—not the suavest tactic but efficient. Each time he hit the deepest spot in her, her toes curled into his bare rump.

She was pulling her pussy up him, making his thrusts harder. The hair on his scalp prickled. She was stronger than he expected, maybe as resilient as she'd claimed.

Even if he wasn't willing to test her limits, the idea that he didn't have to be *too* careful triggered more excitement inside of him. His hips started churning faster, and that started her groaning. The sound was like pepper itching on his bulbus gland. He couldn't control himself. He sped up more, needing to rub the slight swelling at the base of his shaft. His balls ached with fullness. God, he was going to go. Wanting to bring her with him, he gripped the dash with his left hand and worked the right between them.

The shift placed the electrum cuff between their abdomens. Even as Rick searched out her clit with his thumb, the low grade tingling in the metal flared. Cass's back arched off the seat, her nails digging excitingly into him.

Her swollen button throbbed beneath the pressure he exerted, the satiny skin slippery and hot.

He simply had to rub it harder.

She cried out and clenched, and Rick's orgasm catapulted over the tipping point. He poured himself into her with a groan, thrusting and thrusting, until his balls squeezed out the last shot of ecstasy. His mating gland had *almost* activated. Even now, it twitched like it was considering it.

"God," Cass sighed, hands stroking up and down his back.

Too relaxed to worry, Rick lifted his head and smiled at her. She smiled back, the curve of her mouth mixing naughtiness and languor.

"You're really good at that," she observed.

"I'm glad you think so."

"I know so, Detective Lupone. Sex that good deserves an award."

He laughed. "I should make love to you more often. I like seeing you sassy." He kissed the tip of her nose and then her soft full lips. "Don't think I won't take a rain check on the other."

"The other? Oh." He adored her blush as she recalled how she'd started off this encounter. "Well, that will be my pleasure."

He stroked her dampened hair from her face. Their bodies remained connected. Probably, he ought to move and pull on his clothes, but he was damned if he wanted to. "Speaking of pleasure, I didn't bonk my hip or my funny bone even once in the thick of it. You must have done a spell."

"Oh no," she denied earnestly. "I was too distracted to do magic. That was just faerie luck." She yawned. "Gosh, I could drop off right here."

"If you do, be sure to talk in your sleep like before."

"I don't talk in my sleep."

"You do," he insisted teasingly. "'Where's my shovel,' is what you said last time."

"'Where's my shovel?'" Her eyes were wide.

Because he was looking right at her, he saw the instant her gaze blanked out.

CHAPTER
SIX

CASS Maycee had the best daddy in the world. Not only did he bring her presents when he went away on trips, he taught her to do spells so she'd know he was all right.

Tonight, she was curled in a blanket in the big story chair beside her window. Her daddy's pocket watch lay open on the sill. If she sent it a pulse of energy from her faerie half, the face lit up. A green glow said he was safe and sound. Blue was the sign he missed her, and white meant he was almost home.

Cass had been pulsing the watch every fifteen minutes, refusing to fall asleep. Despite her constant checking, it wouldn't change from green to white.

Wondering if she'd done the charm wrong, she pushed up on her knees. She could see out the window then. Her bedroom took up one end of the attic, which was nicer than it sounded. She liked the slope of the rafters and the pretty princess bed her mother had let her pick. Best of all, the rest of the huge floor was empty—the perfect place for her and her daddy to practice tricks. Cass's mother didn't want her learning spells. She didn't approve of magic. Cass thought that was silly. You couldn't get away from magic in the Pocket, but her dad said they ought to be considerate.

He only taught her tricks when her mother wasn't around.

Cass didn't see his car coming up the drive, so she guessed she hadn't been mis-spelling his special watch. When she checked the hands, the time was eleven thirty and a bit. She frowned at that. She'd turned seven years old today. He'd promised he'd be back for her birthday. He didn't have much longer to keep his word.

Annoyed, she flopped back in the chair. He'd already missed her party with the kids from school. The half elf cousins she liked had come, the ones she'd told him about. They'd picked their own present, instead of just handing one over from their moms. Bridie had wrapped theirs with extra stars stuck onto the paper. That was nice, Cass thought. Bridie and Jin might turn into real friends. Cass wanted to share that with her dad but couldn't until he was home.

She wondered why her mom didn't mind when he went away. She was down in her room sleeping, not at all angry or worried.

"How's my girl?" the best voice in the world asked softly from her doorway.

"You're back!" Cass cried happily. She ran to him for her bear hug, loving how he picked her up and squeezed her until she squeaked. "I checked your watch, Daddy, but you snuck up on me!"

"I'm the grownup," he said with a teasing smile. "I have to have my secrets."

He let her chatter about school and the party and all the things she'd been storing up since he went away.

"That's good," he said when she told him about Jin and Bridie. "Friends are nice things to have."

"So you really think they'll be my friends?"

He framed her face in his hands. His blue eyes were serious. "I think you're the most amazing little girl in the Pocket. You'd make a lovely friend to them."

"I want to," she said. "They're more fun than anyone."

He patted her head and straightened. "Do you think a special gift from your old dad would be fun?"

"A *special* gift?" The back of Cass's neck tingled. She'd learned that word meant something when he used it.

"Three special gifts, actually. I've been saving them for you. I think you're old enough to take care of them."

Cass felt her eyes go round. "Are they what you took your trip to get?"

"They are. Why don't we sit in your chair, and I'll tell you."

He pulled her onto his lap in the story chair. The big moon shone through the window, so he didn't turn on the lamp. "Remember when I told you about T'Fain?"

"T'Fain was the bravest dragon in Faerie. You raised her from a hatchling. She gave her life to form the Pocket."

"That's right." He let out a little sigh that told her he was sad. Cass put her cheek on his chest to make him feel better. He hugged her but just gently. "What I didn't tell you was that T'Fain wasn't really the last dragon."

"She wasn't?" Cass tilted her head to him.

"No. The Dragon Guild—"

"Your bosses."

"Yes, my bosses kept three final eggs a secret from the kings of the fae. They knew their rulers wouldn't be able to resist using up the dragons' magic if they knew they existed. They didn't want the race to die out forever."

"They gave the eggs to you," Cass concluded. "Because you were the best dragon keeper."

"I don't know about the best, but they trusted me to do what it took to protect them."

He petted her hair as she nodded sleepily on his chest. She liked this story so far. She'd always thought the last dragon dying was a sad thing.

"Cass," her father said. "You're my daughter. You're the last of my keeper line."

"I'm half," she said.

"Half is enough. In fact, half is perfect. You're going to take care of the dragons now."

The sleepiness fell away from her. Shocked, she sat up straight on his lap. "Not really!"

Her dad touched her cheek with one finger. "You can do this, honey. You're good at hiding things. Of all the powers I've taught you, that's the one you're best at."

"But—"

"All you need to do is hide them in a good safe place you never tell anyone about. Not even me, Cass. If my enemies ever found me, they'd steal the location out of my head."

"You have enemies?"

He smiled crookedly at her disbelief. "They won't guess I'd trust you with this, that I'd give up control of this treasure to a half human. I promise I'll do everything . . ."

He stopped. To Cass's amazement, her dad was crying. He wiped his eyes and went on. "I promise I'll do everything to keep you safe and out of sight from them. After you do this, you won't have to . . . lift the burden again until you're much older."

Two more tears rolled shining down his cheeks. He brushed them away and simply looked at her. She realized he was waiting for her decision—as if she were grown up too.

"The dragons need me," she said slowly.

"Yes," he agreed. "You're the perfect person to protect them."

She didn't see how she was perfect, but she knew her father didn't lie. "What if I accidentally tell you where I hid them?"

"I'll glamour you when you're done. You won't remember this happened."

That sounded a little scary, but she supposed forgetting would be safer. "Could I see the dragons?"

He smiled. "They don't look very exciting now."

"I want to see anyway."

He was so good at magic he made it seem like no work at all. "*Open*," he said quietly in high fae as he dragged his right index finger across the air. Sparkles trailed prettily behind it.

A space that hadn't been there before appeared, a shelf supported by nothing, with a gray velvet bag in it. Her dad removed the bag, loosened its black silk drawstring, and showed her what lay inside.

The eggs were about the size of a chicken's, but they were round. They were gray with a silvery sheen. Her dad put one in her hand. The sphere was surprisingly heavy.

"It feels like metal," she said, holding it carefully. "And it's cold."

"These eggs are dormant. They won't wake up and hatch until the time is right."

"How will they know?"

"They just will."

She stroked the one she held with her thumb. "When will I have to hide them?"

"Tonight," he said. "The full moon gives you more power to draw on."

Cass had a lump of fear in her throat. This responsibility seemed too important to leave to her. She remembered the stories her dad had told her about T'Fain: how sweet the dragon was, how mischievous sometimes, and how clever. She knew people cried when they lost their pets. Her dad must have felt ten times worse than that.

A keeper and his dragon were as close as father and child.

"Okay," she said. She held out her other hand for the velvet bag. "You should wait downstairs, Daddy. You won't want to know what I do next."

~

The vision snapped away from Cass. Rick had shaken her back to reality.

"The dream," she said, caught between different memories. "I dreamed about that night right before my father's picture fell off the wall."

"What night?" he asked, looking relieved that she'd responded.

She told him as efficiently as she could. While she did, he helped her find her clothes and dress. Taking them off had been much easier. Somewhat to her disappointment, Rick pulled his shirt back on.

"Your dad gave you the dragon eggs?"

"Evidently." She was scared and excited at the same time—not unlike she'd been as a girl. "I think we should get them."

Rick paused in the process of zipping up his jeans. "What if they're safer where they are?"

"What if they're not?"

"Shit," he said, recognizing the dilemma.

"I feel like we should," she said. "I feel like maybe we need to hurry."

Rick scratched the side of his square jaw. "You dad did lead the faerie who was looking for them away . . . Does getting them involve breaking into your old house?"

She shook her head, vividly recalling how she'd climbed out her attic window and down the long rainspout. "I hid them in some parkland. We need to drive thataways a bit."

Rick let out his breath as he decided. "Okay. Thataways it is."

Having him trust her instincts was gratifying—though it made her nervous that she was right. Finding the nature reserve relatively easily steadied her. It was good to know her newly recovered memories weren't false.

The entrance she told Rick to stop at wasn't the park's main gate. The only thing that marked it was a wider stretch of gravel on the side of the quiet two-lane. They couldn't see the hiker's path until they got out. The entrance to that was a break in the low guardrail. The trees were a mix of evergreens and wind-stripped oaks. As the brisk breeze hit her, Cass wished her suit jacket were heavier.

"Cass," Rick said. "This has to be three miles from your home. Are you sure you walked all this way when you were seven?"

"I'm sure. Faeries are strong. And I could move faster than most kids."

Rick ran his hand through his thick brown hair. "All right. Lead the way."

Trees grew a lot in three decades. The packed-dirt path was narrower than she remembered, and of course the landscape looked different in daylight. Despite this, she only hesitated a time or two. She *knew* which way to take at the forks. The right direction tugged at her breastbone.

Rick was a wolf and had no trouble following. He wasn't out of breath from the pace she set, just surprised as she went deeper and deeper in.

"You were a ballsy kid, coming here by yourself in the dark."

"I was scared," she admitted. "Especially when I had to find my way out again. These aren't faerie woods, but I kept thinking that I heard trolls."

A short distance off the path, one of the trees caught her eye. The oak wasn't marked, but it was larger than its neighbors. The shape its lower branches formed stirred a shiver of recognition.

"There," she said, pointing.

Rick took her hand to help her through the tangled brush. She probably didn't need the assist, but she welcomed it anyway. His palm was warm, his strength more than a physical support.

"Damn," she said, looking down at the big tree's roots. "We didn't bring a shovel."

"The ground is soft," Rick said. "We can use a fallen branch."

He found one and started digging with its sharp end. "Sit," he told her. "Wolves are good at this kind of thing."

She supposed they were. She had five minutes to perch on a nearby boulder and admire his arm muscles in action. On the night her father gave her this mission, she recalled having a kid's garden shovel: pink with white polka dots.

Suddenly Rick bent, cleared some soil with one hand, and looked at her. "I think I found it."

She could see the wolf in him. His eyes were bright, his body language vibrating with interest. She went to his side. Down in the hole he'd made, partially covered by dark brown dirt, was a stained but recognizable scrap of gray velvet. Cass's heart began to pound. A wonder Faerie hadn't seen for centuries was in there.

She went to her knees and pulled it out.

Rick dropped beside her as she set the bag on her lap. The drawstring loosened after a struggle. She spread the gray velvet mouth.

"What?" Rick said, seeing the astonishment in her face.

"They're rocks." Dismayed to her foundations, she spilled the contents onto the ground. "We tramped out here for rocks."

They weren't special rocks. Not polished. Not egg-shaped. Not sparkly or colorful. Just common-old, chuck-'em-out-of-your-flowerbed rocks. Cass probed them to be certain, but they didn't give off the slightest whiff of magic.

"Huh," Rick said, picking one up and turning it over in his hand.

"Sheesh," Cass said. "What kind of crazy ploy was my father pulling? Why would he go through that rigmarole to have me bury these?"

"These aren't what you remember burying?"

"No. The eggs he . . . The eggs I *thought* he gave me were round and metallic. Of course, since he glamoured me, he could have made me believe I was hiding the Hope Diamond."

"Huh," Rick said again thoughtfully. He retrieved the other rocks and stuck them in his pockets.

"What are you doing?"

"We came all this way. We may as well take them with us."

"But they're rocks."

"They're *your* rocks," he said with exaggerated gravity.

In spite of her disappointment, Cass found herself laughing.

~

Since Tony was still babysitting at Rick's place, they decided to drive to hers. Cass stared out the window and bit her thumbnail, finding it hard to get over her letdown.

"This is embarrassing," she said.

Rick glanced at her, and warmth washed her cheek. "You mean because your secret dragon cache was as empty as Al Capone's vault? That's pretty normal for police work. Sometimes the lead you follow goes nowhere."

She squirmed around to face him. "You like being a cop."

"It's what I was born to do. I don't mean because I'm a wolf either. I'm not the smartest or the bravest, but I like protecting people."

"You liked that when we were in high school too."

He was watching the road ahead, but she saw his face color up. This was a more date-like conversation than they'd had up till now. "I suppose I did. Mind you—" he turned his head to flash a quick grin at her "—I *am* a wolf. Sometimes I just like kicking ass."

She smiled, her amusement letting her relax against the door. He was silent for a few seconds.

"Your dad did teach you magic," he observed.

"I guess he did. He waited until he'd glamoured away my memory to stop our lessons. He could pretend I'd never had any. Even now, with my recall back, that girl I was, waiting so trustingly for him to come home . . . She feels like a stranger."

"You're angry at him."

She was—too angry to hold it in. "He took away my memory of us being truly close. Maybe he had his reasons, but that's kind of horrible."

Rick nodded. He was good at that: letting people talk, absorbing what they said. He merged into the lane that would take them onto the freeway. "What does doing magic feel like?"

The question surprised her. She didn't think she'd been asked before. "Probably it feels like shifting does for wolves when the moon is full. Once you get the hang of a spell, it's like tying your shoes. If you don't think about it, it's natural."

"Do you ever wonder how powerful you really are?"

"No," she answered without thinking.

He looked at her, his green eyes more intelligent than he gave himself credit for. "Do you ever wonder why you haven't wondered?" he asked softly.

This wasn't him indulging his curiosity. This was a professional query.

"Well, I'll wonder now," she said, trying not to sound huffy.

As unsettled by his question as she was by him turning cop, she gnawed at her nail again.

~

The Maycees had their own reserved area in the store's underground garage. Rick parked between a rain-spotted navy Cadillac and a gorgeous vintage limo he'd seen Cass's gran riding in a time or two on the news. *Maycee Matriarch Opens Youth Center* or *Renoir Donated to Museum by Patricia Maycee*. Possibly in honor of her granddaughter, the grill ornament was a winged faerie. Rick had a sudden longing to see Cass dressed up to paint the town, swinging her endless legs out of the ritzy vehicle. But this was a fantasy for another day. After a brief struggle with himself, he took Cass's rocks from his pockets and tucked them out of sight under the front seat of his Buick.

Cass watched him with raised eyebrows.

"They'll be safe there," he said.

Shaking her head, she waved for him to follow her to the penthouse's private elevator. Out of habit, he memorized the code she punched in to access it.

He wasn't as vigilant as he should have been. Whatever shit was going to hit the fan, it seemed like Cass's father had led it out of town. Cass—so it appeared—had been left with a red herring. He was semi-relaxed as they stepped off on her floor, but she stiffened.

"Someone's in the house," she said.

Rick's warning bells went off then. He drew his gun and held up a finger for her to be quiet. He touched the door, which was no longer locked and swung slightly. Gesturing to the wall beside it, he made a sign for her to stay. A peculiar sound issued from the apartment, reminding him of an unhappy and not-quite-human child.

The cat, Cass mouthed, her eyes gone wide with alarm.

Wanting some idea what he faced, Rick pricked his ears harder.

"Put that creature in the other room," he heard a low voice say.

Cass must have heard it too, because she stifled a small gasp. Great. Now she was worried about her cat. No way would he coax her to go to Security and wait.

The idea of handcuffing her to the elevator rail was a little too distracting.

Resigned, he pushed the door fully open and slipped inside. Wolves knew how to track prey in silence and so did Rick. He noted a pair of cleaning carts parked in the round entry. Their plastic sides bore the logo for the Merriment Maids service. This *might* have reduced his tension, except none of the supplies had been removed. No vacuums hummed farther in, no scrub brushes swished, no brooms swept across marble. He did hear drawers being quietly opened and shut again. He wished he heard them opening and shutting in the same area.

He wished even harder that Cass hadn't crept after him.

When he frowned at her, she held up nine fingers. He guessed she was better at counting energy signatures than him.

Goblins, she mouthed with exaggerated lip movements. She held up her cell phone, clearly offering to call for back-up.

Nine goblins were pretty many, but they were small as a rule. Rick probably could take them if Cass had sufficient juice to dampen their limited magic. Waiting for back-up would give the intruders more time to find what they were searching for.

If Rick's half-baked theory about Cass's rocks was wrong, the dragon eggs could be here. Cass would have been in and out of her grandmother's house as a girl. So would her father. Rick wasn't convinced she'd remembered everything that had gone down all those years ago.

Wherever the truth lay, they couldn't afford to let the clutch fall into the wrong hands.

He looked at her, not knowing how to ask if she was up for this. There she stood in her prissy I'm-a-member-of-the-Board pantsuit, not so much as a smudge to prove she'd been hiking through the woods—in four-inch heels, no less. On the other hand, her pristine appearance kind of proved the amount of casual power she had.

No harder than tying shoes, was how she'd put it.

"I can help," she whispered as quietly as she could. She seemed nervous but not afraid—no more than the downspout-scaling seven-year-old she'd been.

He nodded and squeezed her arm, wanting her as steady as possible. Even in the midst of facing danger, touching her felt incredible.

You love her, he thought. *It's too late to stop that from happening.*

This made him feel a little grim, so maybe he was lucky he didn't have time to think. He peered around the corner to the central hall, the one that did double duty as a portrait gallery. Three goblins were in a confab around its midpoint. The tallest was four foot nothing, the shortest maybe three. Only one appeared to be a woman, though all wore the female version of the Merriment Maids' baby blue uniform. They shared the same mud green skin tone, suggesting they were members of the same low-ranked clan.

Vibrant colors were the mark of goblin aristocrats.

The lower ranks supplied the city with cheap labor. Because they were strong for their size, rarely sick, and usually hardworking, penny-pinching employers overlooked their tendency to petty larceny. Certainly intelligent enough for skilled jobs, goblins sometimes pretended to be stupid. Rick had interrogated quite a few who conveniently "forgot" they knew English. He had mixed emotions about them being approved Pocket residents—sympathy and suspicion generally fighting for dominance.

At that moment, suspicion was winning.

Deciding a direct approach might gain useful information, Rick tucked his gun into the back of his jeans and strode into the hall. He looked like a bodyguard. He'd let them assume he was one.

"Excuse me," he said as the three goblins froze and gaped. "What are you doing in Miss Maycee's home?"

"Cleaning," said the shortest, none too believably. He held a framed oil portrait nearly as tall he was. "See?" He dusted it ineffectively with his ill-fitting sleeve.

The four-foot goblin took the picture from him and—by stretching up on his toes—hung it crookedly on a waiting hook. "We have a standing appointment. Security let us in."

Rick let this pass temporarily. If these "maids" had been here before, why was the cat so upset? He glanced at the newly hung painting. It depicted a sour-faced woman in 1920's dress. The plaque on the bottom said it was Millicent Maycee. Rick was no expert, but he'd never heard of her.

"This doesn't belong here," he said sternly. "Older family members go near to the door."

He hoped to herd the trio toward it. Maybe he could rout them without the others he'd heard moving around the penthouse piling on.

"Of course," said the middle goblin—the female. She reached the portrait down. "Pardon us. Our mistake."

The mistake was Rick's. As soon as the picture was off the wall, the female hopped like lightning onto one of her companion's shoulders, using him as a springboard to bash the heavy wooden frame against Rick head. The blow didn't knock him over, but he staggered. At the same time, a door opened behind the trio and to the left. Two more goblins plus Poly the cat streaked out. She must have recognized him and decided he was a friend. She clawed up his leg like he was a tree she wanted to hide in.

Rick ended up on the carpet beneath five goblins and a panicked cat.

This isn't going to earn me a medal, the calmer part of him thought.

His wolf reflexes and greater size enabled him to block the barrage of kicks and punches. He got in a few himself, tossing one attacker at least ten feet. Not liking that, another goblin muttered a weakening spell. Luckily, it sputtered out before it had a chance to sap Rick's muscles.

Unluckily, he wasn't alone in guessing why it failed.

"The halfling!" someone called. "She's here."

Four more goblins rushed out of various doors and ran toward where he'd left Cass.

Crap, Rick thought. With a burst of strength, he pitched off the remaining goblins. This allowed him to roll to his feet. His hand flashed to the small of his back . . .

And came out with nothing.

"Looking for this?" the smallest goblin inquired. Rick stared down the barrel of his own Smith & Wesson, dismayed to find it in someone else's unexpectedly competent grip. The safety was off, the gun primed to fire. The goblin's four-knuckled finger curled over the trigger.

"She's in the parlor!" another goblin cried. "Help me control her."

The goblin with the gun let his focus split. Rick didn't wait for a second opening. He unleashed a kick from his hip, neatly knocking the weapon from his opponent's hand. The goblin cursed in Goblin and shook stinging fingers. The middle-sized one, the female, scrambled for the pistol before Rick could. Simultaneously, chaos erupted in the parlor. Rick knew he had to settle this group before he could help Cass.

"Go ahead," said the female, pointing his gun at him. "Make my day."

Really? Now he had to deal with goblins who thought they were Clint Eastwood? Frustration swelled inside him, a growl rising from his belly as if he were his wolf. Evidently, his opponent wasn't immune to the primal threat. A shot rang out but went wide, the female's nerves not up to aiming. Seeing she'd missed, she ran. Rick launched himself over her, landing in front of her in a beastlike crouch. That really rattled her. Still crouched and too quick for her to dodge, he swung his arm in an uppercut.

As he did, flame engulfed his right hand. Had another of the goblins gotten off a spell? In that instant, he didn't care if they'd set him on fire. This punch was going to connect.

His fist landed with a crunch he wasn't prepared for. Something flew and bounced off the wall. It was the goblin's head. He'd ripped it clear off the female's neck. Rick gawked at his hand, no longer burning but encased in an exquisitely articulated knight's gauntlet. His electrum cuff had transformed again. Slender spikes sprouted from the metal glove's knuckles—sharp ones, apparently. A *thunk* announced the rest of the goblin collapsing to the floor. Since the species was rather gristly, there wasn't a lot of blood.

A scream he thought was Cass's sent him running to the parlor.

Four goblins had her backed against a wall of glass-fronted display cabinets. Using what looked like all the room's floor lamps, Cass had erected a fence between her and her attackers. A magical force field shimmered between the posts, which the goblins were wildly throwing themselves against. Cass flinched each time they hit—and no wonder. Snarling like mad things, their lips were peeled back from their pointy teeth, their eyes bloodshot and bulging. Two were actually drooling.

This wasn't the image goblin leaders tried to promote. Right then her assailants resembled true monsters. If Rick had filmed them and shared the footage, he could have gotten the entire species' visas revoked.

"Hey!" he called to get their attention.

He succeeded a bit too well. All the goblins rushed him at once. Fury undermined their ability to coordinate the attack. His new accouterment dispatched two handily, the impact of the metal on their skulls knocking them unconscious. The third went for his throat with its pointy teeth. Rick gutted it on his gauntlet's spikes.

The fourth he had alternate plans for.

Catching it by the neck with his metal fingers, he body-slammed all four feet of it to the floor.

"You resist, you die," he said, his voice gone guttural and wolfy.

The enraged goblin spat at him.

The spittle missed, but Rick was not amused. He smashed the goblin's head against the carpet. "Who are you working for?"

He'd stunned the sturdy goblin enough to weaken it. It curled its lip and answered. "You aren't worthy to hear her name, Wolf Man."

Her name? That was interesting.

"Rick!" Cass cried before he could ask more questions.

The goblins from the hall had regrouped. Now blocking the parlor door, two were holding mops as if they were rifles. He'd have found that funny, except the handles started shooting golf ball sized electric bolts.

"You resist, *you* die," the goblin he'd trapped chortled.

Rick ran out of patience and snapped its neck.

"Come on," he said, waving Cass to him. She released the force field she'd spun around the lamps and raced over. She got to him as a bolt winged his elbow, the charge jolting uncomfortably through his nerves. He deflected the next shot with his electrum glove. Apparently, it did possess Wonder Woman bracelet qualities. Wising up, the mop-wielding goblins split apart to shoot at them from different directions.

"Crap," he said, wondering how he'd get him and Cass out of here unfried.

Cass took his left hand and squeezed it, but she wasn't trying to comfort him.

"*We're not here,*" she said in a strange intense tone.

Because his main focus was the shooters, Rick only watched Cass from the corner of his eye. All the same, he couldn't fail to notice when she disappeared. Registering that he'd blinked out of view as well took a few more seconds.

The goblins who'd been firing at them exclaimed to each other in their own language.

"Don't let go," Cass murmured, her invisible hand gripping his harder. "And hurry. I can't hold this spell long."

The confounded goblins blundered into the parlor, trying to find them by waving their arms around. Rick slipped Cass between them and out the front entrance. Her spell was flickering as they reached the elevator. Without wasting breath on cursing, she punched in the code and hit the call button. Rick pulled her inside the car the instant the doors opened.

Poly yowled from the threshold to the penthouse.

"Well, come on," Rick hissed, but the frightened cat didn't understand.

An electric bolt singed the floor mere inches from her back paw.

Damn it, he thought, dashing back across the foyer for her.

Naturally the goblins saw him the moment he released Cass's hand. Hoping to avoid being shot, he weaved and feinted like his old soccer-playing days. He feared the cat might run from him, but he managed to grab it around the middle before it could decide what it was most scared of.

He dove with it cradled to his chest, sliding on his side across the polished marble back to where Cass waited. With a strength that probably shouldn't have surprised him, she hauled him and his cargo in.

One last bolt sizzled on the elevator doors as they hissed closed.

"Jesus," he said, repeatedly pressing the "P3" button in a stupid attempt to make the car hurry.

"We'll reach the garage first," Cass said. "I melted the mechanism on the door to the stairs."

She was pleased with herself. A tiny smile played around her gorgeous mouth. What she didn't realize was that one of the goblin's bolts must have exploded near her head. Most of her raven hair was floating up with static.

Combined with her smugness, this was pretty adorable.

"That was quick thinking," he acknowledged, not giving the joke away.

"Shall I take her?" Cass offered, indicating the wriggling cat.

As soon as Rick passed her over, the ungrateful feline began purring.

"We didn't like those goblins, did we?" Cass cooed into Poly's ruff. "They had terrible coffee breath."

Rick's knees might have been shaking in the aftermath of the fight, but he still found energy to chuckle.

~

To Cass's amusement, the first thing Rick did after they jogged into the garage was retrieve the rocks from his car. The second was pull out his cell phone. He seemed to be struggling over whether to use it.

"Make up your mind while I drive," she said, opening the door to the tricked-out dark blue caddie.

He gave her a look.

"The Cadillac is nicer," she said, "and Gran always kept it charged. Plus, I can disable the GPS chip. You know, in case the goblins try to use it to track us."

She dropped the now-mellow Poly in the back seat.

Rick shoved the cell phone into his front jeans pocket, an interesting process what with the gauntlet's spikes. "Fine," he said, "but I'm driving."

"Can you?" She looked pointedly at his hand.

"The day I can't is the day I turn in my Y chromosome."

She laughed and let him take the wheel, aware that her giddy humor was probably the result of too much fear-driven adrenaline.

She took a moment to be proud of herself. The magic she'd used wouldn't win a prize, but she hadn't choked in the thick of things. She'd helped her and Rick get free. She couldn't deny she'd enjoyed teaming up with him.

She directed him to the private exit from the garage. As they emerged on Sixth Avenue, police sirens began to wail on Fifth. Someone must have heard the fight and reported it.

Rick touched the pocket that held his phone again.

"You don't know if you should call your pack," she realized.

His face twisted, his expression more strained than it had been for the goblin attack. "My wolf wants me to. It's what we do when there's danger: pull together and face it as a group."

"But?"

His hands—one gloved, one bare—slid restlessly on the wheel. The gauntlet's spikes were clean and shiny and strangely cheerful, as if they'd drunk the goblin blood and liked it. "But maybe we *do* have the dragon eggs. I know. You think those rocks can't be them, but if it's another trick you or your dad pulled . . ."

"They're not magic. I double-checked."

Rick stopped for a red light. A hot dog vendor rolled his cart across the intersection in front of them, followed by a huge Spink demon walking a bouncy pug puppy. Cass took advantage of the car being stationary to remove the GPS chip from its hiding spot behind the radio.

"Squish it?" she asked Rick.

Still troubled, he nodded.

"You should turn off your phone if you're going to," she said. "As long as you use Elfnet, shutting it off will prohibit it pinging off cell towers."

He'd know this of course. Any cop would. Grimacing, he dug out his unit and handed it to her.

"We're dealing with two faeries now," he said as she switched off his cell and hers. "That goblin said they were hired by a she. And the portrait they were hanging? I think whoever she is sent the fake cleaners not just to search the penthouse, but also to replace the picture you threw in the trash chute. I think it must have been the faerie version of a nanny cam—spelled to keep an eye on the place and you. The question is are the male and female faeries working together or rivals to find the eggs? If I call in my pack, will they be caught in a faerie crossfire? And then there's you."

"Me?"

He glanced at her, then put the car in motion for the green light. Despite his distraction, he drove more smoothly than anyone she'd ridden with. "What if you'd be safer with all of us protecting you? What if I'm not enough by myself?"

"I'm not helpless," she pointed out.

"I know." He smacked the wheel in frustration. "I wish my brain worked faster."

"Your brain works fine the way it is!"

He smiled at her defense of it. "We would hide more easily if it was just the two of us."

"Then that's what we'll do." She was struck by the surrealness of the situation. How had her return to Resurrection turned into her and her old crush going on the lam from dragon-obsessed faeries?

"Can you be tracked by photos like you said your dad could?"

She blinked. So much for his "slow" brain. She hadn't thought of that. "Maybe. Being tracked that way is a faerie-specific thing, because purebloods radiate extra energy. I'm not certain it works on halves."

"Could you burn out your images like he did?"

"I don't know. Doing it long distance might be tricky."

"I think you should try," he said.

"O-kay," she agreed slowly.

He spun the wheel for an unexpected turn, one that doubled back on their route thus far. "I'm making sure we aren't followed," he said. "Once I do, I'll decide where we'll hide out. Concentrate on your erasing. I'll take care of us for now."

He talked as if her accomplishing the feat was a foregone conclusion. Apparently, he had as much faith in her as he did in those stupid rocks.

CHAPTER SEVEN

AS a cop and a wolf, Rick knew back ways into Wolf Woods. Though the land reserved to his kind for hunting stretched many miles, run-ins between packs could get rowdy. Rick's squad had been called in to assist the rangers a time or two.

Because the full moon had passed a week ago, he was likelier to face a standoff with a bear than one of his own species. The bear he could handle. It wouldn't blab that it had seen them.

He squeezed the borrowed Cadillac into a work shed behind an empty cabin. Cass and the cat were asleep. Cass had conked out after spending an hour looking like she was meditating—presumably burning out her image from people's pictures. Rick hoped asking her to do that was overkill. He also hoped her friends didn't find out he was responsible. His sister Maria taught him women got pissed over ruined photographs.

Happy to let Cass nap, he rummaged through the cabin for supplies he could liberate. The magic gauntlet—which he wished he could figure out how to turn back into a cuff—made his search awkward. That didn't matter. This wasn't their final stop. Though Rick knew faeries drew strength from nature, he wasn't sure how Cass felt about roughing it. Thoughts of the luxuries she was used to led him to shove more into the bags than he would have for his own sake. His conscience pricked at the thefts. Hopefully, he'd get a chance to pay back the owner. Hopefully, this crazy situation wasn't going to end with the Pocket imploding.

His illegal foraging complete, Rick returned to the car.

Cass woke when he opened the door she was leaning on. Her eyes were sleepy, her cheeks and lips as rosy as a child's. She was too effing beautiful for comfort. Rick's restless cock started stretching inside his jeans. His control wasn't helped by his whole body itching for a post-fight release. He'd have loved to let go and take her now.

"Are we there?" she asked, her voice husky from waking up.

"Almost." He held up the woman's moccasins he'd found by the cabin door. "I know you can walk in heels, but we've got a ways to go. These might be easier."

She slipped them on. Either he'd guessed her size, or she made them fit with a spell. She looked out the door of the weathered shed, toward the trees that surrounded them. The Pocket might be just a few centuries old, but this forest looked as if it had been around longer. Pines as tall as ship masts grew here; oaks with trunks three grown men couldn't circle with their arms. He'd heard rumors actual wood sprites had been seen dancing in some clearings.

"Where are we?" she asked.

"Wolf Woods."

"I thought it felt familiar."

"You've been here before?" Non-wolves were allowed in the park if they had permits. He tried to imagine Cass camping and couldn't.

"I've driven past the gates. The original Maycee farmstead is out Route One. When I was a kid, Gran took me on a couple pilgrimages to see it. I think she was glad for the company. My mom absolutely refused to go. There's a lot of woo-woo energy on the property."

"The farm buildings are intact?"

"More or less. Gran paid a caretaker to keep them from falling down."

"I didn't know that. I'm surprised the place isn't a museum."

"I think Gran wanted it to stay a family thing."

Since Cass was ready, Rick offered her a hand out of the car. Her warm palm slid over his like silk.

"I'll get the cat," she said, opening the back and leaning in to do it.

Sweat prickled on his skin, his jeans tightening even more. Her trousers might be prissy, but her rounded ass was killer. Poly let out grumpy *mew* before falling back to sleep draped on her shoulder.

Rick wasn't ready for Cass to turn around.

"What?" she asked, seeing the tension in his facial muscles.

"Nothing," he said, grateful he had no problem lying. "I left some supplies outside."

She followed him into the tall weeds of the cabin's yard. Rick heaved the larger duffel over his head and shoulder.

"I can carry both," he offered. "I forgot about the cat."

Cass lifted the smaller backpack by one strap. "Oh my God," she moaned, pretending to be bent double by the weight.

"It's not *that* heavy," he said without thinking.

She laughed and straightened with it on her shoulder. Her blue eyes twinkled with amusement. "I guess my faerie princess cred has expired."

"I said I'd carry both."

"No, no," she demurred. "You're tired of treating me like a fragile flower.

I'll just have to bear up."

Since she seemed to prefer this, he shut his mouth.

"You could offer to take Poly," she teased.

"Thanks but no thanks. She likes you way more than me."

He enjoyed that Cass was smiling as they set off into the trees. Because he'd decided to avoid trails, they had to rely on their similar aptitudes for navigating wild places. The air was nippy, the autumn sun well on its downward path. Rick looked back to check Cass for shivers, but she seemed all right.

"Are we going somewhere in particular?" she asked after a few minutes.

"Yes," he answered, reluctant to explain he wasn't certain he could find it.

She waited a beat and then broke into a laugh. "That's all I get? A *yes?*"

Rick sighed in surrender. "I haven't been to the spot myself. A member of my pack described it after he stumbled onto it."

"I thought you'd decided not to involve your pack. Won't it occur to him that's where we'd go?"

"Nate won't *want* to think it. Something bad happened to him there."

The something bad was a power-mad part faerie forcing him into his wolf form without the civilizing effect of his human consciousness. As a result, he'd hunted and nearly killed his future wife. Under the circumstances, Rick thought he could be excused from bringing up all that.

"The way Nate described it, it wasn't a normal place. I can't be sure, but I have a feeling we'll be safe there."

Cass resettled the backpack on her deceptively slender shoulders. "Okay," she said. "I believe in feelings."

~

What Cass felt most at the moment was freezing. The woods grew darker, the mercury plummeting along with the sun. She and Rick had good night vision. They continued quietly and at a good pace. Whether they were actually making progress was a separate issue.

Poly was awake again and seemed to find the nighttime journey interesting. She peered this way and that from her safe post on Cass's shoulder, ears flicking at forest creatures and snapping twigs. Cass was grateful for her furry warmth to bury her hands in.

Don't ask, she ordered as the urge arose yet again to inquire if Rick was sure he could find this place. She already knew he wasn't. His packmate had described it, not traced the route on a map. Rick had stopped half a dozen times already to get his bearings and take a different tack.

She clenched her teeth against chattering. Maybe it would be okay to suggest they make camp now and try again in the morning. Rick wasn't as uptight about being right as some men.

She opened her mouth to ask and bumped into his broad back. He'd stopped without warning. God, she could have put her head on his shoulder and slept standing up.

He reached behind him to rub her hip. "I think it's up ahead."

Her heart rate perked up. There did seem to be a clearing. By leaning around him she spotted an increase in moonlight. Rick walked faster and she followed.

"Wow," he said, coming to a halt. He stepped aside so Cass could see.

The lake before her was as magical a spot as she'd ever encountered. Not huge but considerably bigger than a pond, the tall dark forest surrounded it. Nearly as still as glass, its slowly wavering surface turned everything it reflected ethereal. The trees looked ready to start walking, the stars to float down to earth. Though it was night and almost winter, the scent of flowers perfumed the air. A milky boulder rose from the water's center—a great chunk of quartz, she thought. Power emanated from it in gentle waves, not fae power but similar to it. Despite Rick's story of his packmate stumbling here, it seemed a place no civilized person had disturbed.

"Wow," she agreed, her breath gusting white in front of her.

"This has to be it," Rick said. "Nate described that rock perfectly."

They were whispering, too awed by their surroundings to speak loudly. Poly meowed and wriggled to be let down. With some trepidation, Cass set her on her feet. The cat ran to the lake edge and lapped a drink.

"She won't run away," Rick assured her. "She's a house cat. She'll want you to feed her."

Cass hoped this was true. She'd grown attached to her grandmother's orphaned pet. Rick rubbed her sleeve. The comfort she received from the gesture reminded her—or warned her—she'd grown attached to him as well.

"Look over there," he said, pointing across the water toward where the bank was taller and overhung with vines. "I think there might be a cave."

Goose bumps skipped across her shoulders. Didn't dragons traditionally like them?

"Let's go see," she said.

Rick had been caught up in goggling at the lake. At her words, he turned and smiled at her. Her heart jumped into her throat and stuck. She'd thought of him as a knight before, but he truly looked it then. Bathed by the soft moonlight, his brow was noble, his grin game for anything. His green eyes flashed with his wolf's excitement as he took her hand in his.

He squeezed her fingers for the entire walk to the cave. The shimmery moonlight went in a little ways.

"It looks big," she said, craning to see farther into the opening.

Rick dug a flashlight out of his duffel and scanned the beam around. "It *is* big."

The bit Cass saw was empty and dry and blessedly out of the frigid wind.

"Wait two minutes while I check it," he said.

Cass hugged her hands beneath her armpits and humored him. She couldn't have checked it from outside anyway. Right then, her energy sense was as numb as the rest of her.

Rick didn't keep her waiting long. The smile he returned with was cheery. "No bears, no snakes, no trolls. Maybe a couple field mice, but Poly will scare off those."

"Good," she said, her teeth chattering a bit.

Rick's face altered with concern. "Why didn't you say you were cold?"

Cass let out a sheepish laugh. "You were so impressed with how tough I was. I didn't want to ruin it."

Rick pulled her to him and rubbed her back briskly. Cass buried her head in his chest and sighed with pleasure. Wolf that he was, his body had remained warm. Before she could really snuggle, he dropped a quick kiss into her hair. "Let's get inside and set up. I've got supplies for starting a fire."

As it turned out, he'd stolen three canisters of Duraflame Smokeless Log-Coater.

"You're a genius!" she exclaimed as he dabbed the enchanted gel onto an armload of branches he'd piled in the cave's center. They'd burn many times longer now—and without giving them away.

He'd packed food in the duffel too, plus spell-shrunk bedrolls, and an empty Christmas cookie tin in which he very carefully placed the precious rocks he'd carried along with him. He set the metal container a foot from the flickering fire, thought about it a moment, and nudged it an inch closer. Cass bit her lip against teasing, but he saw what she was thinking.

"Laugh now," he said. "You'll eat those sniggers if these things hatch."

"God knows what we'll do with them if they do."

"We'll figure it out," he said. "We've done all right so far."

They'd done more than all right, considering. Without warning, Cass's eyes teared up. How pathetic was it that sharing this adventure with him was more fun—and more excitement—than she'd had in two decades?

~

Canned hash and protein bars made up dinner. Cass appeared not to have eaten hash before. After a cautious bite, she finished her portion without complaint.

Being lakeside was handy for washing up and seeing to calls of nature. Cass returned from her trip outside with the cat trotting behind her. Poly fell on the final slice of hash like it was filet mignon. The bell on her collar jingled with the fervor of her chomping.

"Good thing she isn't fussy," Cass observed fondly.

"Mm-hm." Rick sat on a rock a foot from the fire. He hadn't built a blaze, just enough to warm them and stare into. He turned his deactivated cell phone round and round in his hands. It clinked on the electrum gauntlet, the rhythmic sound soothing his edginess.

Cass paused by him and rubbed his shoulder. "Sometimes you can't know in the moment whether you made the right decision. Sometimes you have to wait and see."

He looked up at her. "Am I that easy to read?"

She smiled, bending to pick up the two bedrolls. They were heavy but no thicker than wrung towels. "I'm knackered. I'm going to set these up." She found a flat spot she liked and pulled the spell tabs on both. The sleeping bags decompacted and unrolled. Cass knelt and zipped the pair together, forming a double sack.

She noticed him watching her. "This is okay, right? You don't want to sleep separately?"

"It's good," he said, his voice husky.

Cass's lips curved, causing the heat spreading through his chest to spike. "You know, I never really saw the charm of camping until now."

Rick couldn't speak. He was so grateful she wanted him. He stood and peeled off his shirt, only just avoiding ripping the material on the gauntlet's spikes. He unzipped his jeans left-handed, loving how Cass went motionless and watched wide-eyed. Once he'd removed his running shoes and socks, he shoved the denim down.

His cock rose without obstruction as he shucked his boxer briefs.

All he wore then was his saint medal.

"*Man by Firelight*," she murmured like it was the title of a painting she admired. Inspired by the attention, his shaft strained longer.

"Take off your clothes," he rasped.

She rose, removing her garments as unfussily as he had. Then she stood without moving, seeming to understand he needed to drink in the sight of her. No painter could have captured her. Her skin was as white as sugar but at the same time alive with color. Tiny rainbow glints sparkled on its surface wherever the firelight licked. Her breasts were beautiful rounded handfuls decorated by tight nipples prettier than rubies. Her thatch was a neat raven triangle, her waist and hips mimicking the curves of an hourglass. Her proportions were so precise and pleasing a watchmaker could have constructed her. She was real, though, and for this night entirely his. Looking at her literally made his mouth water. When his gaze finally traveled back to her face, a wash of rose pink stained it.

"I like the way you look at me," she confessed.

"That's good," he responded breathlessly. "I don't think I can stop."

His cock was so hard it pounded. Cass's eyes dropped to it. When she licked her lips, he felt a drop of pre-come squeeze from the tip.

"I've heard a good fight makes werewolves horny."

"That isn't false," he agreed hoarsely.

"You've been showing some restraint."

"We had things to do."

She stepped onto the joined bedrolls, each long white leg enchanting him in turn. She sank to her knees as gracefully as a water sprite, then stretched out on her side. A second drop of wetness squeezed from his dick. She patted the quilting in front of her. "Do we have anything better to do right now?"

He moved to her, awkward with desire and emotion. He dropped to his knees, to his side, and pulled her against him.

"Shit," he cursed, hugging her for a new reason. "You're still cold."

She tipped her head up and licked his chin. "Why don't you warm me?"

He moaned when one of her chilly thighs insinuated between his. "Hold still," he said gruffly, wrapping her close full length. He wanted to warm her up a minute. Her shivering while he made love to her wasn't his fantasy.

Cass had her own agenda, he guessed. She nuzzled the crook of his neck. "Your penis is burning me."

She undulated against it, the curve of her belly smooth. Rick's hand—the hand with the gauntlet, as it happened—clamped tight around her butt.

"I want to roll you under me," he whispered, craving that control. "But these damn spikes will tear up the bedroll."

She kissed him: deep, strong, with plenty of tongue action.

"Fuck," he gasped, just about seeing stars once she released him. He couldn't look away from her. Her blue eyes glowed with desire, soft and fiery at the same time. Maybe the fight had torqued her up as well.

"I want you to fuck me," she said, her voice as incendiary as her gaze. "I want you to take me from behind like your wolf would."

He jerked but not with shock. A flood of hormones had surged into his bloodstream. She'd thrown a switch in his nature she couldn't have known was there. In spite of how much he wanted to do it, he held back. "I might go too hard at you if I do. I . . . That position really brings out my dominance."

"You want to let it out."

He did . . . but maybe not with her.

"Rick," she scolded, and—oh—his name was magic on her lips. "I used to sneak-read werewolf bodice rippers. I've been dreaming of you taking me like that since high school."

The idea of *her* dreaming about *him* set his skin on fire. He growled as he flipped her onto her front. She was half faerie. She wasn't weak, and she could move fast. All the same, she hadn't a hope in the world of stopping him.

She ended up on her hands and knees, back dipped, pretty ass in the air, neck held carefully captive within the circle of his gauntlet. He pushed until her brow rested on the pillow that came with the bedroll. Then he stopped. She didn't need more force in order to react.

She sucked in a startled breath to find herself where she was—though she'd literally asked for it.

Sensing she could take more, he nudged her knees wider with his own. She struggled for just a moment, then settled obediently. The trust this implied humbled him.

He could have gone at her. He was ready, and so was she. He didn't need his wolf's gifts to scent her arousal. His cock pounded like a demon, goading him to pump into her, its thick flesh stretched to the aching point. Knowing he didn't have to wear a condom made him want it even more.

He remembered the tight hot heaven of sliding into her.

He didn't do it. Her beauty—and her longing—spread before him like a feast. No lover worth the name wouldn't have played with her beforehand.

He folded himself around her, his knees between hers, his throbbing length laid up the cleft of her ass. He released her neck so he could kiss her nape. The hand in the gauntlet rubbed over and around her breasts. Despite the metal's ability to stop projectiles, the thinness of the cleverly fashioned plates practically let him feel her flesh through them. He knew the electrum wasn't cold. His heat had transferred into it. He slid his left hand, his bare hand, across her belly to hug her waist.

Then he tucked his chin over her shoulder.

"Now I'll warm you," he said.

He held her, blanketing her with his body. All he moved was his hands. He liked stroking her hip and belly, liked cupping her dangling breasts and slowly plucking their taut nipples.

He especially liked how she responded.

"Rick," she whispered, moving restlessly under him. "That glove . . ."

He shifted back a few inches, kissing her between her shoulder blades. He could tell she wasn't complaining. "Don't move."

"Rick—"

He put both his hands behind her head, holding it down as gently as he could. "Stay," he said softly.

When he thought she would, he let go. He drew his palms down and up her back, down and up, the shining white of her skin brightening with each pass. Petting her was like stroking velvet, a special version woven from silk and faerie dust. He squeezed the halves of her ass, a sound of admiration breaking from him at the sumptuous give of her curves.

"Rick—"

"Shh." Relishing how her squirms increased, he kissed a path down her vertebrae. His canines had slid out, upper and lower. He dragged them across her buttocks, then bit each cheek lightly.

The sound Cass choked out was a muffled yip. The scent of her arousal grew heavier.

"I'm warm now," she insisted breathily.

Hot was more like it. Her heightened core temperature beat out at him. He licked all the way up her spine. She tasted delicious: human salt, faerie spice, and some indefinable sweetness that was all her. He nuzzled her nape, drunk on her and the magic they made together. Aroused almost beyond bearing, he smoothed her wavy hair aside for his mouth.

His balls were pulsing nearly as hard as his cock.

"Can I hold you here?" he whispered. "With my teeth? Male wolves like to . . . restrain their partners during sex."

She shuddered. He ran the electrum gauntlet down her front, sliding one metal finger through her curls, over her swollen clit, and into her wet heat. He guessed she enjoyed the slightly alien intrusion. She was already drenched, but she gasped and creamed over him.

"Yes," she breathed. "I'd like you to restrain me."

His dick jerked like she'd stroked it.

He angled his head and got his teeth where he wanted them: secure around her skin but not breaking it. She began to tremble, and his breath came harder. Had he ever wanted anyone this much? He backed his finger slowly out of her, leaving it pressed beside her clitoris but not rubbing. His hips weren't in the right position. Lifting them dragged his erection around her ass.

That felt so good he groaned.

"You're wet," she said, the trail of his arousal difficult to miss.

He didn't want to let go of her to answer. He grunted against her nape. A little too eager, he jabbed the head of his cock at her and missed.

She reached for his hip, tilting her pelvis higher. The next time he pushed, he glided easily into her.

Each of them let out a low pleasured sound.

He went in and in, until her warm wet flesh clasped him all around.

He closed his eyes. His bulbus gland was itching. He didn't think he'd escape it going off this time. He hoped those werewolf bodice rippers prepared her for the shock.

"Push up," he said.

Cass straightened her slim arms. He braced his left hand over hers with his thumb behind her wrist, symbolically holding her captive. His gloved hand found occupation in gently circling her clitoris. Her hot button was engorged, slippery with excitement.

"Rick," she urged. Her ass cheeks squirmed deliciously against his pelvis, her pussy tightening on his cock.

He wouldn't let her rush him, no matter how strong the temptation was. He pulled back and thrust in slowly, savoring taking her again. She moaned, and he fell in love with the sound. He thrust once more like the first time, his teeth gripping her nape a little more securely. He kept this up, caressing her sheath with his raging hard-on for long minutes. It wasn't easy. Contrary impulses tugged at him. Beauty like hers invited worship *and* pillaging.

It seemed Cass was in the mood for plunder. Her neck arched with longing beneath his grip. "God," she groaned. "You're killing me."

He treated her to a more forceful stroke.

"*Unh*," she said, her hips backing into it.

He gave her another one.

"Yes," she gasped, and abruptly he couldn't stop.

He drove at her like his lust wanted: hard long thrusts, his pelvis moving faster and faster until this wasn't the sort of coupling a human could have given her. He guessed he liked that idea, because he turned as unthinking as his wolf, his body following its instincts for what he and she would enjoy. *It* found the angle that let him deeper. *It* judged the force they needed to go over. Cass had to brace hard to take his fucking, but she was in it all the way, pushing back at him for each stroke. Her little cries excited him, the rising heat of her body, the snug clamping of her cunt.

They couldn't have picked a better place for this. The rocky walls of the cave, the dancing fire, the ragged slapping of their flesh all brought out his wild nature. The gland at the base of his shaft was burning, too tender for the vigorous friction it was getting. Despite this, he couldn't stop. The nerves in his gland and cock kept demanding more and more.

"More," she groaned, echoing his thoughts. "Please."

He let loose. She slapped her hand around his gloved wrist, trapping his metal-encased fingers against her clitoris and pussy lips. He squeezed her the way she seemed to want, massaging all of her with the strange metal. She moaned, and sensation twanged through his mating gland. He couldn't tell if the feeling was pain or pleasure, and frankly he didn't care. He slammed into her, balls contracting in preparation to spill their load, bulbus abruptly swelling to twice its normal size. The enlargement frightened him for a second, but the extra pressure hit some good spot in her. She cried out hoarsely and climaxed.

Her contractions set off his own explosion. He roared like his beast as every cell in his penis came. It felt like her pussy was dusting him. The ecstasy was unearthly. Her faerie power combined with his heightened mating sensations to create an orgasm strong enough to blind. His nerves fired until they tingled, muscles kicking uncontrollably. He shot more seed than he knew he had in him.

The pulses went on and on, the swelling of his bulbus wedging him tight in her. He didn't know if he could pull out, and he wasn't about to try. He needed to be as deep inside her as he could get, needed to lay claim to her by every means possible.

Since she was grinding desperately closer and gasping out her pleasure, that seemed to be all right.

Gradually, almost reluctantly, the swelling in his gland subsided. Cass's sheath stopped greedily seizing him.

They both seemed to have been struck speechless. The first to be willing to separate, Cass pulled free and collapsed onto the bedroll.

Rick's left hand still held her wrist captive.

"Mm," she said, eyes closed, cheek turned sideways on the bedroll's pillow. The inky fans of her lashes were indescribably pretty.

As fascinating as her relaxed features were, Rick couldn't ignore his own condition. His cock was heavy and exhausted, seed dripping down its length onto her. If she noticed, she didn't care. As he lowered his weight next to her, he realized his limbs were shaking.

He was too overheated to crawl into the sleeping bag. Mindful of her human half's lower tolerance for the cold, he draped an arm and leg over her.

"Mm," she said again, unexpectedly turning to snuggle into him.

He held her in both arms then, taking advantage of her closeness to kiss her brow lightly. Her arms were folded up between them. Her mouth curved softly before her body went limp in sleep.

"I'll keep you warm," he murmured.

Mostly, though, he wanted to keep her.

~

Cass wasn't sure how long she slept wrapped up against Rick's chest. Feeling almost laughably good, she stretched her toes and wriggled her spine looser. If it wouldn't have disturbed him, she'd have groaned with pleasure.

She extricated herself from his hold instead. The fire was dying. He might not miss its warmth, but she would. As quietly as she was able, she dabbed some Duraflame on a log from the pile he'd gathered and placed it atop the rest. The cat was curled up next to Rick's cookie tin of rocks, her nose tucked beneath her tail. Cass petted her, rolled her eyes at the rocks, and went to stand over Rick.

God, he was a beautiful man.

The way he'd made love to her was a revelation. She hadn't known she could feel that close to another person, or that being controlled by him would be a thrill. She hadn't been frightened—not even by the strangeness of the gauntlet. That Rick had found the experience exciting she couldn't doubt. She knew a bit about werewolf biology—apart from the shifter romances she'd read back in high school. She knew his *bulbus glandis* had swollen up at the end, and that this meant the two of them were genetically suited for having kids. Some thought the gland's activation signaled that partners were soul mates, but Cass wasn't going to jump to that conclusion. Even romantics admitted werewolves could react this way to more than one person. She was half faerie. Faeries often inspired unnaturally strong erotic responses.

Rick made a snuffling sound in his sleep, then rolled onto the warm spot her slipping off the sleeping bag had left. Cass grinned at the new real estate this revealed. Her werewolf lover had an amazing ass: muscular and tight with dimples decorating either side of his strong tailbone. She wondered what his wolf's tail looked like. If it were able to sprout like his claws did when he was in human form, would it have been wagging?

She covered her mouth to keep herself from laughing.

Because she could, she sat down cross-legged and stroked his back.

"Sleeping now," he mumbled, but as if he might be smiling.

She kissed his shoulder before rubbing her face across his olive skin. "What if I wanted to give you your rain check?"

"Mmph," he said, not seeming to remember this topic coming up before.

She trailed her touch down his lovely muscled arm, gathering up his hand so she could kiss it. Rick shifted onto his side and blinked sleepily at her. The tenderness that rose within her was probably dangerous. Ignoring that, she brushed his tousled hair from his forehead. "I want to be nice to you."

He drew her hand to his mouth and kissed it. "You're always nice."

She snorted. "Rick, roll onto your back."

"Huh?"

She pushed his shoulder, and he toppled without protest. She straddled his hips, taking the opportunity to knead his impressive pecs through his dark chest hair. His small nipples tightened, his sex beginning to stir. Cass dragged her hold down his sides. When she reached his hipbones, she fanned her thumbs over them.

"Oh," he said, finally getting it. "Cass, you don't have to do that."

She bent to drop a kiss to his sternum. His manhood jerked in reaction, briefly touching her belly. "Wouldn't you like me to?"

"Sure, but I don't—" He gasped as she licked his left nipple. "I don't want you to think you owe me."

"Strictly speaking, I don't."

"What?"

Her thumbs rasped through the hair above his scrotum, tugging the skin that held his testicles. His cock had lifted to forty-five degrees and was swiftly heading toward ninety. His *what* sounded like thinking was difficult.

"Strictly speaking, I don't owe you. You haven't performed this particular act on me."

"Well, I'd be happy to. Believe me."

She had to laugh at him. "Rick, shut up and enjoy."

She grasped his shaft firmly at its root and pulled up.

"Uh," he said. "Cass—"

She switched hands and repeated. Watching his eyes cross was pretty fun. "Be quiet. I like the thought of stealing a march on you."

He sucked in air as she switched hands again. "You think a simple wolf like me understands fancy metaphors?"

"I think you understand way more than you let on."

This time when she gripped his root, she used her second hand to circle the top of his scrotum. She pulled both holds in opposite directions, careful not to hurt him but with sufficient firmness to insure he felt the stretch. She was counting on her bookworm tendencies paying off again, since she'd learned the technique from a manual Bridie had raved about. Happily, Rick reacted as if she'd employed it successfully.

Just to be sure, she did it again.

"Cass—" His hips thrust upward, his thigh muscles shifting as he squirmed. "Maybe I should—"

"What does a girl have to do to shut you up?"

His eyes met hers, his irises glowing green with lust. His shaft was fully rigid, its big head flushing ever darker as she repeated her two-way stroke. A bead of pre-come squeezed from the slit. Cass pushed the slippery drop across him. Werewolves were especially sensitive to touch. Rick bit his lip with teeth that weren't completely human anymore.

"That's better," she purred. "Now let's see if I can keep you from arguing."

She crawled farther back and bowed over his obelisk. It shuddered very nicely when she licked up its underridge. His erection stood very straight, like an illustration of an ideal hard-on.

"So pretty," she murmured with her lips against its skin. "So thick and hard and ready to be pleasured."

She took the knob of him in her mouth, rubbing the flat of her tongue gently across the slit. Rick moaned and bent one leg up beside her. She liked that. His warm inner thigh felt like it was hugging her, like it was safe to do what she wanted even if she wasn't a pro at this. She sank farther down him, loving the heat and smoothness of his organ. He tasted wild and alive. His cock bucked with excitement as she sucked it. She steadied him with her hand.

She felt his fingertips press behind her ear, settling there light but tense.

She drew her mouth off him. "Do you want to guide me?"

He was up on one elbow, raptly watching her suck him. He shook his head.

"I might not guess what you like."

He smiled slow and male and sexy. "I like everything you do."

"That's not possible."

The smile turned into a grin. "Maybe it's your faerie luck."

He was full of it, but she liked the compliment anyway. "My faerie luck is telling me something else you might enjoy."

She pushed his cock onto his flat stomach, amazed by how far it reached. Had she really had all that inside her? The idea aroused her, but she wanted to concentrate on him. Holding the head trapped against his belly, she moved so that her shadow didn't block the firelight. A flushed area the size of a quarter, located near his base, revealed the spot she sought. The color made it look hotter than the rest of him. She rubbed the pad of her thumb experimentally over it. The gland was firmer than the surrounding flesh.

Rick jerked and sucked in air.

"Too much pressure?"

Once more, he shook his head.

She smiled and continued her light rubbing. "I know a bit about wolves. I felt this get bigger when you came."

He blushed, which she found endearing. His voice came out as a growl. "I think *you* know more than you let on."

She hoped what she knew was useful. She lowered her head, sealed her lips around the area in question, and worked her tongue over it. Her actions had more of an effect than she expected.

"Oh God," Rick moaned, his hips struggling to stay still. "God, that feels really good."

With praise like that, how could she stop?

To keep herself and him steady, she wrapped one arm around the thigh he'd bent up. Even with her weight to brace him, he heaved up and down. His gasps and groans assured her the torture was successful. The muscles of his straight leg began to twitch.

"Cass," he finally pleaded. "I can't take anymore. Please suck me off."

She dragged her tongue up his thudding underside and teased the other hot spot beneath the head.

"Christ," he hissed, wriggling like a fish.

She let his erection lift into her mouth. His moan as she pushed her wet ringed lips along him was wonderful. She decided she was done with teasing. She wanted to drive him straight to his pleasure now. He must have felt that; must have trusted her to pay off. Rather than grip her head, he wrapped his left hand around his erection's base—probably to prevent himself from thrusting down her throat. As soon as he had the safeguard in place, he gave in to temptation and pushed his cock at her.

She suspected he'd wanted to fuck her mouth for a while.

She let him, his eagerness more exciting than she could describe. Overcome, he flung out the hand in the gauntlet, fisting it on top of the bedroll.

Cass's only job then was to make what he did feel better.

He cried out at her cooperation, pumping in quick short motions over her busy lips and tongue. She sucked him, licked him, treated him to the subtle scrape of teeth. That made him grunt with pleasure. His hefty thigh muscles tensed, his breath huffing in uneven pants. His fingers tightened on the stretch of shaft he held. She thought he might be considering pulling out when he came. Not inclined to allow that, she cupped his balls and squeezed lightly.

His spine arched a second before he choked out a raw cry and went over.

He'd ejaculated so much the first time, this time's volume couldn't overwhelm her. She liked his climax surprisingly much—not just the way his cock jerked inside her mouth but also the taste of him. This was a different intimacy from intercourse. This was spying on his most private responses.

She rested her cheek against him when he was done.

"Cass," he said, extricating his hand from between them to stroke her head.

She grinned at the gratitude in his tone. "I know. I did that pretty good."

His stomach moved with a laugh. She crawled up him and laid her head on his shoulder. His arm came around her as if it belonged there. Sighing, he tucked her hair behind her ear. "Now I owe you."

"Nuh-uh," she said, enjoying her chance to rub his chest. "No debts. No strings. People should do what they want in bed because they feel inspired to."

"That's your philosophy?"

"It is tonight. If I took you for a slacker, I might develop a different one."

He chuckled, the sound a pleasant vibration beneath her palm. He was quiet then—thinking, she suspected, and not drifting off to sleep.

"Cass?" he said like he wasn't sure he ought to.

"Mm?"

"If this is too personal a question, you don't have to answer. I'm wondering, though. Why doesn't a stunning woman like you, who obviously enjoys sex, have more experience?"

Cass lifted her head and looked at him.

"I'm not saying you seemed inexperienced," he backpedaled. "You mentioned that you were the first time."

Cass let out a resigned sigh.

"You don't have to tell me. I can just assume the men you met Outside were idiots."

"They weren't idiots. I mean, some of them were of course, but there's probably the same ratio of keepers to discards that there are here. I . . . had a bad experience."

The arm he'd wrapped around her back tightened. "Some male hurt you?"

"No." She considered how to explain what happened. "Outside . . . my magic wasn't as much of an issue as it is here. I still had faerie mojo, but it was damped. I met a guy through work. I was in real estate in Manhattan, and he was buying an apartment."

"Okay." Rick shifted under her as if settling in to hear the tale.

"We hit it off. Damian was more outgoing than me, but we had interests in common. He was funny and smart and reasonably good looking."

"Reasonably."

"Okay, he was gorgeous. Especially in a suit and tie."

Rick snorted but didn't seem put out. "So this gorgeous guy and you had a thing."

"We had enough of a thing that three months later we were engaged. We had rings and a date and I was shopping for wedding gowns."

"And then?"

"And then I had a long lunch with his big sister from out of town."

Rick moved back so he could look at her. "You didn't like his sister?"

"Shelley was awesome," she admitted. "All the qualities I loved in Damian, she had in spades. If I'd fallen for her instead of him, this story might have ended differently."

"But you didn't fall for her."

"No." Cass patted Rick's chest, gathering herself to tell the rest. "Shelley loved her brother but hadn't seen him in a while. He was the family's black sheep. He'd stolen a chunk of money from her and her best friend, who he'd been dating *and* cheating on. Apparently, he was kind of a cokehead—"

She hesitated, but Rick nodded that he knew the Outsider term.

"Anyway, the family called him on his transgressions, and he took off in a huff for New York. He'd pulled his act together somewhat when I met him, but not enough to apologize or pay back what he'd stolen. According to Shelley, he blamed *them* for the estrangement."

"And you didn't know that side of him."

"I didn't have a clue. To me, Damian was Prince Charming: kind, responsible, considerate to me and everyone we met. I never saw him use drugs or even drink too much—which was what his sister spent the better part of two hours complimenting me on. She couldn't believe how much I'd changed him. She claimed I was a miracle worker wrapped in a saint. The more credit she gave me for his transformation, the more my stomach sank."

"You'd glamoured him," Rick deduced.

"I'd glamoured him. Without realizing I'd done it, I'd turned him into what I wanted him to be. He didn't love me. He loved the charge he got from my faerie half. He'd traded his old addictions for a dependence on faerie dust." She shook her head. "At first, I didn't want to believe it. Maybe Damian *did* love me. Maybe I'd just nudged him. As soon as I figured out how to do it safely, I de-glamoured him. That wasn't pretty. Within a day, he reverted to being the childish prick his sister had described."

"What did you do?"

"I broke off the engagement, but— I don't know if it was right, but I couldn't leave him the way he was. I re-glamoured him a little. So he wouldn't go back to the drugs. And I tried to give him more self-confidence: the real stuff, not the obnoxiousness he used to compensate for insecurity. I think it worked. I hope it did. I didn't see him after that."

Cass touched the Saint Michael medal that hung around Rick's neck. "I'm *really* glad you have this, that it's spelled to protect you from glamour. I *never* want to go through that again."

Her voice was choked, which seemed to startle him.

"You don't have to," he assured her.

She was embarrassed that she'd been so impassioned. If she didn't watch what she said, he'd think she assumed *he'd* fallen in love with her.

If he was thinking this, he didn't say. He pulled her against him and rubbed her arm gently. The warmth of the re-stoked fire radiated against her back.

"Rick," she said. "Could I ask a favor?"

"Anything."

Anything didn't really mean anything, but she continued. "Could you say a prayer for my father? That he comes out of this all right?"

"Me?"

She'd surprised him again. "You said effective prayer was your specialty in the squad. Faeries aren't big churchgoers."

"Sure," he said. "I . . . I'll say one in my head."

She knew he would. Feeling better and unable to resist, she wriggled closer and shut her eyes.

~

Rick lay awake after Cass dropped off. What an odd duck she was sometimes: asking *him* to pray when she had so much juice she'd glamoured a human while she was still Outside. That was disconcerting when he thought about it —maybe as disconcerting as the idea that she'd almost married an Outsider. He wouldn't have guessed a half faerie could change a whole personality. He couldn't recall her glamouring anyone in high school. Oh, kids had been dazzled by her beauty, but that wasn't the same thing. Cass must be good at being careful.

Her dismay over causing her fiancé to fall in fake love probably explained why she kept people at arm's length.

He rubbed his Saint Michael medal, relieved when the subtle tingle assured him the spell was there. Of course, as uncomfortable as his feelings for Cass were, he should have known they were real. Glamoured people didn't fear they were being stupid when they fell for their glamourers.

CHAPTER EIGHT

CASS had no real reason to wake up grumpy, but she did. Rick was gone from the bed. She hoped they weren't having another awkward morning after. She hadn't enjoyed the first. When she looked toward the cave mouth, where the curtain of vines hung down, she saw it was raining. She realized the pattering drops weren't the noise that had roused her. That honor belonged to Poly playing bat and rattle with Rick's stupid tin of rocks.

"Leave that alone," she snapped.

The cat froze, gaping at Cass with big gold eyes. She must have decided she didn't like Cass's expression. A second later, she streaked off like an ogre was after her. She disappeared into the shadows at the back of the cave, where two small tunnels led who knew where.

Great, Cass thought. Now she owed the cat an apology.

She didn't feel better when she sat up. Her nipples pebbled in the damp cold.

"Not a morning person?" Rick suggested. He was coming in from outside. He wore an unfamiliar flannel shirt with his jeans. Though his hair and shoulders were dewed with rain, he was relatively alert looking. He gave her nakedness a glance and smiled.

"I guess not," she said, doubly embarrassed now.

Rick gestured with the small saucepan he carried. "I've got water to boil for coffee. All I found to steal was instant."

"That's fine. I mean, thank you. Instant is great."

He laughed, setting the pan on the metal shelving he'd rigged above the fire. "Instant is *not* great, but it does have caffeine."

She started to ask if he'd stolen creamer but shut her mouth. She *wasn't* a princess. She'd choke it down black if she had to.

"Sugar and non-dairy stuff is in your backpack," he said.

"Oh thank God," she exclaimed.

He seemed to find her amusing. "I've got this covered. Why don't you get dressed and do . . . whatever."

He'd pilfered a fresh flannel shirt for her too. Much more practical than her silk blouse, it must have belonged to a boy. Even spelled, the fit across her breasts was tight. She did "whatever" as quickly as she could in the mud and drizzle. She admitted the little lake was pretty in the mist—just disgustingly drippy.

Rick had a steaming mug ready for her when she returned. He'd put the fake cream and sugar in already. Poly sat at his feet. She threw a haughty look at Cass, as if to say: *This one is my friend now.*

Ignoring the ticked off feline, Cass propped her butt on the boulder next to Rick's. It didn't occur to her that he was suspiciously quiet until the coffee was inside her.

"So," he said, turning his cup between mismatched hands. "As pleasant as last night was, I'm sure you've realized we can't hole up here forever. For one thing, once we eat all the food, I'll have to go out and hunt Bambi. For another, if it turns out we don't have the real dragon eggs, we need a plan for finding them."

Anger flashed through her too suddenly to hide the reaction.

"I know," he said, his gloved hand lifting to calm her. "I'm only asking you to entertain the possibility that my gut isn't wrong. We need to know for sure one way or another."

"We do know," she said hotly.

When Rick put his hand on her shoulder, she struggled not to shrug it off.

"You're powerful, Cass," he said much too soothingly. Maybe your dad isn't the only one who can make you forget things. Maybe you glamoured yourself."

"I was seven!" She set her empty mug down and crossed her arms.

"You were seven and good at hiding things. I've heard stories of purebloods erasing whole lifetimes of their own memories."

"Purebloods," she objected. "I'm only half."

"You've got more juice than you knew. You're the daughter of a dragon keeper. Maybe you were a half faerie prodigy."

"They're rocks!"

"Why are you so insistent?" he asked softly.

She swallowed a rude retort—but only so she wouldn't seem more in the wrong than him. She wasn't wrong, and she wasn't lying. She'd have known if she was.

Rick got to his feet and looked down at her. She knew she was glaring but couldn't stop. "I'm going to take a walk to patrol the area," he said. "You meditate or whatever you do to pull in more mojo. Make an honest attempt to crack through any camouflage you might have put on those things."

Telling her to be honest was a low blow. "I don't lie."

"Then promise to really try, and I'll believe you."

She clenched her jaw in refusal. He released a weary sigh. "Fine." He turned and strode toward the cave entrance. "Do what you want. I'll be back in an hour or so."

Immediately, she felt terrible. Naturally, she and Damian never fought. Her glamoured ex thought she'd hung the moon. Rick probably thought she'd kicked it. In that moment, she wanted to.

"Stupid waste of time," she muttered to herself.

Almost to herself, at least. Given Rick's sharp hearing, he likely heard every word.

The cave seemed empty and boring without him, nothing but a big hollow of rocks and dirt. Because she had to prove he was wrong, she dragged the bedrolls to the side of the fire where he'd set the cookie tin. From there she could see the entrance and the two tunnels in the back wall. Neither mice nor bears could sneak up on her.

Other creepy crawlies she didn't know about.

"Camping blows," she said.

This time she knew Rick was too far away to hear. Unimpressed, Poly settled in to grooming her back leg. Cass heaved a last irritated huff before arranging herself in the classic Buddha meditating pose.

Drawing up more energy was no problem. The lake and its surroundings were stuffed with it. Cass's aura started expanding before she'd regulated her breathing much. Her mind was another matter. It resisted quieting. Her thoughts circled back to Damian and the story she'd told Rick. When she met Damian, she'd wanted so badly to be in love. Her mother had already met the man who'd become her second husband. She was happy and didn't need Cass so much. Looking back, Cass didn't know why she hadn't returned to the Pocket then. She could have spent more time with her grandmother. That would have been logical.

"Crap," she burst out as recognition hit. "That fucking bastard glamoured me to stay away."

It was the only explanation that made sense. Cass had always been closer to her grandmother. If her human mother only had so much time on earth, Patricia Maycee had even less. By compelling Cass to choose the former, her dad had robbed his daughter of sharing her favorite person in the world's last years.

"Damn it," she said, tears springing to her eyes at the aching loss.

Cass guessed the cat had forgiven her. At her exclamation, Poly hopped into Cass's lap and climbed her chest with both paws.

"That was wrong of him," Cass said, rubbing her cheek against the cat's. "Dad shouldn't have made that choice for me."

Sadly, she couldn't work up a good fury. Wherever her dad was, he might be in grave danger. No matter what he'd done, she wanted him to be all right.

"Loving people is complicated," she informed Poly.

Poly *mrrp*'d and offered her an ear to scratch.

Cass indulged the cat for a minute before closing her eyes again. She hadn't promised Rick she'd try this, but she was going to. Her breathing settled, her heart rate gradually slowing. Something that was at least a relative of peace began seeping into her.

I see through illusion, she told herself. *I call up the power of Nature, and the veil falls away.*

Energy tingled more strongly on her skin. Her fingertips were numbing, the top of her skull increasingly floaty. She barely noticed Poly clambering over her crossed ankles.

I see through illusion . . .

I call up the power of the earth . . .

A sudden clatter and an alarmed *miaooww* snapped her eyes open. Unable to resist the allure of the forbidden cookie tin, Poly had overturned it. The rocks inside had tumbled into Rick's campfire.

No! Cass thought.

She was on her knees in a flash, reaching between the burning logs to rescue them. The power she'd pulled up protected her somewhat, but the flames still singed.

"Ow," she complained as she grabbed the things. Since they were too hot to hold, she dropped them onto the bedroll.

She looked at them. They didn't appear harmed, but they remained unadorned chunks of stone. She shook her fingers and hissed. Her skin was reddened and stinging. To jumpstart the healing process, she got up and pressed her palms to the cold wet wall near the opening. As the burning faded, her brain began to work again.

Okay, she thought. Why had she pulled a bunch of rocks from a red-hot fire if she honestly believed that's all they were?

Returning to the bedroll, she narrowed her eyes at the homely trio of objects.

"I *don't* believe you're just rocks," she said experimentally. It must have been true. Her head didn't suffer the slightest twinge.

She pointed at them. "You're dragon eggs," she accused.

For a second nothing happened. Then the air around them shimmered like heat waves. The rocks were rounding and changing color and suddenly they were *there*—three golf-ball sized silvery dragon eggs.

"Oh my God." Stunned, Cass picked them up, cradling the now cool spheres against her flannel shirt. The eggs were as she remembered from that long-ago night with her father: heavy and smooth and solid as metal.

Rick was right.

They had the treasure the faeries were hunting.

~

Rick stood on the bank of the misty lake, hands laced behind his head with his elbows out. He couldn't decide about going back to the cave. He'd patrolled the area and found no danger, but it hadn't been quite an hour. Would Cass have cooled off by now? Would she have done as he asked? If she hadn't, what should his next move be? More than once, he'd overheard Maria telling her husband Johnny not to "handle" her. According to Rick's big sister, women had zero tolerance for that.

The problem was, sometimes the handling worked. Also, from what he could tell, Maria had no problem turning the technique back on Johnny.

He dropped his arms and frowned at the water's intersecting raindrop patterns. This was why he sucked at the girlfriend thing. He didn't want to handle Cass. He wanted them to be on the same side.

Well, you can't always be, he thought. *And if the situation is this important, you might have to stand your ground and let her be mad at you.*

He was pretty sure he was right—really sure, if he were honest. If Cass had been a suspect and not a woman he'd fallen for, he'd have had no trouble playing hardball with her.

The sound of moccasins running toward him turned him around. He'd known the person approaching him was Cass, but the state she was in inspired a grin. Seeming to have forgotten they were at odds, she was as excited as his five-year-old nephew Ethan when he mastered a new trick on the monkey bars.

"You were right!" she exclaimed. "I did it! Okay, the cat did it, but you were right!"

She grabbed his arms to bounce up and down. Rick steadied her under the elbows. "I was right?"

"About the . . . you know whats," she said in a lower voice. She took his hand and tugged. "Hurry. I don't want to leave them alone with the cat too long."

Liking the way she touched him, he let her pull him after her.

Despite having expected something along these lines, when he saw the eggs, he had to gape for a few seconds. She'd made a little nest in the cookie tin from ripped up pieces of her silk shirt.

Rick scratched the back of his head. "They're small."

"They're exactly the size they're supposed to be," she huffed. She held the tin against her stomach as if ready to defend it.

Fighting a smile, Rick gently picked up one of the silvery spheres. The surface was slightly textured but still smooth. "They're heavy."

"Yes. And apparently hard to break. Poly knocked them in the fire."

"Do you suppose that's how they hatch?"

"I don't *think* so," she said. "I mean, if it were that simple, couldn't anyone do it?"

"Nate's contact at the U was vague. He said when conditions were right, they would." Rick picked up the other eggs, balancing the three together in his palm. He should have been nervous, but he felt oddly soothed holding them. "I know I expected this, but I can hardly believe I'm touching them. If we figure out how, we could bring an extinct species back to life."

"I know," Cass said. "I'm in awe myself."

Their gazes met, drawn close over what he held. Cass gnawed her luscious lower lip. "I'm sorry I was stubborn."

He smiled at her. He didn't need an apology. "Did you remember disguising the eggs?"

"No. But I don't remember my dad erasing my memories either. I guess some things are destined to stay blank." She shivered at the idea.

"It's weird," he suggested.

"Very." She stroked the eggs, both their hands cupping them. When she looked up, her dreamy blue eyes were big. "Do you think we should hatch them?"

"You *are* a dragon keeper's daughter. The presence of that bloodline is probably one of the conditions the professor referred to. If we go on the assumption that nothing in Resurrection happens by accident, it stands to reason we're meant to give it a shot."

Cass's mouth pulled uncertainly on one side. "You don't think it's arrogant of me to want to try?"

Her self-doubt was easier to deal with than his own. "Cass," he said. "The last thing I'd call you is arrogant."

She liked that. A flattered pink rose into her cheeks. "Okay. I'm going to make a list."

She bounced off to do it. Love and amusement and a strange sort of helplessness tangled in his chest. He wasn't crushing on her or dazzled or even falling anymore. Rick loved Cass Maycee just like a grown person.

~

The list Cass scratched in the cave floor dirt wasn't long.

Food. Shelter. Protection. Warmth.

After some thought, she added *Magic* with her stick. Dragons were made up of a lot of magic. They might need a good supply to grow big and strong. She snorted at the goofy way she was thinking. Next thing you knew she'd be knitting baby dragon booties.

Rick set the eggs back in their tin by the fire. He came over to read what she'd jotted down. Gesturing for her to hand him the stick, he added *Gorgeous Keeper.*

"Cute," she said.

He scratched with the stick again. When he let her see, she read: *Cute Keeper-Protector with Big Sharp Teeth.*

"Haha," she said, though she really was laughing.

120

Rick hugged her and kissed her temple. "We have everything on your list. Those dragons should be hatching any minute now."

"Not food," she said. "Unless you think dragons eat hash too."

"Well, there's food around. Deer, rabbits, squirrels—these woods are great hunting grounds."

"Do you suppose they can sense that?"

"I have no idea," he admitted.

"Maybe we should kill something."

He lifted one eyebrow.

"Okay, maybe *you* should." She knew she didn't sound very certain. She didn't feel it either. "Wouldn't you like to eat something meaty that didn't come from a can?"

"Yes," he said without hesitation, which made her smile. "All right. I'll catch a couple rabbits and establish my provider cred. If you don't want to see bloody bits, stay away while I'm dressing them."

~

Rick had hunted in human form before. Because whether he'd catch something wasn't in doubt, he took his time, selecting two healthy full-grown rabbits to chase down. The gauntlet didn't get in his way, so he supposed he was getting used to it. He brought his prizes to the lake for the messy business of skinning, gutting, and otherwise preparing them for cooking. As he did, he marked a patch of wild onions and some edible herbs and greens. Cass might want to impress incubating dragons, but he saw no reason why he shouldn't impress *her* while he was at it.

In spite of warning her away, he'd hoped she'd come out and keep him company. This she didn't do until he was nearly finished. Since he was crouched down and wrist-deep in rabbit innards, he only turned his head to greet her.

She looked cautiously over his shoulder, visibly trying not to make an *ew* face. Rick controlled his amusement. "Everything okay with the eggs?"

"Yes." She seemed distracted. Interestingly, her hands were behind her back. "I rigged a thingie to keep Poly from batting them into the fire again. And I collected a bit more wood."

"That was good thinking." He waited for her to get to her hidden point.

"Um," she said. "I hope it's okay. I caught a fish." She brought it out dripping from behind her back. It was a shiny, still alive lake trout—not huge but big enough to eat. "Tada. I thought the cat would like it. I felt a little bad, because I lured it to me with a spell, and then I wasn't sure if I should kill it right away or if it would be fresher if I waited. Can you kill fish by bashing them on the head with rocks?"

She looked proud of herself and embarrassed at the same time.

"You could kill them that way. A good sharp knife is quicker. Would you like me to do it?"

"Please," she said in relief. "And, um . . ."

"Yes," he said, his grin breaking out as she trailed off. "I'll clean it and cook it too."

"I'm sorry. I'm just not Camping Girl."

"Lucky for you, you hooked up with me."

"Yes." She let out a laugh. "My faerie luck outdid itself on that."

Her saying that gave him such a warm feeling he had to look away. His next words were slightly gruff. "I stuck a skillet in the duffle. I could use it for carrying the meat when I'm done."

She brought it to him. She watched him work on her fish for a minute, laid her hand briefly on his shoulder, and then left him alone again. This time he didn't mind. She was waiting for him back there, thinking about him probably.

He couldn't have felt more primally satisfied if he'd been a real cave man.

~

When Rick returned to the cave, Poly was hunkered in front of the cookie tin, staring at the eggs intently. Rick thought the smell of raw meat would interest her, but her only reaction was the tip of her tail twitching.

"Why is she looking at them like that?" he asked Cass.

Cass had been digging through the duffel and sat back on her heels. "I'm using a magic cage to keep her from swatting them. I set it to channel extra energy from the area around the lake, in case the eggs need more amperage to develop. I think Poly can see the flow."

Rick couldn't see it, though he squinted. He turned back to her. "Searching for something in particular?" he asked, gesturing to the bag.

She grinned. "Just seeing what else you stole."

"Liberated," he corrected, moving to set up his camp kitchen. "For the possible Public Good." He noticed she'd found the meat skewers and had placed them on a nearby rock.

"Do you need help?" She didn't sound convinced she could provide it.

"I saved the pelts. For lining the cookie tin. I scraped them mostly clean, but if it's not too icky, maybe you could finish them magically."

"I think I can do that," she said.

She didn't take long. Once she'd tucked the furry pieces around the eggs, she came back to watch him cook. He liked the way she pulled her legs up and wrapped them in her arms. "You've done this before."

"Once or twice. Nate is the pack's gourmet, but when we're roughing it, I'm in charge of meals."

"You don't eat as your wolves?"

"We do, but sometimes we stay out longer than the full moon and have a pack retreat. We haven't done that in a while. Not since Adam and Nate got married."

"You should." Cass's eyes twinkled with mischief. "I bet the wives could entertain themselves while you're gone."

"Maybe that's why Adam hasn't suggested it."

She put her cheek on her knees and smiled. It was nice that she got his sense of humor—nice that he got hers, come to that.

"You and your friends like your girls nights out, I bet."

"You aren't wrong. I missed the three of them while I was Outside. Seeing them once a year after Christmas really wasn't enough."

He didn't say he'd missed her too, but he was thinking it so hard he turned tongue-tied. They didn't speak much until he served. Cass had a good appetite —not as good as a shifter, but good enough to let him know she enjoyed his food.

"Mm," she said, licking rabbit juice from her thumb with unconscious seductiveness. "Messy but delicious."

"I hope you saved room."

She'd relaxed against a boulder, but at his comment she sat straighter. "What for?" Her eyes widened. "Is this a sex thing?"

God, she was cute. "It's not a sex thing, though when you see what you *didn't* find in that duffel, you may want to kiss me."

"What didn't I find?"

He unzipped one of the bag's side pockets and brought it out. Cass's face lighting up was as gratifying a reaction as he'd ever inspired.

"Chocolate," she breathed. "Good chocolate. Oh my God, I love you!" She blushed bright red the second the words were out. "I mean—"

He smiled and handed her the small Celestial Milk bar. "I know what you meant."

She unwrapped the foil and inhaled. "I haven't had one of these in *ages*. I used to dream about these Outside. Do you want some?"

He shook his head, preferring to watch her. She broke off one square, popped it in her mouth, and sighed orgasmically as she sucked.

"Maybe this is a sex thing," he laughed.

"Mm," she hummed, then rewrapped the candy and tucked it safely into the bag again. Her expression was serious. "Okay. I do."

"You do?" He seemed to have missed part of this conversation.

She braced her shoulders. "I do love you."

He blinked, his mind gone completely blank.

"It's true," she said. "See? No headache. Sorry if you didn't want to hear that."

"Cass. I . . ." From being completely blank, his mind went to way too full. "There isn't anything I'd rather hear. Not anything in the world."

"Really?"

"Really."

"Oh." She sagged back in shock. "Wow."

"I should say, in case it wasn't clear, that I love you too."

"I inferred that. You know what *inferred* means, right? Simple wolf that you are?"

For the first time in his life, he growled and laughed simultaneously.

~

Cass hadn't planned to admit she loved him. She'd simply felt like a coward for pretending she didn't when the words came out accidentally. Even after Rick said he loved her too, she was a bit aghast at herself.

"I'm rushing this," she blurted. "I shouldn't—"

Rick got up, pulled her to her feet by the hands, and kissed her.

That calmed her nervousness like a charm. She wrapped her arms around him and sank in, loving how he squeezed her close to his hard body.

His *extra* hard body, to go by the long thick ridge forming between his thighs. The kiss intensified deliciously. For quite a while, neither of them let go.

His eyes glowed when he pulled back. With a quickening of her pulse, she realized the time for simply kissing was over. He quickly undid his flannel shirt, then started in on hers. The motions of his fingers turned her pussy nuclear.

"How can I want you so much?" she marveled.

Rick stilled, his touch paused in the act of sliding over her bare breasts. When he resumed breathing, the sound came faster. "Must be my wolf luck."

He deserved to get lucky for sure. She unzipped her tailored trousers, wriggling them past her hips until they fell. Her hands now free, she attacked his button and zipper. His boxer briefs were bulging, the heat and heft of his erection enticing her. She reached into the cotton to stroke his thudding shaft. As always, his skin was amazingly silky. Out of respect for the genius that made him yummy, she had to explore him.

Pushing and pulling her hold up and down him was truly a pleasure.

His eyes drifted shut, a moan breaking in his throat. "Cass . . ."

"Take me," she said, wanting to be crystal clear. "Don't make me wait for this."

She pulled her hand free and set her palms on his broad shoulders. Wolf light flared in his irises. Without arguing, he hiked her to his waist, her legs needing no urging to part around his hips. The denim he wore rubbed her thighs pleasantly.

"Right," he said, hands tightening on her bottom.

She wasn't prepared for him to use shifter speed on her. The cave blurred a second before her back hit a smooth stone wall. Her pulse and her arousal jumped. Rick didn't give her time to recover. He kissed her, and adjusted her, and then his big rounded crest forged into her.

She groaned her enjoyment down his throat. No one felt like he did inside her—that smooth, that big, that incredibly alive. He was too much and just right at the same time. He pressed deeper, stretching her, answering her groan with an equally hungry one.

His head dropped once he was in all the way, the huffing of his breath hot on her shoulder. She stroked his thick hair and wriggled on his spear, not wanting him to stop.

"Okay," he said in response. He braced his knees on the rock. "Okay."

Then he went to town on her.

The rapid pounding of his hips was perfect, the depth and force of each inward drive. Every grunt excited her, every sensation. The heady scent of his arousal rose higher as he got sweaty. Cass couldn't contain her reactions. She slid her hands under the back of his flannel shirt and let herself soar with him.

The pair of them came in under two minutes.

His gland swelled for the finish. She felt the snugness within her gate as her muscles tightened helplessly on him. He growled and ejaculated, his enjoyment at the increase in pressure obvious.

"Good," he said, in case she had any doubt. "God, I love fucking you standing up."

His thrusts had slowed but not stopped. Pleasure continued to twist his face as he went in and out. She'd heard male wolves were like this. A single climax didn't always finish them. The idea that he'd want more was welcome. She squirmed on him as her interest recovered.

"Do it again," she gasped.

He'd dropped his head to nuzzle and suck her neck. He lifted it at her words. His lids were heavy but not with sleepiness. "Right now?"

She smiled. "If you'd be so kind."

She guessed he would. His cock hadn't softened much, but now it jerked fuller inside of her. His weight held her securely against the rock, the strength of her legs sufficient to keep the motions of their hips where they both wanted them. Rick took her hands, moving them from his back and up the rock to either side of her head. He held her there, not allowing her arms to move. When he wove their fingers together—some metal and some flesh— she knew he was imagining what truly trapping her would be like.

"I'm yours," she promised. "I can't get away from you."

His expression flickered, going darker and wilder. "Cass—"

His tone held more wonder than worry.

"Do it," she encouraged.

He didn't go as fast as the first time, but he went hard. He was very focused, as if each jolting plunge mattered. He brought her twice, after which he disengaged and carried her to the soft bedroll. She'd have conked out after all those orgasms, but he kissed his way down her body and wound her up again. Lord, he was good at giving head—teasing and nibbling and sucking her tirelessly. His tongue was agile, his fingers hard as iron as they controlled her wild thrashing.

Her wildness was due to his refusal to let her come, which she wanted quite a lot by then. He wouldn't enter her either, not until she begged him.

He might have held off longer, but her moaning *please* pushed buttons he had trouble resisting.

"You're a bad, bad man," she panted, smacking his sweating chest when he finally rose over her on his arms and pushed in.

"No, I'm not." He paused to groan at how wonderful the long penetration felt. He was *really* hard now, having held off his pleasure while he teased her. A lovely swivel and grind of his pelvis lodged his throbbing cock all the way in her. "You're annoyed because I'm just that good."

She laughed, unable to deny it.

"God," he breathed, seeing her break up. "I feel like I've loved you forever."

She touched his face, sudden tears stinging in her eyes. He smiled.

"Now we'll be sweet," he predicted.

They were sweet, riding each other slow and easy to their last sighing peaks. They didn't rush, though they both wanted to. Watching Rick unravel delighted Cass as much as her own climax.

When it was over, he rolled off her and collapsed.

They both were a complete mess, and Rick was down for the count. Laughing softly, Cass went to warm some water for washing up.

Loving people wasn't just complicated; it was sticky.

CHAPTER NINE

SOMETHING warm and furry stretched across Cass's feet.

"That better be the cat," Rick said. He sounded remarkably awake. Probably it was a wolf thing—being able to snap alert at a pin drop.

"Pretty sure it is," she mumbled. They were in the sleeping bag for once, though Rick had only pulled the covering to their waists. "What time is it?"

"Midnight. You sure she can breathe down there?"

Cass sat up and shoved her hair from her face. "Cats like to be where it's warm."

"I never had one. I guess she's getting used to me."

"Poly is a girl. How could she resist a big, strong—"

Rick touched her arm. "Sh," he said, his head cocking to the side. "I hear something."

Cass shushed, but all she heard was the fire crackling.

Rick rose onto his elbow, his dark brows climbing his forehead. "I think the eggs are hatching."

Cass's heart gave a big hard thump. This couldn't be happening so soon. "I'm not ready."

Rick grinned. "Better get ready," he advised.

Cass scrambled out of the bedroll, grabbing her shirt and panties to pull on. Rick seemed to find this amusing.

"I don't think they'll know if you're naked."

"What?"

"I don't think—"

"Oh hush," she said before he could repeat himself. "Get out of bed and help."

She heard him complying but didn't watch. When he joined her on the boulder that overlooked the improvised nest, he'd dragged on his jeans. His broad chest was bare, his smooth tanned side warming hers. Like her, he leaned forward across his knees. Cass still couldn't hear anything, but one of the silvery spheres seemed to have the tiniest fracture.

"I don't think we're supposed to help," Rick said. "On nature shows, turtles and whatever get themselves out of their own eggs."

"Right," she said, "but we should keep an eye on them."

He rubbed her back through the flannel shirt. She glanced at him, and his head tilted. "I hear heartbeats. All three of them are stirring."

Barely able to breathe, Cass pressed her hands together before her mouth. A hole appeared in the egg that had the crack. Unable to help herself, she clutched Rick's bicep. Despite his calm exterior, he seemed excited too.

"I see it," he said softly.

Letting the dragons peck their own way into the world might have been the hardest thing she had ever done. If Rick hadn't been there to assure her they all were fine, she probably would have tried to assist them. Luckily, he held her hand very tightly for the next quarter hour. The first little dragon had wriggled out by then, only to collapse in an instant nap. The second got its head and one leg out and was working on widening the opening. The third took so long Cass was gnawing her thumbnail by the time its small nose poked out.

Her heart rate settled when she saw it too was all right.

Finally all three dragons had clawed and clambered shakily from their shells. Cass took her first non-panicked survey of them.

"Hm," she said. "They look really . . ."

"Homely?" Rick suggested, like he was about to laugh.

"I was going to say *puny*, but that too."

"Those eggs *were* small," he admitted, as if he too found their newly hatched charges underwhelming. "I'm sure they'll get bigger."

Like their eggs, the little dragons were gray with a silvery sheen. Their semi-transparent skin, through which their tiny veins and organs could be observed, looked like it might get scaly. At the moment, it resembled a plucked chicken's. Though the hatchlings had four legs and tails like lizards, they definitely weren't as mobile as babies of that species. Their wings, which they intermittently spread and twitched, were clearly not much use except to prevent them from falling over. Cass was glad for the cookie tin's rabbit fur lining. Seemingly unable to travel in a straight line, the newborns wove and bobbled like they'd had too much dragon wine.

"They look drunk," Rick observed.

Cass started to laugh but stopped. "Oh my God, maybe they are. Maybe I channeled too much magic to them through the protective cage."

"No," Rick soothed. "They probably don't have a sense of balance yet. If you'd been stuck in an egg for a couple centuries, you might be dizzy too. Also, I don't think their eyes are open."

This could explain why one of the dragons bumped into its brother or sister and toppled on its side. Opening its little nose or muzzle or whatever the hell it was, it let out a birdlike wail.

Suddenly, its unimpressive looks didn't matter. Cass had to comfort it.

"Aw," she said, gathering it gently into her palm. Its itty-bitty claws tried to grab onto her skin as it continued to tremble and cry out. "You're okay, little man. Or girl. Whichever." The hatchling was warm, its baby heart beating rapidly. Its apparently prehensile tail chose one of her fingers to wind around. As it settled on her palm, its cries quieted. Cass felt a surge of affection, but also helplessness. "I was hoping they'd be able to protect themselves after they hatched. Breathe fire or fly away or *something*. These little guys couldn't make a flame as big as a match head."

"On the plus side, as small as they are, they won't be too hard to hide."

"Pocket dragons," she said, unable to resist the pun.

Rick chuckled. The rich low sound startled the other two. They started cheeping and wailing like the first one.

"Oh boy." Giving in to the same urge as her, Rick reached into the nest to pick them up. The magic cage wasn't designed to keep him out, and he held them gently against his chest. "We better figure out what they eat. All this noise would give them away."

Cass stroked the head of her dragon with one finger. Its miniature dorsal spikes were rubbery. "We could try milk, I guess. Or blood in an eyedropper. I didn't see teeth when they were wailing."

The dragon's head bobbed at her stroking, a croon swelling from its throat. Cass crooned back, and it opened dual eyelids.

A shock snapped through her. She sensed . . . awareness. A little thinker lived behind those silver eyes—a baby, yes, but something more than a baby animal.

She looked at the pair Rick held. With perfect timing, they opened their eyes too. Immediately, all three dragons stopped crying. They were staring at her, their bright scarlet mouths agape. They couldn't really be shocked, but they looked it.

"Holy cow," she murmured.

"What?" Rick said.

Cass felt slightly embarrassed. "Um," she said. "I think I just imprinted them."

~

Rick was no authority on dragon beauty, but the hatchlings' appearance seemed improved by the next morning. Their former chicken skin was now opaque and scaled, and had developed a sheen of color over its silvery base. One of the dragons looked like it might turn green, another gold, and the final one deep red. They were toddling more confidently around their nest, even peeking over its edge curiously.

Poly, naturally, found their jerky movements enthralling.

"I'm keeping that enchanted cage up," Cass warned the cat, stooping to give her a pet and scratch. "We'll introduce you when they're bigger."

"They don't seem afraid of her," Rick observed. The red dragon, the smallest of the three, stretched its foreleg over the edge of the cookie tin toward the cat.

"That doesn't mean they shouldn't be. Or vice versa, for all we know."

Rick handed her the snaptop plastic container into which he'd poured a few ounces of rabbit blood.

"I hope they drink this," she said. "I don't know what we'll rig for a bottle if they need to be fed that way."

The greenish dragon—the biggest, relatively speaking—sniffed at the meal she'd set down.

"Try it," Cass encouraged. Goose bumps rippled across Rick's shoulders. The dragon looked up at her as if it understood.

After a hesitation, it dipped its muzzle into the blood . . . and nearly fell in as it overbalanced. Shocked by this, it scrambled back sneezing. The gold dragon ran to it worriedly. The greenish dragon licked its red snout. This was a better surprise. Rick smiled as it creeled out the reptilian version of *yummy!* Within seconds, all the hatchlings were bellied over the plastic container slurping their breakfast.

"They're pigs!" Cass exclaimed, a hint of pride in her tone.

They were. They ate the entire serving he'd supplied, nosed at the bowl for more, then curled up together to sleep off their gorging. They didn't seem to mind that blood had spattered them all over.

"Well, that went all right," he said, belated realizing he and Cass were holding hands. "Maybe later we'll try some mashed liver."

"Yum," Cass said, pulling a face at him.

When she laid her head on his shoulder, the feeling that washed through him was singular. He couldn't recall ever being so right with the world and his place in it.

~

The mashed liver wasn't a go until the third day. By then, the dragons were as long as Rick's hands—not including their whippy tails. Because they'd grown so much, Cass had been obliged to remove their protective cage. Free to roam, they darted around the cave too quickly for the cat to catch. They did seem to like playing chase with her, deliberately pausing close enough to be pounced on until Poly was lured in.

The intelligence this suggested impressed Rick. If they could outsmart the cat already, how smart were they going to get?

True to legend, they were hoarders. He caught the green dragon trying to steal a can opener heavier than it was, probably because it was shiny. The gold one amassed a stash of pyrite pebbles gathered from the lakeshore. The red one learned to breathe fire first, nearly setting Poly's tail on fire in the process.

"No," Cass scolded, immediately grabbing it by the scruff. "No burning up the cat."

The little dragon let out a piteous wail, dangling dolefully from Cass's hold. Cass petted it soothingly. "Yes, I love you," she assured it. "And, yes, you're clever to learn that trick, but not everyone is fireproof like you."

As if it were ashamed, the red dragon hid its head underneath its tail.

Cass kissed it and set it down, where it ran off happily enough to rejoin its siblings.

"They're smart," Rick said, coming to her side.

"Very," she agreed.

The dragons had found an old rabbit bone and were now playing three-way tug of war with it. Cass watched them indulgently. She glowed, he decided, her fae beauty taking on a Madonna-esque loveliness. She seemed to have forgotten her initial nervousness about taking care of them. Ironically, her lack of concern spurred Rick's anxiety. Their exotic brood was growing fast, but maybe not fast enough. Whoever was searching for them wouldn't have given up.

"They need names," Cass said.

Rick had a feeling they needed way more than that.

~

Cass was basking. She'd wrapped herself in one of the bedrolls and rested her back on a tree trunk. Though the lakeside was nippy, sunbeams angled through the tall forest. The dragons—her dragons—were safe and accounted for. Rick had identified the boys from the girls. Verdi, as she was calling the green dragon, was perched on her right shoulder. He was the most vocal of her babies and the most operatic in temperament. Belly plump from breakfast, his warm weight leaned against her ear while his tail curled behind her neck for balance. Auric and Scarlet, the second boy and the only girl, watched their reflections shimmer from the lake's edge. Poly the cat had claimed Cass's lap, not about to give up her seniority.

Cass stroked her furry head and shoulders, so relaxed she almost could have been asleep.

She was semi-aware that her unwavering tranquility wasn't normal. No one felt this wonderful morning, noon, and night—even with a lover as amazing as Rick around. For once in her life, she experienced no particular need to do anything.

She simply wanted to be with her babies.

As if they sensed her thinking about them, Scarlet and Auric glanced back at her. Their red mouths gaped in what she'd come to think of as dragon smiles. Their silvery eyes seemed to radiate love to her. When they looked at her like that, she could believe she was the best mother in the world, and they were the best babies. Her dragons might squabble and play-fight, but they were never mean—not even to Poly, who they teased quite a lot. The cat forgave them their antics, letting them snuggle up with her for naps. This wasn't simply because the baby dragons were extra warm. The older cat seemed to have appointed herself their honorary aunt.

"Nice Poly," Cass murmured, scratching her purring throat beneath her collar.

A high-pitched cheep drew her attention to Auric. The gold dragon had been acting interested in swimming, but each time he dipped his toes in the water, its autumn chill discouraged him.

"All right," Cass surrendered, setting Poly on the ground so she could rise. Verdi clung to her hair with both paws. He jumped down to join his siblings as soon as she knelt on the pebbly bank. All three dragons looked up at her, a rapt and curious audience.

Cass noticed with a start that they were half as big as the cat now. She'd lost track of time. Was it really just a week since they'd been born?

"If I do this," she said, "you have to promise you stinky little piggies will take a bath."

Verdi chittered at her and bobbed his head. Whatever he was expressing sounded affirmative.

Cass smiled, closed her eyes, and held her palms a few inches above the surface of the water. Wherever in the world she went, the earth possessed the same resonance. If she matched her frequency to it, energy would naturally flow to her. When she lived Outside, this had been a challenge. Here, magic was easier to channel than anywhere in the Pocket. Cass drew it up from the planet's seemingly endless reservoir. Letting her fae half stretch without worrying was nice. Her body hummed as the current entered her. Before the sensation could grow uncomfortable, she sent it into the lake with a whispered direction.

She knew she'd been successful when she saw wisps of steam rising.

Auric dipped his paw in the water and made a happy sound. Never shy, Scarlet slipped into the heated wavelets before he could. Auric had to flounder after her in a hurry or lose his bragging rights. Not to be outdone, Verdi jumped so far from the bank that he went under. He rose spluttering and flapping his wings, a game his siblings couldn't resist joining. As they churned up the surface, Scarlet snorted tiny fireballs at everyone, a trick her brothers couldn't yet imitate. This led to squawking, splashing chases to the edge of the area Cass had warmed up.

"Looks fun," Rick said, coming up behind her. "I didn't know you could do that."

She rose, their arms winding naturally around each other's waists. "I only heated this corner. I couldn't do the whole lake."

Rick kissed her hair and hugged her, watching the dragons play. He'd been patrolling the woods. His relaxed body language told her he'd found nothing alarming. He let out a contented sigh. "Too bad we can't stay here forever."

His words surprised her. Cass felt this way herself but didn't expect him to. She studied his handsome face, which was unusually calm. He'd said he loved her, but wasn't he itching to get back to work? She couldn't remember the last time he'd fidgeted over his cell phone, wondering if he should call his pack. A week was a long time to be out of touch. Didn't he long to put some plan into action to defeat their enemies?

She guessed he didn't. When he felt her gaze on him, he simply looked at her and smiled.

Verdi burst out of the water, half hopping and half flying with his wings flapping crazily. None of the dragons had flown for real, but she could tell they were getting close. Verdi landed at Rick's feet and chattered a loud greeting.

Rick squatted in front of him and laughed.

"Hey, Verdi," he said, giving his scaly head a knuckle rub. "I saw how good you were at swimming."

The others crowded up to get their share of Rick's attention. Knowing what they liked, he stroked Auric's wings and scritched Scarlet along the sides of her sharp dorsal spikes. As always, Cass loved seeing the affection between them. Different from always was the cold shadow that brushed her awareness.

Her dragons were small and cute, but they also were magical—maybe more magical than she or Rick had any defense against. Were they responsible for her surge of maternal bliss? And if they were, had the effect spread to Rick? Could they be drawing him and her closer to increase their chances of survival? Babies did do better with two parents.

Understanding the possibility but not liking it, she shivered and bit her thumb.

~

"Where are my clean socks?" Rick asked. "I spread them on the boulder by the fire to dry."

Cass was washing up after dinner, part magically and part with warmed up water from the lake. Rick had caught and roasted a young wild pig—an event that stirred considerable excitement. Evidently, dragons were mad for pork. They'd eaten so much their smooth scaly stomachs bulged. Only Auric wasn't sleeping off the feast. Rick held him in the crook of his right forearm, where the dragon was engaged in one of his favorite activities: trying to pull apart Rick's shiny electrum gauntlet. Thus far he hadn't succeeded, but he didn't tire of gnawing it with his new teeth or poking at its plates with his claws.

Socks, Cass reminded herself, distracted from Rick's question by her affection for their gold dragon boy.

"I don't know," she said, looking around the firelit cave that had become their home. "Maybe—"

Her gaze fell on Verdi. He'd been sleeping in a pile on the bedroll with Scarlet and Poly but lifted his head when he heard voices. He froze in a manner that struck her as suspicious. Mouth agape, he widened his eyes as if trying to look innocent.

"Ah," she said. "Try the stash the dragons stuck in their tunnel. They might have decided they wanted something that smelled like you."

Rick shifted Auric to his shoulder and went to check. "I washed those socks," he objected. "They're not smelly."

The dragons' tunnel was one of two craggy slits in the cave's back wall, about five feet off the ground. The hole was large enough for the youngsters but not people. Muttering about little hoarders, Rick reached in his left arm.

"The flashlight!" he exclaimed, coming out with it. He stuck in his arm again. "And here's the rest of the chocolate bar. They didn't eat it. They must have been attracted to the foil. Don't ask me how they unzipped the duffel." Auric chittered in protest as Rick removed more items. "Rocks. Rabbit bones. Hm. This might have been a bird they or Poly caught. And my socks!"

He brought them out triumphantly. Something fell out as he slapped off the fresh dirt they'd collected. The object was small and shiny. It clinked to the floor and bounced.

"That's Poly's collar bell." Cass strode over to retrieve it. Auric tried to get there first, but Rick had a good hold on him.

"You little thieves," she said, closing her hand around it. Auric flapped his wings and cheeped grumpily.

"They *could* keep the bell," Rick said, petting him. "We're not squeamish like your gran. If Poly wants to hunt birds out here, they don't necessarily need to hear her coming."

Cass supposed this was true. She began to uncurl her fingers but realized her palm was tingling.

She looked at Auric. His now eight-inch tail lashed back and forth on Rick's chest, expressing his disapproval over them confiscating the brood's treasures. She read no other motivation behind his silver eyes, but—really— how would she know what he was thinking?

"What?" Rick asked, seeing something in her face.

"There's a spell on this bell," she said.

He laughed at her rhyme, then stopped. Cass wasn't trying to be funny. "They couldn't have put it there, could they?"

By *they*, he meant the dragons. "I don't think so. I think . . ." She paused to consider. "I think the spell has been there all along. I think I'm noticing it now because I'm more open to magic here."

"Is it another spy spell?" Rick was whispering. "Like the fake Maycee portrait those goblins were trying to hang?"

Him mentioning this event reminded her how long it had been since either of them had thought about anything unpleasant. They'd been here . . . could it be ten days now? They'd been living in a dream, a dream spun—deliberately or not—by three young magical creatures.

Not sure how to handle the knowledge, Cass cupped both hands around the enchanted bell. Ignoring the sick feeling in her stomach, she blew out her breath and told herself to relax. As she did, an image came to her of her father's final visit to the penthouse, of him petting Poly into a feline stupor. Hadn't she noticed the bell soon after? Her father had led a dangerous pursuit away from them, risking his immortal life to do so. Would he truly leave himself with no means of checking in on the parties he was trying to protect?

"I think it is a surveillance device," she said. "But I don't think it was planted by the bad faeries."

"Your dad," Rick deduced, still speaking in an undertone.

Cass's hand tightened on the bell. "I can track him. If he laid this enchantment, I can discover where he is."

"Should we?" Rick asked. Auric was rubbing his head against Rick's temple, as if the dragon were seeking comfort or trying to give it. Cass wished she could see the gesture as one of mere sweetness.

"Rick," she said. "You're a cop. Don't you think it's strange you're considering *not* following this lead?"

"Uh." He looked at Auric, and at the bell, and then his gaze returned to her. "Oh boy," he murmured, and she knew he'd understood.

He didn't object when she coaxed Auric off his shoulder to perch on her forearm. Stashing the bell in her pocket, she carried him to the bedroll where the others were sleeping. She tucked him among them.

"Stay," she said, petting his golden head until his eyes closed. She repeated the order to Verdi. A few more strokes closed his eyes as well.

Thankfully, their big meal would keep them in dreamland. She and Rick slipped silently from the cave. Side by side at the lake, they contemplated the rippling water. After a minute, they turned to each other.

Rick's expression held more worry than she'd seen in it recently. "The dragons wouldn't have whammied us on purpose. They're too young to be that devious. Plus—" He struggled to sort through his perceptions. "They're too affectionate. I'm not magic, and I can feel how fond of us they are."

However fond they were, the end result was the same. Cass and Rick had acted in ways that weren't natural to them. Rick had taken Cass's hands as he spoke. Now Cass caressed his gauntlet, carefully avoiding the knuckle spikes.

As she rubbed the smooth gleaming surface, a new thought occurred to her. "You've been hunting with this, haven't you?"

"Well, it's there," Rick said. "Handy. And it's not like I can remove it."

She nodded, not accusing him of anything.

"It . . . doesn't get messy," he confided, like maybe he'd been wanting to for some time. "It seems to drink in any blood I get on it."

He looked at her. The furrow in his brow seemed to say, *That's weird, isn't it?*

"This situation has changed us," she said.

"Not for the worse. I'm glad we're together."

Did he mean that, or was he enchanted to think so? Cass wasn't ready to face that particular answer. She dropped his hand and pulled the bell out of her pocket.

"I'm going to give this a shot," she said.

Her shot went nowhere. Though she pulled up power and concentrated, Poly's jingling collar bell didn't give up its secrets. "Shoot. This thing has to connect both ways. If my dad can spy on us, I should be able to track the spell back to him."

"Your dad's no bantam weight when it comes to magic."

This was true, but it didn't help her crack the puzzle.

"Try this," he said, holding out his gauntlet. "Put your hand in mine. Your dad is a dragon keeper. This is a protector's glove. Maybe its magic will help you fine tune your search."

Willing to try, Cass rested the hand with the bell in his. She breathed in and out, keeping the motion smooth. The night was quiet but not completely so. Branches whispered against each other. Water lapped the pebbled shore. Rick's heart beat slow and even, his hand as firm as the ground under her. Suddenly, her brain seemed to swoop, and Rick steadied her elbow. She saw a funnel made of stars against a field of black.

She knew she had to go where it led.

In her imagination, she slid in like the shape was oiled. Before she could start thinking this would be easy, her progress stopped. The tunnel she'd glided into narrowed to a point.

I need to shrink myself, she thought. *There's a way through this.*

She moved again as the idea took hold. Faster she went, and faster, an Olympic bobsledder rounding hairpin curves. She gripped her focus tighter, concerned she'd overshoot her mark. *Father,* she thought.

A real world scene appeared.

She was aware of being in two places: with Rick by the lake and outside a dark outbuilding. She knew she needed to get inside it, not stand out in the weeds.

Rick is watching over my body, she thought. *It's safe to go in there.*

Her astral melted through the planks of the wooden wall.

Her father was inside. A hurricane lantern sat on bare ground to one side of the barnlike space. Its paradoxically homey light lit a horrific scene. A long electrum-plated chain—presumably spelled to prevent its links from snapping —bound her father's unconscious body to the side of a green tractor. Blood had spattered the vehicle's paint and its giant rear wheels. More blood coated the silvery chain, soaking in darkened patches into the dirt. Such a quantity had spilled that the area beneath the old farm machine was mud. No one body could contain so much . . . unless that body belonged to a pureblood fae.

Faeries like Cass's father could replace almost any amount of loss almost any amount of times.

Dad, she thought. *What have they done to you?*

He moaned, lifting his head unsteadily. His face was a mess—swollen, broken, the soft blue eyes they shared peering from puffy slits. Other parts of his body were broken too. His arm bones were crooked, and both his shins. From what she could see, his flesh had been cut and ripped, dark blood seeping sluggishly from many wounds. Cass took a little comfort in the fact that his blood wasn't glittering. He wasn't dying, though maybe he wanted to.

She didn't think he knew she was there. Though his head came up, he didn't look in her direction.

A second figure stepped into view.

The tall male was as beautiful as a fairy tale. His thick hip-length braid was silver, his snowy skin sparkling like he'd been rolled in tiny stars. Cass's breath caught in her throat at the fluidity of his stride. Though he was slender, his shoulders stretched straight and broad. His arms were bare beneath a laced chamois vest, and his legs looked strong in brown leather pants. A long sheathed sword hung diagonally across his shoulder blades.

Given the guns his arms were sporting, she imagined he'd be able to swing it fine.

"Good." The stranger's voice was a breeze over sun-warmed sand. "You're ready to play again."

"Why don't you . . . get it over with?" her father rasped.

"When I have what I need." The stranger held an iron instrument in both graceful hands, a fireplace poker with a sharp hooked tip. Cass knew the properties of iron allowed it to harm faeries but not kill them.

"I already told you," her father said. "I'd rather die than give those eggs to you."

Those eggs, Cass thought. Didn't her father know they'd been hatched?

"They're ours by right," said his torturer. "We have the boldness and the vision. We spent centuries laboring in secret to get this close to them."

"Ceallach—" Her father coughed and spit blood. "The only thing that's yours and that cunt's by right is a one-way trip through a hell portal."

In a blur of motion, Ceallach lashed out with his hooked bar. A fresh slash exploded across her father's face. Bone cracked beneath the impact. Her father gasped but didn't cry out. When he looked up again, his skull was distorted on one side.

A human being couldn't have survived that much damage.

Ceallach stepped to him and grabbed his broken jaw. "Where is the Sevryn clutch?"

The fae's electric blue eyes glowed. He was right in her father's face, the light from his gaze probing her father's. Cass realized he was pulling up extra power to read his thoughts. Considering the pain her father must have been in, it should have been easy.

"*Where are the eggs?*" Ceallach demanded.

"Safe from you and your demon-fucking whore," her father spat.

The insult angered the other faerie, but he wrestled his temper under control and stepped back. Cass didn't understand. Her father knew where the dragons were. He'd been watching her through the bell. Ceallach should have been able to steal that knowledge from him.

That he hadn't was obvious. He stared at her father from the distance he'd stepped to, looking weary but determined. The arm that held the poker at the ready dropped.

"I shall return," he said. "As you know, I'm willing to spend as long as it takes breaking you."

He left the weatherworn outbuilding. Cass wanted to follow and see what he did, but she was tethered to her father. In Ceallach's absence, he'd begun breathing unevenly. Cass wondered if his injuries bothered him more than he'd let on in front of his enemy. Then a broken sound tore from him.

She knew what was happening.

Her father was crying.

She sensed more than pain fueled the reaction. He believed he was alone; believed no one in this world or any other was coming to save him. He thought he'd chosen a path that rendered rescue impossible.

When Cass realized that, her heart broke for him.

~

Rick didn't want to get in the way of Cass's magic, but just standing there while tears trickled down her cheeks was tough. When she jerked from the vision and lost her balance, he caught her arms.

"I'm okay." She dragged her palms down her face. "I found him."

"Your father?"

"Yes." Her voice was rough with emotion. She composed herself with a ragged breath. "I recognized the location. He's at the old Maycee farm."

Rick's brows drew together. This seemed a less than ideal choice.

"I know," she said. "He's not a Maycee, but it's still a place a thorough person would think to search. Maybe he wanted to be found. Or maybe he thought the extra magic from the Pocket's birth would give him an edge."

"I gather it didn't."

She scrubbed her face again. "One of the faeries had him chained up. My father called him Ceallach. From what they said, it sounds like the two faeries who want the dragons are working together. I didn't see his partner. I couldn't tell if she was there."

Since Cass was shaking, Rick led her to a fallen tree trunk and sat her down. Her eyes were haunted by what she'd seen. She took his wrists and looked up at him.

"He hasn't given us up. Ceallach is torturing him, trying to break down his resistance to having his thoughts read. Purebloods can heal a lot of damage. My dad has got to be in incredible pain, but somehow he's maintained his barriers. Ceallach believes my dad has hidden the eggs but won't say where."

Rick squeezed her fingers.

"We have to save him," she pleaded. "He thinks no one is coming."

Rick's chest tightened, but he had to stand firm. "You need to leave this to me. It's my job to help people who are in trouble. This is too dangerous for you."

"It's too dangerous for you! Rick, this Ceallach is a pureblood. And probably royal. He's very strong. You can't go after him on your own. Even with your pack . . . Anyway, we can't wait for them. Ceallach warned my father he would return. My dad was in bad, bad shape. I don't know how much longer he can hold on."

"Your dad is trying to protect you and the dragons. If we go rushing to the very people who are trying to steal them, you undo his sacrifice."

"Just us," Cass said earnestly. "We'll leave the babies behind. I'll order them to hide."

"Cass—"

"They'll behave. I'll make them." Her face tightened with resolve. Despite the strange expression, he didn't guess what was coming when she stood; didn't sense any threat from her at all. She ran both hands around the thin chain he wore . . . and yanked off his saint medal. "I've got your protection now," she said, holding it in one fist. "I can glamour you. So help me, if you try to force me to stay behind, I'll compel you."

She shocked him to his core. He looked into her hot blue eyes and saw she meant every word.

"I *can't* let you go alone," she said softly.

He didn't want to give in to her. She meant too much to him to risk. They shouldn't go at all. It wasn't strategic. One man's death . . . Except the one man was her father. Truth be told, Rick couldn't abandon him either. At least if he went alone, he could pray to come up with some sort of Hail Mary pass.

Unfortunately, him going alone wasn't in the cards. Because Cass was determined to be involved, she needed more protection than just him.

"We call the pack," he said. "No arguments."

Simply saying the words was a relief. He hadn't realized how much he minded going his own way without them. He could see Cass didn't want to agree. He gave her his hardest face, the face he'd have led men with if he'd been alpha.

"We can't wait for them," she insisted. "We have to get to the farm right away."

"We won't wait. I'll tell them to come here. They can look after the dragons."

This much of a delay she'd accept. He didn't add that once his fellow squad members were so close, they'd damn well find a way to help him and her. They'd try to protect the dragons; they'd just care about people more.

Cass threw her arms around him. "Thank you," she said into his neck.

Rick hugged her back grimly. He didn't feel guilty over misleading her. Whether he'd just signed his pack's death warrants did trouble him a bit.

Cass didn't waste any time hurrying back to the cave. Rick followed almost as quickly, though he wasn't eager to get this rescue mission on the road. As of that moment, he didn't foresee it ending well.

His Elfnet phone was where he'd left it, in a snapped pocket of the duffel. His thumb hovered above the button that turned it on. Cass was waking the dragons, clasping each scaly head to look into their eyes while murmuring stern instructions. As the hatchlings listened, their mouths gaped like surprised toddlers.

Rick hoped this meant her strategy would work. He didn't want the dragons hurt. Preferring privacy for his call, he stepped to the vine-draped cave mouth.

Naturally, he had Adam on speed dial. His pack leader answered halfway into the second ring.

"Hey, boss," Rick said somewhat sheepishly.

"Jesus," Adam responded. "Where the hell are you? Are you all right?"

"I'm fine," Rick said. "But I don't have much time. Is this line secure?"

"Of course it is. What the hell is going on?"

"We have the dragons. We need you and the pack to protect them. Don't involve anyone you don't trust a hundred and ten percent. The second faerie is still unaccounted for."

"And the first?"

"Is torturing Cass's father for information. We're hoping to rescue him."

"Rick," Adam said, his frustration and worry clear. "Wait for us. Wherever you are, don't do anything crazy by yourself."

"We can't wait. Track my cell phone. If you lose the signal, we're in a spot only Nate and Evina know about."

"Only Nate and Evina . . . Rick—"

Rick disconnected the call and turned off the ringer. Adam would be furious. Unable to help that, he joined Cass at the rear of the cave. She'd tucked the dragons into the tunnel they used for their treasure hoard. Verdi's green head was sticking out, craning around to watch her shove supplies into the second opening in the wall. For whatever dragonish reason, her babies weren't as fond of this hidey-hole.

"I'm almost done," she said. "In case the wrong people come looking, I don't want the cave to seem like we camped in it."

"You moved fast." He was slightly stunned by how much she'd done.

She glanced at him over her shoulder. "Did you reach your alpha?"

"Yes. They'll be here as soon as they track my phone's signal." At the sound of his voice, Auric and Scarlet peeped out of the burrow too. "Don't chew on this," he requested, slipping the phone in with them. "My pack will find you a lot quicker if Nate doesn't have to remember exactly how to get here."

He petted Auric and scratched Scarlet beneath her chin. An inquiring *mew* informed him Poly was hiding in their hole too. He looked at Verdi last. The normally playful dragon seemed serious.

"You're the eldest," Rick said. "Look out for the others and be nice to my pack when they arrive. They'll smell like me, so you'll know it's them."

He doubted the dragons understood him as well as they did Cass, but they certainly understood something. Auric cheeped mournfully.

"Time to hide now," Cass said.

The dragons looked at her for a moment, then retreated into the hole until the last glimmer of their silver eyes winked out.

Cass turned away with her jaw clenched against crying.

"*Out*," she said, waving her right arm in the direction of the campfire.

The flames didn't just go out, the whole fire collapsed, the branches that fed it transformed into a random tumble the wind might have blown in. The sweep of her arm had also erased their footprints. If he hadn't known better, Rick would have sworn no one had been here.

His wolf came alert within him, gearing up for action.

"Okay," he said, his adrenaline spiking. "Let's you and me get this thing going."

~

They moved quickly through the dark woods—not as quickly as Cass wanted, but Rick reminded her they'd didn't want to arrive exhausted. So much anxiety coursed through her she had trouble reining herself in. If they didn't reach her father in time . . . if he goaded Ceallach into inflicting more damage than he could heal . . .

They took forty minutes to hit Route One. Being able to commandeer a car would have been useful, but the area was remote, and they saw none. At least, they were able to get their bearings. Twenty more minutes loping down the two-lane brought them to the rutted turnoff for the old family farm.

A ranch-style gate marked "PRIVATE" was the only sign the ruts led anywhere. A magical tripwire stretched across this barrier. If a person had the eyes to see it, the alarm was easy to avoid. Cass sensed no other warning spells. Obviously, Ceallach wasn't overly concerned about being found.

The forest that surrounded the property wasn't as wild or varied as Wolf Woods. It had been harvested once upon a time, for building materials or firewood. Rick pulled Cass down behind a big oak within sight of the two-story farmhouse and its handful of outbuildings. Her heart gave a sickening clench as she recognized the barn in which she'd seen her father.

"Okay," Rick said, sitting with his shoulder pressed close to hers and his back braced against the tree trunk. "Here's my gun. Pay attention while I show you how to shoot it."

"Rick—"

"No arguments. It's not much of a weapon against a pureblood anyway. The bullets are only electrum plated, so the best you can hope is to slow him down. If we had an Uzi with full electrum ammo, we'd stand a better chance, but we'll make do with what we've got."

"Maybe a head shot . . . " Cass suggested.

"I thought of that, but faeries move too fast. Plus, we'd have to hit his brain in just the right area, possibly more than once. I'm an okay shot, but I don't think even my aim is up to that."

"Okay," she said, trying to sound calm. "Then how do we take him out?"

Rick lifted his gauntlet and fisted it. The spikes glinted faintly where they stuck out from his knuckles. "This is pure electrum. And magical. And I'm pretty sure rival faeries are one of the threats it's meant to protect dragon keepers from. I already know it can rip off a goblin's head. We'll see if it does the same to fae."

Decapitation would kill a faerie—probably permanently, if it were done with spelled electrum. This, however, wasn't all there was to it.

"Rick, you'll have to get really close to do it. If he senses you coming, he'll spell you off or worse."

"That's why I need a distraction." He blew out a sigh. "Trust me, I hate this plan. I just don't have a better one."

"I'm the distraction," she realized.

"He'll be disinclined to kill you," Rick said. "If you overheard correctly, and your father's captor is working with the second faerie, she'll have told him you might have knowledge of the dragons' whereabouts. I suspect you could empty that clip into Ceallach, and he'd still want you alive for questioning."

Cass swallowed. She'd seen his method of questioning.

"You don't have to do this," Rick said, seeing her reaction. "If you feel too unsure, we'll both be safer if you wait here."

She looked at the gun he'd brought out to lay on his thigh. She didn't understand how it could seem big and deadly and completely insufficient at the same time.

"You trust me not to choke?" she asked.

"I do."

His gaze didn't flinch from hers. Cass wished she could say the same. She dropped her eyes with shame. She'd been wrong to threaten to glamour him. She saw now he'd have given her pleas a fair hearing. He trusted her—even after her betrayal. She dug his charmed Saint Michael medal from her pocket.

She held it out contritely. "I need to give this back to you."

Rick looked at it and at her. His expression was neither angry nor accusing.

"Ceallach might be able to compel you in spite of it," she warned, "but not as easily."

"Can you mend the broken latch?"

"Yes," she said as a blush rose into her face.

Rick bowed his head so she could place the chain back around his neck.

"I'm sorry," she whispered as she did.

He cupped her cheek, stroking her skin with the gauntlet's thumb. His lack of anger notwithstanding, he didn't say *it's all right* or *don't worry about it*. He demonstrated how the gun worked instead.

"This is cocked and locked," he said. "That means there's a round in the chamber and nine left in the clip. When you're ready to shoot, you disengage the safety, line up the sight with your target, and pull the trigger. You don't have to cock the gun again after that. One pull equals one bullet. Don't worry if you don't hit the faerie. A .45 rushing by will get most people's attention. The gun will buck, so it's best if you use both hands."

Cass repeated what he'd shown her.

"Good," he said, squeezing her shoulder. He turned toward the farm and narrowed his eyes. She sensed the wolf in him searching out heartbeats. "I read two people, one in that barn and one in the house. You?"

She nodded in agreement, not wanting to dwell on how thready the lifeforce in the barn was.

"Chances are, the faerie has another alarm spell set near your father. If you trip it, you should draw him out." He thought for a moment. "Can you cloak me like you did from the goblins, but make it work while you're not touching me? This will go better if he doesn't know I'm there."

She nodded for that too.

"Okay then, we'll keep this simple. I'll hide behind the door while you warn your father. You see Ceallach, you start shooting. You see me in the line of fire, please try to stop."

"Oh God." Cass pressed her hand to her mouth in horror.

In spite of everything, Rick laughed. "One shot probably wouldn't kill me. Hurt like hell, but not that."

"I'd rather not find out," she said.

He laughed at that too. Stupidly, the sound made her feel better.

As she spun the concealment cloak around him, she reminded herself she was stronger than when she tried to disappear Rick's brother in high school. As to that, she was stronger than when they'd fought the goblins. Their time at the cave had charged her up. She only wished Rick faced nothing worse than grounding if her charm went awry tonight.

"Can you tell where I am?" asked his disembodied voice.

"I cast the spell so I can still see your energy. It should hide you from other people, but I won't lose track of you."

"Good," he said. "Wish me luck."

"Wait." She caught his invisible arm. "Ceallach set another tripwire across the barn's entrance. It's shaped like an *X* and stretches from corner to corner. If you don't want to set it off right away, crawl through on your belly."

"Got it," he said.

The glimmer he'd become moved across the scruffy farmyard to the open door of the outbuilding.

Cass watched him for a moment before sprinting in a crouch toward its rear. She'd seen loose boards there she thought she could squeeze between. She stopped when she reached the spot and checked again for spells. None protected the building here. She wriggled in, biting back a curse as she scraped her side. Once she was through, she hurried around the dark hulk of the tractor.

Her father was still chained to it, still lit by the hurricane lamp. He wasn't conscious, but he was alive. Hoping it wasn't cruel to wake him, she carefully tipped up his fallen head. The contact revealed how low his reserves had sunk. His energy felt almost humanly ordinary between her palms. She saw the bash in his skull had healed but not much else—magical prioritizing, she supposed.

"Dad," she said, soft but firm.

Not surprisingly, he didn't respond.

She sensed Rick slipping into position beside the door, which was rolled back from the opening on an overhead track. When she glanced toward him, the concealment spell was functioning. Not sure how long it would hold, she knew she couldn't afford to spend a lot of time trying to rouse her father. On the other hand, she'd rather he wasn't completely vulnerable when the fireworks went off.

"Dad." She fed a bit of her energy into him, not daring to expend too much in case she needed it for fighting. "Dad, wake up."

His eyes rolled behind their swollen lids. He swallowed a small pained noise as one set of dark lashes succeeded in lifting.

"Daughter," he said, his gaze slowly focusing. "What are you doing here?"

"I'm getting you out of here. I brought a friend to help."

Her answer seemed to confuse him. His bruised and puffy face pulled downward in a frown. "I am very weakened. I cannot assist you in a fight."

"We're here to assist *you*. We're here because I love you."

"Cass," he said very gravely. "You shouldn't have come for me."

She wasn't going to let him make her cry. "We have a plan. Do what you can protect yourself."

Her father looked at her with his one good eye. Approval wasn't exactly beaming from it, but she saw his intelligence sharpen. "There is a spell on the tractor," he informed her. "If I try to break the axel to get more play in these chains, my captor is alerted."

"He's alone here?"

"He is enough," her father said.

Given her father's acerbic tone, this wasn't meant to lift her spirits. Well, too bad. They were going ahead with this anyway. She looked toward Rick's shadow form. She pointed to herself and then at the axel and mimed breaking it in her hands. She couldn't tell if he nodded, but his ears were sharp enough to have heard what her father said. She assumed he understood the gist.

Because her strength wasn't up to snapping tractor parts like twigs, she was glad all it took to trigger the alarm was a solid kick. A pulse of nearly visible energy burst out. The fist-sized ball zoomed out of the barn, presumably on its way to notify Ceallach.

Here we go, she thought, stepping back to her father's side.

She removed Rick's gun from where she'd tucked it in the small of her back. Thumbing off the safety, she lifted it with both arms to aim.

"Gods save us," her father groaned, but not like he thought they would.

Cass suspected she felt as dire as he sounded.

CHAPTER
TEN

CEALLACH took his sweet time appearing. Fighting to stay calm and ready, Rick listened hard for movements in the farmhouse. He thought he heard water running and boots descending stairs. Perhaps the fae had been resting up for having another go at Cass's dad. The back door creaked open on old hinges. The faerie's slow heartbeats came closer, though his feet made no noise striding through the grass. Maybe soundlessness out in nature was a faerie trait. Cass had moved almost silently through the woods.

Then again, maybe this fae was using his power to levitate.

Rick didn't get a chance to check. The sparkly pureblood appeared in the opening to the barn, visible from the side of Rick's vision. Rick froze and held his breath. He should have asked if Cass's spell muffled sounds.

"So, keeper," the faerie said, not looking around at him. "I assume by your struggles that you're ready to talk again."

A different sort of light ignited in the shadows near the tractor. Cass had begun firing.

Somewhat to Rick's surprise, she winged Ceallach's right shoulder. His arm was knocked back but not by much. No more troubled than if he'd been given a friendly punch, he put his hand to the injury. He looked at the blood on his palm, and Cass pulled the trigger a second time. This time, her shot went wide. Ceallach didn't bother to duck or streak forward and attack her. He seemed not to care that a giant long sword hung nice and handy behind his back.

Of course, if he didn't think he needed it, Rick wasn't about to suggest differently.

"How nice," the faerie said in a perfectly normal tone. "You've arranged a reunion with the family member I most wanted to meet."

Cass hit him twice in the chest. The faerie jerked slightly and took a step toward her. He was wearing trousers and a medieval-ish leather vest with no shirt. Two dark spots appeared on the leather above the sword, not the exit wounds Rick expected from a .45. A moment later, the center of the spots spit out the bloody slugs. Seeing them hit the ground, Cass's eyes got bigger, but she didn't lose her nerve. Steadying her stance, she shifter her aim higher —trying for a headshot, Rick assumed.

Ceallach opened his mouth, perhaps to stop her with an incantation. Judging that his attention was fully occupied, Rick rushed forward with all the speed he had. The fist with the gauntlet was drawn back beside his ear, his muscles coiled to release the instant he was close enough. He aimed the electrum spikes toward his target, where the faerie's vertebrae met his skull, so focused he felt as if he were seeing *through* Ceallach's sleek silver braid. He let out no battle cry, not wanting to give himself away. In truth, he barely let himself think one.

Two white glows flared to life on the back of Ceallach's head.

Rick had a second to wonder why they looked like eyes. Then something hit him, a punch of invisible force as solid as a wall. The force knocked his breath from him, flinging his body like a toy high into the air. He braced himself for a crash, but none came. He'd stopped moving abruptly. The magic held him dangling among the barn's rafters. In the process, it shredded Cass's concealing cloak. Not that the faerie knew this.

He hadn't bothered to turn around.

"Really," he said, no more than mildly irritated. "Did you think I'd let a *puppy* sneak up on me?"

Cass wasn't out of bullets, but she dropped her arms anyway. She didn't say a word, just stood trembling with the useless gun hanging by her thigh.

"That's better," Ceallach said.

"Leave her alone," said her chained-up father. "I'm the one who has what you want."

Ceallach tipped his head to the side to consider him. "That's the problem with torture," he observed. "I've put you in so much pain you no longer mind the discomfort of lying."

Cass's father clenched his jaw, his irises beginning to kindle with anger. Seeming amused, Ceallach moved toward him. He didn't look like he planned to hurt his captive, but Rick had already noticed he didn't telegraph his intentions.

"Hey," he called, deciding an interruption might be in order. "Let me down from here."

Ceallach dropped him as easily as thinking.

Rick's shifter reflexes allowed him to land on his fist and feet without breaking bones. His falling weight drove the gauntlet's spikes into the ground. Grunting, he yanked them out and straightened.

Apparently unconcerned with him, Ceallach pointed at Cass. "Breathe the wrong way, and I'll end them both."

Only when he was sure she'd behave did the faerie turn to Rick. Before Ceallach, Rick had never met a pureblood who didn't damp his looks in mixed company. Despite everything that had happened, Ceallach's gazillion watt glittery beauty sent a mind-blanking stutter into Rick's brain. Evidently, the anti-glamour charm on his medal wasn't up to nulling power like this.

Rick needed all his concentration to blink and recover. As his mental functioning returned, he realized Ceallach had taken possession of his hand. Turning it this way and that, he examined the gauntlet.

"I wondered where this went," he said. "You must have been the best replacement that female protector could summon on short notice. But I suppose that's to be expected in a dimension for idiots and mongrels."

Maybe Rick hadn't returned to normal yet. He snatched his hand back belatedly. "You killed her."

Ceallach shrugged as if to say, *what of it?*

He had a point, considering Rick was currently in no position to arrest him.

"There is one advantage to you being a lowly wolf," Ceallach mused. "I'll have no trouble glamouring you into serving us."

"Like hell," Rick denied.

Ceallach smiled creamily at him. His electric eyes were eerie in the dimness, his confidence unnerving. Rick was at least an inch taller and more substantial by many pounds. Nonetheless, the faerie suddenly seemed bigger in every way. Understanding they were being threatened, Rick's wolf trickled out a snarl.

"Pup," Ceallach said silkily, "you can't comprehend how easy compelling you would be. My queen would enjoy making a pet of you."

"Your queen would fuck a dog if she were bored enough," Cass's dad contributed.

Rick didn't think Roald le Beau was trying to insult him, only to ruffle his enemy's smooth feathers. In this, he succeeded. Ceallach's glowing blue eyes narrowed.

"Keeper," he growled as if he were a wolf himself. "You speak of one whose slippers you're not fit to lick."

"Maybe we should talk about this," Cass interrupted. "Work out a trade we can all live with."

Ceallach let a portion of his tension go and laughed. "By all means, halfling. Tell me what you propose to trade."

Cass didn't tell him. He was a foot away from her and overconfident. She whipped up the hand that held Rick's Smith & Wesson and shot him point-blank through the forehead.

That had an effect all right, all right. Ceallach toppled back, body stiff and eyes wide with shock. He lay like that on his sword—not a comfortable position, Rick expected.

"Fuck," Roald exclaimed, not seeming pleased by his daughter's bad-assness. "Cut off his head. Cut off his head *right now!*"

He was so desperate to do it he threw his broken body against the chains. Recovering from his shock at Cass's actions, Rick leaped to behead the downed man with his spiked gauntlet. He didn't get to the fae in time. Ceallach made a nasty growling noise and sat up. The grisly bullet wriggled from the hole in his brow and fell.

He spoke a guttural word that was not English.

Cass screamed and dropped the gun. Rick didn't understand what had happened until he saw the semiautomatic had gone red-hot. Cass's hand was blistered, the skin on it smoking. Roald whispered something soft, and the smoking stopped. Then Roald moaned. By healing Cass, he'd reopened a gash on his own temple.

"Dad!" Cass cried in alarm.

"Enough," Ceallach said, struggling to his feet. *He* had plenty of juice to heal himself. The bullet's entry wound was now nothing but a dent. With an ominous *zing*, he drew the blade that until then had been safely sheathed. "No more tricks. One of you tells me where the eggs are or I start removing body parts."

"There are no eggs," Cass declared truthfully.

"There are," Ceallach shouted, losing all patience. "Damn you, we will have them!"

Great, Rick thought. Now they had a crazy über-powerful fae to deal with.

Ceallach placed the tip of his sword over Roald's heart.

Rick was the first to hear the approach. The sound was soft, like pillowcases flapping on a clothesline. For a single heartbeat, elation rose. Then he realized this couldn't be a good development. Too little time had passed for his pack to have the brood in their protection.

Cass's babies had come alone.

Ceallach's head swiveled toward the door, listening. "Don't move," he ordered Cass, his blade continuing to press Roald's breast.

Two shapes swooped through the building's door, revealed by the hurricane lantern as one green and one red dragon. The dragons seemed bigger with their wings spread and their tails trailing. Maybe they were. They grew so fast it was possible.

Ceallach's expression transformed to dazzled awe. "Two," he breathed, turning to watch them circle between the rafters. "*Two* of them survived."

Rick tried to clamp his brain down tight. Whatever advantage there might be in Ceallach believing only two dragons lived, Rick wanted to cling to. He glanced at Roald, who seemed similarly amazed. Rick wanted to say *really?* He'd entrusted the clutch to his daughter but hadn't thought she'd hatch them successfully?

"Those eggs were ancient," Roald murmured in wonder.

Cass exchanged a glance with Rick and shrugged. Like him, she was impressed the dragons were flying but also worried that they were here. Perversely, Auric's absence annoyed Rick a tiny bit. Of the three, the gold dragon was Rick's bestie. Did Auric lag that far behind the others in motor skills?

Verdi and Scarlet landed—only a little awkwardly—on one of the barn's cross beams. Verdi lifted his wings and puffed out his crop in a victory squawk. No matter the danger he'd just flown into, Rick couldn't repress a smile for the dragon's pride. Scarlet cheeped and scrabbled closer to her brother. The dragons were breathing hard. The flight from the cave must have been an exertion.

Ceallach stepped away from Cass and her father to crane at them. The crushed-star glister of his skin brightened.

"Little darlings," he crooned. "Fly down to me, sweethearts. I'll take you to your new mother."

Cass stifled a surprised gasp. Either the faerie didn't hear it or didn't consider it important. For his part, Rick was as stumped as Cass. She'd imprinted these dragons. As far as he knew, that only happened once. If this was true, how could the brood get a new mother?

"Come," Ceallach coaxed. He tucked the sword underneath one arm, his fingers and his shining power beckoning. "I'll protect you, darlings. I'll bring you to the one queen who deserves you."

The dragons sidled unsurely on the beam. Cass's father let out a snort. "You . . . expect your whore . . . to 'mother' them? There isn't . . . one drop of keeper blood . . . in Joscela's veins."

Ceallach shot him a hooded look. "You'd be surprised what magic my queen has amassed since you fled with our treasure to this pocket of pestilence."

"They won't come to you," Cass predicted.

Ceallach simply smiled at her.

Rick didn't know why she'd challenged him until he noticed her edging closer to the fallen gun. His heart sank at least a foot. He gave her points for bravery but maybe not for sense. The dragons were here. Ceallach might want a spare swordsman for his queen, but he no longer had an incentive to keep Cass alive. If they failed to kill him again, Rick doubted the fae would bother reining in his temper.

He tried to catch Cass's eye to tell her *no*. Before he could, something tugged at his jeans' leg. Every hair on his scalp stood up. Fortunately, his wolf's instincts stopped him from turning to see what it was. The tug came again, right around the level of his knee.

Auric, he thought. The gold dragon must have crawled between the loose boards at the building's rear, using his siblings' showier entrance as cover. Not sure what Auric wanted but willing to find out, Rick shifted his position so that his back angled more fully away from Ceallach. The tugging was replaced by the pricks of Auric's claws as he swiftly climbed Rick's pants leg. When he reached Rick's waist, he butted him with his head. Sincerely hoping this was more than a game, Rick bent the arm with the gauntlet and stuck it behind him. Auric crawled onto it.

Scarlet chose that moment to flap down from the beam to land on Ceallach's shoulder.

Looking utterly enchanted and slightly smug, Ceallach petted her. "That's a girl," he praised. "You know who you belong with."

Auric wasn't gnawing at the gauntlet the way he usually did. Wrapping his tail around Rick's upper arm for balance, he'd crouched down to hum to it. The sound was so low it was barely more than a vibration. Low or not, it was powerful. Rick's arm bones began to resonate. The glove took up the vibration next, tingles touching the skin under it. Rick felt an almost silent click-click-click as the clever plates that encased his fingers peeled back one by one from their tips.

He tried to keep his face impassive, but Cass glanced over. He guessed she could see Auric from where she stood, because her eyebrows went up.

Verdi cawed, drawing attention to himself. Ceallach was trying to lure the green dragon down from his perch. The dragons' behavior reminded Rick of a pack coordinating to hunt prey. One wolf would dart in and distract their target while the others crept closer. Even as the thought arose, more plates unpeeled from his glove. The segments were folding together, forming an uneven sphere in his palm. Rick's hand felt oddly cold without the covering. His job apparently done, Auric scrambled down his leg to the ground where he hid behind Rick's ankles.

Okay, what was Rick supposed to do now? Obviously, the dragons expected a contribution. They'd consider him part of their pack too. He rolled the electrum ball in his hand. Should he throw it at Ceallach's head? It felt unfinished, but would it do some special magical damage?

Before he could decide, Verdi darted down from the beam to land on Ceallach's other shoulder. The faerie's sword was tucked beneath the same arm. Verdi stretched his neck to nibble the glinting hilt.

Ah, Rick thought, finally getting it. That's what the gauntlet was supposed to turn into. He wanted it to do that like he'd never wanted anything before. How could he protect Cass without it? How could he protect their dragons?

The overwhelming desire to defend them was a catalyst. The metal ball blazed within his hand. Rick didn't drop it. He knew by now its transformations wouldn't harm him.

Ceallach was too busy chuckling at Verdi's antics to see Rick's sword stretch full length. Scarlet shifted on the fae's other shoulder, her toothy mouth gaping by his ear. Cass must have guessed what was coming. She stooped to grab the fallen gun. That Ceallach noticed. He spun toward her.

Scarlet breathed a blistering fireball at him.

It didn't set him alight, but the faerie cried out and swatted her. At the same time, he tried to regain a fighting grip on his sword. Cass aimed but couldn't shoot with the dragons flapping and squawking so nearby.

They were in Rick's way too. Unable to swing at the faerie's head, he went low, sliding across the dirt on his knees to him. From there he thrust upward, impaling Ceallach through the belly and out his ribs. Blood gushed, but it wasn't a killing blow—possibly because Rick wasn't used to wielding a blade that big. Ceallach coughed and spat blood. Rick knew he needed to strike again, through his heart preferably, but discovered the sword was stuck. Though he pulled as hard as he could, he couldn't wrench it free.

The idea that the faerie's flesh was healing around it didn't make him happy.

With a bloody grin, Ceallach brought his own weapon up.

"Fuck," Rick cursed, tugging harder.

He was about to let go and roll out of reach when a gold shape zoomed by. Auric crashed into Ceallach's arm, knocking the sword away. Seizing his opening, Rick put all his strength into one massive heave.

He stumbled as the blade tore from Ceallach's body. Verdi saved him from falling by flying into his back. Ceallach hissed a spell that made Rick's feet go numb and stick to the ground. As if that weren't enough confusion, Rick heard his gun go off. Cass was standing behind the faerie, firing methodically into his torso. The faerie couldn't recover quickly enough between bullets to spin another spell. Even better, each shot knocked him nearer to where Rick was stuck. On the fifth shot, he was close enough. Rick swung his blade back and then forward.

He suspected he looked more like a baseball player than a swordsman. Even forgiving his bad form, he definitely needed more practice. The blade hacked halfway through Ceallach's neck and stopped.

Ceallach still didn't give up the ghost. His eyes flared like lasers in the low light. The air beside him did a weird unzipping thing. The opening didn't look like a portal, but it wasn't regular space either. Rick blinked, and Ceallach disappeared into the slit of Otherness he'd created.

"Damn it," he said, ears ringing from the abruptly ended fight.

The dragons didn't seem disappointed. They were flapping around and creeling like kids hopped up on sugar. Scarlet landed on Rick's tired shoulder and chittered excitedly.

"Okay," he conceded, petting her for her bravery. "You guys did really good."

Roald le Beau began to laugh raggedly. "As did you, wolf." He nodded at the ground in front of Rick.

"My feet!" Rick exclaimed, only then noticing they were encased in blocks of ice. No wonder he hadn't been able to move them. To his relief, the ice seemed to be melting.

"Not your feet," corrected Cass's father. "Look at the blood Ceallach spilled."

The edges of the dark splatters were sparkling, the glitter gradually eating away the blood—the same as happened to the protector in the subway.

"You severed enough of his spinal cord," Roald said. "Ceallach may have escaped, but it won't do him any good."

"I killed him," Rick said, hardly believing it. "*We* killed him."

He looked at Cass, who was rubbing her forehead with the back of the hand that held his now-empty gun. When her gaze met his, it was troubled.

"Right," Rick said. "If he was dying and bothered to spell himself away, where in hell was he going?"

~

Cass was shaking worse than after their fight with the goblins. She'd fired a gun and helped kill a man. Most trying to her nerves, she'd almost watched Rick die. Though she didn't want to think about it, she kept flashing back to Ceallach grinning and raising his sword to strike. In that moment, she'd known what she had to lose, that her life would continue minus a piece of her heart and soul. Having a crush on the teenager Rick had been couldn't compare to getting to know the man. He'd added so much to her happiness. She didn't want to learn how to go on without him.

Annoyingly, Rick took a minute to stomp off the ice and went back to his usual self. He was in cop mode now. He'd found a pair of bolt cutters to free her chained-up father from the old tractor. Because her dad couldn't stand, Rick got his arm around him.

"There's probably a land line in the farm house," he said. "We can call my pack and get you medical attention." He looked at Cass. "You okay?"

She wanted him to hold her, to squeeze him tight and breathe in his scent. She supposed this wasn't the time for that.

"I'm okay," she said, ignoring the twinge the misstatement sent through her skull. "I'll corral the dragons and make sure they stay close."

He nodded but with less than his full attention. *Oh grow up*, she ordered her irritated self. Rick had more important things to do than cosset her.

She joined him in helping her father cross the yard. Despite his weakness, he watched the dragons fly rings around them with wondering eyes.

"They tracked you here," he said. "That's marvelous."

"Is it really surprising?" she asked.

"It's good," he said. "They've bonded to you the way they should."

She had the impression he wasn't telling the whole story. "Dad—"

He stumbled on a tuft of grass, necessitating that she help catch his weight.

"I meant to ask," he said. "How did you find me?"

"Through the spy bell you put on Poly. When I realized what it was, I traced the spell back to you."

"The spy bell?" He looked confused for a second before letting out a rough chuckle. "That wasn't for spying. I didn't *want* to know what you were up to. It was an alarm system. If things went . . . seriously wrong for you, it would send me an alert. Knowing what you'd done with the eggs would defeat the purpose of handing them off to you."

"Oh." She was disconcerted. "I should have thought of that."

They'd reached the old farmhouse, where Ceallach had left on the lights. Her father squeezed her hand as Rick supported most of his weight up the worn back steps. The house had the same strange energy she remembered from visits with her gran, as if it were stuck in the past like amber and overstuffed with life at the same time.

The kitchen bore evidence of Ceallach having made himself at home. An empty milk carton stood in the sink, a sandwich plate with crumbs left out on the counter.

In a more startling discovery, they found the caretaker dead in the bedroom on the same floor. From the glimpse Cass caught, he'd been desiccated—like a thousand year old mummy in work boots and overalls.

"Okay then," Rick said, switching off the light and shutting the door hastily. "We'll deal with that later. Let's get your father settled in the living room."

Cass perched on the couch where they'd laid her father while Rick called his pack leader on the kitchen phone. The conversation was businesslike and male—just the facts and no drama. When he rejoined them, she saw speaking to his alpha had improved his mood. He was still . . . vigilant, she guessed she'd call it, but no longer so tightly coiled.

"They'll be here soon," he said to her dad. "Are you up for a few questions in the meantime?"

"As long as I don't have to dance a jig while I answer," he said.

Rick smiled and lifted a straight-backed chair closer. He'd stuck his new sword underneath his arm—not unlike Ceallach, actually. As he sat, he began to set it on the floor.

"May I?" her father asked, extending one trembling hand.

Rick hesitated, then laid the weapon across the blanket that draped her father's lap. They'd propped him up on pillows, and he didn't have strain. His fingertips stroked the runes the sword maker's art had chased into the blade.

"This is Blood Drinker," he said as if introducing Rick to a person. "All protectors' swords have names. Yours is a very old blade. Many protectors carried it with honor."

"Ah." Rick seemed interested, but a shadow crossed his face. "Ceallach had one too."

"So he did. His was a younger blade. I don't know where he got it. Forced one of the old makers to forge it for him, perhaps. He must have found a way to activate the magic that binds these weapons to their owners."

"That's why they zap some people. And why Ceallach said he'd compel me to work for his queen. He couldn't just take my blade and give it to someone else."

"That's correct," her father confirmed. "I couldn't claim your sword or force it through its changes, but it doesn't 'zap' me because I'm a hereditary Guild member. Your sword recognizes my blood line."

"Did you know the woman Ceallach killed in the subway?"

"I did." He didn't name her even though she was dead, proving faeries were indeed weird about that stuff. "I hadn't spoken to her or my other colleagues since coming here. The Guild thought cutting off contact would make me more difficult to find. When I—" Her father sighed. "I sensed my time of safety was running short, but when I heard about her death on the television, I knew the Pocket's enemies had tracked me down at last."

"The *Pocket's* enemies," Rick repeated.

Her father regarded him, weary but clear-eyed. "You heard Ceallach speak of his queen. Joscela has ever been King Manfred's adversary. Manfred won the High Council's approval to sacrifice my . . . the dragon T'Fain and create this dimension. He dreamed of the magical world and the mundane interacting as in days of old."

"And Joscela disapproved of that."

"She would have hated any idea Manfred came up with but, yes, she found the mixing of fae with human abhorrent. When a being is immortal, grievances have a way of becoming magnified. Ceallach is . . . was her most loyal minister."

"Would he have returned to her when he escaped?" Cass asked.

"He'd try," her father said. "I believe he genuinely loved her—and she him in return." He released another sigh. "I am sorry, daughter. I hoped to delay your involvement in these matters until you were older."

His soft blue gaze held hers earnestly. He didn't seem to realize she minded being glamoured to do things against her will a great deal more than she minded being involved. Of course, considering her recent behavior, this was a tricky complaint to bring up in front of Rick.

She rubbed her father's arm. The shirt he'd been wearing when he and Ceallach first battled in his apartment was in shreds, no doubt due to his torture here. All her life, this was his personal uniform: button-down Oxfords in nice cotton. Sometimes he wore them with jeans and sometimes with good trousers. She'd never seen his attire bloodied and torn before.

She knew she was very lucky he hadn't died.

"Just concentrate on healing," she said. "That's what matters to me now."

Her father patted her hand, his tired eyes beginning to drift shut. "You exceeded every expectation I had for you. One living dragon was the most I dared hope for."

He was asleep then, leaving Cass strangely uneasy. He spoke of *expectations* in a way that suggested a long-term plan—and an elaborate one. She knew he'd set whatever it was into motion when she was a child. The question was, did his plotting go further back than that?

Verdi made a trilling noise from the windowsill he and his siblings were perched on.

A second later, Cass heard what had caught the dragon's attention: the distant *thwap* of a helicopter approaching. It circled the house with its searchlight directed downward before landing in the level area between the farm buildings.

"Okay," Rick said. "Let's get out of here."

Rick helped her dad while Cass called the dragons to her. The pilot wasn't turning off the rotor, and she didn't want them accidentally hurt by it.

Rick's alpha, Adam Santini—who she also remembered from high school —leaned out the open side to haul them up and in. When he caught her hand, his eyes widened. At first, she thought he was surprised to see the dragons, but his jaw dropped too. Her looks had dazzled him just a bit.

She realized she hadn't missed people reacting to her like that.

Two more wolves were in the bay, plus a third acting as pilot. Rick did a double take when he saw him.

"Johnny," he said. "When did you get your license?"

"Yesterday." Hands staying on the controls, he glanced back with a grin. "I guess you miss stuff when you go AWOL and don't check in."

The chopper lifted off as the stylish wolf she'd met at Tony's buckled her into a harnessed seat. "Nate," she said, remembering.

He flashed a lady-killer's smile. "Nice to see you again. And in one piece."

Intrigued by all these new people, Scarlet cheeped at him from her huddle with her siblings on Cass's lap. Nate chucked her beneath the chin. "This one's pretty," he said.

Scarlet must have understood his tone, because the red dragon preened.

Cass smiled. Some men could win any female's heart.

Settled now, she noticed Rick hadn't chosen to sit beside her in the rear. Nate took the empty spot next to her. Rick faced her from the front with Adam, the two big men shoulder to shoulder. Her father had gotten the full invalid treatment. He was strapped to the floor on a pallet with an emergency blanket to warm him. Cass doubted he like this arrangement, but he wasn't protesting. The final wolf, a stocky older man, slid the open door shut and sat on a side seat opposite. He nodded, pleasant but businesslike, and picked up a serious-looking automatic rifle.

Rick raised his voice above the engine noise. "Where's Tony?" he asked his boss.

"I sent him, Ari, and the kids to stay with Evina. I know her tigers are tough, but I wanted at least one set of cop's eyes with them."

Rick nodded like he approved, but also like the precaution jostled his equilibrium.

"My wife Evina is a fire chief," Nate explained. "A tiger shifter. She and her pride will keep everyone safe until we can settle this."

Now Cass was off balance too. "I'm sorry we've brought this danger into your lives."

Nate shrugged. "It isn't your fault. Those crazy purebloods need their asses kicked."

Her father, as the sole pureblood in the chopper, smiled crookedly from the floor.

"Tony has your cat," the stocky wolf informed her. "We found her in the cave with Rick's phone. We thought she might be a magical feline, but when we tried to interrogate her, all she did was meow."

Cass snorted a startled laugh at that idea.

"I'm Carmine, by the way," he said. "Since the oaf has forgotten his manners."

"Cass," she said, understanding Rick was the oaf he referred to.

"What?" Rick said.

Carmine said something teasing in Italian. The byplay relaxed her, probably the wolf's intention.

"So, boss," Johnny the pilot said. "Where am I flying this circus?"

Adam looked across the helicopter bay at her. He held the same big mother rifle as Carmine. "That depends on Cass."

"Me? Do you want permission to use my house?"

"No," Rick and Adam denied in unison.

"We can't stay there," Adam said. "You live on top of a department store. If the other faerie mounts an attack, we can't risk the public getting caught in the crossfire. What I need to know is how well you trust your friends Bridie and Jin Levine."

"I'd trust them with anything. I've known them all my life." Her face went abruptly cold. "Are they all right?"

"They're fine," Adam reassured her, watching her reactions like the sharp cop he was. "They're just worried about you. They reported you missing and in danger when their photos of you burned up."

"Shoot," she said. "I forgot that might frighten them."

Her dad was on his elbows, giving her a strange look.

"You gave me the idea," she said in self-defense. "You burned out your photo so I couldn't track you through it."

"I'm aware of that. I hadn't realized you knew how to do that spell."

"I fudged it," she said. "Like I do most things." The reminder of all the magic he could have taught her but hadn't ticked her off. Her dad was probably lucky Adam spoke again.

"Fudging aside," he said. "Your friends own a large isolated property in Westchester. If they'd allow us to take it over, it wouldn't be a bad place to set up temporary headquarters."

"They'll allow it," Cass predicted, familiar with the cousins' generosity. "The trick will be convincing them not to turn your stay into a party."

CHAPTER ELEVEN

JOHNNY landed the helicopter on the lawn next to Jin and Bridie's stone-clad horse stables. Tasteful landscape lighting revealed grass too green for November and perfect enough for a real carpet. Autumn leaves had fallen into the rear garden's reflecting pool, their colors so pretty Cass wasn't surprised the cousins had left them there. Beyond that rose the two-story, two-winged house, Jin and Bridie's "treat" to themselves for making a success of their TV show. Cass had been here a couple times during holiday visits to her gran. The mansion was over-the-top, but so them she couldn't help but be fond of it.

"I guess we don't have to worry about roughing it here," Rick observed.

His tone was dry. When Cass glanced at him questioningly, he turned his head away. She saw he'd rigged a make-do sheath for the sword to secure it on his back. How right it looked on him was uncanny.

"I'll get these buckles for you, sir," Carmine said to her father. Her dad had nixed the idea of going to the hospital or summoning a medic. He'd claimed time would heal him better than any professional. Cass was aware he'd used a push of glamour to get his way. She supposed this meant he really was improving.

She *was* slightly troubled by the failure of the pack's anti-compulsion charms to fend off his influence.

"Go on," her dad said to her as she watched him being helped to his feet again. "Your friends need to see you're all right."

She could have jumped out the door herself, but Nate waited on the grass to help. Shoving aside her wish that he were Rick, she accepted his assistance and thanked him.

Jin and Bridie stood side by side a short distance behind him, wrapped up in warm sweaters. Bridie actually had her hands clutched together at her breast. Jin had painted fresh pink streaks in her short hair—adding a festive

159

note to their welcome. Cass smiled at the sight, loving her friends more than she knew how to say.

As Cass began to walk, Bridie ran to hug her. "I know you don't really do this," she said, squeezing her in a tight embrace, "but we were so worried!"

Cass laughed and let her have her way. Just this once, Bridie would survive a stray speck of faerie dust. "I'm fine," she said. "Sometimes you've got to hug."

Bridie released her and wiped her cheeks. "We've got bedrooms ready. And we cleared out a stall in the stables for the you-know-whats."

The you-know-whats had hopped out of the helicopter and were clustered a little shyly around Cass's feet.

Jin stared at them openmouthed. "Three . . . Wow. They're adorable."

"Jin sent Felipe to the butcher," Bridie said. "We figured everyone ate red meat."

Felipe was their gorgeous Brazilian-Japanese stable master and Jin's live-in lover. He was a human with a Talent for soothing animals. Though he probably was trustworthy, Cass added him to her mental list of staff she planned to compel to keep their mouths shut. Her father needed to conserve his power for healing, and better safe than sorry.

Rick's alpha seemed to be thinking along the same lines. "You've told your employees how important it is not to mention we're staying here?"

"Oh yes," Bridie assured him. "We have lots of celebrities come for parties. Every six months we require staff to submit to being spelled against gossiping."

Cass looked at Jin, who was quieter than normal. Of the two very social cousins, she was the most outgoing.

She jerked when she noticed Cass's eyes on her. "Sorry," she laughed. "You don't often catch me speechless, do you? I fixed a special room for your dad to convalesce in. Why don't I take him there now?"

Her father was leaning on Carmine. "That's kind of you," he said, then added a bit too casually: "Might I ask, is your friend Rhona safe and well?"

"Rhona? She's fine." Jin seemed not to hear the carefulness of the question. "We figured it was best not to ask her over and put her or Pip at risk."

"Of course," her father said.

"We told her Cass is all right," Bridie added. "Just that she wasn't up for visitors."

Her father inclined his head.

Hm, Cass thought, but decided solving this mystery wasn't on her priority list.

~

The gold elf cousins' mansion was posher than Cass's penthouse. Rick wasn't the only wolf to feel out of place. His packmates tiptoed along the expensive rugs for fear of doing damage with their big feet. Even Nate was overawed. Twice Rick caught him slack jawed. The first time was for a probably famous painting of a rearing horse. The second was for the dazzling gold-leafed dome that topped a marble garden room so lush it put him in mind of a tropical oasis. He heard sleepy bird cries up among the palm fronds and smelled orchids. A single one of the fancy wrought iron cafe tables would have cost him a month's salary.

Roald's guest room opened onto this undeniably lovely space.

Rick had tagged along here with Cass, though his mental state regarding her was disturbingly conflicted. Surviving the fight with Ceallach had hyped him up of course. He could have bedded her for a week and not gotten enough of her. Unfortunately, he was also uneasy over her apparent willingness to glamour him. He'd put off thinking about it until they rescued Roald, but it was back in his face again. He knew he needed to decide how to handle it.

Just because he loved Cass didn't mean he'd let her treat him a like a puppet whenever they disagreed, not even if she only did it when she thought it was important. That was no sort of relationship—and no way to keep her respect for him.

Respect seemed more important than ever. At the cave, he'd forgotten their differences. Seeing her at home amidst this luxury dragged them back to the forefront. If he hadn't had a few more questions to ask her father, he'd have holed up somewhere far from her to think his way through the dilemma.

Because he couldn't, he followed the little group into Roald's guest room. He concluded plants aided convalescing. In addition to the proximity of the garden, two French doors led onto a terrace with a view of the beautifully groomed back grounds.

Carmine helped Roald onto the bed, his aptitude for fussing learned from his warmhearted wife. He left once Roald was settled, slapping Rick's shoulder along the way. When Rick looked at him, he mouthed *Snow White* and wagged his thick eyebrows.

Tony must have spread the news about Rick's high school crush.

"This is beautiful," Roald said to Jin, who hovered at the doorway. "My spirit feels refreshed already."

"I'm glad," their hostess said. "Shall I open the patio doors or bring more pillows? Perhaps our housekeeper could bring tea."

"I need nothing more. And I believe my daughter's friend wishes to speak to me privately."

"Oh." She put her hand to her throat. "Of course. I'll leave you to it. Cass, your usual room is ready."

Seeming reluctant, Jin left and shut the door. Rick supposed even celebrity interviewers could be dazzled by purebloods. Despite his advanced age, her father didn't look a day older than forty.

Seeming unaware of the interest he'd attracted, Roald straightened the blanket at his waist. His motions were gingerly, but the cuts and bruises on his face weren't as bad. He looked at Rick out of two eyes instead of one. "You have more questions for me?"

"A clarification. Ceallach mentioned he was going to bring the dragons to their new mother. I thought they could only be imprinted once."

"I wondered about that too," Cass said.

The sound of her voice caused Rick's spine to tingle all the way to his tailbone. Doing his best to ignore this, he kept his attention on her father.

"Ah." Sheets rustled as Roald shifted on the bed—perhaps in embarrassment. "Ceallach may have been under the impression Cass couldn't form that bond with them. Because she's only half faerie."

"But I did form it," Cass said. "Are you saying I shouldn't have been able to?"

Her father rubbed a fading bruise on his jaw. "In your case, there are . . . other factors in play."

"What factors?" she pressed.

Her father looked extremely reluctant to answer.

"*Dad.*"

He gave in with a sigh. "It's because your human half is Maycee. When T'Fain gave her life to form Resurrection, their farm was at the epicenter of her energy nova. The genes of every Maycee there were infused with dragon power. You imprinted the Sevryn clutch because of her."

Emotion brightened Roald's eyes. He seemed to plead with his daughter—for what, Rick didn't understand. Looking at Cass revealed her mouth hung open, her manner taken aback by what he'd revealed.

"But then—" She stopped and continued. "When you married Mom . . ."

"Daughter," Roald said. "Don't ask questions you don't want answers to."

Cass shut her mouth, though her face struggled. She composed herself and gave her father a steady look. "You know I'll want the truth at some point."

"Not tonight. Tonight we can simply be grateful we're alive."

Their exchange sounded like family business. Rick waited to question Cass until they'd left her father and were walking down a long hallway.

"Do I need to know what that was about?" he asked.

She stopped, and he did too. Her expression was troubled. "I don't think so."

He wanted to take her hands, to feel her warm slender fingers sliding between his own. He could have done it. She wasn't even a foot away. His flesh stirred between his legs, the unavoidable effect of her nearness and her gaze holding his.

He saw her breasts lift with quickened breaths.

"My usual room is up those stairs," she said, tipping her head toward them.

The heat in his groin spread to his chest. "I should check on Nate. Make sure he has everything he needs to stand guard over the brood."

Cass nodded and looked down. "I understand. I'll . . . catch up with you later."

As he strode away, arousal thrummed through his body. Rick wondered if Cass did understand. He wasn't certain he did himself.

He rounded a bend in the corridor, almost bumping into Jin as he did. Their hostess was rearranging calla lilies in a large silver urn.

"Something wrong?" she asked. Her shiny manicured nails matched the pink streaks in her cropped hair. She was pretty with her sun-kissed skin and her twenty-four carat locks, but something about her struck him as too sharp. Was she really one of Cass's dearest friends? She didn't seem natural enough for that.

"Everything's fine," he said. "This is the way to the stables, isn't it?"

"Yes." She hesitated, then spoke again. "I forgot to ask. Did you want a separate room from Cass? Body language says a lot, but I don't want to assume you're together."

Rick regarded her without answering. Her slanted elf eyes were also golden, like honey shot through with sun. For just a second, he wondered who the hell was looking out of them. He shook himself and the thought faded, though maybe not his caution. Cass's friend or not, this female was a slicker operator than he knew how to be comfortable with.

"We'll sort it out," he said. "Thank you for making space for us."

"No problem," she responded. "Any friend of Cass's is a friend of mine."

He nodded curtly and walked away. Probably Cass's friend thought he was as big an oaf as Carmine claimed.

The stables weren't far from the back exit. Nicer than many people's homes, they had thick stone walls, shuttered windows, and brick-lined floors with drains for cleaning. The interior was warm, so they also had central heating. Rick's wolf preferred the scent of hay and horses to the various perfumes inside the house.

He followed the rise and fall of Nate's voice to the space that had been cleared for the dragons.

Nate seemed to be telling the trio a bedtime story. Rick grinned over the stall door at the picture they presented. The ponytailed wolf sat on the floor on a blanket, his back propped on a hay bale with the youngsters ranged around him. Auric and Verdi listened with their mouths open. Scarlet had clambered onto Nate's legs and was having her chin scratched.

The Little Tiger Who Saved the Deva?" Rick teased, recognizing the tale.

The light was low, but he thought Nate blushed. "It's the cubs' favorite. These guys wouldn't settle. They were waking up the horses."

Auric cheeped at Rick as he stepped into the stall and swung the half-door shut behind him. He crouched to pet all three dragons, who seemed happy to see him. "Anything happen since you've been guarding them?"

"Nothing since Bridie—the one with the long gold hair—left us here."

"Did Adam mention having an actual plan?"

"Only what you'd imagine. We don't have much chance of finding the second faerie, so we'll use the dragons to lure her here. Adam figures she and her co-conspirator knew more about Roald le Beau's activities in the Pocket than he realized. They must have split their efforts between him and his daughter, waiting to see where the eggs showed up. Unless the second fae is an idiot, she's watching everyone close to Cass. Even if the staff don't gossip, she'll read the signs that we're holed up here."

Unable to argue, Rick accepted Auric's invitation to rub his belly. "I wish we had a better plan. I don't like using these little guys as bait. Or involving Cass's friends."

"We've got manpower," Nate pointed out. "And firepower. And don't forget, you and your girlfriend killed that first faerie by yourselves."

"She's not my—" Rick shut his mouth and frowned. Maybe Cass was his girlfriend. How the hell would he know?

"What's the matter?" Nate asked.

Rick considered how to answer. "I'm uneasy about this whole situation. What if we got lucky when we killed Ceallach? This other pureblood is a queen. Maybe she has more mojo than he did. Maybe she'll want revenge for us killing her lover. Faeries keep secrets from the rest of us. We don't know what we're up against."

"We'll figure it out. You've got the pack with you now."

He did, and it should have made him feel better. In some ways it did. His wolf was calmer with them around him—or maybe it was just lulled.

"How do you stand Evina being more powerful than you?" he blurted.

"I wouldn't say she's more powerful. We each have different strengths."

"But she's alpha." Though Rick knew this had to be a sensitive topic, he needed the answer. "Theoretically, she could order you to do something, and you'd be obliged to obey."

"Actually," Nate said, suddenly finding petting Scarlet's wings extra interesting. "Within Evina's pride, I am alpha. I'm not sure what about my energy does it, but her tigers recognize me as their co-leader."

Rick gaped at him. How could Nate not have mentioned this before? If nothing else, his healthy ego should have driven him to it.

Nate let out a breathy laugh. "I know. It's weird. And sometimes those macho cats do not like answering to a dog. We're smoothing out the rough spots as we go."

"No wonder you've been mellower since you married her," Rick said.

"Yeah." Nate went back to scratching Scarlet's outstretched throat. "I guess you could say not coming first or second in this pack nettled me. Not that I don't respect you and Adam. I just thought . . ." He trailed off and let it go. "The truth is, even if I weren't co-alpha with Evina, I think I'd trust her to treat me as an equal in the relationship. She's not the sort of person who wants to make anyone feel small."

Rick wasn't comfortable with the sympathy in Nate's eyes. Cass didn't want to make him feel small. She just . . . well, he wasn't sure what she wanted.

Everything considered, maybe it was time he found out.

~

When they were younger, Jin taught the half-and-halfers her motto: Everything looks better after a good long soak. Cass intended to test the theory now. One of the reasons she loved her usual guest room was its adjoining bath, which was a spa-like blend of white and black tile, shiny silver fixtures, and a sleek slipper tub.

She saw no reason to follow her father's reluctant confession to its unpleasant conclusion, not when there were bath salts and plenty of hot water to distract her. She'd distract herself from Rick while she was at it. So what if her own stupidity seemed to have rung the death knell on their romance? Worse, she hadn't done it by accident like with her ex. No, she'd screwed up her and Rick with her eyes open. But to hell with that. She was under-washed and overtired and she was damn well going to enjoy her wallow.

Then again, maybe she'd lock the door and cry.

Clucking at herself in disgust, she dropped the robe Jin had lent her and stepped into the steaming water. The tub was deep enough to submerge her to her neck. The heat was heaven, the lilac-scented oil soothing to her skin. She stretched her arms along the rim and let her head tip back.

Unfortunately, the moment she relaxed, her body remembered how much it wanted Rick inside it.

"Damn it," she said just as the door opened.

It was him of course.

"Sorry," he said, starting to withdraw.

"I wasn't cursing at you, or not exactly."

He stopped leaving and smiled. "Need help . . . unwinding?" he suggested.

"You don't have to sound so smug." *She* sounded petulant, which stretched his grin wider.

"Who's smug?" he asked innocently. "We did face death together. And you're the one who looks so delectable lolling there any sane man would sell his soul to have you."

She sat up and looked at him. "Rick, I don't want you to sell your soul."

Her seriousness stole the humor from his face. Suddenly, she feared what he'd say. Thoughts were definitely rolling behind his eyes. In the end, he said nothing. He stepped to the side of tub, grasped both her hands in his, and pulled her dripping onto her feet. The way his gaze slid down her wet body set all her nerves on fire. Her nipples tightened, and her thigh muscles tensed. Her pussy went liquid with readiness for him. She knew he was aroused too. The front of his jeans had stretched as far as it could without his erection actually ripping the worn denim. His cock was thick, his balls seeming to have swelled bigger too. Cass shivered at the sight and grew hotter.

Rick saw her do it. By the time her gaze returned to his, his irises were glowing.

"Cass," he said. "God."

Afraid to speak, she slid her hands up his chest to his broad shoulders. He wore the same flannel shirt he had in the cave. The firm path her palms took up it made him shudder and catch his breath. The green fire in his eyes flared higher.

A second later, he kissed her.

He wasn't gentle about it. His lips and tongue ravaged hers, probing, claiming, his arms tightening around her like steel bands. His hands cupped her bare wet buttocks to lift her off the floor.

The way he squeezed and caressed her said he enjoyed the gauntlet no longer hampering him.

He wasn't the only one. His kiss made her feel like she was flying, the excitement he stirred in her too powerful for anything earthbound. She clutched his shoulders and sucked his tongue deeper. That inspired a good response. The room spun as his groan burned her ear. He took a step, and her back met the slick black- and white-tiled wall. His hips shoved her into it, the hardness of his erection drawing a gasp from her.

Getting that hard and thick was supernatural.

When he tried to pull back, she didn't want to let him.

"I just need to get this off," he panted.

He meant the sword harness. "Oh," she said, instantly on board with that idea. "Let me help."

He smiled, and she freed him from it, leaving him to lean the weapon safely somewhere. She didn't see where he put it. She only cared about having more skin to touch. "This too, please," she said, speedily undoing his shirt buttons.

She rolled her lip between her teeth as his lovely olive flesh appeared. Feeling greedy, she pushed the sleeves off his arms.

"You move fast when you want to," he joked.

She would have offered a smart retort, but he kissed her before she could. His warmth was summery, his chest perfect for rubbing hers against. His seriously muscled back absolutely had to be investigated from trapezius to tailbone. He made a noise when her fingers squeezed under his back waistband.

Cass didn't let the sound stop her from wedging both hands around her goal.

"Such a fine, fine ass," she complimented an inch away from his ear. "So tight and hard. You really shouldn't wonder that I want my hands on it."

"What about what I want my hands on?" he growled.

He slid them up her front to her breasts, kneading them with a possessiveness and a skill that soon had her squirming.

"You're distracting me," she panted.

"Really." Amused, he popped one nipple out between two fingers and bent to suck the tip. His tongue flicked between his pursed lips to tickle it.

Cass's body jerked. He'd found the exact right nerve to stimulate. An electric pulse streaked from what his mouth was doing to the heart of her clitoris.

"*Rick*," she said and writhed for him.

He liked having her at his mercy. He moved his head to her other breast, subjecting it to the same sharp delight. Her entire pussy twitched, her hands pulling from his jeans to thread through his soft dark hair. Her hold couldn't keep him where he was. He switched breasts again, dragging her to the trembling verge of coming.

She hadn't known her body could do that. Her startled inhalation echoed off the bathroom walls.

"Rick," she said. "Please."

His mouth left her. "Stay," he ordered in his best I'm-the-boss-now voice.

"Stay? But—"

He dropped a hard kiss onto her mouth, his aggression silencing her. She didn't know why she liked him this way, but she did. He slid his hands to her hips and held them immobile on the wall.

"I want this," he said, low and rough. "I want to feel you unravel."

He sank to his knees in front of her.

"Oh God," she said, realizing what he intended.

He looked up her body, his eyes on fire, his lengthened canines changing his lips' shape. He kissed her navel, then dragged his face across her thatch. His hands cruised down her legs to her ankles.

"My wolf likes the way you smell," he said.

He lifted her left foot and then her right, widening her stance for him.

"Keep these spread," he said.

The order was unnecessary. She couldn't have closed her legs even if she wanted; his broad shoulders were in the way. His hands came up her thighs again, the smooth caress causing more of her nerves to jump. His destination reached, he parted her labia with his thumbs, watching in fascination as he revealed her sex. Though she couldn't see what he did, she felt her clitoris standing out and pulsing. When he stroked her gently around it, more cream ran out of her. More than anything, that exposed her: her desire for him, her intense longing for a release.

He looked up into her face.

"This is mine," he said, increasing the pressure of his thumbs as they moved up and down to either side of her clit. "You're going to let me do what I want to it."

What he wanted was to draw the sensitive button into his mouth. Cass moaned with pleasure, her hips bucking close for more. He let her do it, though his position and the lean of his weight trapped her against the tile. The suction of his cheeks created a quick rhythm on the bundle of swollen nerves. His canines were another pressure—and his tongue. Cass's neck arched, her fingers burrowing into his hair. He growled his approval as she broke into a million pieces of ecstasy.

"Good," he said . . . and made her do it again.

She was drunk from the second climax, but she still wanted him. He rose, and she needed the wall to hold her up. His hands moved to the bulging front of his jeans, undoing the button and starting to unzip.

"I can help," she slurred, reaching one arm to him.

"You can watch," he corrected.

She shivered, just a little reaction but one he couldn't miss. He pushed the denim and his briefs down his legs. They were hairy and strong and—to her—totally sexy. Even his knees got her going; they seemed so capable and male. Her hands fisted with longing on the tiles. She was half afraid to look at his erection.

He didn't let her get away with avoiding it.

"Look," he said. He stroked down abs that gleamed with perspiration, then caught up his thick flushed pole. He stroked that too, showing off how hard he was by squeezing as he pulled. Cass was hypnotized. He ringed his fingers beneath the tip, stopping where it flared out. He held himself out for her, letting her look her fill.

She couldn't deny he was beautiful. Straight. Full. Throbbing with vigor and impatience. She licked her lips, her thighs tensing at the thought of him pushing that prodigy into her.

"Do you want this?" he said, steadying it with one hand. His voice was so harsh she barely recognized it as his.

"Yes," she said. "Please give your cock to me."

He liked when she said *please*. He was on her—and in her—at shifter speed. He cried out as his cock plunged up her into her sheath. Her legs were already spread for entry, her sex fully prepared for his intrusion. He didn't hesitate to take advantage. The penetration lifted her to her toes. Loving that but wanting even more, she swung her legs up and around him. His fine, fine ass made the perfect shelf for her bare heels to dig into.

Rick let out a low growl for that.

"Take me," she urged. "Every step I take tomorrow I want to know you were inside me."

That idea got to him. His lips curled back, showing her his wolf fangs. She didn't think he meant to do it, but he couldn't control himself. His grip on her bottom tightened, his claws sliding out as well. The throbbing of his cock increased as he withdrew partway. Like her, this part of him looked forward to what was coming.

He let loose as never before, humping her fast and hard and as deep inside her as he could get. He fucked her like the world was ending, and this was their last chance to be together. Their mingled cries were noisy: groans of pleasure, pleas for each other to never stop. He came, and it didn't matter. He was just as desperate to go again.

A tile cracked behind her and shattered on the floor.

"Fuck," he said.

He carried her to the bedroom, hurrying with their groins locked together and grinding greedily. Eagerness made him awkward, along with the kisses he couldn't stop giving her. He bumped them into a chair and stumbled against the bed. They fell onto the soft mattress together.

Cass was very happily under him.

Directly above her was a headboard painted with a scene of shepherds and sheep grazing. Cass doubted Rick noticed the decoration as he stretched over her to grab it. The coiling of his muscles said he intended to resume what they'd been doing in the bathroom.

"Oh God," Cass moaned, spreading her legs wider.

As it turned out, he hadn't been going as fast and hard as he could.

"Am I hurting you?" he panted when she cried out. He couldn't have been too worried, because he wasn't easing up. Maybe he couldn't. She felt that special gland of his swelling.

The headboard rattled epically.

"No," she promised, meeting him thrust for crazy thrust. Each concussion felt life-and-death important. She clutched the mattress for leverage. "Rub your gland on me. I want to . . . feel you lock us together."

She tightened her sheath to give him more friction. To her surprise, he pulled out. Why quickly became clear. Cursing with urgency, he flipped her over, hitched her up on her knees, and shoved into her from behind—his favorite position for when he was cranked up. Cass slapped her hands on the headboard just in time.

"Ah," he cried, the swelling at his base increasing.

His new angle was good for her, her passage most sensitive exactly where the engorged gland pumped over and over it. Hearing her excited cries, he wrapped his hand around her vulva and rubbed.

The strength of his hold sent her sensations into overdrive.

Her peak crashed through her with the force of a tidal wave. Rick was going too. His wolf teeth clamped on her neck, holding her prisoner as he slammed in for his finish. It was a big one. Hot ejaculate flooded her. He growled out his pleasure, the vibration tingling down her vertebrae. His body wrapped hers, speared hers, overwhelming her inside and out. She didn't want him to stop shooting. Given her way, she'd have let him drown her in his ecstasy.

That he didn't split the headboard was a miracle.

"God," he finally said.

He'd released his grip on her neck. They both were shaking, both slippery and hot with sweat. Rick nuzzled her shoulder, his hand slipping from her pussy to rub gently up her front.

Then he pulled out of her.

Cass had just enough energy to fall onto her back. She knew he'd enjoyed what they'd shared, but when she looked up at him, he didn't seem happy.

He sat back on his heels and touched her cheek with one fingertip. She suspected he was going to bring up the topic she'd been afraid he would before.

"Cass . . ." he began.

"I'm sorry," she said, hoping to head him off. "I'm sorry I threatened to compel you."

If anything, his expression grew more somber. "I believe you. The problem is you can't promise you won't do it again, not if you think you have a good reason."

"Could *you* promise, if you were in my shoes? If I wanted to face something terrible by myself?"

"I don't know, which is why I can't judge you."

"And why you can't trust me."

She saw she'd hit the bitter nail on the head.

"Yes," he said. "And now I have to decide if I can live with that."

CHAPTER
TWELVE

RICK collected his sword and left. He claimed he needed to talk to his alpha, but Cass suspected putting space between him and her was just as important. She wished she could blame him. She understood how he felt. Her father had taken choices from her, and she hadn't liked it one bit. She could promise she'd try to show more restraint, but that might not be good enough for Rick.

People had a right to chart their own course in life.

"Crap," she said to the empty room.

She wiped her eyes, annoyed by her tearfulness. She wanted her dragons with her something awful—though she knew their energy and mischief would wreak havoc in Jin and Bridie's beautiful home. Her babies were housebroken, but not house-safe. Guarding them in the stables was a reasonable solution.

Well, fine, she thought. She'd go to them if they couldn't come to her.

She pulled on the comfy sweats Jin had been kind enough to leave her. The house was quiet as she strode through it, the mansion's many rooms easily swallowing a handful of lupine guests.

When she reached the stables, the first glimmer of coming dawn was turning the sky pearly. Given how early the cousins left for the studio, Cass didn't expect to find Jin there. The charming half elf leaned over the swinging door to the dragons' stall, but Cass recognized her from behind. Her one figure flaw, if it truly were one, was that she thought her butt was flat.

"Hello, darlings," Jin was murmuring. "Come up and meet me."

She seemed to be having trouble coaxing the brood to her.

"I think they're shy with strangers," Cass said.

Jin spun, her gold eyes wide with surprise. She looked like she'd been caught with her hand in the cookie jar. "Oh," she said, recovering with a quiet laugh. "I know I probably shouldn't be here, but I couldn't resist peeking in on them. They're so wild and beautiful. That little red one is a heartbreaker."

She was whispering.

"Where's the guard wolf?" Cass whispered back.

Jin pointed into the stall and smiled. Nate was indeed inside, as Cass saw when she joined her friend at the door. He was sound asleep sitting up, his back leaning on a hay bale, his mouth open but not snoring. Scarlet really had taken a shine to him. The boys were cuddled to either side of his black-jeaned legs, but she'd curled up on his chest with her ear over his heartbeat.

As if the weapon were a baby too, Nate's second arm draped his big-ass machine gun.

Watching Rick's pack mate slumber struck Cass as an invasion of his privacy. Jin didn't seem to see anything wrong in it, but she was bolder with men than Cass.

"Isn't he supposed to be on duty?" Cass asked softly.

"Oh you know wolves." Jin waved her pink manicure in dismissal. "I'm sure he'd wake up in a snap if anything were wrong."

Cass imagined that was true. She'd seen Rick do it enough times. Then again, she'd expect the sound of their voices to wake him. Verdi stirred when he heard her, lifting his head and opening his silver eyes.

I'm here, Cass thought at him, though she wasn't certain they could communicate this way. *Everything's fine. You rest up, and we'll play tomorrow.*

He seemed like he understood. He gazed at her, and she felt the love all her babies were good at sending out. Her troubles fell away as she wished it back to him. *I love you too, sweetheart.*

Apparently reassured, the green dragon let his head drop onto the werecop's thigh. A little sigh issued from him, followed by a wisp of smoke. Cass smiled. If that meant what she thought it did, Scarlet was about to lose her fire-breathing monopoly. She watched Verdi's cute rounded belly rise and fall in his sleep, her own body relaxing as she leaned on the stall door. How attached she'd grown to the brood was its own sort of magic. It was difficult to imagine what she *wouldn't* do protect them.

She realized she'd found the purpose she'd been searching for when she returned home to the Pocket.

"Do they all do that?" Jin asked.

"Do what?" Cass responded, turning her head to her.

"Send that little love fest to you."

Cass's brow puckered. Jin's tone held a trace of bitterness, as if she might be jealous. Cass couldn't think why she would be. Jin had tons of people in her life who loved her, including her and Bridie's audience.

"I suppose they do. I didn't know you could sense that."

"I may not have your pedigree, but half elves aren't rocks. We're sensitive to magic too."

Jin smiled, but Cass felt a need to apologize. "I'm sorry. I wasn't thinking."

Jin waved her hand that it didn't matter, then leaned sideways on the door like Cass was. The pose invited confidences, something her job demanded she be good at. "Tell the truth," she said as if Cass were an interviewee she was wooing. "You imprinted them, didn't you?"

Cass's mouth fell open.

Jin broke into a laugh. "Come on," she said. "I'm more than on-air talent or a pretty face. I do my research."

"I guess I did," Cass admitted. "My dad said it's because I'm half Maycee as well as half faerie. He claims Maycee genes were changed when the last dragon's energy washed across their farm."

Jin looked thoughtfully over her shoulder into the stall. "Not the last dragon anymore."

"No. Not anymore."

"The red dragon is a girl."

"Yes," Cass agreed.

"Since they're magical, they probably have a way to overcome the hazards of inbreeding."

"They're too little to think that way!" Cass objected.

Jin faced her again and smiled. "They're not people."

"I know. But they're still too young."

Amused, Jin rolled her eyes at her. "You always did have a moral streak."

"Someone had to. You and Bridie were juvenile delinquents. Still are, I'd say, sneaking out in the dark to watch men you don't even know sleeping."

Jin flashed a gleaming grin. "What they don't know won't hurt them. And speaking of sexy, why aren't you denned down with that hot hunk of wolf who can't keep his eyes off you?"

Cass's good humor dropped from her like a stone.

"Oh boy," Jin said in response to her expression. "This seems like a conversation that requires more privacy—and possibly good liquor."

~

Jin kept a stash of triple-blessed Bénédictine and Brandy in her and Bridie's shared sitting room. According to the store that sold it, the blessings were for health, happiness, and avoiding hangovers. Bridie wandered in from her bedroom as Jin began to pour. Wearing pajamas and with her naturally straight blonde hair in soft rollers, she plopped into a flowered armchair and sprawled her legs.

"I don't know if it's too early for alcohol or too late."

"Man trouble," Jin informed her cousin, handing her a snifter.

Bridie swirled the liquor and took a sip.

"Don't you two have to go to work?" Cass asked.

"Not today," Bridie said. "We're off."

"We couldn't abandon you anyway," Jin assured her. "Not with a broken heart."

Was her heart broken? Hearing Jin say so depressed her.

"Rick and I *could* work through this," she said tentatively. She took the glass Jin offered but didn't drink.

"You don't believe that. You only wish you did."

"What does she wish?" Bridie asked sleepily.

"That the big wolf actually loved her and wasn't just caught up in the romance of having to rescue her."

"I didn't say that!"

"Is there another reason you think he can't love you?" Jin's hands were on her hips, her golden eyes kind but stern. It seemed impossible not to answer her.

"I don't know about *can't* . . . He's mad because I threatened to glamour him."

"Really?" Bridie sat straighter with wide eyes. "I thought you had rules about that."

"I do. He wanted me to stay behind while he faced the faerie who was torturing my father. I couldn't let him do that by himself."

"Of course you couldn't," Bridie said soothingly. "He's an idiot if he's annoyed by that."

"*Men,*" Jin said, tossing back half her drink.

She sounded brittle, like she had back in the stable. Was Jin having trouble with Felipe? She frowned when she noticed Cass's attention.

"Men always break your heart," she declared.

She said this with such confidence it seemed it must be true. Her beautiful honeyed gaze held Cass's.

"Maybe," Cass agreed unsurely. Her stomach felt unhappy.

"Look at your dad," Jin went on, gesturing with her glass. "How many times did we watch him disappoint you? Never loving you back as much as you loved him. And that human you met Outside, the weak-willed druggie you compelled to fall for you."

"Accidentally."

"Does it matter? He broke your heart the same as the others. Half the time, when men think they've fallen in love, they're kidding themselves. The only people you can count on are female friends."

"Friends are forever," Bridie put in helpfully.

Cass looked at her. Bridie generally agreed with her cousin, but Cass would have preferred she didn't then.

Giving up on staying awake, Bridie pushed up from her chair, yawning. "Sorry about the wolf. Gosh, I need to go back to bed."

"I should too," Cass said, inexplicably reluctant to stay. Confiding her troubles to the cousins usually made her feel better. She set down her untouched glass.

"You sure?" Jin asked. "My shoulder is yours as long as you need it."

Cass gave her a quick hug. "Thanks, Jin. I appreciate you being here for me."

Probably Jin was surprised to be embraced. She stiffened for a heartbeat before she held Cass back.

Her hesitation increased the heaviness of Cass's spirit. She trudged back to her room with cement feet. Maybe she'd never be loved by anyone. Maybe a lifetime of keeping up her guards so she wouldn't inadvertently dust her friends made that impossible. She didn't think to wonder why she'd gone from being merely unhappy to miserable so fast. She *ought* to be miserable. Her life was a hopeless mess.

In her current mood, the cold spot she passed through outside her door seemed appropriate. Maybe it was a draft, but ghosts chilled the air pretty much the same way. Given that Cass was haunted by her past, why shouldn't a stray specter be drawn to her?

She curled up on the bed she and Rick had rumpled, a bolster hugged to her stomach. Nice though the pillow was, it was no substitute for him. Tears squeezed from the corners of her eyes, pathetic but somehow right.

Sleep tight, she thought she heard someone say.

~

The house Cass's friends lived in was too damn big. Rick resorted to using his nose to track down his alpha. He found him in a book-lined study lit by a Tiffany lamp. Adam was asleep at the dark wood desk, his cheek resting on his folded arms and his ElfBook open in front of him. Knowing Adam, he'd skimped on sleep since Rick went AWOL.

Even alpha werewolves had to catch up sometime.

The room was cooler than even shifters liked. Rick grabbed a throw from a nearby chair to spread over Adam's back. His boss didn't stir as he covered him.

Amused and absurdly touched, Rick patted Adam's arm, then drew the notebook closer to himself. The computer's screen woke to a search Adam had been doing on Jin Levine.

That was weird. Had Jin done something suspicious? He glanced at the files. Apart from quite a few parking tickets and a two-year-old Disturbing the Peace complaint for a loud party, she had a clean record. Rick contemplated his sleeping boss. Adam was the one who'd suggested they bring the dragons here. Rick assumed he'd gotten the idea when Cass's friends reported her missing, because they'd seemed trustworthy. But perhaps the opposite was true. Perhaps Adam thought they were in league with Ceallach's female accomplice.

That certainly would insure the queen heard about their presence, though not sharing his misgivings with his pack meant Adam was playing a deeper game than usual. As a rule, he kept his team informed.

Rick shut the ElfBook and rubbed his jaw. To hell with it. He was Adam's second. Adam ought to trust him with whatever was in the works.

"Hey," he said, shaking the pack leader's shoulder. "Adam, wake up."

Adam grunted and turned his head the other way.

"Adam."

Still the wolf didn't wake. Concerned, Rick pushed him bodily upward in the chair. When that failed to rouse him, Rick took a steadying breath and slapped him across the face. He'd hit him hard enough for his palm to sting . . . and earned no response at all.

Fuck, he thought. He sniffed the coffee Adam had been drinking but scented no drugs in it. Was the pack leader spelled? Or maybe the whole house was. He remembered how Ceallach had sent a block's worth of apartment residents to sleep in order to attack Cass's father without raising an alarm. Could the faerie queen do the same? Was she at the house already? Was she even then kidnapping the dragons?

He ran for the door, grateful he'd remembered to strap the protector sword to his back. He touched the knob, so eager to reach the brood he noticed too late that it was icy. As he flung it open, a damp chill enveloped him. His instincts kicked in then. He retreated, trying to get away from the invisible wintry patch, but the chill came with him. His breath puffed white and his knees buckled. Sleep sucked him down in an irresistible undertow. His eyelids were leaden, his thoughts as sluggish as cold honey. He reached for his Saint Michael medal, but the charm on it had been overwhelmed. His cheek thunked onto the carpet. He couldn't move . . . couldn't remember why he should.

Cass, he thought worriedly.

Sleep tight, said a whispery male voice.

~

Cass felt herself bobbing, up and down, up and down, like a cork on rough ocean. That anti-hangover blessing must not be working. Or maybe it was no good for seasickness. Either way, Jin ought to return the bottle for a refund.

You weren't drinking, she reminded. *Not even a single sip.*

She opened her eyes and looked down at herself in bed . . . five feet below where she was floating.

Holy smokes, she thought. *I hope I'm not dead.*

She wasn't; she could see herself breathing. She was having an out of body experience, something she couldn't recall happening in her sleep before. Not that she'd necessarily remember. People often forgot dreams. Cass especially was good at forgetting.

This seemed so funny she snickered.

Daughter, said her father's voice. *You need to concentrate and come to me.*

Visiting her father was not on her to-do list. She should wish herself to

Morocco. Or spy on hot naked men.

Cassia, her father insisted.

Oh fine, she snapped mentally. In the time it took to blink, she reached the palm-filled conservatory outside his room. Seen with her astral vision, the indoor garden wasn't all pretty. The vines had grown as big as serpents, their thick black stems a sinister tangle that barred his door. Sleeping Beauty wouldn't be able to win free of that prison.

Whether her father could seemed iffy.

If he couldn't come out, she'd have to go in. He was her father, and she loved him—even if he'd done infuriating things she couldn't quite remember. Because it seemed to make sense, she held her breath and pushed through the barrier. *Whoa,* she thought, looking around inside. More tendrils from the vines had infiltrated here. They'd wrapped her father from neck to ankle, binding him and his spirit to the bed.

He was awake at least—and highly irritated, to go by the blaze in his soft blue eyes.

"That doesn't look comfortable," she observed.

"It doesn't matter. You need to stop Joscela. You're the only one who can."

"Joscela?"

"The queen," he said. "The one who wants to steal your dragons."

"Oh. The evil queen." Cass fought a shiver. "Are you sure that's a good idea? She's a queen. I'm only half faerie."

"Come here," her father ordered, and of course she had to. He was impossible to disobey when he used that voice. "Listen to me, daughter. There's no *only* to what you are. You have power. Not just faerie power either. Remember how strong your grandmother was."

Cass did. She remembered something else as well. "You compelled me to live Outside. You spelled me away from her."

"Only to keep you safe. Parents do that for their children. Keepers do that for their broods."

Cass's astral shoulders straightened. "Those dragons don't belong to her."

"No they don't. They belong to themselves and you."

Cass considered that. "I have my mother's blood in me too. She isn't very strong."

"Isn't she?" asked her father. "Irene convinced herself the Pocket isn't real. She lived here for forty years. Don't you think that takes mental power? You have what it takes to defeat Joscela."

"You're trying to glamour me to believe in myself."

Her father smiled at the accusation. "Because you should, sweetheart. Trust me, no truer spell was ever spun."

She looked down at him. She knew he meant well, but he was wrong.

"I have to trust *me,*" she corrected. "Without being tricked into it. That's the only way I'll be strong enough."

To her surprise, he didn't argue. "As you prefer," he said. "The queen is in the garden behind the house. You need to hurry. The sun is rising. Royals draw strength from that."

Awesome, Cass thought sourly. Like a plain old pureblood wasn't strong enough.

She kept her doubts to herself and nodded.

"Go now," her father urged, like she could just *do* these things.

But she needed to prove she could. Forcing herself to calm, she imagined the reflecting pool: the scarlet leaves floating on its surface, the glimmer of the new day. A breeze would ripple the lush green grass . . .

I'm just a breeze, she thought, wanting to arrive unnoticed.

Air rushed through her, and she was there. Joscela wasn't. Jin stood barefoot on the lawn in a long sundress, facing away from her. She looked beautiful and romantic, though maybe not warm enough for the time of year. Cass felt a rush of fondness. She was lucky to have friends—even if they couldn't always cheer her up. She opened her mouth, forgetting she didn't have vocal chords and couldn't greet her friend normally.

Jin turned. "There you are."

She wasn't speaking to Cass. Her gaze was directed to a faint cloud of mist hovering in the air a few feet from her. Jin's face suddenly seemed odd. Her nose wasn't the right shape, and her cheekbones seemed to have been dusted with glitter. Her irises were lavender, when they should have been gold. Cass jerked, her brows shooting up in shock. Jin's hair was growing longer, and longer, until it reached her waist. The strands had changed color too. No longer twenty-four carat streaked with pink, they bore the silvery sheen of electrum.

Oh, she thought, finally getting what her father must have realized. This wasn't Jin. Joscela had used glamour to impersonate her. More than glamour, actually. She'd known exactly how to act like her friend—recreating her memories, her personality, right down to keeping Rhona and Pip away. Jin was smart and considerate like that. Apart from a fraction less warmth than the original, the copy was perfect.

Cass didn't see how this was possible. Joscela had fooled Bridie, who'd known her cousin from infancy. Almost everything the queen had uttered had been a lie. She should have been in terrible pain, but she'd never betrayed it. Could a pureblood hide that much discomfort?

More importantly, what had she done with the real Jin?

Dismay clutched the stomach Cass didn't have, but she had to push the concern aside. She needed to know who Joscela was talking to.

"Come out of there," the queen demanded, beckoning with a hand that was whiter and more elegant than Jin's. "I need to talk to you."

The misty spot in front of her unzipped.

If Cass had been in possession of her lungs, her gasp surely would have audible. Ceallach stepped out of the opening in the air, the same Ceallach Rick had supposedly killed. An electrum collar braced his neck between his collarbones and jaw, similar to what EMTs used to immobilize accident victims.

Having your head half cut off probably qualified as a risk to your spinal cord.

Ceallach must have reached Joscela in time for her to apply the fix magically. Cass didn't think he'd done it himself. He looked considerably de-juiced from when she'd seen him blazing bright as the sun in the Maycee barn. Joscela seemed to notice this as well.

She frowned as she regarded him. "Is the household asleep?"

"Yes," he said, his voice also wan-sounding.

"And T'Fain's old keeper?"

"Trapped by the vines, as you instructed."

"Good." Despite her positive response, Joscela's exquisite mouth thinned with displeasure. "You don't look well. Do you need me to charge you again?"

The formerly vital Ceallach shook his head. "I have the power I need to carry out your wishes."

Since his answer was nearly lifeless, Cass understood why the queen scowled harder. "Did you bring the girl?"

Ceallach turned to lean into the unzipped mist. His body disappeared to the waist. Suddenly, Cass realized how he'd escaped after Rick wounded him. He'd used an interdimensional carrying pocket, the one accessory no pureblood would be caught dead without. The spelled spaces were meant to transport inanimate objects. Ceallach had upped the capacity of his by sending himself to the queen instead.

Cass was spared admiring his cleverness by what he pulled from the pocket next. It was her: her unconscious body hanging limp in his arms, thankfully modest in Bridie's borrowed sweats. The pureblood set her none too carefully on the grass, her arms and legs flopping down after.

That was disturbing, to say the least.

"Are you certain we need her?" Ceallach asked.

Okay, that was more disturbing.

"Yes," Joscela confirmed. "The dragons have bonded with her. They'll be impossible to handle without her to control them."

"But can you control her?"

"Of course I can. I've already made a start on breaking her spirit. It won't be long before I've convinced her I'm her only friend in the universe."

Her cohort looked down at Cass's awkwardly sprawled body. "She was strong enough to imprint them."

"That only delays our plan. Once a new brood is born, I'll take control of them. We'll finally put an end to this . . . repulsive experiment." She waved her hands to indicate the world around them. Cass didn't know what Joscela saw. To her, their surroundings were beautiful—the grass, the sky, the scents of autumn and horse, even the lovely faeries lit by the morning sun. The scene reflected the essence of the blended realities: grounded, homely, yet magical.

Ceallach appeared neither disgusted nor enthralled. "What if the halfling discovers how to speak to the dragons mind-to-mind? What if she becomes a true keeper?"

"She won't. She can't." Joscela reached to squeeze Ceallach's shoulder. "Don't you see? That was her father's plan. He whelped a child who could imprint the hatchlings, but who'd lack the mental power to fully exploit their potential. I felt her and the brood communicate. It was all primitive emotion, barely any words at all. There's simply no way she could convey the detail needed to create or destroy worlds. It's a shame no one else can claim the creatures, but whatever jumped-up human her sire found to breed her on, she'll never be more than a mongrel."

Ceallach nodded, the collar that held his neck gleaming. He hesitated. "When you have what you want," he asked carefully, "then will you let me go?"

"Darling!" Joscela cried. "How can you ask me that?"

He gazed pleadingly at her. "I don't feel . . . right. Ever since you put this collar on me, it's like black ice is eating the edges of my spirit. I'm cold, Joscela, and I feel myself slipping. It won't be long before there's no *me* in here."

"We'll fix that," Joscela promised, the set of her features fierce. "As soon as we've wrapped up this inconvenience, I'll feed you all the power you need to recover. We'll make this rabble pay for what they've done to you."

"Joscela." Ceallach covered the hand she'd rested on his shoulder. "If you didn't know in your heart they'd killed me, you wouldn't care about punishing them."

For just a second, tears glimmered in her lavender eyes. "Don't talk like that," she said, blinking them away. "You're not yourself right now. You'll be grateful I saved you later."

The pleading drained from Ceallach's expression—and much of the life as well. "As you wish, my queen. Shall I collect the dragons or will you?"

Cass snapped alert. She wasn't just here to watch. She needed to do something. She could attempt to get back into her body, but what if that sent her astral to sleep as well? Her heart wanted to go to Rick. He had the sword, for one thing, but he wasn't the closest to the most imminent danger.

Nate, she decided, picturing him knocked out on that bale of hay with his arm crooked around the big gun. Rick had mentioned an automatic weapon with electrum ammo might kill faeries.

She was beside the snazzy wolf almost before she realized she'd chosen him as her goal. The dragons woke when she knelt. Evidently, they could see her energy body.

She shushed their chitters and thought quickly.

Because Verdi was the leader, she took his head between her ethereal hands.

"I want you to hide," she said, showing him pictures of what she meant. "You and your brother and sister need to stay out of reach of the bad faeries. I'm going to wake this nice wolf and Rick, and we're going to finish them."

Verdi let out a cheep that sounded like an objection.

"Don't join the fight," she insisted. "I don't want the bad faeries to get angry and hurt you. You three are very important."

She added an urge to hurry. To her relief, the green dragon heeded her. He nudged Scarlet and Auric with his snout, and the trio flapped off—nearly silently—to another stall farther in. The horse they'd joined whuffled and then fell quiet.

Cass gazed at Nate. He was seriously out. He hadn't moved while she chivvied the dragons. Without a body, she couldn't slap him and couldn't yell. Hinges creaked. The outside door to the stables was swinging open. The glittery radiance that shot through the gap warned her the queen was approaching.

Crap, she thought, and then: *Here goes nothing.*

She willed her astral *into* Nate's physical form.

He jerked as if he'd been jolted with a taser. *Wake up!* she thought as loudly as she could.

"Jesus," he muttered, which she perceived both as a sound and a thought inside her mind. "Ergh," he added, so she guessed he didn't like the sensation of her consciousness inside his.

Stay awake, she ordered. *Ceallach is still alive. He and the queen spelled everyone to sleep. Joscela is at the door. Ready your weapon to hold her off. I'm going to wake Rick.*

"Where . . . dragons?" he wondered sleepily.

Ruthless, Cass pumped more energy into him.

Nate's eyes flew open. He sat up straight and grabbed the gun. Acting on reflexes too quick for her to follow, he had it braced on his shoulder with his finger on the trigger.

"Time to take a trip," Joscela cooed halfway between the outer door and the stall. Nate sighted down the thick barrel.

Go, he thought more or less at Cass.

She couldn't afford to stay and see what happened. Nate's gun *seemed* like it could cut through anything, but she knew how powerful the faeries were and how good at recovering from attacks. Nate needed Rick to back him up. She forced her focus to return to the house. Her astral moved sluggishly. She'd given Nate a lot of juice to help him stay awake. She couldn't shift from place to place lightning fast anymore.

Rick, she thought, concentrating harder.

She wished he were there to say a prayer. God help them all if she didn't reach him in time.

~

Something—or someone—nudged at the borders of Rick's awareness. He put up his guards automatically. He was Adam's second, a power in his own right. People weren't allowed to hop into his dreams whenever they wanted to.

"Oh for God's sake," he heard the would-be intruder huff. "I'm not trying to glamour you, only wake you up. The flirt let me do it. Why do you have to be stubborn?"

That was Cass's voice. What was she doing here?

"Rick," she pleaded. "The dragons need your help. No matter what you think of me, try to wake up for them. Wake up for Nate. Your pack mate is defending them all alone."

He was awake. He was listening, wasn't he?

"Damn it." Hands grabbed the sword he'd strapped to his back, two sets of fingers wrapping the electrum hilt. Instinctively, he knew she planned to use it as a magical conduit to him.

Hey, he thought a second before what felt like a bazillion amps of electricity zapped his spinal cord.

"Aughh!" he cried out aloud. He sat up and rubbed his twitching back muscles. Okay, now he really was awake, instead of dreaming that he was. He looked around, but the only other person in the room was Adam, and the alpha was sound asleep. "Cass?"

Here, she said. *I'm on the astral.*

He saw a shimmery shape that resembled her. His heart thumped hard and he lost his breath. "Tell me you're not a ghost."

No, she said. *But I should try to get back into my body. Joscela and Ceallach want to abduct me.*

"Ceallach!" Rick struggled to his feet and swayed.

He's alive. Sort of. You should behead him all the way this time. He spelled everyone in the house to sleep. Please don't let Nate accidentally shoot you. And Joscela was disguised as Jin, but I don't think she looks like her anymore.

Cass's voice sounded funny, even allowing for it being inside his head. Actually, it sounded like she was about to cry. Had he hurt her that badly when he walked out on her earlier? The thought made his throat feel tight. "Cass—"

Go, she urged. *I'll follow as soon as I catch my breath.*

Every muscle he had protested leaving her. Should he tell her to wake Adam, or would that take too long? He didn't like the idea of her physical body being vulnerable, but he didn't like sending her consciousness into the line of fire either.

Make up your mind, he ordered himself.

"Be careful," he told her glowing form.

Then he was off at werewolf speed. He descended a set of stairs in two bounds, his shoulder bumping the wall as his balance recovered from his involuntary nap. A long corridor blurred by, the carpet runner buckling slightly behind his feet.

As he ran, he tried to think with the same swiftness. He wished he knew a way to approach unseen, but the back grounds didn't offer much cover. Whipping out his sword and hoping for the best hardly seemed like a surefire plan.

The *brup-brup-brup* of a submachine gun sounded outside. That was good. Probably. As long as Nate was wielding it. Maybe Rick should have found Carmine and grabbed his firearm. A sword *and* a gun would have improved his odds.

It was too late for that. He'd almost reached the doors to the rear terrace. The gun barked again. Suddenly the air flared bright and made a whumping sound. Rick heard a canine yelp. *Shit.* That was Nate. One of the faeries must have forced him into wolf form. Nate wouldn't like that. The last time that was done to him had been nightmarish.

More motivated than ever, Rick burst into the open with his sword drawn.

Rather than make himself a stationary target, he accelerated and overleaped the three combatants. His eyes had to work fast as he vaulted them. He saw a slender female faerie with Nate crouched snarling on his paws before her, both of them near the stable door. Rick landed and rebounded off the grass, striking the earth again closer to Ceallach.

The electrum neck brace the faerie wore startled him. Even so, he calculated the angle needed to lop off his head beneath it. He swung, all his power behind the long sword's hopefully fatal strike.

Then he saw what Ceallach had in his arms: Cass's body, limp and helpless without her soul in it. Rick had to check his swing, in case the faerie decided to use her as a shield. Ceallach smiled, not as brightly as before but bright enough. His muscles gathered, and he threw Cass at Rick.

This he wasn't expecting. Rick caught her awkwardly with one arm. Her weight made him stumble, and her skull hit the grass. Fortunately, her spirit had jumped back in.

"I'm okay." She pushed upward on unsteady legs, shaking her head to clear sleep from it. "I'll help Nate with the queen."

He had to let her. He couldn't take on both fae himself.

Ceallach saw his dilemma and grinned wider. He drew his sword with a metallic hiss. "The halfling is mincemeat," he promised, "whichever way this goes."

~

Cass was probably lucky she didn't have time to be afraid. Nate was circling

Joscela, hackles lifted and ears laid back. Could wolf's teeth rip off a faerie's head? Nate certainly seemed game to try if given an opening. The queen was on her feet, staggering in her now-holey sundress but still dangerous. Nate had shot her many times. From each bullet wound, light radiated—her pureblood power healing them. If Cass could retrieve the gun, which Nate no longer had hands to shoot, maybe she could weaken her further.

As she scrambled forward to grab it off the lawn, an odd thing happened. At the exact same second, Nate leaped at the queen with a horrible growl. He hadn't looked around, and Cass hadn't tried to reach him mentally. He'd simply intuited what she intended and provided a distraction.

He was behaving as if *she* were his pack member.

Predictably, the queen's magic threw Nate off before he could get to her, smashing him into the stone stable with a nasty crack. As worrisome as that was, Cass now had the chance she needed to squeeze off a line of shots without hitting him. She braced herself for the gun to buck, and got a good hold around the grip. The magazine held a lot of rounds. She pulled the trigger and kept it down, refusing to lose her nerve as Joscela strode through the hail toward her. The royal waved most of the bullets off but not all. Those that didn't come near her head, she simply let hit her. Cass did her best not to waver. She meant to keep shooting until she ran out. This wasn't about killing Joscela. This was about forcing her to use her power for something other than attacking them.

At least it was until Joscela snatched the gun by the barrel and tossed it behind her like a toy. Its strong recoil had knocked Cass onto her butt. Though the queen wasn't big, per se, she stood over Cass like a giantess.

"You *dare*," she said, power gusting from her like wind. "A mongrel like you cannot be my equal. You couldn't get a lowly wolf to love you without glamour."

She put magic behind those words, twisting Cass's worst fear into what felt like truth. But so what if Rick didn't love her? So what if no one did? *She* knew how to love. As long as she did, she'd never give up fighting for what she cared about.

"You're one to talk," she panted. "You're the one who's forcing your lover to serve you against his will."

She'd scored a point with that. Anger glowed in Joscela's lilac eyes.

And then her attention split. Ceallach cried out in pain. Rick must have wounded him. Joscela sent her power to him in an arc like a solar flare. The sending stretched higher than the stables and was intense enough that Nate also perceived it.

He'd limped back from where the queen had thrown him. He looked at Cass, his eyes beast wild and human determined. He jerked his wolf head toward Rick and Ceallach's fight. She thought she understood what he was saying. Ceallach was Joscela's Achilles heel. No amount of electrum ammo could weaken her like him.

Cass had no time for indecision. Joscela and Ceallach were the superior force. Though capable of moving faster than wolves or halflings, they'd grown used to thinking in terms of decades for achieving victories. Split-second actions *could* work against them—if they were the right ones.

Cass sped to Rick so fast she knew she'd called on magic to get her there. He had Ceallach on the ground. The male fae had lost his sword somehow, and the pair was wrestling for control of Rick's. Rick's blade zapped Ceallach with buzzing blue bolts of power, but the fae was ignoring the discomfort. Royals really must have high pain thresholds. Cass reached through their straining arms and took a death grip on his collar.

Doubting she could snap it, she didn't try. She'd honed one particular skill when she lived Outside: drawing power from sources that didn't naturally give it up. She drew Ceallach's energy through the conduit of the neck brace faster than the queen could replenish it, faster in fact than her half human body was designed to absorb it. Ceallach felt her draining him. White began to show around his eyes, his breath panting from him in distress. Rick hadn't allowed himself to react when she appeared at his side. This, however, caused him to glance at her.

"No," Ceallach said, trying to compel her with his glamour.

Cass clenched her jaw and pulled harder. Nate was attacking the queen again, giving Cass precious seconds to build up momentum. Already the stolen power was altering her perceptions. Some sense she hadn't known she had could see in every direction without turning. When Joscela hurled Nate into the stable wall again, Cass threw him power for healing.

As she did, the queen sent more to Ceallach. Cass sucked that up as well. Ceallach moaned, caught in the tug of war. His face resembled a death's head, his skin sinking inward toward his skull. Cass knew this was a terrible thing she did, but as his energy overfilled her, the strongest emotion she experienced was exhilaration. She'd been half a power all her life. Finally, she knew what it meant to be whole.

Her skin started shooting sparks like a pureblood's.

Joscela swore in high fae and tried to attack her and Rick with raw magic.

Cass grabbed that power too before it could harm them.

"Careful," Rick said.

He put his hand over hers where it gripped the collar. Anger rose quick and hot. Who was he to drag her back to smallness? She'd had more than enough of that. Then she saw what his eyes were saying. That he loved her. That he trusted all she needed to return to herself was a single word of caution.

This was a faith she couldn't disappoint. She spun the magic she couldn't hold into a protective bubble around them. Ironically, that gave her room to draw up more.

"Stop!" Joscela screamed, beating the barrier with her fists. The power she continued to try to feed to Ceallach streamed over its surface like water.

"Please," Ceallach gasped, his veins standing out in ropes.

Cass read the struggle in him: that he wasn't certain what he was begging for. He'd stopped fighting Rick, his body splayed helpless beneath the two of them.

"You want to let go," she said, knowing she spoke the truth. "You want to be released."

"I don't . . . want to leave her alone."

"You'll leave her alone if you stay. She can only heal your body. Your spirit will be dead. How will you love her once that happens?"

Ceallach closed tortured eyes, and a single tear rolled out. "Will you kill her?"

Cass wasn't sure how to answer, but Rick squeezed the fae's shoulder. "I'm pretty sure Death isn't the horror immortals fear it is."

Cass felt dangerously lightheaded. "I'm going to finish this," she said, her voice seeming to come from a great distance. "Are you ready?"

Rick nodded. He had the sword, his grip on it prepared. Cass tugged a final spark from Ceallach.

The pureblood exploded in a brilliant white glitter bomb.

Joscela keened. Cass dropped the protective shield. Rick blurred to the queen and swung his sword with a warrior cry.

This time, he gauged the force for decapitating a royal fae correctly. Joscela's head flew free, pale hair whipping as it tumbled. Her skull landed with a thump a number of yards away. She didn't burst into faerie dust like her lover had, though her separate pieces did sparkle where they'd been parted from each other.

Well? Cass thought, abruptly exhausted as the stolen energy drained from her. *Is it over?*

"I've got this," came Nate's weary voice.

He was human again, and he'd retrieved the big black gun. Naked—though somehow still stylish—he braced the stock on his shoulder, sighted down at Joscela's head, and kept depressing the trigger until it too disappeared in a Fourth of July display.

Hearteningly, the queen's headless body flashed out of existence at the same time.

Nate watched the last twinkles wink out among the grass as Rick and Cass moved to stand by him. Nate turned his head to her. "We had to do that. They would have kept coming if we gave them the smallest chance."

"Yes," Rick agreed. "Joscela wouldn't have been satisfied until she'd destroyed the Pocket and everyone in it."

Both men were looking at her. Cass wasn't sure why until she noticed her cheeks were wet. "Oh," she said, touching them. She hadn't known she was crying.

"It's hard to take a life," Rick said. "Even when it's justified."

She met his serious green gaze. The kindness that had always moved her glowed behind it. Was love in there as well? Or had she imagined that in the heat of battle?

Nate patted her back, pulling her attention back to him. "You did well. I'd fight alongside you any day."

She suspected this was high praise. Nate gave Rick a look that seemed to be a warning and began walking toward the house. Abruptly, Cass wasn't sure she wanted to be alone with Rick. Was he going to dash her hopes again?

"Well . . ." he said right before all hell broke loose.

CHAPTER

THIRTEEN

THE dragons must have decided it was safe to come out of hiding. They zoomed squealing from the stables, circling her and Rick so excitedly they were obliged to duck.

"Settle," Cass called, trying to calm them.

She hadn't made much progress when three big men jogged out of the house. The hyped up dragons couldn't resist dive-bombing them playfully. Nate hadn't gotten inside yet. Scarlet landed on his shoulder—her werewolf-crush, Cass guessed—but the boys weren't so easily lured down.

"*Verdi*," she scolded as firmly as she could. "You and Auric come here *now*."

They made one more circle and flew back to her and Rick.

"Wow," Adam said, for it was he, Carmine, and the pilot Johnny who'd trotted out. "They really are something."

Understanding this was a compliment, Verdi stretched up full height on her shoulder, flapped his green wings, and crowed.

"I sense we missed something," Carmine said. He leaned on the gun he'd carried out with him. "The last time I saw Nate he had clothes."

"We killed the bad faeries," his packmate said, his gift for drollness on display. His handsome face split into a grin. "You sleepyheads can go back to bed."

"Where's Jin Levine?" Adam turned his gaze around as if she might appear.

"She wasn't in cahoots with the queen," Rick informed him. "The queen was impersonating her."

This comment took Cass *and* the alpha aback. She hadn't known Jin was suspected of collaborating with the enemy.

"Ah." Adam scratched his cheek awkwardly. "About that . . . I didn't mention that before because I wasn't sure how easily the faeries could read our minds. I figured the fewer of us who knew my strategy, the better chance it had of working."

"Jin *wouldn't*," Cass said. "She's a good person."

"Well, she seemed a little off when she came with Bridie to report you were in trouble. She said the right things. She just didn't feel authentically upset." Adam pursed his mouth in consideration. "I suppose she already wasn't her at that point. We'll need to discover where she's . . . gotten to."

Rick slid his hand around Cass's, which made her feel simultaneously better and worse. If he'd thought there was nothing to worry about, he wouldn't be comforting her.

Her dad limped out then, and the dragons went strangely quiet. Roald stopped at the edge of the stone terrace. His smile was faint and a little wistful as he gazed at each of her brood in turn. She wondered if they could tell he'd been a keeper too. Cass was pretty sure he was remembering T'Fain.

Wherever the dragon's essence still existed—in this world or some other —she had to be glad her species would continue.

"Dad," Cass said. "You're all right."

"Yes," he agreed. "When Ceallach and the queen died, the spell they'd set to trap me unraveled." Something flashed in the grass before him. Brow furrowed, he leaned down to pick it up. Blue fire sizzled around his fingers but at a whispered word, it stopped. He straightened, turned what he held over in his hands, and looked musing. "Ceallach's protector sword. This will need a new owner."

"You could—" Cass stopped, because she wasn't sure he'd welcome the suggestion that came to mind. "You can contact the Dragon Guild now, can't you? The danger has passed, and you're out of hiding. They'll know what to do with it."

"Yes," he said and looked even more thoughtful.

Verdi snuggled against her ear, and she petted him.

Rick's hand tightened around hers. "I smell someone new."

Every wolf there drew at least one weapon.

"Don't shoot," said a tired but familiar voice.

"Jin!" Cass cried.

"Jin?" Bridie asked, having shuffled out to join the others. She must have rolled straight out of bed. She wore her polka dot pajamas and hair rollers.

"It's me," Jin confirmed. "The real me."

Felipe had carried her to the rear of the house, romance hero style. The handsome stable master seemed reluctant to put her down. The last Cass heard, the fake Jin had sent him to the butcher. She realized she never saw him return.

"Felipe found me," Jin said, her head on his broad shoulder.

"Because you were clever enough to escape your captors," her hero praised.

"You were captured?" Bridie said, more than a bit confused.

"By a gang of goblins. I was coming out of Star's Brew with my mocha latte, and they grabbed me right off the street. I screamed like a banshee, but they used a muffling enchantment, and nobody heard a thing. I'm telling you, it was a nightmare!"

Now Bridie looked aghast. "When was this?"

"The morning after Cass's welcome back party. Oh, I am *sick* about that bitch interviewing Talulah Banksworth instead of me. That was a serious get." Miffed at the memory, she patted Felipe's chest. "You can put me down now, sweetheart."

The stable master set her on her Jimmy Choos but kept her at his side. Not seeming to mind this, Jin brushed her short gold locks back from her face. Being her, she'd recently applied makeup. She didn't believe in making an entrance looking less than her best. Nonetheless, Cass could tell she'd been through the wringer. Her short-skirted, ultra-stylish suit was crinkled beyond repairing.

"What happened after they captured you?" she asked.

"Just the most disgusting experience of my life. That faerie . . . the 'queen'"—Jin put this in quote marks—"stuck a spell inside my brain, like one of those horror film creepy crawlies, only made of magic. She chained my mind to hers so she could rifle through it at will and imitate me in front of you. I saw it all but couldn't stop a thing."

Jin shuddered and made a face.

"How did you escape?" Bridie asked, sympathetically horrified.

"What's-her-face started losing her grip when her boyfriend showed up wounded. I watched for my chance and wriggled out of the ropes the goblins tied me up with. Luckily, she'd dismissed Felipe—"

"Because *I* would have seen through her charade," he declared.

Jin smiled indulgently at him, maybe believing him and maybe not. She turned to Adam more seriously. "I got a good look at all my captors. You sit me down with your mug shot files, and I'll do whatever it takes to help you prosecute. First, though, I'm burning everything she wore. I can't believe that bitch had free run of my closet!"

Amused, Cass gave her a long but gentle hug. Bridie joined in a moment later. Neither of them mentioned Jin was shaking.

"I'm so glad you're all right," Cass said.

"Me too," Jin agreed. She laughed dryly. "On the bright side, this is going to make the best *As Luck Would Have It* episode ever."

"Oh my gosh," Bridie gasped, obviously jumping onto the same page. "It totally is!"

Verdi had clung to Cass's head throughout the hug. He cheeped when she backed away from it.

"You are beautiful," Jin praised, which he enjoyed of course. Seeing he'd allow it, she stroked his neck and crop. "How would you and your siblings like to be famous?"

"Uh," Cass said, not sure about that idea.

"It'll be safer," Jin insisted. "You imprinted them, and no one else can claim them, but there's still the future to think about. If the dragons aren't secret, no stupid faerie factions can move against them without the rest noticing."

"That's true," Bridie said. "Just don't call faeries 'stupid' on air."

"Hm," Cass's dad responded, clearly considering the merits of the suggestion.

Auric chittered his two cents from his perch on Rick's shoulder.

"We need to think about this," Rick cautioned. "Don't start planning promo spots."

"Of course not," Jin and Bridie assured him in unison.

Cass hid her smile against Verdi's warm scaled side. Nothing short of Armageddon would keep the cousins from dreaming up promotions.

"Why don't we take this inside?" Adam said, his quiet authority turning all heads to him. "We can notify the rest of the pack, Jin can . . . purge her wardrobe, and then we'll start on identifying the goblins who captured her."

"Rick and I might be able to help with that," Cass said.

When Rick's boss looked at her, he wasn't dazzled like he'd been when he helped her into the helicopter. Though he seemed calm, she sensed a bit of annoyance that he'd missed out on the big fight.

"We, uh, had a run in back at my penthouse with some goblins Joscela hired."

"We were aware of that," he said.

"Don't be a jackass," Nate said. "How does she know what we've been doing since she and Rick took off?"

Adam shot the naked man a cool look, but this simply made Nate grin. "Alphas and their seconds," he observed. "The bromance is beautiful until you add women."

"Now who's a jackass?" Adam said in an eye-rolling undertone.

"Put on some clothes," Carmine threw in. "You're blinding me with your pretty abs."

Rick wasn't alarmed by their exchange. "Ignore them," he said to her.

His hand had found its way into hers again, its reassuring squeeze addictive. She wanted to ask him many things but didn't have the nerve. Right then, fighting evil faeries seemed like a piece of cake compared to romance.

~

Adam set up a temporary cop-shop in the ground level sunroom that overlooked the back of the estate. He took Cass's formal statement while Carmine questioned Rick. The pack leader was thorough but didn't badger her. Cass found herself gradually relaxing around him.

He didn't really disapprove of her; he was just being cautious about the woman his beta had hooked up with.

"This is good," he finally said. "The Founders Board may have some questions about how and why Queen Joscela died, but I think we'll be able to keep them away from you."

Cass appreciated that. Though reputedly pro-Pocket, the group of faeries responsible for overseeing Resurrection was an intimidating bunch. She'd just as soon they didn't cross-examine her.

"Thank you," she said as she rose. "If you need anything else, I'll be outside talking to my dad."

"I'd like to interview him too," the alpha said.

Cass smiled for the first time since sitting down with him. How much actual authority Resurrection's police had over purebloods could be tricky.

"I'll pass your request along," she said dryly.

The weather outside was bright and crisp. Here and there, wispy clouds brushed the rich blue sky. Cass's father sat on the coping at the edge of the reflecting pool, watching the dragons devour a lunch of raw hamburger.

Cass lowered herself beside him with their sides touching. "They're not traumatized," she observed.

"No," he agreed. He glanced cautiously at her. "You have questions."

"Just one really." His injuries had healed, and he was back to his normal solemnly handsome state. Something was different about him—or maybe the difference lay in her.

Despite him having much more power, she felt closer to being his equal.

"You enchanted Mom to fall in love with you," she said.

The topic didn't surprise him. He let out a resigned sigh. "Yes. I searched long and hard to find the right human to bear my child, someone who could hatch the dragons but not abuse their power. I was wrong to do this without Irene's permission. I stole many years from the path she would have chosen for herself."

"And you'd do it again," Cass said.

"In a heartbeat." He leaned forward, his forearms resting on his knees. "There was only one thing I didn't plan on, one thing that made my actions difficult."

The sun twinkled off his perfect features as his emotion rose. The charm that normally damped his sparkle wasn't so firmly in place right then.

"What didn't you plan on?" she asked.

"To love you. As much as I ever loved T'Fain. You, my daughter, became so precious I sometimes thought my heart would break for putting you in danger."

"I love you too, Dad."

"You . . . forgive me?"

She could give him a complicated answer, but she knew the humble question hadn't come easily for him. "I do," she said simply.

How could she not when he'd withstood torture to protect her?

He straightened on his seat. The dragons had finished eating, and had flopped down for a snooze on the sunny grass. Verdi's head was draped over Auric's side. He opened one eye to check that she was there. Satisfied, he closed it again.

"You could have a real life now that you're done hiding," Cass suggested. "You know, do what Mom did: find someone to be with who you genuinely like."

"Daughter," her father said repressively. "I'm too old for romance."

The pucker that dented the center of his brow told a different story. He was lying . . . and Cass could guess about whom.

~

Rick expected it would be some time before he and Cass got to talk alone, and he wasn't mistaken. Adam, understandably, wanted to go over everything with everyone. The pack leader was good at compiling a full picture of a case, seeing the different angles, making sure all the *T*'s were crossed.

Everyone was tired by the time he was satisfied, including Cass's brood. They'd enjoyed being fussed over by new people, but as that novelty wore off, they retreated into a huddle on his and Cass's familiar laps.

A number the pack's significant others joined them at the Levine estate, and that took up time as well. Rick's longing for his own bed and his own shower was powerful. Wanting Cass with him made the longing more difficult.

Whether she'd want to come seemed troublingly uncertain.

As morning wore into afternoon, Cass's friend Bridie snuck over to the couch where they were holed up.

"You two look bushed," she said, crouching in front of Cass. Like everyone, she couldn't resist petting the dragons. "Do you want to borrow my car and get out of here?"

Cass turned to see what he thought. What he found in her dreamy blue eyes was both mysterious and moving. His memory of them blazing like a conqueror's while she drained Ceallach was hard to square with how she seemed now.

"We could go to my place," he said unsurely.

"With the dragons?"

"Of course. Grant is probably there. He's a good watchdog."

"Grant?"

"He's a gargoyle. He has nesting rights on our building's roof. I don't expect there's more danger, but he'll keep an eye out regardless."

She smiled, her face so beautiful he ached. "You have gargoyles as friends."

"We do," he said, extra glad of it then.

"Yes," she said. "I'd love to go to your place."

~

The dragons liked riding in Bridie's car but not being restricted to the back seat. Convincing them not to scramble up front took some sternness on both Rick and Cass's parts. Introducing them to Grant on his roof perch atop the brownstone was another surprise for them. The gargoyle was as big as a minivan, with a goblin's head, a lion's body, and bat wings. Only his golden eyes had color; otherwise he resembled stone—especially when he didn't move. His size brought out the dragons' shyness, though this new magical creature who could fly like they did fascinated them. Cass was fascinated too. Rick concluded she'd never met one of Grant's race up close.

"Friend of Rick," Grant said in his rumbling voice. "Thank you for allow me meet dragons. Them very healthy and beautiful."

"Thank you," she said. "I . . . I'm honored you think so."

Grant winked at Rick as they left. His Pidgin English was a put-on, useful for maintaining the stereotype that gargoyles weren't very bright. His goblin mouth moved in a silent comment that looked like *hubba-hubba*.

Somewhat to Rick's amazement, Tony had straightened up his place. The dishes were washed, his bed was made up with fresh sheets, and clean towels hung in both bathrooms. Considering Tony's aversion to housework, this was a miracle.

It seemed a lifetime since he'd been home.

"We could put these guys in the guest room," he said. Scarlet was sleeping on Cass's arm while the boys swiveled their heads around from the floor. Having three dragons in his apartment was surreal.

"How does that sound?" Cass asked them. Auric craned up at her and yawned.

Thankfully, they weren't hard to settle. Of course, once they were tucked together on a heap of blankets, nothing remained to delay the discussion he and Cass were overdue to have.

Almost nothing anyway.

Leaving a crack so they wouldn't wake up afraid, Rick shut the door on the sleeping brood. "Would you like to use the shower in my bathroom? It's bigger than the one for guests."

"Rick," she said. "You know we didn't drive to your place so I could shower."

He walked ahead of her into his room, setting the sword beside the door. His neatly made bed seemed to accuse him of something—stupidity, maybe. Feeling her waiting, he laced his hands behind his neck in frustration.

"I trust you," he said, the words that seemed most important coming out.

"You're not power-mad or you wouldn't have leveled down Ceallach's energy when I warned you to."

"My father enchanted my mother to fall in love with him."

He turned, not having expected that response. Her expression twisted ruefully.

"He confirmed it today, but I think maybe I always suspected. Kids aren't stupid and I—" She blew out her breath. "Even when I was little, I had a phobia about making people like me against their will. The more times a faerie glamours a child, the bigger chance they have of getting faerie-struck. Even when they're not spelled, the child can get caught up in trying to please whoever affected them. It won't harm them physically, but it's not healthy—and they don't get over it as quickly as adults."

"So when you were a kid . . ."

"I had to be careful not to dust my friends too much."

Rick remembered her reputation for being standoffish; Snow White implied cold as well as beautiful. He'd never believed the slur, but there were those who had. "Why are you telling me this?"

"I want you to understand I know what I did was wrong. I shouldn't have threatened to compel you. I should have found another way."

He hesitated, then gave in and asked. Right now, knowing the truth mattered more than politeness. "Why didn't you?"

"I think because I believed it had already happened. The dragons whammied us to want to stay in the cave with them, to want to be closer to each other."

She thought he didn't really love her? The idea stole his breath for a few seconds. "Cass, we threw that off."

"Did we?"

"*Yes*. Cass, I fell for you before the dragons existed, before the dying faerie gave me the magic cuff, before it led me back to you. Look, if I were enchanted, could I hurt you the way I did? Could I even take offense at you threatening to compel me?"

"I suppose not," she said slowly.

He took her shoulders in his hands, not knowing whether to shake her or laugh. "This is *real*, Cass. It's too awkward not to be."

"So, um, does this mean you've decided you can live with it? You said you had to decide if you could live with me being able to compel you when you walked out at Jin and Bridie's house. I mean, I can't have a power-ectomy. My magic is always going to be there."

He stroked her arms with his thumbs. "I can live with it."

"You're sure? Because—"

"Cass."

She fell silent and looked at him worriedly. He smiled. She'd proven a point he should have realized already.

"We have power over each other. Probably any two people who care about each other do."

"Who care about each other . . ."

"Who love each other," he clarified. "Part of you *is* the person who exulted in stealing Ceallach's power." She flinched, but he went on. "Part of me exults in my wolf's—in being stronger and faster; even in being deadly, if that's required. That's only a portion of who we are, not the whole. I promise you, I love you as you are, Cass: magic and all."

The recognition lifted a weight off him. He wasn't power-mad any more than she was. He loved her for all the qualities that were inside her, and because she called the most loving part of him to his surface. She made him bigger than he was without her.

In more ways than one of course. His cock was eager to prove its devotion.

Happily, she rose on tiptoes for a kiss. Her tongue teased his lips and slid between them. His grip tightened on her shoulders. He wanted to tug her close and claim her, but her mood was lighter. He ordered his hands to relax as she dropped her feet back onto the floor. Her blue eyes glowed mesmerizingly into his, her thick lashes dark as ink.

The connection between them steadied and excited him.

"I love you so much," she marveled. "I hardly know what to do with my feelings."

This was an opening no red-blooded male could resist. "Tony put fresh sheets on my bed," he said, a smile playing at his lips.

"Should I be embarrassed?"

She was smiling too. Rick chafed her warm shoulders. "More like amazed. I just thought if you needed a suggestion for what to do with your feelings . . ."

"Ah." Her hands slipped up his chest and down, fingers splayed, thumbs caressing his pectoral muscles and causing them to hum. "You're thinking no clean sheet ought to go unmussed."

Her touch bumped over his waistband and closed over his bulging crotch. Rick stopped thinking altogether as she squeezed the pounding there. She must have known how much he ached to have her hands on him. She kneaded every part of his covered erection that her fingers could stretch to. Delicious sensations poured through him, longings that multiplied for everything she did. She made a comment he couldn't decipher.

"Huh?" he said, not wanting to miss something important.

She laughed, soft and delighted. "Sometimes you are too easy, wolf."

"Too easy? Are you saying you want me to play hard to get?"

She pushed his chest, and he sat on the mattress edge. Her slender legs fit between his gapped thighs. Holding her with his knees, he slowly unzipped the buttercup yellow hoodie her friend Bridie had loaned her. "You half-and-halfers seem to buy your not-really-for-sweating clothes at the same store."

She laughed. "We buy them at Maycees. And I promise not to tell you how much they cost."

"Good." The satiny inner curves of her breasts appeared between the halves of the lowering zipper. Bridie, bless her, hadn't loaned Cass a bra.

Rick nuzzled his head inside to close his mouth around one sleek nipple. "Mm," he said, loving how the peak tightened for his sucking lips and tongue, how her breath caught in her throat, and her whole body squirmed. He held her waist, his knees and hands securing her.

"Rick," she gasped as he switched to the other breast.

He treated the second nipple like the first and then drew back from her. "What do you want?" he asked, the offer rising from deep within his soul. "Name anything at all, and I'll try to give it to you."

Her lush red lips fell open and she blinked at him in surprise. Suddenly, she blushed, her cheeks going as pink as her nick-namesake's.

"Well, there's an answer," he chuckled.

She blushed harder and stammered unintelligibly.

"Spit it out," he teased, kissing the knuckles of her hands in turn. "Trust me, whatever you're thinking, I've had pervier fantasies."

"Could I . . ." She swallowed and tried again. "Could I use your handcuffs on you?"

His face split into a grin. He wouldn't have guessed she was a closet badge bunny. "You want to use them on me."

"Yes. I know you like to—"

"—control you?"

"Yes, but just this once, I'd like to . . . have you at my mercy."

Her cheeks were scarlet. He couldn't resist yanking her chain a bit. "Just this once? What if you really like it and want a repeat performance?"

"Oh shut up," she said, shoving at his chest.

This time, he ignored the push and kissed her—deeply, hungrily, claiming her as he'd wanted to from the first. When he released her, she was pleasingly out of breath.

"Stay here," he said. "I have to grab a pair from my weapons closet."

She watched him go with big eyes, sitting on her heels in the center of his bed, looking like she didn't believe he was actually doing it.

He returned from the hall with a set and a key, which he set on his slightly wobbly bedside table from the thrift store.

Cass wasn't paying attention to the differences in their furnishings. "Those are real handcuffs."

"I don't have fakes."

"So . . . no one has locked you up before?"

Her breathlessness entertained him. "No."

She rolled her pretty lips together. "You won't hurt yourself? You know, tugging at them?"

Rick let his smile win free. "I don't know, Cass. Will you make me?"

She shook her head and muttered, then patted the covers. "Come up here. I want to attach your hand to the head rail. Wait—"

He stopped mid-motion and looked at her.

"Please take off your clothes first."

He set down the cuffs to do it. Cass snatched them up and held them against her breasts.

"I'm not going to change my mind," he said as his arms came free of his shirt.

She smiled like the Mona Lisa and gestured for him to continue. He was a bit self-conscious with her watching, though—as a rule—wolves weren't uptight about nakedness.

Self-conscious or not, his cock pressed hard against his jeans. Cass didn't look away as he unzipped.

"I like your body better than your pack mate's," she said consideringly.

Rick was pushing down his jeans. Disconcerted, he hesitated for a second. "You mean Nate's? You checked him out?"

She bit her lip and grinned. "Your muscles are more substantial, and you're a bit hairier. You make me shivery when I look at you naked."

He was glad of that. She made him shiver too. So erect he was throbbing, he stepped out of his pile of clothes. He climbed onto the bed, intending to kiss her. Before he could, she backed out of reach.

"Right hand or left?" she asked.

He didn't know if she was purposefully keeping him off balance. "Left."

He had a simple cottage-style iron bed—secondhand rather than antique. He liked it for its hominess, and because it was sturdy. Cass snapped the first of the handcuff's bracelets shut on a rail.

"Did I do that right?" she asked.

He checked. "Yes," he said, his voice gone slightly hoarse.

Hearing the reaction, a glow flared behind her eyes. "Lie on your back, please."

He shifted into position and lifted his left hand. Cass had to lean across his chest to squeeze the restraint closed around his wrist. He'd have made it snugger for a perp, but it would hold him.

She didn't let go immediately, running her thumb across the sensitive skin just beneath the metal. Her lovely breasts dangled inside her unzipped top. A longing to maraud all her treasures momentarily dizzied him.

"This is electrum," she said, tapping the bracelet.

"Plated," he said in the same roughened tone as before. "Even with my shifter strength, it wouldn't be easy for me to break."

"You can reach the key?"

He glanced to where it lay on his bedside table. "Yes."

"Are you comfortable?"

His cock was as stiff as one of the bed's iron bars, his lungs refused to fill completely, and his spine had tensed on the verge of writhing helplessly with lust. He hadn't expected this to be so exciting. He thought he'd do it as a treat for her.

Because her cheeks were pink and her nipples sharp, he didn't try to pretend she hadn't affected him.

"Everything considered," he said wryly, "I'm comfy."

She smiled, leaning down to kiss his lips with butterfly softness. "You're almost perfect."

She slipped off the bed to remove her clothes, leaving him to wonder what actual perfection would require. Okay, mostly he watched her strip her gorgeous body bare, but the wondering was there somewhere.

"May I look inside your closet?" she asked politely once every stitch was gone.

He blinked, his attention having been directed toward other things. "Sure. It's that door there."

She opened it and lifted two of his three neckties from the hanger inside the door. He wore the things for court appearances. He gathered Cass had a different use for them.

Jesus, he thought, a muscle in one thigh jumping involuntarily.

"You seem to be enjoying this," she explained. "I thought I'd fasten your feet to the bed as well."

"My feet?"

She nodded. "I know you could rip these, but I'd like to spread your legs apart."

The muscle in his thigh wasn't the only thing that jumped. His cock did too, the sudden coolness at its tip telling him it had started leaking with arousal. Cass had sharp eyes. Her face flushed at his reaction.

He imagined his cheeks were similarly dark.

"I'll just, um, get these on you now," she said.

She shifted his legs apart. The care she took was weirdly arousing—considering how not fragile he was. His height insured the foot rail was close. The silk ties were smooth where they wrapped his ankles, as comfortable as the cuff was hard on his arm. Rick tested each of his legs for play. He could move, but she'd knotted the bonds securely. Air tickled his exposed ball sac and inner thighs.

She didn't ask if he liked what she'd done. A blind woman would have known he did. His breathing harshened as she climbed up between his bound legs. She pushed her fingertips up his thighs, over his hipbones and torso, and finally onto the underside of his arms. Tingles jumped from nerve to nerve, linking his touch receptors into a single erogenous net.

She bowed toward his mouth. "Now you're perfect."

The kiss she dropped on his lips was light. She pressed another to his jaw and continued down his throat. His right hand was free. Wanting to touch her, he curved it behind her head and stroked.

Her gaze rose to his, but she didn't tell him to stop. She moved lower, her hands on his ribcage to steady her. Her teasing mouth found his right nipple.

"Cass," he gasped as she sucked it.

She didn't interrupt herself to respond. Her wavy hair whispered over him soft as silk. His toes curled at the combination of delights, reminding him that his feet were tied. That did strange things to him. His back arched, his buttocks tightening on the covers. Cass smoothed her hands down to them.

"Hold onto your control," she said, her warm breath fanning his cockhead.

The order made him long to let go, but he did as she asked. He shifted his body higher, using the handcuff to lift his weight. He guessed what was coming and didn't want to miss seeing her give him head. Despite expecting it, the first touch of her lips on his tip shocked through him deliciously. Her mouth surrounded the crest, pushing down the shaft with her tongue rubbing. A moan broke inside his throat. Cass wrapped one fist around his base and squeezed tightly.

She seemed to know exactly how much compression he could stand.

"God," he breathed, thrusting his pelvis up.

She sucked him above her hold—wetly, strongly, but not so fast that he went over. Fearing how much he wanted to urge her farther downward, he removed his hand from her hair. He gripped the covers in his fist instead, writhing and twisting with bliss at what she did.

When his gasps came closer together, she pulled her mouth from him. His cock felt immense, held straight up in her fist. Her thumb rubbed the underridge.

"So pretty," she murmured.

Noting his enraptured gaze on her, she made a show of licking him—tongue flat, dragging the pressure from her enfolding fingers, up his raphe, and onto his pulsing head. There she pointed her tongue, tickling it over and over the welling slit.

Watching her, feeling her, was more than he could take.

"Cass," he said. "Please."

Her grip left his base. This was the one word she couldn't say without flipping his switches. Grinning in recognition that their roles were reversed, she stretched up him with a catlike roll. The satiny skin of her belly rubbed up his throbbing length. He wanted more, but he couldn't help enjoying that. His groan betrayed him, and Cass did the full body roll again, this time strafing him with her breasts as well.

"Like that?" she teased, obviously guessing he couldn't speak.

The next time she undulated, he caught the back of her neck. One-handed, he held her prisoner for a long deep kiss.

Her body responded. Even with him cuffed and tied at her request, she loved him dominating her. Her shoulders quivered, and her weight went softer on top of him.

"Stay," he ordered against her lips.

Testing to see if she would, he relaxed his hold on her neck. Her lashes lifted, her burning blue gaze locking onto his. He slid his right hand down her spine to the dip just above her buttocks and over those tempting mounds. He squeezed the taut rounded flesh, traced its curves with his fingers, then gripped it hard again.

Cass wriggled and breathed harder. *Who's easy now?* he thought.

Smiling, he lifted his hand from her, paused . . . and brought it back for a stinging smack.

"Rick!" she exclaimed. She rubbed her bottom but didn't seem angry.

"Now we're even," he said, grinning.

Cass's eyebrows went up. "You think so, do you?"

Rick had a feeling he was in trouble now.

~

Cass had briefly forgotten what she intended to do to him. The spank reminded her. She backed out of reach, sitting on her haunches facing him. She was pleased to discover his ankles remained secure.

If he hadn't broken free, he still accepted her command.

"Let's see if you're ticklish," she suggested.

"I'm not," he said.

She took one foot in each hand anyway. "Sure?" She worked her thumbs into his arches. Pleasure flickered across his face, and his hips shifted restlessly.

"Pretty sure," he answered a bit thickly.

Cass smiled and shot a small burst of faerie dust directly up his soles. She felt very daring doing this on purpose, but she guessed he truly did trust her. He groaned, his torso twisting as his cock jerked. His stomach muscles gleamed with increased sweat.

"Cass." He'd screwed his eyes shut for the jolt of erotic sensations. When his eyelids opened, his hot green gaze was blurred. "Come up here and fuck me."

The growled instruction was difficult to resist, given how much she loved being controlled by him in bed.

"Soon," she promised.

Her fingers raked up his impressive legs. If he wanted to force the issue, he could. Since he didn't, he must like her tormenting him. She caressed his kneecaps, shooting a few sparklers into the nerves there. His feet kicked as she triggered his reflexes.

The fire in his eyes burned brighter. "Cass," he said warningly.

Her explorations reached his thighs.

"You have good legs." She dragged her nails over and around the thick muscles, ruffling his brown hair. "I'd be remiss if I neglected them."

"*Remiss*," he repeated, shaking his head at her.

"Playing simple wolf again?"

She cupped his balls gently enough that he sighed with pleasure.

"Don't dust me there," he said as he squirmed for her caresses. "That spot is too tender."

She leaned forward to drag her lips over his breastbone.

She knew the moment he realized he could hold her. His right hand released its clutch on the bed covers. His gaze probed hers as he placed it on her waist. He rubbed her there, a sweet reassurance that trumped any game they might play.

"I love you," she said.

"I'll never stop loving you," he swore.

Emotion gleamed in his eyes, but he didn't look away. Neither did she. His soul was naked to her—good and brave and calling the same from her.

She swung her legs over his, her knees now planted outside his hips. His cock extended up his stomach, pounding with excitement. She tipped it toward her, stroking, tugging, drawing out the suspense the few seconds more she could bear.

His fingers dug into her waist, his cuffed hand curling around the iron bar next to it. She didn't ask if he was ready. She knew he was.

She pressed his glans to her gate and sank.

His breath rushed out, her pussy's wetness and heat making the inward glide silky. He lifted his hips to complete it and let out a throaty growl.

The sound was as satisfying as the stretch of him inside her.

"Shall I fuck you now?" she whispered.

His eyes flared hotly. "Maybe I'll fuck you."

He did it before she could argue, with just one hand and the amazing strength of his bound body. Cass gasped for air as his hips shoved up to and dropped from her. His control of his movements wasn't lessened in any way. He targeted her pleasure spots just as brilliantly as before—with his cock, with his fingers, with his mouth on her breasts and throat when she bent close enough. She rode him, but he was the one in charge.

Utterly unable to mind, she came moaning into his corded neck. Each flutter of her inner muscles around his thickness was sumptuous. As the delectable spasm eased, she realized he hadn't come with her.

His cock was diamond hard in her.

"Fuck," he breathed like this was killing him. He yanked his right leg, and she heard a snap—one of the neckties ripping. This allowed him to roll them onto their sides. Their groins were still locked together. He wasn't going to let them part. With that goal clear, his free hand clamped her bottom, his free leg urging hers higher. His burning green eyes searched hers.

She thought she knew what they were asking. As good and caring a man as he was, his wild side needed satisfaction too.

"Yes," she said. "Give me everything you've got."

He kissed her, filled his lungs, and let his inner wolf gallop free.

The result was fast and hard and totally breathtaking. Every thrust was powerful, every grunt an aphrodisiac for her ears. He let himself enjoy her, let himself speed into her and pump without worrying she'd be overwhelmed.

She was overwhelmed of course, but only with excitement.

"Again," he urged. "Come with me this time."

She clutched his back, fingers slipping in the sweat that mantled his big shoulders. The rhythmic pounding of his hips was so wonderful she had to help it along. His lengthened teeth nipped her shoulder as her pelvis swung to his more strongly.

"Cass," he groaned. "God."

Her sensations rose toward another peak, muscles tightening all over her body. She wanted to smash them together into one being and one climax. The gland at the base of his cock jumped a size bigger, throbbing so violently she could only imagine how hard a time he had holding back climax. His claws slid out to dent her bottom, which she couldn't help but find thrilling. Her spine arched, her neck stretching with longing . . .

Rick's chest rumbled a wordless plea. She knew he wanted to come. He drove into her so deeply she seemed to feel it in her throat. *God, yes,* she tried to say. Maybe he heard somehow. Their orgasms broke together, long hot bolts of pleasure seizing their neural pathways until they blazed like the sun. Cass dusted him as her sheath contracted. She didn't have the control not to. Feeling it, Rick groaned louder, shooting so copiously his seed spilled out. She heard the creaking moan of metal put under stress.

She thought nothing for a long time.

Eventually her mind recovered, as did her pleasurably sore body. Her cheek lay on his chest, where his heart still raced and his breath still sawed in and out. Curious as to what had made the noise she heard, she looked up. She bit her lip to stifle a snicker.

"What?" he mumbled.

"You pulled your bed out of shape."

"Mm?"

"When you were coming. You bent one of the iron bars."

He craned his head to see and swore.

"I like it," she said, smiling against his skin. "You should leave it that way —as my personal badge of honor."

"*Your* personal badge . . ."

"Aren't I the fabulous lover who inspired it?"

He gave in and chuckled. "Tony is going to tease me if he sees that."

"All right," she said. "We'll just leave it a little while."

He hummed a vague response, probably already planning how to hammer out the bend.

"I could get an iron bed for my place," she mused. "Or maybe titanium."

He reached over her, found the key for the cuffs, and unlocked them. He sat then, rubbing his slightly reddened wrist as he looked down at her with his brow furrowed.

"Have I alarmed you?" she asked.

"No," he said, drawing the word out like he wasn't sure. "I was . . . Are you suggesting we move in together?"

"Should I not suggest that?" She wasn't afraid to ask. She had an inkling what he was working through. He was a proud man, and the Maycee money was an issue.

"Your place is larger," he conceded.

"It is."

"And we won't want to be apart too much."

"No," she agreed, beginning to be amused. "We'd probably go crazy if we weren't having sex regularly. Plus, the dragons would have that big rooftop to run around."

"You're laughing at me," he accused.

She kissed the hairy thigh that was nearest her.

"Okay," he said. "I accept your invitation, but you don't get to ask me to marry you."

Her heart gave a lovely swoop. He *could* jump ahead of her when he wanted to. "I don't?" she asked.

He shook his head decisively. "I want to be sure you're ready. It's not just me you'll have to adjust to. It's my family and my pack and the whole shebang. Even if I'm careful, your life won't be the nice civilized existence you're used to."

Cass wriggled up and hugged him. "Civilization is overrated."

His arm came companionably around her. "We'll see if you say that a month from now."

As luck would have it, he didn't sound worried.

CHAPTER FOURTEEN

CASS and Rick threw their engagement party on a clear night in January. Actually, their friends threw it, though the venue for the celebration was Cass's roof.

Cass's dad spun a wonderful warming spell for the terrace. The enchantment turned the winter cold to summer, allowing the kids—and a few of the adults—to run around in swimsuits. The air smelled like flowers that grew in heaven, except near the barbecue. That smelled heavenly in a different way, thanks to Rick's brother-in-law Johnny and a mountain of charring meat. Nate's wife Evina brought her all-male firefighting crew to help consume the feast. The universally imposing weretigers mixed drinks behind the bar . . . in between causing female hearts to flutter.

Rounding out the entertainment, Jin and Bridie hired a jazz quartet. Rick's *really* nice parents were close-dancing with each other, looking more like newly minted sweethearts than folks who'd been married half a century. Every so often, Cass's friend Rhona would look over at them and smile. Her adopted son Pip was doing a bouncy baby dance standing on her lap. Cass's dad sat beside them with his legs stretched out and his ankles crossed. The attempt was valiant, but he wasn't quite pulling off casualness. Now that he didn't have to worry about embroiling Rhona and Pip in danger, he'd agreed to serve as the werefox boy's faerie godfather. According to him, that was all the arrangement was: not romance or dating or the ultra-respectful courtship it coincidentally resembled.

Cass was pretty sure no one who'd seen them together believed a word of it.

"I so should have seen that coming," Jin declared at Cass's shoulder. "Rhona was always saying how nice your dad was, and how she couldn't understand why your mom divorced him."

"They're adorable," Bridie chimed from Cass's other side. "And who cares about the thousand-year age difference? Your dad's a pureblood. It's not like he's going to get wrinkly. Plus, hanging with him will keep her young. Faerie dust is rejuvenating."

"That's a practical attitude," Cass observed, amused as ever by the cousins.

"Whenever possible, love *should* make sense," Bridie said. She handed Cass one of the mango martinis she'd carried from the bar. "These are dee-licious, by the way."

"So is that big weretiger," Cass teased. "I saw you both batting your eyes at him."

"Mm," Jin agreed. She took a contemplative sip of her sunset-colored drink. "If I thought he was interested, I'd let him give Felipe some competition."

"You're always talking like that," Bridie said. "And still Felipe's your number one."

"What can I say?" Jin tossed her glamorous short gold hair, striped with blue tonight to match her miniscule swimwear. "I'm faithful by default."

Cass caught sight of Rick over by the pool, lifting one hand to get her attention. He looked completely scrumptious in his worn jeans and polo shirt.

"Love calls," Bridie said, spying him as well. She kissed one of Cass's cheeks while Jin bussed the other. "Congratulations, sweetie. This is a great party."

It was a great party—a different crowd from one of her gran's but similarly convivial. Cass crossed the grass toward her inamorata, neatly sidestepping squealing kids and almost as ebullient adults. She didn't know everyone, but the general vibe of the gathering was easy to be around. She felt like she belonged, maybe a funny thing to say since this was her house. Funny or not, she enjoyed the sensation. All around her, people smiled and wished her well. They knew who she was, and all of them liked and respected Rick. That was nice to witness. Her fiancé had a humble streak, but he definitely deserved to be esteemed.

She kissed his cheek when she reached him, noting Poly the cat was draped over his shoulder. Poly wasn't asleep, just watching the exciting activity from the safest perch she knew. Rick's protector sword was back to a cuff that gleamed on his strong forearm. To their relief, it hadn't magically chained him to her side since they'd killed Ceallach and the queen. Humorously enough, Nate's son Rafi had helped Rick develop the mental discipline he needed to put the mystical object through its various phases on demand. The six-year-old's encyclopedic knowledge of every episode of *Mini-Dragons to the Rescue* had proved invaluable.

"What's up?" Cass asked, enjoying the glow that lit Rick's eyes as he regarded her in her bikini and sheer cover-up.

Her swimsuit wasn't as small as Jin's, but apparently it was small enough. Rick lifted one brow and smiled wolfishly.

"Grant the gargoyle wants to know if he can take the dragons on a short flight a little later. He thinks they'll be less wound up if they stretch their wings."

Wound up was putting it kindly. Good-natured though they were, the brood was completely hyper from the attention they were getting—not only tonight but also as a result of making their existence known. Cass had reluctantly brought them on Jin and Bridie's show, the ratings for which had been stratospheric. School trips had followed, a ribbon cutting for a new park, and a special invitation to meet the mayor. Considering her babies had grown as big as Saint Bernards in the last few months, anything that expended their excess energy was welcome.

Cass squinted across the roof at Verdi. As if all four of his legs had springs, the green dragon hopped around to the music provided by the band. Always the flirt, Scarlet posed like a sphinx at the bassist's feet, bobbing her head in time. Cass looked around for gold wings, spotting them a short ways off from the other siblings. The final dragon's situation was a wee bit concerning.

She nudged Rick's elbow with her own. "Is that your nephew trying to ride Auric like a horse?"

"Hm," he said. "It certainly looks like him."

"Ethan!" Rick's sister Maria cried, dashing toward the boy and his would-be steed. "I told you not to do that!"

"Ethan makes raising dragons look relaxing," Rick commented.

Cass turned to smile at him. The world went away as their gazes locked. God, she was a lucky woman. "I'm so glad you asked me to marry you. Think how boring my life would be without all this."

Rick's grin broadened. "Shall I tell Grant *yes* then?"

"*Yes* and *thank you*. I always feel safe when the brood is with him."

Rick kissed her on the mouth, slipping her his tongue for a few wet, steamy seconds before he pulled away. He stroked the side of her face tenderly. Then he handed her Poly.

"Think of me while I'm gone," he said.

He knew she would. Living together hadn't been without hurdles, but they'd grown surer of each other. Their love would last. Cass felt it in her bones.

Poly perked up suddenly on her shoulder, letting out an interested *meow*. Rick's brother Tony had just climbed dripping up the pool's ladder.

"Hey, cat," he said, giving a Poly a damp scratch between her uplifted ears. Ever since he'd rescued her from the cave, Poly had been fond of him. Not satisfied with a scratch, she jumped down to nose at his ankles.

"Hey, Tony," Cass said, affection and pleasure spreading out from her breast. Tony made getting used to Rick's family easy. Rick loved her, so Tony did as well. It was as simple and as miraculous as that. "You having a good time tonight?"

Tony's grin was very like his brother's. "Better than usual."

"Ooh. *Better* than usual. You know that piques my curiosity."

He squeezed her shoulder and kissed her cheek. "Don't want to jinx it," he said. "Interrogate me again later."

He sambaed off toward the band, his body also like Rick's but more graceful. Cass smiled at the extra wiggle he gave his butt. He looked awfully cute in his snug red swim shorts. Rick wasn't enough of an exhibitionist for either of those things.

Rick had other charms of course—as the new iron bed in the new master suite could attest. Her girlhood room was history. She and Rick had chosen a new space to make their own. Cass's lips curved smugly. They'd given their big bed quite the workout since it arrived from the furnishings department. Rick had proposed to her in it, which made it extra dear to her.

Her fingers strayed to the ring he'd given her. The design was vintage, the setting sparkly with sapphires and diamonds. He'd confessed his sister had helped him pick it out. Apparently, he'd been anxious that Cass like it and hadn't trusted his own judgment. Cass had found his nervousness endearing, along with him buying it at Maycees—keeping it in the family, as he'd put it.

Her eyes welled up with emotion, realizing how much her gran would have enjoyed him.

This is good, she thought through the poignancy. This was everything her grandmother would have wished for her and more.

The softest sound caught her attention, an inquiring dragon chirp cutting through the laughter and splashing and jazz music. When she turned, she discovered all three of her babies gazing at her.

I'm well, she thought to them, hands crossed over her heart to send them love. *Just being sentimental. Go back to having fun.*

To her surprise, they didn't. Verdi's silver eyes narrowed, and he jerked his head meaningfully. *Look behind you,* his unusually serious expression seemed to say.

Cass looked.

A line of silent pureblood faeries, nine in all, stood like statues behind the French doors that led out of her penthouse. Some were men and some women, and all of them wore long robes. The different shades of silk gleamed with embroidery stitched in electrum thread. Cass had no doubt the patterns held powerful spells. She could feel the magic the group emanated as if the air around them were boiling.

Her breath lodged in her throat, a lump of instinctive fear she couldn't quite swallow. What could she do if they caused trouble? What could anyone?

No, she thought. That's how purebloods like Joscela wanted her to view herself—a helpless halfling doomed to defeat. But she wasn't doomed. Between Joscela and her and Ceallach, Cass was the one standing.

The music—indeed, the entire party—fell silent. Cass reminded herself she'd been expecting this. Once they let the dragons out of the bag, so to speak, some Old Country authority was bound to show up. She relaxed her shoulders and the rest of her body too. From the corner of her eye, she saw wolves and tigers cross their arms, universal body language for *what are you doing on our turf?*

Cass's father took up a similar pose, moving between the new arrivals and Rhona and her son.

Cass's personal hero appeared at her side as swiftly as if he'd apparated there. Rick's arms weren't folded. They hung by his sides with his protector cuff beginning to hum softly. Though he seemed outwardly unruffled, he was ready for action. Cass hoped he'd signaled Nate to keep the weretigers under control. They were bigger hotheads than werewolves.

"Looks like we have party crashers," her fiancé said calmly.

Cass was certain everyone, including the aforementioned crashers, heard him with their sharp ears.

She looked at Rick and smiled faintly. "I'll talk to them."

"Sure?" he said for her alone.

"If it were Gran's party, she'd handle this herself."

He cupped her cheek and let go, trusting her but ready to back her up if she needed it.

Reassured by his support, Cass walked the length of the poolside to the house. Halfway there, a quick flapping sound resolved into Scarlet landing nimbly on the pavers. That surprised her. Scarlet's brothers were more attached to her. Not tonight, she guessed. The beautiful red dragon assumed a stately pace as Cass proceeded, her head held as proudly as a queen's.

No one would have guessed she'd shredded six rolls of toilet paper just that morning.

One of the doors to the terrace opened and a male fae stepped out. His shining long hair was black, his eyes an interesting calico. Embroidered dragons decorated his silver robes. The chain that belted them at his narrow waist was forged from electrum. The clasp was a dragon's head biting a dragon's tail, and its eyes were rubies that shot small sparks. Cass interpreted the sartorial theme as signifying he came from the Dragon Guild.

This was a better option than the Founders Board; Guild members were by definition pro-Dragon. It was, however, far from a guarantee of good tidings.

Since the leader was coming out to meet her, Cass stopped and waited for him.

"I am Dubh," he said. "Head of the Dragon Guild."

He most assuredly wasn't "Dubh." Cass didn't know the symbolism of all fae names, but *Dubh* only meant black-haired.

"I am Cass," she returned, inclining her head as stingily as he had. "Keeper of the Sevryn clutch."

Scarlet contributed to the girl power anthem with a short caw. Dubh unbent enough to smile paternally down at her. Cass didn't appreciate the implied ownership in the look.

"Before you put your foot in it," she said, deciding a dose of her gran's plain speaking was in order. "If you've come to take these dragons back to Faerie, you'll find that plan is a non-starter."

She'd hit the nail on the head. She saw that from the startled flicker that crossed the faerie's face.

"We're the Dragon Guild," he said.

"And I'm a free citizen of Resurrection." She laid her hand on Scarlet's warm scaly skull. "As are my brood. The mayor himself put them on the city's rolls."

At the time, she'd assumed this was a ceremonial honor—something the Guild didn't need to know.

Dubh blinked his calico eyes. "The brood will be safer in Faerie, under our protection."

Cass allowed herself to snort. "Hardly. Queen Joscela wasn't born to a keeper line, but she expected to imprint these dragons. I can only infer she infiltrated your guild—whether through torture or trickery—and stole your secrets. And then there's Ceallach's sword. How did that fall into his hands? I'd say your 'protection' hasn't been stellar."

"Are you certain you'd have done better?"

His tone was glacial, his body stiff with injured arrogance. Fearing she'd gone too far, Cass moderated her tone.

"Look around you," she said. "Most of these folks would lay down their lives for the brood. They protect everyone they care about—and perfect strangers too. They don't need magical swords or kings or a guild to drive them to it. Their hearts guide them, and their sense of justice. The Pocket has become much more than a fae creation. It belongs to its people. The Sevryn clutch is going to grow up here. They're lucky this is their home."

"But—" The Guild leader's jaw worked briefly. "You can't raise dragons on top of a department store!"

"We can for now," she said. "When they grow too big, we'll move them to the Maycee farm."

"Do you even know what you're doing? The challenges you'll need to overcome? Dragons are more complicated than house cats!"

His calico eyes were practically shooting flames. Cass was happy she had a response ready.

"We've been working with a local foundation, the Society for the Protection of Rare Creatures. I hear they have a board position open. I'm sure they'd be honored if one of your members volunteered to fill it."

Dubh shut his mouth on whatever curse he was tempted to let out. Since it might have been a literal curse, Cass was grateful for his restraint. The Guild leader glanced down at Scarlet, who was looking up at him. Cass had to fight a sudden surge of humor. Scarlet's ruby red wings were slightly lifted, her head tilted fetchingly. The little minx was doing the dragon version of lash batting. The strategy must have worked. The Guild leader's stiff face softened.

"They do look healthy," he conceded grudgingly. "And they're certainly socialized."

Scarlet butted his hand and creeled softly.

"Fine," he said, succumbing to her invitation to pet her head. "The Guild accepts your offer, but we'll want two board seats instead of one."

Cass refrained from pointing out that without her dragons, the Guild wouldn't have much relevance.

"I expect they'll make room for you," she said.

Sensing some irony, Dubh lifted his multi-colored eyes to hers. His gaze shifted toward her father and back again. "You certainly are Roald's daughter. He was stubborn at your age too."

Amusement tugged her lips. "I don't believe he's outgrown it."

"Hmph." The beautiful faerie looked down his nose. "I suppose you're hoping we'll award Ceallach's protector sword to him."

"That's your business," she said, though the idea had occurred to her.

"Your father has new commitments," Dubh said flatly. "He's no longer an appropriate choice."

Cass didn't argue. She suspected she'd already won more concessions than the Guild wanted to give her.

"You will need two more protectors," he continued, making it sound more like a threat than a benefit. "Since you have three dragons."

That caught her flatfooted. She tried to think quickly. "Well," she said. "I trust the Guild will select candidates both I and the brood find acceptable."

She supposed this was an intelligent response, because Dubh leveled a tri-colored glower at her.

"Keeper," he said, offering her a short bow.

"Guild head," she returned the same way.

Old Country bureaucrats didn't do long goodbyes. He turned and stalked back into the penthouse, drawing his fellow Guild members into an obedient line behind him. She watched them recede down the repaired portrait hall, thinking who-knew-what about her human ancestors. Party sounds started up again as they went, but Cass wasn't ready to return to the festivities.

Her knees still shook a little in reaction.

Rick came up behind her, his warm hands settling on her shoulders. "Everything okay?"

She turned to rest her palms on his chest. "I think so. I told them about the SPRC. They're leaving the dragons here in return for two board seats."

"Good." He put a lot of feeling into that single word.

"I love you," she said.

"Don't I know it," he teased. He hugged her and held her until her legs steadied. Then he held her a little longer, just because it was nice.

"You're my heart," he murmured, his lips brushing her temple.

She squeezed him back, then turned her head toward a swoop of movement in the sky. The lead aviator was Grant the gargoyle, circling the terrace with her babies. Party lights illuminated the dragons' wings from beneath, gleaming gold and green and red as they glided on thermals that rose from her father's spell. Cass's heart swelled with pride. Though the brood was small compared to Grant, they didn't seem less strong.

"They're so graceful," Rick said, awe coloring his tone. "When did that happen?"

They might have been graceful, but they weren't grown up yet. Unable to resist showing off for so many lifted faces, Auric did a loop-de-loop, followed in neat succession by Verdi and Scarlet. The kids watching on the roof *oohed* excitedly.

The joy of the moment was quite perfect.

"They're magic," Cass said.

Rick met her gaze and smiled. "The whole world is."

Cass concluded her wolf was a wise man.

# # #

ABOUT THE AUTHOR

EMMA Holly is the award winning, *USA Today* bestselling author of more than thirty romantic books, featuring vampires, demons, faeries and just plain extraordinary ordinary folks. She loves the hot stuff, both to read and to write!

If you'd like to discover what else she's written, please visit her website at http://www.emmaholly.com.

Emma runs monthly contests and sends out newsletters that often include coupons for ebooks. To receive them, go to her contest page.

Thanks so much for reading this book!

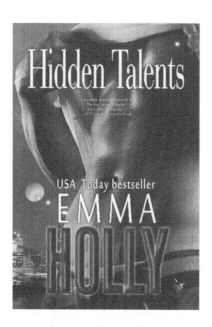

WEREWOLF cop Adam Santini is sworn to protect and serve all the supes in Resurrection, NY—including unsuspecting human Talents who wander in from Outside.

Telekinetic Ari is hot on the trail of a mysterious crime boss who wants to exploit her gift for his own evil ends, a mission that puts her on a collision course with the hottest cop in the RPD.

Adam wants the crime boss too, but mostly he wants Ari. She seems to be the mate he's been yearning for all his life, though getting a former street kid into bed with the Law could be his toughest case to date.

"*Hidden Talents* is the perfect package of Supes,
romance, mystery and HEA!"—**Paperback Dolls**

available in ebook and print

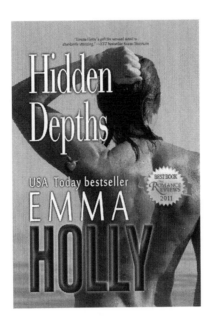

JAMES and Olivia Forster have been happily married for many years. A harmless kink here or there spices up their love life, but they can't imagine the kinks they'll encounter while sneaking off to their beach house for a long hot weekend.

Anso Vitul has ruled the wereseals for one short month. He hardly needs his authority questioned because he's going crazy from mating heat. Anso's best friend and male lover Ty offers to help him find the human mate his genes are seeking.

To Ty's amazement, Anso's quest leads him claim not one partner but a pair. Ty would object, except he too finds the Forsters hopelessly attractive.

"The most captivating and titillating story I have read in some time . . . Flaming hot . . . even under water"—**Tara's Blog**

available in ebook and print

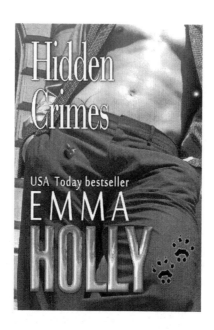

Hidden Crimes

USA Today bestseller
EMMA HOLLY

CATS and dogs shouldn't fall in love. Like any wolf, detective Nate Rivera knows this. He can't help it if the tigress he's been trading quips with at the supermarket is the most alluring woman he's ever met—sassy too, which suits him down to his designer boots.

Evina Mohajit is aware their flirtation can't lead to more. Still, she relishes trading banter with the hot werewolf. This hardworking single mom hasn't felt so female since her twins' baby daddy left to start his new family. Plus, as a station chief in Resurrection's Fire Department, she understands the demands of a dangerous job.

Their will-they-or-won't-they tango could go on forever if it weren't for the mortal peril the city's shifter children fall into. To save them, Nate and Evina must team up, a choice that ignites the sparks smoldering between them . . .

"Weaving the police procedural with her inventive love scenes [made] this book one I could not put down."—**The Romance Reviews**

available in ebook and print

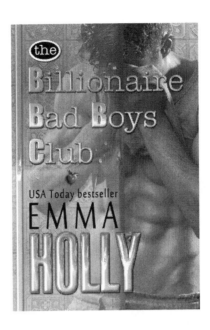

the
Billionaire
Bad Boys
Club

USA Today bestseller
EMMA
HOLLY

SELF-made billionaires Zane and Trey have been a club of two since they were eighteen. They've done everything together: play football, fall in love, even get smacked around by their dads. The only thing they haven't tried is seducing the same woman. When they set their sights on sexy chef Rebecca, these bad boys just might have met their match!

"This book is a mesmerizing, beautiful and oh-my-gods-hot work of art!"
—**BittenByLove** 5-hearts review

available in ebook and print

Made in the USA
Middletown, DE
16 April 2017